Praise for John Harvey

"Harvey's series about Charlie Resnick, the jazz-loving, melancholy cop in provincial Nottingham, England, has long been one of the finest police procedural series around." —*Publishers Weekly*

"The characters in John Harvey's urban crime novels are so defiantly alive and unruly that they put these British police procedurals on a shelf by themselves."

—Marilyn Stasio, *The New York Times Book Review*

"Without doubt the best cop on the Britcrime beat. Harvey has set a benchmark which the genre must now measure up to."

—*Literary Review*

"One of the masters of British crime fiction."

—*Sunday Telegraph (London)*

"Harvey reminds me of Graham Greene, a stylist who tells you everything you need to know while keeping the prose clean and simple. It's a very realistic style that draws you into the story without the writer getting in the way." —Elmore Leonard

"Much like Elmore Leonard and James Lee Burke, John Harvey has far transcended his genre." —Jim Harrison

"Charlie Resnick is one of the most fully realized characters in modern crime fiction … Lifts the police procedural into the realm of the mainstream novel." —Sue Grafton

"Harvey's Resnick novels are far and away the finest British police procedurals yet written." —*GQ*

"Nobody writes police procedurals better than John Harvey. Nobody." —*Booklist*

Enjoy the complete Resnick series from Bloody Brits Press

Lonely Hearts
Rough Treatment
Cutting Edge
Off Minor
Wasted Years
Cold Light
Living Proof
Easy Meat
Still Water
Last Rites

COLD LIGHT

JOHN HARVEY

BLOODY BRITS PRESS
Ann Arbor and Alnmouth
2008

Bloody Brits Press
PO Box 3671
Ann Arbor MI 48106-3671

BLOODY BRITS PRESS FIRST EDITION
First Printing July 2008

First published in Great Britain in 1994 by William Heinemann

Printed in the United States of America on acid-free paper

Cover designer: Bonnie Liss (Phoenix Graphics)

Bloody Brits Press is an imprint of Bywater Books

ISBN 978-1-932859-57-7

One

She slid out from beneath Gary's sleeping body and eased herself to the edge of the bed. Always the same, the way he would turn towards her each night, arm and the heft of his thigh heavily upon her. Weighing her down. Since they'd been moved here it was worse. He couldn't sleep without her. Holding her breath, Michelle waited for the thin squeak of the bedframe to still. Cracked lino cold at her feet. Gary sighed and when she looked round she could see his face, young in the faint light, open-mouthed. She saw the way one hand gripped the sheet, the knot of skin above his eyes, and was thankful she knew nothing of his dreams.

Slipping one of Gary's sweaters over her T-shirt, a pair of his socks on to her feet, she left the room.

The children had a bedroom of their own along the narrow landing, but these past weeks it had been too cold. Ice overlapping on the insides of the windows and their breath pigeoning the air. Get an oil stove in there, neighbors had said, keep it low. But Michelle knew of two house fires less than half a mile from here since winter had set in, ladders reaching up too late and never close enough, kiddies trapped upstairs and overcome by fumes.

Now they banked up the living-room fire with slack, made sure the guard borrowed from her parents' home was fixed in place. Natalie's cot they lifted into the middle of the room once the TV had been switched off and Karl's bed was the settee, curled beneath a nest of coats and blankets, thumb in mouth and dead to the world.

Downstairs, Michelle smiled at the baby, who had wriggled round again until her head was pressed against the bottom corner of the cot, one leg poked through the bars. Raising both hands to her mouth, Michelle warmed them before touching her daughter's tiny foot and easing it back, carefully, out of the cold. Both of them would need changing when they woke. She was reminded that it was her bladder that had woken her and she braced herself for the bathroom, the old scullery that had been converted and badly, quarry tiles laid on bare earth and made uneven by the frost.

She rubbed a circle from the inside of the window and the dark looked back at her. No more than two or three blurred lights pale along the street. If she were lucky, she might yet sit with yesterday's paper and a pot of tea, a little stolen time before the children woke to crying and she heard Gary's feet upon the stairs.

Resnick had been awake since four. So attuned to disruption, he had been blinking back sleep and reaching towards the telephone before, it seemed, he had heard its first ring. Kevin Naylor's voice was indistinct and oddly distant and Resnick, irritably, had to ask him to repeat everything twice.

"Sorry, sir, it's this mobile phone."

All Resnick heard were particles of words, breaking up like starlings in the early morning air.

"Redial," Resnick said, "and try again."

"Sorry, sir. Can't hear you."

Resnick cursed and broke the connection himself and when Naylor rang back he could hear him perfectly. A taxi driver had been taking two youths from the city center to an address in West Bridgford; as they neared Lady Bay Bridge, one of them had tapped on the window, asked the driver to pull over as his mate was feeling sick, like to throw up. When one young man got out of the car on to the pavement, the other went around to the driver's side and threatened him with an iron bar. Before the driver could pull away, the windscreen had been splintered in his face. The youths dragged him out of the cab and beat him around the head and body. He had been crawling across the center of the road when a milk lorry turned on to the bridge and stopped. The youths had run off and the driver's takings had gone with them.

"The weapon?" Resnick asked.

"Tried to chuck it into the Trent, sir, but only landed in the mud."

"And the driver?"

"Queen's. Accident and Emergency."

"Who's with him?"

"Uniform patrol should be there now, sir. There's nobody ..."

"Graham Millington ..."

"Leave, sir. He and the wife, they were going away. In-laws, I ..."

Resnick sighed; he should have remembered. "Divine, then. But I want someone with him all the time. The cabbie. We don't know how many chances we'll get."

"I could ..."

"You stay where you are." Resnick narrowed his eyes towards the bedside clock. "Twenty minutes, I'll be there. And see no one gets their sticky fingers all over that cab."

Absent-mindedly, he lifted away a cat that had folded itself into his lap and set it back down on the bed. One of the others was over by the bedroom door, scratching its head against the heavy edge of wood. The last time something like this had happened, the weapon had been a baseball bat and the taxi driver had died. Quickly, he showered and dressed and went downstairs, grinding coffee for a cup he would only half drink before stepping out into the cold light of another day.

"Bloody hell!" Gary said. "What sodding time is it?"

"It's late."

"It's what?"

"It's past seven."

"And you reckon that's late, do you?"

Michelle arched her back and shifted the baby's weight against her arm. She didn't think Natalie was taking any milk now, just suckling for the comfort of it. "Depends how long you've been up," she said.

Gary was leaning sideways inside the doorway, head stooped, still wearing the boxer shorts and County shirt he had slept in. "I've been down since before six," Michelle told him, though he hadn't asked.

Gary gave himself a scratch and walked past the end of the table where she was sitting. "I suppose that's my fault, too," he said, not quite loud enough for her to be certain.

"What?"

"You heard."

"If I heard, why would I ...?"

"You waking so early, I suppose it was my fault."

"Don't be silly."

"What's silly? Don't tell me I'm fucking silly. Everything else is my fault, why not that?"

"Gary …"

"What?"

Sitting between them, eating a mush of warm milk and cornflakes too big for his mouth, two-year-old Karl's eyes flicked from one to the other.

"Gary, no one's saying it's your fault. Not any of it."

"No?"

"No."

He tossed his head and glanced away. "Wasn't what you said the other day."

"Gary, I was angry. I lost my temper, right? Don't you ever lose your temper?"

She knew it was a stupid thing to say. She watched his fingers tighten around the curve of the kitchen chair.

"Gary …"

Michelle stood carefully with the baby still at her breast and went to him. He turned from her and she rested the side of her face soft against his back, unkempt curl of her hair brushing the nape of his neck. The baby wriggled a little between them and Michelle shushed into the feathery down of her head.

The last job Gary had had, six months back, laboring on a building site, cash in hand at the end of the week, no questions asked, had ended when the firm went bankrupt. Gary had turned in one morning to find the whole place cordoned off, all the heavy machinery being repossessed. Before that it had been the night shift in a factory that manufactured plastic switches for the fitments on table lamps. Then there had been piece-work, Sellotaping free floppy disks to the covers of a short-lived computer software magazinc. Three jobs in as many years. More than a lot of people they knew; more than most.

"Gary?"

"Mmm?"

But he knew. Michelle's free hand was stroking him through the striped cotton of his shirt, sliding up against the edges of his ribcage, along the flat of stomach just above the top of his shorts. She craned up to kiss him and his mouth was slightly sour from sleep. Behind them, Karl spun his spoon around the bowl too fast and it landed on the floor. Michelle lifted Natalie away from her breast as she turned and at once the baby screwed up her face and began to cry.

Mist rolled off the river in swathes. Hard against the curb, its offside door wide open, the cab sat cordoned off with yellow tape. Bright in the headlights of Resnick's car, glass sparkled on the surface of the road like ice. Immediately beyond, the road narrowed to a single lane across the bridge and Resnick knew that within an hour the traffic would be building up into the city worse than ever: Christmas Eve, for many the last day of this working year.

The scene of crime team were dusting the outside of the taxi now, the interior would be more safely and thoroughly examined when the vehicle had been removed. Uniformed officers were sifting carefully through the frosted mud and sparse grass of the riverbank below, others checking the path which led back off the bridge towards the city. This was the direction in which the driver of the milk lorry had seen two men running, down the slope towards the all-night garage and the road that would take them—where? On towards Colwick and the Country Park, the race course, or left into Sneinton. Yet according to the message the driver had called into base and the entry he had made in his own log, the destination for this fare had been across the river. A ruse, or had they simply run off, unthinking, panicked by what they had done?

"Sir?"

Naylor stepped towards him, the usual hint of deference and apology in his voice. At first Resnick had found it grated on him, waited for it to change with use and time; now he simply accepted it, the way the man was. The reverse, perhaps, of Mark Divine's bullish eagerness. How had Lynn Kellogg described Divine? All mouth and trousers? Resnick's mouth widened, letting in a smile.

"The cabbie—they've moved him to Intensive Care."

The smile faded: an all-too-familiar pattern falling into place.

"Mark wants to know, should he stick around or come back in?"

"He stays. As long as there's any chance he'll get some answers, he stays put."

"Yes, sir," said Naylor, hesitating. "Only ..."

"Well?"

"I know it's not ... it's just, he seemed a bit het-up about getting stuck there all day. The shops, you see, they close early some of them and ..."

"And he wants to be let off duty to do a bit of last-minute Christmas shopping?"

"It is for his mother," Naylor said, not believing it for a moment.

"Tell him he'll be relieved in the usual way, as and when we can."

"I'll say you're keeping it in mind, then." Naylor grinned.

"If you like," said Resnick. One of the scene of crime team was walking towards him; likely they were ready to winch the cab on to the waiting lorry and drive it away. The last thing Resnick wanted cluttering up his mind—thoughts of what Divine might be putting into someone's Christmas stocking.

Two

She'd been getting things for the kids for months now. Oh, nothing much, not a lot, not expensive. Just, you know, little things that had caught her fancy—a Dennis the Menace T-shirt for Karl, bright red on black, a toy dog for the baby, yellow, with blue stitching for its paws and nose, not too big, soft, something she could cuddle up to in her sleep. Michelle had joined the Christmas Club at the shop on the corner, opposite the old Co-op. Putting by a pound a week, not telling Gary, slipping in when she was on her own.

As long as there was something there for the children Christmas Day, enough to make it feel special. Not that either of them really knew, not yet, what it was all about. Too young to understand. They had been to the fair, though, the one in the Old Market Square; walked around the Christmas tree in its red tub outside the Council House, staring up at the colored lights and the star at the top. A present from Norway or Sweden or somewhere, though no one seemed to know why.

Gary'd bought them a jumbo hot dog, running over with tomato sauce, onions crisped, some of them, till they were black and brittle. They'd sat on the wall behind the fountain, sharing it between them, Michelle blowing on a piece of sausage and chewing it a little before pushing it into the baby's mouth. All around them, other kids with parents, kids on their own in gangs. Pushchairs and prams. Arms and coats to tug at. "Dad, can I have this?" "Can I have a go on that?" "Can't I? Can't I? Can I not? Oh, Mum! Dad!"

Michelle thought their Karl was like to carry on the same when he first saw the carousel, all the horses, brightly painted, prancing up and down. But she did his work for him, taking hold of Gary's hand to ask him softly, "Do look at his face, you can see how much he wants to have a go."

"You're all right," said Gary. "Just this once."

They had stood back and waved at him, Michelle shaking the baby's hand as well, and Karl, for all his smiles, had never quite felt sure enough to loose his grasp of the saddle and wave back.

"Snowman," said Gary later, pointing at the figure in front of the dodgems with its yellow hat and gloves. "See the snowman, Karl?"

"Noman," Karl had replied, excited. He had seen snowmen in his cartoons on TV

"Snowman," Gary laughed. "Not noman, you daft pillock! Snowman."

"Gary," Michelle said, starting to laugh herself. "Don't call him that."

"Noman!" sang out Karl, jumping up and down. "Noman! Noman! Noman!"

He lost his footing and went sprawling, bruising his face and grazing the fingers of the hand from which he'd earlier lost his glove. Not long after that they all caught the bus home.

Michelle looked up from what she was doing and listened; footsteps that might have been Gary's outside on the street. As they went on past, she slid her hands back into the soapy water, washing out a few clothes in the sink. Natalie she'd put down half-hour back and mercifully she'd stayed. Last time she'd checked, Karl was belly down in front of the TV lost in a program about lions; at least he was quiet.

She lifted the clothes clear of the water while she emptied the bowl ready to rinse. She only hoped Gary would be pleased with what she'd got for him, a replica goalie's shirt, twenty-eight quid it'd set her back; they'd kept it on order for her at the County shop, twenty-eight pounds less one penny.

Well, it was only once a year after all.

The door stuck as she was taking the washing through to the back yard to peg out and when she nudged it with her hip the bottom half of the door came away from the frame.

"Michelle! Michelle! You there?"

"I'm out back."

"You might've shut the door behind you. Like a bloody fridge in here." He stopped short, staring at the twisted hinge.

"I'm sorry," Michelle said. "It wasn't my fault."

Gary turned on his heel and a moment later she heard the front door open and slam shut. Upstairs in her cot, the baby woke up crying.

"Ion," said Karl from the doorway. "Ion!" And he made his tottering run towards her, hands stretched high like claws, growling loudly.

Mark Divine was three degrees short of pissed off. First they'd told him, sorry, he'd have to wait outside the Intensive Care unit, they'd be certain to let him know the minute Mr. Raju regained consciousness. So he'd sat there, his bulk awkward on the low chair, legs at all angles, watching various other Rajus as they were shepherded in and out, whispering and wailing. The one time he wandered off in search of the WVS canteen and a decent cup of tea, one of the staff nurses came out looking for him.

"He's come to, then, has he?" Divine asked when finally she found him.

As well as the plastic cup of tea, which was threatening to burn a hole in his fingers, he was trying to balance two chocolate cupcakes and a lemon puff.

"Concerned about your sugar levels?" the staff nurse asked, raising an eyebrow in the direction of Divine's one-handed juggling.

"Not as I know of," Divine said cockily.

"Well, perhaps you should be."

One of the cupcakes fell to the floor and rolled underneath the nearest chair. "Don't worry," she said, "the cleaners will find it. Why don't you put the rest of them down on the table over there and come through?"

"You mean now, like? This minute?"

"You do want to see him, don't you?"

"Yes, but …"

"Ask him some questions?"

"Yes."

"Then I should do it before they take him down to theater."

Divine took a large bite from the lemon puff, risked burning his tongue on a swig of tea, and followed the staff nurse through the double set of doors towards the ward. Nice arse, he thought, wonder if they've got any mistletoe strung up in Intensive Care?

✦✦✦

Resnick arrived back in his office after a brisk thirty minutes with the superintendent, to find a large parcel stuffed into his waste basket. Brown paper and string inside a pair of plastic bags. Around ten pounds, he thought, weighing it in his hands. One of the plastic bags contained quite a little puddle of blood. He hadn't realized Lynn Kellogg was due back in the office so soon.

The files detailing the night's events, messages and memoranda, the movement of prisoners in and out of police cells, still lay on his desk barely touched. Half-a-dozen men and one woman drunk and disorderly; Resnick recognized most of the names. Likely by now they'd been cautioned and pushed back out on to the streets. By noon most of them would be drunk again, winding themselves up for the night. After all, it was Christmas, wasn't it? Wasn't that what Christmas was about?

In the outer office two phones began ringing almost simultaneously and Resnick switched them from his mind.

Considering the possibilities—so many homes left empty, all those expensive presents ready-wrapped—the increase in burglaries was less than might have been expected. Even so, enough people would have returned from their firm's annual pre-cooked Christmas dinner, the ritual risqué jokes and innuendo, to find the golden goose had flown. All those expensive tokens of status and admiration liberated in under fifteen minutes by eager hands using a pair of the home-owner's socks as gloves.

The phones were still ringing. Resnick pushed open the door to his office, ready to shout an order, and realized there was no one there. A filing cabinet with the drawer not pushed fully back, mugs of tea staining deeper and deeper orange, typewriters and VDUs all unattended. Resnick picked up the nearest receiver, identified himself and asked the caller to hold while he dealt with the second. A postman had been cycling to work at the sorting office off Incinerator Road when a taxi had turned past him, heading for the bridge; he'd got a pretty good sight of the two youths in the back. A woman on her way back from the garage shop with a packet of cigarettes and a carton of milk had nearly been knocked off her feet by two lads rushing past. Resnick made a note of their names and addresses, was still arranging for the postman to come into the station, when Lynn Kellogg came backwards through the door.

When she turned to face him she had two sandwiches in her hands, two cups of filter coffee, one of them black. Medium height, hair medium brown, red-faced, stocky, Detective Constable Lynn Kellogg, back from her parents' poultry farm in Norfolk, by way of the deli across the street.

"Mozzarella and tomato," Lynn said, handing Resnick a brown paper bag already leaking French dressing. "I thought you might not have eaten."

"Thanks." He prized the plastic lid from the coffee and drank. "I thought you weren't due in till this afternoon?"

Lynn widened her eyes and moved to her desk.

"Things at home not so good?" Resnick asked.

Lynn shrugged. "Not so bad." She shook some loose pieces of lettuce from the paper bag and pushed them back inside her sandwich.

"I found the turkey," Resnick said, nodding in the direction of his office.

"Good." And then, suddenly grinning, "It's a duck."

"I was just wondering," Divine said. He was on his way out of the ward, interview over, and he'd timed his move to perfection, coinciding with Staff Nurse Bruton's purposeful walk towards the drugs trolley. Lesley Bruton— tall, her height accentuated by the mass of dark hair untamed by her nurse's cap ... it was there on her badge, printed out for all to see. "Like I say, Lesley, I was wondering ..."

"Yes?"

"What time you got finished? You know, came off shift."

"I know what it means."

"So?"

She gave him a look that would have scuppered a more sensitive man and lifted a clipboard from the side of the trolley.

"Look, it's not a chat-up, you know. No way."

Amusement flirted across her eyes. "Help you with your inquiries, can I? Something like that?"

What? Divine thought. Give me half the chance!

"No," he said, "not official ..."

"I thought perhaps not."

"See, what it is, I've got to stay here till he gets back on the ward. Raju. Could be— well, what?—hours."

"Could be."

"Thing is, there's this present I've got to get. You know, for tomorrow."

"Special, is it?"

Divine nodded, looked sincere.

"Girlfriend?"

"Sort of."

"Underwear, then?"

Divine treated her to his lop-sided grin; he was starting to sweat more than just a little.

"Black and sexy?"

"Could be. Why not?"

She looked at him, saying nothing. Waiting.

"There's this place," Divine said. "That arcade back of the Council House. Real posh."

"I know it," Lesley Bruton said. "My boyfriend buys me stuff there all the time."

Jesus! Divine thought. His eyes slithered down her uniform, wondering if she was wearing any of it now.

Lesley slid her hands along the rail of the trolley. "And you'd like me to pop in there when I finish?" she said. "Pick up something for you. For your girlfriend. A bra and pantie set. Maybe a camisole top. One of those teddies."

"Yes," said Divine, "that sort of thing." Wondering if a teddy was what he hoped it was, one of those all-in-one jobs like a swimsuit made out of lace.

"Maybe try them on for you while I'm there?"

"Why not?" Divine said, not quite able to believe his luck.

"Why not?" Lesley said, fixing him with her eyes. "For you?"

"Well, I ..."

For a moment, voice lowered, she leaned towards him. "In your dreams," she said. And without a second glance, she walked away.

Gary had been working on the door the best part of two hours, more, if you included the time it had taken him to walk up the street to his mate Brian's house and borrow a decent-sized screwdriver and a rasp. Michelle had finished a second lot of washing, fed Natalie, given Karl fish fingers and beans, and made herself some toast. Gary had said he wasn't hungry. Her mum had asked her to take the kids round some time that afternoon so she could give them their presents and even though it meant carting the pushchair off and on two buses, Michelle thought she'd better make the effort. First thing in the morning, her parents would be off up the A1 to Darlington to have their Christmas dinner with Michelle's older sister, Marie, and her family. Three-bedroom semi, that's what they had. Picked it up dirt cheap after it was repossessed.

"Michelle!" Gary's voice from the back.

"Yes?"

"Lend us a hand, will you?"

"Be there in a minute."

"No, now."

The kettle was coming to the boil, Natalie was getting into a right old grizzle, Karl was calling something from the front room and she couldn't tell what; she'd thought while the tea was mashing, she'd see if there was mincemeat enough left to make some more mince pies. Last she'd made were almost as good as you could buy in the shop.

"Michelle! You coming or what?"

Michelle sighed and pushed the teapot to one side. Through the open front-room door, she could see Karl painstakingly climbing on to the settee so he could roll back off.

"You be careful now," she called at him on the way past. "You'll only hurt yourself."

"Here," Gary said, pointing. "Steady that for me there."

"Where?"

"Jesus Christ, girl! There!"

Michelle pushed two fingers against the top of the hinge, her thumb against the bottom.

"Okay, now budge over, give me room to get the screwdriver to it."

She could hear his breathing clearly, loud and slightly ragged beneath his shirt. He hated doing jobs like this.

"Right. Whatever you do, don't let go. Hold it firm. Push."

There was a shout, sudden and loud, from inside the house and she knew that Karl had fallen and hurt himself.

Gary sensed her move and stopped it. "I'll be done in a minute. Hang on."

"It's Karl, he …"

"I said bloody hang on!"

Gary gave a final turn and the screw splintered sideways through the wood of the frame, jerking the screwdriver from his hand. The hinge fell away from Michelle's fingers and the whole door slid sharply outwards, wrenching the bottom hinge away with it

"Fuck!" Gary yelled. "Sodding bastard fuck!"

"Gary!" Michelle called. "Don't."

From somewhere, blood seemed to be running between her fingers, collecting inside her hand.

Karl was standing close by the doorway, fists jammed against his eyes, mouth widening through a succession of screams.

"Fuck!" Gary swore again, kicking at the frame. "And you," he said, grabbing Karl by both arms and lifting him into the air. "You want something to bloody cry about!" He dropped his son towards the floor and before he could land, had cracked his hand, hard as he could, back across Karl's face.

Three

"Crying out for it, she was?

Meal time in the canteen and Divine, relieved from his duties at the hospital, was telling Kevin Naylor about his encounter with Staff Nurse Bruton over the drugs trolley. A year or so back, Naylor would have been impressed; now his expression was, to put it mildly, skeptical.

"No, she was. Straight up."

"Told you, did she?" Naylor asked. "I mean, you know, came right out and said it?"

Divine dipped one of his chips into the pool of brown sauce spreading across his plate. "Don't need to *say*, do they? Know what's what, you can tell." He pointed his fork across at Naylor, sprinkling the table with sauce. "Lot of your problem, you and Debbie ..."

"Debbie and I don't *have* a problem."

"For now, maybe."

"We don't have a problem." Naylor's voice getting louder, attracting attention.

"All I'm saying," Divine went on blithely, spearing another chip, "all the evidence shows, you know bog all about bloody women."

"Whereas you," Lynn Kellogg leaned over from the next table, "expert by now, aren't you, Mark?"

Sarcastic cow! Divine thought. "Don't believe me," he said, "catch me in action, this do tonight. The man who made pulling an art form."

"I can't wait!"

"No?" Divine forked up a piece of meat pie. "Well, shame but you just might have to. I mean, I'd like to help out, but there's just so many others in line before you."

Lynn pushed back her plate and stood up. "What do I have to do to keep it that way? Wear a cross round my neck? Eat garlic?"

Divine gave her a swift appraisal. “No need. Just keep looking the way you do.”

He leaned back and winked across at Naylor, as Lynn walked away, muffled laughter from some of the other officers flushing her face.

“You didn’t need to say that,” Kevin Naylor said quietly.

“Nobody asked her to stick her nose in. Any road, it’s no more’n true. I mean, would you fancy it? Be honest.”

Naylor looked back down at his plate and made no reply.

“That prick,” Lynn said to herself on the stairs, “knows as much about women as the average five-year-old.” She remembered him picking a magazine off her desk once, attention drawn by blonde hair and bright red lips and the headline, *Shere Hite and the Clitoral Tendency*. Divine had thought they were a new pop group.

Gary James had been waiting close to two hours and there were still five people in front of him, two of them Pakis. Turn a place over to them and the next thing it’d be swarming, aunts and uncles, sisters and cousins, floor to ceiling like bugs. He’d seen it happen. Next to them, this couple lolling all over one another, tongues in each other’s ears half the time, looked as though they should still be at school, not in the bloody Housing Office. Tattoos all up their shoulders and necks, her with enough little rings in her nose to open a shop; bloke with his hair twisted round like some Rasta, though he was white as Gary himself. Down the row from Gary there was this West Indian woman the size of a sodding house herself, three kids clinging to her and another one on the way.

Jesus! Gary didn’t have a watch and the clock on the waiting room wall had been at twenty-five past seven the past three times he’d been there.

“Hey, mate,” he said, tapping the nearest Paki on the shoulder, then pointing to his own wrist in case the bloke didn’t understand. “What time you got?”

“Very nearly a quarter to four,” the man said politely and smiled.

Don’t smile at me, you smarmy bastard, Gary thought as he sat back down, save that for when you get in there. And then, Christ, that’s nearly three hours, never mind two.

“Hey!” he shouted. “Hey, you!” He pulled one of the metal-frame chairs out of line and pushed it hard towards the wall. "Think I'm going to sit here all bloody day? I want to see somebody and I want to see them bloody now!"

"Sir," the receptionist said. "Sir, if you'll just go back to your seat, you'll be seen as soon as possible." All the while her fingers moving towards the panic button underneath the counter top.

Resnick had gone to talk to Mavis Alderney himself. Mavis thankful for the chance to catch a fag out back from the laundry off Trent Boulevard where she worked.

It had been Mavis who had come close to being sent flying by two youths that morning. "Arse over tip," was how she put it. "Someone wants to get hold of the like of them and give them a good thrashing. Well, don't you think? Should've been done to 'em long time back. Then happen they'd not be the way they are now."

Resnick had grunted something noncommittal and pressed for her to be more specific with her descriptions. "A pair of them tearaways, you know, them boots and jeans, no respect for anyone, not even themselves," wasn't quite going to do it

Now he was in the market, upstairs in the Victoria Centre, all the seats around the Italian coffee stall taken and having to stand to drink his espresso, listening to an animated discussion about why both the city's soccer teams were languishing near the bottom of their respective leagues.

"Ask me," someone said, "best thing could happen, bloody managers ship 'emselves either side of Trent, swop jobs."

"Now you're talking rubbish, man."

"Well, they couldn't do a lot worse."

"No," put in somebody else, "I'll tell you what. Best present they could have, both clubs. Christmas morning, chairmen of directors gets 'em both, Cloughie and Warnock on the phone, wishes them a Merry Christmas and tells them they're both sacked."

"What? They'll not sack Cloughie, they'd never dare. They'd have a full-scale bloody riot on their hands."

"Aye, maybe. But not as much as if they go down."

Resnick smiled and reached between two of the men, setting his cup and saucer back on the counter. On his way out of the market he'd buy a little Polish sausage to go with his duck, a chunk of Gruyère and some Blue Stilton, a good slice of apple strudel and some sour cream to take the place of a Christmas pudding.

Down below, crowds were pushing their way from store to store and last-minute shoplifting was in full swing. Even more people than usual were gathered around the Emmett clock, holding up small children to see the fantastic metal animals revolve and laugh with wonder as streams of water splashed off its gilded petals as they opened. Again, again, again.

Suspended from the high ceiling, a Santa on a bright red sledge chased polypropylene reindeer through stale air.

Resnick was out on the street when he heard the first siren.

Nancy Phelan had emerged from her office at the sound of shouting, curious to know whoever it was making all that noise. Besides, she could do with a break from her present assignment, explaining to a couple with an eighteen-month-old kid that by leaving the damp basement room for which the girl's mother had been charging her a robbery of a rent, they had made themselves voluntarily homeless.

"Voluntarily sodding homeless," the man kept saying. "What in buggery is that?" Not loud, not even angry, simply swearing by rote.

What it bloody is, Nancy had thought, and not for the first time, was an almost meaningless form of words dreamed up by some official to get the housing authority off the hook.

That hadn't been what she'd said to her client; what she'd said was, "Sir, I've already explained it to you several times."

Several? Half a hundred.

Whatever disturbance was going on outside, it had to be more interesting than that. A little light relief.

Wrong.

Gary James—Nancy thought she recognized him, thought he might even be one of hers, though she could never have put a name to him—was standing pretty much in the middle of the corridor, both hands holding a chair above his head. The metal kind with the canvas seat and back. The receptionist, Penny, was cowering against one wall, bent forward, arms folded up in front of her face. He'd either hit her with the chair or was about to.

Howard, the security guard, was down at the far end of the corridor, squinting hopefully in their direction. Nancy knew for a fact he could scarcely see his own hand in front of his face without his glasses on.

"You!" Gary called over one shoulder.

"Me?"

"It's you I want to see."

Oh, God, Nancy thought, it would be. Her second application to join a TEFAL course, train to teach English to polite, suited business-men in Hong Kong or Japan, had just been turned down. This morning she'd been convinced—though it was difficult to tell—that one of her stick insects had died. And if that wasn't enough she was three days late.

Now this.

"You're the one me and Michelle saw before, right? About getting us out of that dump you moved us into."

"I said I'd try yes ..."

"Look! I'm telling you. You'd better do more than fucking try. And you, just stay where you fucking are or I'll take this tart's head off her fucking shoulders."

Penny flinched and stifled a scream and Howard retreated a few feet more than he had advanced.

"Do you have an appointment?" Nancy asked, keeping her voice as normal as possible.

Gary shot her another glance. "What do you think?"

"Well, if you'll wait till I've finished with my present clients, which shouldn't take long, I'll be happy to review your situation." Nancy, thinking all the while she was speaking that she'd picked up so much official gobbledegook, she sounded as if she'd learned English as a second language herself.

Gary swung the chair through a half-circle and brought it crash against the wall, close enough to Penny's head to make her hair curl.

"All right," Nancy said. "Why don't we talk now?"

"Yeh?" said Gary, panting just a little. "What about Clint Eastwood down there?"

"Howard," Nancy said. "It's okay. I'll see Mister ..." She looked at Gary hopefully.

"James."

"I'll see Mr. James in my office. There's no need to be concerned. But you might look after Penny here, see that she's all right."

Gary was watching her, uncertain. This woman not much older than himself, if that, taking control, coping. She didn't seem frightened at all. Tall, Gary thought, five eight or nine, likely had something to do with it. Not bad looking, either. Standing there in her smart blue jacket and the pleated skirt, waiting for him to make his next move.

When he said nothing, Nancy turned to the couple she'd been interviewing, now agog outside her door, and explained to them this was something of an emergency and if they wouldn't mind waiting a while, she would talk to them again and see if they couldn't sort something out. From her purse she handed them some coins and suggested they try the drinks machine on the next floor.

"Please," she said to Gary, holding open her office door. "After you."

A shade hesitantly, Gary lowered the chair to the floor and walked in. For the briefest of moments, Nancy hesitated; up to now she'd been working on instinct, training, defusing the situation without any special regard to herself. Only now did it strike her, the degree to which she was placing herself in danger. She made a quick face down the corridor that said, do something, and then stepped smartly after him, closing the door behind her.

Four

"Lock the door," he said.

"What?"

"Lock the door."

Nancy sweating a little now, wondering what she'd got herself into. "It's against regulations …" she began, but she could see Gary, increasingly edgy, looking round the room for something to break. Something to break over her. Quietly, she slid open the small drawer to the right of her desk and took out the key.

No sooner had the door been locked and Nancy sat back down than the phone rang, once, twice, three times; looking at Gary for a sign that she should pick it up.

"Hello," she said into the receiver. "Nancy Phelan here."

A pause, then: "No, I'm fine." Glancing across the desk to where Gary was still standing. "We're fine. Yes, I'm sure. No. Bye."

Deliberately, she set the receiver down and, as she did so, Gary bent towards the floor and pulled the wire from its socket above the skirting.

"Well," Nancy said, "why don't you sit down?"

But Gary was staring round her office, taking it all in. The postcards from foreign holidays she'd Blutacked to the filing cabinet, the ivy that needed repotting near the window, the overflowing in-tray, a color photograph of her cousin's twins. In a clear plastic container with an air-tight lid, green leaves and pieces of thin twig. Gary picked it up and shook it.

"Don't!" Nancy cried, alarmed. Then, more quietly, "I'd rather you didn't do that. There's something … there are stick insects in there. Two of them. I think."

Gary held it up to his face and gave the container an experimental shake.

"They were a present," Nancy said, uncertain why she felt the need to explain. "A client."

"I think they're dead," Gary said.

Nancy thought he might be right.

The first response car had only arrived at the Housing Office moments before Resnick walked in, strudel, cheese, and sausage in a plastic bag in his left hand. In the lobby, a young PC was talking to the security guard, another, slightly older, having problems using his two-way radio to call in. Not recognizing either of them, Resnick produced his warrant card.

"PC Bailey," said the officer with the radio. "That there's Hennessey."

Not, Resnick assumed, the one that used so effectively to police the Forest midfield. He listened to a quick run-down of the situation and moved towards the stairs.

"D'you not think we should wait for some support, sir?" Bailey asked.

"Let's see what we can do ourselves," Resnick said. "Whoever he's got in there might not thank us for hanging about."

Most of those who had been queuing to be seen and a growing number from other floors had crowded into the corridor outside the locked door.

"Keep everybody back," Resnick told Hennessey. "In the waiting room with the door shut."

"I spoke to Nancy on the phone just after they went in," the receptionist said. "She said she was all right."

Resnick nodded. "Can I talk to her?"

Penny shook her head. "The line's gone dead."

"The man," Resnick asked, "do we know his name?"

"James. Gary James."

"And did he seem to be armed? Was he carrying any kind of weapon?"

"He tried to hit me with a chair." At the thought of it, Penny's shoulders gave an involuntary shake.

"Gary James," Resnick told Bailey, who was already entering the name in his notebook. "Get him checked out, see if he's known."

"And the backup, sir?"

Resnick half-smiled. "If there's any to spare." Turning back to the receptionist, he asked, "Has there been any shouting from inside? Signs of a disturbance?"

"I went up to the door, close as I dared," Penny's voice, a little breathless, telling it. "On and on about the state of the place where he's living, that's all I could hear. How cold it was and damp and how it would be a miracle if his kids got through the winter without pneumonia. That was a while back, though. I haven't heard a dickybird since."

"Someone must have another key to the room?"

"Oh, yes. The caretaker. For the cleaning staff, you see."

"You've tried contacting him?"

"Oh, no. I'm sorry. With all the fuss, I didn't think. I can try for him now, though, to be honest, I'm not sure where he is this time of day. Somewhere with his boilers, I dare say." She indicated the security guard, blinking behind his glasses. "Howard might know."

"All right, ask Howard for me if he can track him down." Resnick held his carrier bag of provisions out towards her. "And do me a favor, will you? Look after this."

Taking the bag, Penny glanced inside. "Would you like me to pop and put them in the fridge? We've got a fridge."

Resnick shook his head. "Your colleague, Nancy, what's her other name?"

"Phelan. Nancy Phelan."

Resnick thanked her and walked towards the door.

"You know something," Gary said. It was the first time he had spoken—either of them had spoken—in several minutes.

"What's that?" Nancy said.

"I know you."

"Yes, you said. When you and your wife …"

"She's not my wife."

"Well, whatever."

"Me and Michelle, we're not married."

"When you and Michelle came in before, you said that was when you saw me."

"But that's not what I mean. Nothing to do with being here. This place. I mean I *know* you, from before."

Nancy didn't think so.

"From school. We were at the same school. Don't you remember?"

"No."

"Top Valley. You were two years above me. Yeh. You went around with—what's his name?—Brookie. Him and my brother, they was mates."

Malcolm Brooks. Brookie. Watching him play pool in the pub, evenings, sipping a rum and coke, and waiting for him to drive her home. He'd park his old man's Escort round the back of Tesco's till Nancy told him how she'd catch it if she was in late again. She hadn't thought of Brookie in years.

"Nancy," said Resnick's voice through the door. "Nancy, are you all right in there?"

Gary reached across faster than she could judge and caught a hold of her hair. "Tell him," he snarled. "Tell him it's okay."

"Nancy, this is the police. Detective Inspector Resnick, CID."

"Tell him," Gary said, twisting her hair in his hand. "Tell him he'd better sod off and leave us alone."

"Hello? Inspector?" Her voice muffled, difficult to judge the tone. "Listen, there's nothing for you to be concerned about. Really."

Nancy angled her eyes towards Gary, wanting him to look at her. The way he had hold of her hair, tugging against the roots, it was all she could do not to cry.

"Are you sure?" Resnick asked, face all but resting on the cream paint of the door. Nothing solid about it at all, a couple of good whacks and it would be down. "You sure everything's okay?" Listening hard, Resnick could only hear his own breathing. "Nancy?"

She was staring into Gary's face, willing him to let her go.

"Nancy?" Resnick knocked on the center of the door, not hard, even so it moved a little against the frame.

With a look and a sigh, Gary leaned away, loosening his grip on her hair. She read the look and it was that of someone realizing they were deep into something from which there was no easy way out.

"We're talking," Nancy said, raising her voice, never taking her eyes off Gary. "About a problem Gary has with his housing. There was just a misunderstanding, that's all."

"And Gary," Resnick said. "Let me hear your voice, will you? Just say something. Say hello. Anything."

Gary said nothing.

Bailey beckoned Resnick back along the corridor. "James, sir. Quite a tasty little record. Petty stuff as a juvenile. Supervision orders. Right now he's on probation. Aggravated assault. Actual bodily harm. Troops are on their way."

"What it seems to me, Gary," Nancy was saying, "the sooner this is over, the less trouble for you."

"Oh, yeh," Gary said, lip curling. "I can see you being worried about that—trouble for me."

"Gary," she said, "I am. Really, I am."

"Nancy," Resnick said from outside, "as long as everything's all right in there, do you think you could unlock the door?"

She was looking across at Gary, the sweat was beginning to stand out like pimples on his skin and his eyes refused to hold her gaze. Nancy had thought not to leave the key in the lock and now it lay at the end of the table between them, eighteen inches from her right hand. And his. She began to crab her fingers towards it and then stopped, reading his intention clearly.

"No," Nancy said, voice raised but even, "I don't think I can. Not right now."

Bailey signaled that reinforcements had arrived outside the building; soon Resnick would hear their feet as they charged the stairs.

"Gary," he said, "this is your one and only chance. Come on out of your own free will before we have to come in and get you."

"You see," Nancy said, leaning her face towards him, pleading.

"I don't know," Gary said, licking sweat from the soft hairs sprouting round his top lip. "I don't fucking know."

His voice was trembling and he reminded Nancy of the way her younger brother had looked caught stealing from their mother's purse, all of nine years old. Slowly, very slowly, so that he could see what she was doing, Nancy took the key between forefinger and thumb, stood, and walked the four paces to the door.

"Okay, Gary?" she asked, glancing round.

When she turned the key and pushed the door wide, they were inside in a flash: Bailey and Hennessey and two others, grabbing Gary as he tried to move, hands, arms, swinging him hard about and forcing him up against the wall, feet kicked wide, legs spread, arms yanked back and round, the cuffs as they went on biting at his wrists.

"Are you all right?" Resnick asked, touching Nancy lightly on the shoulder.

"I kept telling you, didn't I? I'm fine." She stood aside, arms folded across her chest, her breathing going ragged now and seeking to control it, turning her head as Gary was hauled out into the corridor, no longer wanting to look into his face, see his expression as they bundled him away.

Five

"Things not so good at home," was that what Resnick had said? Lynn smiled grimly, changed down, and indicated that she was taking the next left. Not so good could be measured by the way her mother had stood, tight-lipped and close to tears, still stirring the last of her Christmas puddings with only days to go. Other years, there would have been at least three of them, fat in their white basins, ready in the cupboard by the end of October.

"It's your dad, Lynnie," all she had said.

Lynn had found him mooching between the hen houses, an unlit cigarette loose between his lips, fear in his eyes.

"Dad, whatever is it?"

The electrical equipment used to stun the birds before slaughter had malfunctioned and, at the height of the busiest season, forty-eight hours and several thousand pounds had been lost before it was set to rights. Worse for her father, before the fault was discovered, some hundred force-fed capons had been doused alive in scalding water, their throats slit, feathers plucked—he would wake at four, against all logic, reliving their screams. "Come on, Dad," Lynn had said, "there's nothing you can do about it now."

She should have known there was something more. On the morning she left, she found him in the kitchen at first light, hand round a mug of well-brewed tea. "It's the doctor, Lynnie. He says I've to go to the hospital, see this consultant. Something here, in my gut." He had stared at her along the table and Lynn had hurried from the room before he could see her cry.

It was a little after four in the afternoon and the dark was starting to close in. Still you could read, graffitied in two-foot-high letters on the Asian shopkeeper's wall, *Keep Christmas White—Fuck Off Home.*

Lynn glanced at the street atlas again and readied herself for another three-point turn.

Michelle had not been home long. The buses had been overloaded with shoppers and those whose working day had finished in the lunchtime pub; sporadic bursts of carol singing, most often with the words changed to crude parody, drifted down from the upper deck. A ginger-haired man, still wearing his postman's uniform, sat with his legs out into the aisle, performing conjuring tricks with a deck of cards. As they were veering across the roundabout at the end of Gregory Boulevard, a businessman, wearing a gray pin-stripe suit and a red and white Christmas hat, had leaned wide from the platform of the bus and lost his lunch beneath the wheels of the oncoming traffic.

Natalie had fallen asleep, rocked by the vehicle's motion, and Karl had sat close, clinging to the sleeve of Michelle's coat, wrapped in the wonder of what was going on around him. When the postman leaned across and magicked a shiny ten-pence coin from behind Karl's left ear, the small boy squealed with delight.

"Whatever's happened to him, poor lamb?" Michelle's mother had asked, pointing to the swelling puffing out the side of Karl's face.

"He fell," Michelle had said quickly. "Always rushing at everything. You know what he's like."

"Aye," her mum had said. "Bit of a madcap, like his dad."

There were Christmas lights in some of the windows as they walked back up the street towards home; tiny red and blue bulbs glinting from plastic trees. A neighbor called out a greeting and Michelle felt a sudden rush of warmth run through her. Maybe this wasn't such a bad place after all. If they could just see off the winter, it really could be a new start.

She had called out opening the front door, expecting Gary to be back; the queue at the Housing must have been even longer than he'd thought. Quickly, she'd got the children changed, shipped Karl off in front of the TV with some bread and jam while she spooned rice and apple in and around the baby's mouth. Once fed, she'd put her down and tend to the fire, get it going before Gary returned, settle down to watch *Neighbours* with a fresh pot of tea.

✦✦✦

The knock on the door was clipped and strong and though her first thought was that Gary had mislaid his key, it didn't sound like his knock at all.

"Michelle Paley?"

"Yes."

"Detective Constable Lynn Kellogg. I'd like to talk to you a minute, if I could."

Michelle took in the warrant card, the neat dark hair, the sureness of the stance, cheeks that showed red in the light spilling from the house.

Lynn glanced past Michelle into the room and saw the beginnings of a fire, a cartoon Dracula on the television, volume turned low. On a carpet that had seen better days, a mousy little kid with both legs in the air behind him, squinted round.

"You'll be letting in the cold," Lynn said. Michelle nodded and stood aside, closing the door behind Lynn as she walked in, pushing the folded square of rug back against it to keep out the draught.

Lynn unbuttoned her coat but made no move to take it off.

"What's happened?" Michelle said, sick to her stomach, fearing the worst. "It's Gary, isn't it? Is it Gary? Is he all right? Tell me he's all right."

"Why don't we sit down?" Lynn said.

Michelle swayed a little as she felt her legs starting to go.

"Nothing's happened to him," Lynn said. "You don't have to worry. Nothing like that."

Michelle did sit, uneasily on to the sofa, reaching for the arm to steady herself down. "He's in trouble, then," she said.

"He's at the station," Lynn said. "Canning Circus. He was arrested earlier this afternoon."

"Oh, God, what for?"

Lynn was conscious of the small boy, leaning back against the legs of the TV set, paying them all his attention. "There was a disturbance, at the Housing Office ..."

"A disturbance? What kind of ...?"

"It seems he threatened the staff, physically. At one point he locked himself in a room with one of them and refused to let her out."

Michelle's face had drained of what little color it had.

"I don't know yet," Lynn said, "if he'll be held overnight. It's possible. We thought you ought to know."

"Can I see him?"

"Later. I'll give you a number you can ring."

Upstairs, the baby began crying and then, just as abruptly, stopped.

"Did he hit anyone?" Michelle asked.

"Apparently not. Not this time."

"What d'you mean?"

"He's done it before, hasn't he? He's on probation."

"That was ages ago, what happened."

"A year."

"But he's changed. Gary's changed."

"Has he?"

Karl was rocking backwards and forwards as, on the screen above him, a fading football manager vouched for the splendors of British Gas.

"That's your little boy?" Lynn asked.

"Karl. Yes."

"What happened to his face?"

Divine thanked the sister from Intensive Care and replaced the receiver: Mr. Raju had returned from Recovery, was sleeping, sedated, his condition critical yet stable. It was unlikely he would be strong enough to speak with anyone until the morning.

"You've not changed your mind, then?" he said, as Naylor crossed the room behind him.

"About what?"

"Bringing Debbie along tonight."

Naylor dropped two folders on to his desk: transcripts of interviews pertaining to the taxi driver's assault. Several thousand words and still no clear identification. Two youths in boots and jeans, much like many others. "Why should I?" he said.

Divine's grin was broad as a dirty joke and about as subtle. "Last chance for a bit of spare this side of the stuffing."

"Forget it, Mark, why don't you?" Naylor flipped open the first file and began to read. It had taken all of his persuasion getting Debbie to agree to come with him. "You don't want me there," she'd said, "getting in the way. You'll have a lot more fun on your own." Times were, back when things were going wrong with their marriage, Naylor would have been the first to agree. Jumped at it, the chance for a night out on his own, with the lads. Now it was different; he felt it was different. "All right," he had told her, "if you don't want to go, I'll stay home." That had done the trick.

Now he looked at his watch, the workload on his desk; best give Debbie a quick call.

Lynn was sitting in Resnick's office, telling him about her visit. Earlier, Resnick had interviewed first Gary James and then Nancy Phelan, conversations in still, airless rooms with the tape machine ticking digitally across the long afternoon. Gary had been alternately contrite and angry, constantly bringing things back to rotting wood and sagging doors and damp that ran down the insides of walls.

"You realize," Resnick had said, "behaving the way you did, it's not going to do your case any good."

"No?" Gary had said. "Then tell me what is."

Unable to answer, Resnick had handed him over to the custody sergeant and now he sat sulking in one of the police cells.

Nancy Phelan was adamant that Gary had done nothing to really hurt her, she had never felt in any actual danger. It had simply got out of hand.

"Then he didn't strike you?" Resnick had asked.

"No."

"Never as much as touched you?" A pause and then, pressing her fingers to her scalp, "I suppose he did grab my hair."

"And you weren't frightened?"

"No, he was."

Resnick thought about that as he listened to Lynn describing the marks on the boy's face, the swelling that had all but closed one eye, the bruise coming out strongly, yellow and purple and darkening.

"She said, the mother, that he'd fallen," Resnick said. Lynn nodded. "Running out the back door. The door was actually off, I don't know, she and Gary, they were putting it back on when the boy came running. Went smack into it."

"It's plausible, surely?"

"Yes."

"But you don't believe her?"

Lynn crossed and recrossed her legs. "In different circumstances, I might. But this Gary James, his record …"

"Nothing to suggest any violence towards the children."

"Something must have got him in a state before he got to the Housing Office. Something more than simply having to wait."

"Well …" Resnick got to his feet, walked round from behind his desk. Through the glass he could see Divine speaking into the telephone, Kevin Naylor painstakingly making notes, the pen in that awkward-seeming grip he used, as if it were an implement he was still struggling to control. … "Best have a word with social services." He checked his watch. "If they've knocked off early for the day, you can try the emergency duty team." Though not for long, he thought, rumor was that with the next wave of cuts they were to be axed. Which would mean the likes of Karl waiting till past Boxing Day.

Lynn paused at the door. "James, sir, are we keeping him in?"

Resnick made a face. "Christmas. I'd not want to, not if it can be avoided."

"But if the boy's at risk?"

"I know. Let's get someone round there, get him to a doctor, have him properly examined. Till then young Gary James can kick his heels."

"Right." Lynn stepped out into Divine's raucous laughter and the sound of an ambulance going past outside, another victim of the festivities on the way to Queen's. She paused near her desk and turned back towards the open door to Resnick's office. "I don't suppose there's any good trying to talk to his probation officer? Might throw some light, one way or another."

"You could always try," Resnick said. His expression suggested she would probably be wasting her time. Relationships with the probation service were not the most trusting, either way; and this wasn't the most propitious of times.

"I'll check anyway," Lynn said over her shoulder, "see whose client he is."

"Pam Van Allen."

Lynn was looking at him.

"I gave Neil Park a call. Earlier."

"But you've not spoken to her, sir, Van Allen?"

Resnick shook his head.

"You don't mind if I ..."

"You go ahead."

Back at his desk, for a moment Resnick closed his eyes; he could see her walking out of sight, Pam Van Allen, a meeting that had turned out badly, her hair glinting silver-gray against the light. "Pressure, Charlie," her senior, Neil Park had said later. "Male, high-ranking, used to telling people what to do and expecting them to do it. She resented it." Resnick didn't think he would have any luck there. If Lynn could talk to her, so much the better. Even so, he found himself staring at the phone, part of him wanting to call.

"Sir," Lynn knocked on his door and pushed it wide enough for her head to lean in. "She's gone home for the day. For the holiday."

"All right," Resnick said, "we'll hang on, see what social services have to say. Oh, and Lynn ..."

"Yes?"

"This business at home—whatever it is—if you need to talk about it ..."

For the first time in a while, she found something close to a smile. "Thanks."

Back across the CID room her phone once again was ringing. Someone was humming "Silent Night." From somewhere, Divine had acquired a paper hat, red and green, and he was wearing it as he read off an entry from the VDU, a sprig of mistletoe poking hopefully from his breast pocket.

Six

"So what was he like?" Nancy's flatmate, Dana, asked, her voice blurred beneath the rush and splatter of the shower.

"What was who like?"

"Your kidnapper, who else?"

Nancy pulled her head clear from the spray of water. Opaque, through the thick, flowered plastic of the curtain, she could see Dana on the loo, all but naked, taking a pee. Six months ago, when they had started sharing, Nancy would have been, well, not shocked, but certainly embarrassed. Neither would she have felt comfortable doing what she was doing now, turning off the shower and pulling back the curtain, stepping out on to the tiled floor to dry herself down.

"So?" Dana said, glancing up. "Was he sexy or what?"

Nancy gave a wry smile. "Hardly." She remembered the patchy hair, faint around his mouth, the way he had perspired, the nervous jerkiness of his hands, hollow of his eyes. "Besides, situations like that, sexiness doesn't come into it."

"Doesn't it?" Dana said. Pulling off a length of toilet paper, she folded the sheets again and then again before dabbing between her legs. "Somehow I thought it did."

Nancy was vigorously toweling her hair. "That's because you think it comes into everything."

Dana laughed and sent water flushing round the bowl. "What was he like then?" she said.

"A boy. A kid."

"So?" Dana arched a camp eyebrow and laughed some more.

The time Nancy had come home unexpected and found her flatmate grappling with a seventeen-year-old on the living-room carpet had been, in more ways than one, a revelation. "He's advanced for his age," Dana had explained. "Two A-levels already. Working hard for his Cambridge entrance."

"I noticed," Nancy had said. What she'd noticed were the marks on the youth's back as he'd pulled his Simple Minds T-shirt on over his head.

"Didn't I tell you," Nancy said now, "this Gary, we went to the same school?"

"No, really?"

"Yes, two years below me."

"And that's his name? Gary?"

"Uh-hum."

"And you remembered him?" Dana was standing slightly on tiptoe before the bathroom mirror, examining her breasts.

"Not at all."

"Then he remembered you."

Nancy wound the first towel around her head and reached for another. "I used to go out with this boy, he was a friend of Gary's big brother."

"You see, it all makes sense. There he was, Gary, adoring you from afar and you never as much as noticed him. The stuff that pimply wet dreams are made of."

Nancy grimaced and laughed and pretended to throw up over the toilet bowl.

"You don't think this is a lump, do you? Look, here?"

Serious, Nancy stared at her friend's left breast. "I don't know. I can't see any ..."'

"Feel."

Nancy reached out a hand and Dana took it, guiding it to the right spot.

"Well?"

Pressing down with her fingertips, Nancy rolled the flesh across and back; there was something there, the smallest knot of muscle possibly, not a lump. "No," she said, "I think you're fine. Nothing to worry about at all."

"Of course not," Dana smiled. Another of her friends, just thirty-five, was due in hospital for a mastectomy first thing in the new year.

"Can I borrow your hairdryer?" Nancy asked. "Mine's on the blink."

And then at the bathroom door—"This do tonight, we don't have to get too dressed up, do we?"

Dana's smile was genuine this time. "Only to the nines."

What might have helped, Nancy thought, on her way to the bedroom, if this afternoon had been more of a fright than actually it was, it might have done something to bring me on, get this blasted period of mine moving.

Martin Wrigglesworth no longer considered his working days in terms of good or bad; simply, they were gradations of the latter—bad, less bad, badder, baddest. A classical education not entirely gone to waste. There were days, he thought, his all-but clapped-out Renault Five stalling at the Noel Street lights, when the whole of Forest Fields should be swept into care. Why stop there? Hyson Green. Radford. The lot. Wheel everyone over sixty into residential homes for the aged; whisk children under eleven into the welcoming arms of foster parents, twelve-to-seventeen-year-olds into youth custody. Anyone left could be swept on to a massive Workfare program and work for their dole, performing useful services like cutting the grass on the Forest with nail clippers through the daylight hours. Those were the thoughts that got Martin through his less bad days.

At home in Nuthall at weekends, repainting the bathroom, waiting to collect the boys from swimming, helping his wife fold the washing in from the line, he tried to recall the exact moment, the feeling that had drawn him into social work, a good and honorable profession.

And what, Martin thought, turning into another narrow street in a warren of narrow streets, could he do? What honorable course might he take? Brutus would happily have fallen on his sword, of course, being an honorable man, but so far the mortgage and the pension plan and the irredeemable dream of renovating a dilapidated farmhouse in the South of France had kept any such thought firmly in Martin's scabbard.

"Martin," his wife would say wearily over her marking, "if it's making you feel so low, why don't you hand in your notice? Resign. You'll find something else." With over three million out of work, he knew only too well what be would find. Instead of resigning he was resigned.

Number 37, he said to himself, checking the hastily scribbled note on the seat beside him. A row of two-story, flat-fronted houses, front rooms opening out onto the street. Locking the car, he crossed the narrow, uneven pavement towards the chipped paint of the door. A late referral from a police officer fearful for the safety of a child: Lord knows what he would find on the other side. Not so long ago, here in the city, a young mother had dipped her two-year-old son's penis in hot tea and spun him round inside a spin dryer.

"Hello," he said, as Michelle opened the front door. "Ms. Paley? Martin Wrigglesworth, Social Services …" Showing her his card. "… I've called round about your son, er, Karl. I wonder if we might talk inside?"

"How do I look?"

Nancy was standing in the entrance to Dana's room in a silver crochet top, short black skirt, silver-gray tights with a pattern of raised silver dots, leather ankle boots with a slight heel. When Dana had asked her, back in mid-November, if she would like to go along to her firm's Christmas dinner and dance, it had seemed like a good idea. "Terrific," Dana enthused. "You look terrific."

"I feel ten feet tall."

"Better than five feet wide like me." Dana looked as if she had dived into her wardrobe head first and emerged swathed in color, bright yellows, purple, and green. Nancy was reminded of a parakeet with cleavage.

"No, seriously, I feel stupid."

"You look wonderful. Every man in that room is going to take one look at you …"

"That's what I'm worried about."

"… and be falling over themselves asking you to dance."

Nancy was looking at herself in Dana's full-length mirror. "I look like I'm auditioning for principal boy in *Aladdin.*"

"So, fine. You'll get the part."

Nancy recrossed the room, trying to walk small. She'd met one or two of them already, architects and such, they hadn't seemed too bad. More interesting than the people she worked with herself. "Maybe this isn't such a good idea," she said. "Maybe I shouldn't go at all. They're your friends, people you work with, I shall hardly know a soul."

"*You're* my friend. And besides, I've told them all about you ..." Nancy placed one hand over her eyes. "... and one more thing, there's no refund on the price of your ticket."

"All right," Nancy said, "you talked me into it. I'm coming."

Dana lifted her watch from the dressing table and, held it closer to her face. "Taxi's here in twenty minutes."

"I thought we didn't have to be there till eight?"

"We're meeting first for a drink at Sarah Brown's."

"Won't it be terribly crowded?"

"All the better. Rub shoulders with the rich and nearly famous."

"All the same," Martin Wrigglesworth was saying to Michelle, "I think, just to be certain, I'd be happier if we could just pop him along to the doctor, let someone have a proper look at him." From somewhere he dredged up a smile. "Better safe than sorry."

"You don't mean now?" Michelle asked. "You want to take him to the doctor now?"

"Yes," Martin said, clipping his biro into his top pocket. "Now."

The taxi arrived almost fifteen minutes early and the driver wanted to charge them waiting time, but Dana soon disabused him of that. Nancy had changed out of her black skirt into a pair of loose-fitting black trousers and then back into her skirt again. She had borrowed one of Dana's topcoats, bright red wool, a regular bull's delight.

"You've got your ticket?"

Nancy patted the sequined bag she held in her lap.

"Condoms?" Dana laughed.

Nancy stuck out her tongue. "It isn't going to be that kind of night."

Dana, sitting back in the corner of the cab, smiling. "You never know."

Nancy did: what she had in her bag, ever hopeful, were three Lillets.

The cab swung out of the Park, into incoming traffic on Derby Road. They were approaching Canning Circus when Nancy suddenly leaned forward, asking the driver to stop.

"What's the matter?" Dana asked. "What've you forgotten?"

"Nothing." Nancy opened the nearside door. "I'm just popping into the police station, that's all."

"Whatever for?"

"It doesn't matter. You go on. I'll meet you at the hotel. Go straight there. Bye."

Nancy pushed the cab door closed and stood a moment, watching the vehicle pull away, Dana's face, perplexed, staring back through the glass.

The officer on the duty desk had phoned Resnick's office to inform him he had a visitor, not quite able to keep the smirk out of his voice. It wasn't until Nancy Phelan walked in through the door to the deserted CID room that Resnick understood why.

"Inspector ..."

"Yes?"

"I was here earlier today ..."

"I remember." Resnick smiled. "Not dressed like that."

Nancy gave a half-smile in return. She had unbuttoned the borrowed red coat walking up the stairs and now it hung loose from her shoulders. "Christmas Eve, you know how it is. Everyone out on the town."

While Kevin Naylor held the fort, Resnick had nipped home to feed the cats, brushed his best suit, ironed a white shirt, buffed his shoes, scraped a few fragments of pesto sauce from his tie. The one night of the year he tried to make an impression. "I've got changed myself," he said pleasantly.

"Sorry," Nancy said, "I hadn't noticed."

"Yes, well ... what exactly was it you ..."

"About this afternoon ..."

"Yes?"

"Like I said, nothing really happened, to me I mean. It wasn't, you know, this big traumatic thing or anything."

"But it's on your mind all the same."

"Is it?"

Resnick shrugged large shoulders. "You're here."

"Yes, but that's not because of me. It's him."

"Him?"

"James. Gary James."

"What about him?"

Nancy fidgeted her feet on the office floor. "I'm not sure. I suppose … All it was, I had this thought, like, when I was passing, literally, going past outside … I didn't want to think that he was cooped up in here, in some cell over Christmas because of me."

The social worker had contacted Lynn Kellogg after the doctor had carried out his examination: Karl's injuries were not inconsistent with the explanation that his mother had given—he had run headlong into a heavy wooden door. Social Services would keep a watching brief and if there was any further cause for concern … Gary James had been released a little over half an hour ago, warned as to his future behavior, and made to understand there was a possibility charges might still be brought.

"You don't have to worry," Resnick said. "We've let him go."

Nancy's smile was a delight to behold. "And that's the end of it?"

"Not necessarily."

"But …"

"There are other things, other issues involved." Resnick moved towards the door and she followed him, the worn carpet muffling the clip of her heels.

"You won't be needing me again then? Testimony in court or anything?"

"I shouldn't think so. It's unlikely."

Somehow, close in the doorway, she seemed taller, her face only inches from his own.

"Well, Merry Christmas, I suppose," Nancy said, and for one absurd moment Resnick thought she was going to breach that distance between them with a kiss.

"Merry Christmas," Resnick said, as she walked down the corridor. "And tonight, have a good time."

At the head of the stairs, Nancy raised her hand and waved. "You too," she said.

Resnick turned back towards his office, started putting out the lights.

Seven

How it worked was this: large-scale bookings were given a banqueting room of their own, smaller parties were encouraged to share. Either way the format was the same—long lines of tables on opposite sides of a central dance floor, a DJ in a cream suit waiting to slip Elvis' "Blue Christmas" in between Abba and Rolf Harris doing terrible things to "Stairway to Heaven." Plates of food were bounced down in efficient relays; soup, egg mayonnaise, a blue ticket brought turkey, a pink, salmon; the fruit salad came with cream or without. Two bottles of wine every eight people, one red, one white; any further drinks you fetched yourself from the cellar bar. If that became too crowded, it was always possible to cross the courtyard into the main body of the hotel, pass between reception and the wide armchairs of the foyer, and use the bar there.

"All right now!" the DJ overpitched into his mike above the final scraping of plates and the rising tide of conversation. "Who's gonna be the first ones on the floor?"

"What d'you say, Charlie," Reg Cossall barked into Resnick's ear, "we get ourselves out of here and get a real drink?"

"Later, maybe, Reg. Later."

Cossall scraped back his chair, pushed himself to his feet. "I'll be across the other side for a bit, if you change your mind. Then, likely, I'll head down the Bell."

Times long past, Resnick had closed too many bars with Reg Cossall to forget the mornings after. He'd stick where he was for another half hour or so, long enough to show willing, then slip away and leave them to it. He could see Divine revving up already, on his feet a couple of tables down, trying to encourage one of the new WPCs on to the floor, offering to pull her Christmas cracker.

"Come feel the noize!" called the DJ, turning the volume up on Slade and letting the decibels bounce off the ceiling.

Jack Skelton was wearing a dinner jacket, a midnight-blue bow tie; he was standing against the side wall, deep in conversation with Helen Siddons, recently promoted DCI and using the city as a stepping stone on her fast track to the top. They made an elegant pair, standing there, Siddons in an ankle-length pale green gown.

From his seat, Resnick glanced around, concerned that Skelton's wife might be sitting in need of company. What he saw were Kevin Naylor and his wife Debbie, smiling into one another's eyes, holding hands. Second honeymoon, Resnick thought, and not before time. Like a lot of marriages in the force, this one seemed to have been disintegrating before his eyes. It was more than a sign of the times; even when families had seemed more stable and relationships didn't come with their own sell-by date, police divorce figures had been high. How many times had Reg Cossall bought the CID room cigars and signed his name in the registrar's book? Two? Three? And rumor had it he was trying for one more. Resnick sat back down. Either you were like Reg or you tried once and when that was over, shut the doors and threw away the key.

Which is it with you, Charlie?

He could see Skelton's wife Alice now, three rows down, tilting back her head as she finished her wine, reaching out to refill the glass, tapping a cigarette from the pack on the table before her, small gold lighter from her bag, the head tilting back again as she released a swathe of gray smoke, feathering past her eyes.

"Alice?" He stood alongside her, waiting for her to turn.

"Charlie. Well ... how nice. A social call?"

Resnick shrugged, suddenly uncomfortable. "I saw you ..."

"On my own? A damsel in distress. Alone and palely loitering."

There was a whoop from the dance floor, an attempt at a Michael Jackson going badly out of control, legs and arms akimbo.

"For heaven's sake, sit down, Charlie. You're like a spare prick at a wedding."

Resnick took the chair beside her, calculating how much she had likely drunk, how soon before leaving she'd got started. In all of their infrequent social meetings, stretching back ten years, he had never heard her raise her voice or swear.

"Send you over, did he, Charlie?"

Resnick shook his head.

"Keep an eye on me. Get me talking. Do me a favor, Charlie, keep her happy. Give her a bit of a spin, out on the floor."

"Alice, I don't know—"

Her hand, the one not holding the glass, was on his knee. "Come on, Charlie, don't play naive. We know what it's like, all boys together, doesn't matter how old. You cover my back, I'll cover yours." She drank and exchanged the glass for her cigarette. "That's what it all comes down to, Charlie. In the end. The covering of backs."

Smoke drifted slowly past Resnick's face. At the edge of his vision he could see Jack Skelton leaning lightly against the farthest wall, Helen Siddons turned towards him, both heads bowed in conversation. As Resnick watched, Skelton's hand moved towards his jacket pocket, inadvertently brushing the DCI's bare arm on its way.

"Aren't you drinking, Charlie?" Alice Skelton held the bottle towards him.

Resnick nodded back to where he'd been sitting. "I've got one over there."

"Abstemious, too. Abstemious and loyal. No wonder Jack's so keen to keep you where you are." She emptied the bottle into her glass, little more than the dregs.

"I'll get you another ..."

Her hand had moved from his leg but now, as he made to rise, it was back. Resnick was starting to sweat just a little; just as some would be clocking Skelton and Siddons, how many were noticing himself and Skelton's wife, putting the numbers together to see how well they fit?

"Alice ..."

"What you have to see, she's not just fucking him, Charlie, she's fucking you too."

"Alice, I'm sorry ..." He was on his feet, but she still had hold of him, fingers pressing hard behind the knee. Squeezing past on the other side of the table, one of the civilian VDU operators laughing on his arm, Divine caught Resnick's eye and winked.

"What do you need to know, Charlie?" He had to bend towards her to catch what she was saying above the noise; didn't want her raising her voice any further, shouting it out. "Rules of evidence. How much proof d'you need? Catching them doing it, there in your bed?"

"I'm sorry, Alice, I've got to go."

He prized away her hand and pushed his way between the backs and chairs, the laughter, all the huddled promises and thoughtless betrayals hatching on the night.

Lynn Kellogg was wearing a strapless dress, royal blue, and had done something to her hair Resnick had not noticed before. The man in the dress suit, between them at the crowded bar, was clearly taken. "Let me get those." Smiling, twenty-pound note in his hand. "No, thanks. You're all right," Lynn said, turning away. "Later, then?" "What?" "Let me buy you a drink, later." She shook her head and pushed through the crowd.

Resnick watched her go over to where Maureen Madden was standing, Maureen wearing a dark frock-coat and jeans, looking more like a country singer on the loose than the sergeant who supervised the rape suite. Reg Cossall was shouting at him from the far end of the bar and waving his empty glass.

"A pint of whatever he's drinking," Resnick said to the white-coated barman, "and a large Bells to go with it. Bottle of Czech Budweiser for me, if you've got it."

He had. Resnick pushed his way along and listened for a while to Cossall laying down the law about the unemployment rate, young offenders, overpriced imported beer, Brian Clough, the social benefits of castration. Half a dozen younger officers stood around, drinking steadily, gleaning wisdom. Resnick remembered when he and Cossall had been like them, eager to ape their elders and betters; back when you had to be six foot to get on to the force and either it was draught Bass, draught Worthington or you didn't bother going back for more. Twenty years before.

When he'd heard enough, Resnick moved away and found Lynn Kellogg and Maureen Madden, sitting now on the stairs near the entrance to the lounge.

"Quite an admirer back there," Resnick said to Lynn, nodding back towards the bar.

"Oh, that. He'd been drinking. You know what it's like."

"I wish you'd stop doing that," Maureen said.

"Doing what?"

"Putting yourself down. Assuming that for some man to fancy you he has to be half-pissed."

"It's usually true."

"Don't you think she looks great?" Maureen asked Resnick, craning her neck to look up at him.

"Very nice," Resnick said.

Lynn felt herself starting to blush. "Have you been out on the floor yet?" she asked, covering her embarrassment.

Resnick shook his head.

"He's waiting for you," Maureen teased.

"More like waiting for them to turn the volume down," Resnick said. "Play a waltz."

"Now that's not true," Lynn said. "My first year, you were out there bopping till everyone else dropped. 'Be-bop-a-hula,' stuff like that."

Despite himself, Resnick smiled: something attractive about the idea of Gene Vincent in black leathers and a grass skirt, strumming away at an Hawaiian guitar.

"Well," Maureen announced, setting her empty glass on the floor, "I'm in the mood. What d'you say, Lynn? Game? Before your admirer over there comes and asks you."

The man in the dress suit, glass in hand, was sitting in one of the easy chairs in the lounge, making no pretense of not looking in their direction.

"Come on," Lynn said, getting to her feet "Let's get out of here." Maureen was already on her way. "Coming with us?" Lynn asked.

"You go ahead," Resnick said.

With a last look back, Lynn followed Maureen Madden towards the main door.

"Like watching 'em leave the nest, Charlie?" Reg Cossall said at Resnick's shoulder.

"How d'you mean?"

"You know, young ones, fledglings ..."

"She's scarce a kid, Reg."

"No matter."

"Old enough to be ..."

Cossall's hand squeezed down firm on Resnick's shoulder. "You can be a literal bugger sometimes, Charlie. When it fits your purpose." Cossall treated Resnick to his best philosophical stare. "Kids. Families. Can't get 'em one way, we get 'em another. More's the bastard pity."

He lit a small cigar and cupped it in his hand. "Not on for one in town, I suppose?"

"I don't think so."

"Please yourself, then. You always bloody do."

Resnick turned back to the bar and prepared to wait his chance to order a final beer.

Back in the Friar Tuck Room, things were throbbing towards some sort of climax. Whitney Houston, Rod Stewart, Chris De Burgh, the Drifters—hands clutched shiny buttocks that were not their own. Divine, tie forsaken, shirt all unbuttoned, was executing a limbo dance to "Twist and Shout," sliding his legs beneath a line of brassiere straps linked together. Off to the side of the room, Skelton and Helen Siddons scarcely seemed to have moved, the same urgent conversation, heads angled inwards; one strap of Helen's dress had slid from her shoulder. Lynn and Maureen Madden were dancing with a group of other women, laughing, clapping their hands in the air. Oblivious of the tempo, Kevin Naylor and Debbie were dancing cheek to cheek, bodies barely moving. Resnick couldn't see Alice Skelton anywhere and was grateful.

"Five minutes to Christmas," the DJ announced. "I want to see you all in a big circle, holding hands."

Resnick slipped out through the door.

"Inspector?"

He glanced up and saw long legs, a sequined silver bag, a smile.

"I didn't know we were partying in the same place," Nancy Phelan said.

Resnick half-smiled. "So it seems."

"How's it been?" Nancy asked. Resnick was aware of a car on the curve of the courtyard, waiting. "You been having a good time?"

"Not bad, I suppose."

"Well ..." Smiling, she gestured outwards with open hands. "Merry Christmas, once again. Happy New Year."

"Happy New Year," Resnick echoed, as Nancy walked out of his vision and, hands in pockets, he turned left and crossed the cobbled courtyard to the street.

Eight

For Christmas, Resnick had bought himself *The Complete Billie Holiday on Verve*, a new edition of Dizzy Gillespie's autobiography, and *The Penguin Guide to Jazz on CD, LP and Cassette.* What he still had to acquire was a CD player.

But there he'd been, not so many days before, sauntering down from Canning Circus into town, sunshine, one of those clear blue winter skies, and glancing into the window of Arcade Records he had seen it. Among the Eric Clapton and the Elton John, a black box with the faintest picture of Billie on its front; ten CDs and a two-hundred-and-twenty-page book, seven hundred minutes of music, a numbered, limited edition, only sixteen thousand pressed worldwide.

Worldwide, Resnick had thought; only sixteen thousand worldwide. That didn't seem an awful lot of copies. And here was one, staring up at him, and a bargain offer to boot. He had his check book but not his check card. "It's okay," the owner had said, "I think we can trust you." And knocked another five pounds off the price.

Resnick had spent much of the morning, between readying the duck for the oven, peeling the potatoes, and cleaning round the bath, looking at it. Holding it in his hand. *Billie Holiday on Verve.* There is a photograph of her in the booklet, New York City, 1956: a woman early to middle-age, no glamour, one hand on her hip, none too patiently waiting, a working woman, c'mon now, let's get this done. He closes his eyes and imagines her singing—"Cheek to Cheek" with Ben Webster, wasn't that fifty-six? "Do Nothing Till You Hear From Me." "We'll Be Together Again." The number stamped on the back of Resnick's set is 10961.

So much easier to look again and again at the booklet, slide those disks from their brown card covers, admire the reproductions of album sleeves in their special envelope, easier to do all of this than take the few steps to the mantelpiece and the card that waits in its envelope, unopened. A post mark, smudged, that might say Devon; the unmistakable spikiness of his ex-wife's hand.

The duck was delicious, strongly flavored, fatty yet not too fat. Certainly Dizzy had thought so, up on to the table with a spring before Resnick had noticed, enjoying his share of breast, a little leg, happy finally to be chased off down the garden, jaws tight around a wing.

Resnick sliced away the meat from where the black cat had eaten and shared it amongst the others, Miles rearing up on his hind legs, Bud pushing his head against Resnick's shins, Pepper patient by his bowl.

As well as those he had set to roast around the bird, Resnick had cooked potatoes separately and mashed them with some swede, sprinkled that with paprika, poured on sour cream. Sprouts he had blanched in boiling water before finishing in the frying pan with slices of salami, cut small. Polish sausage he had simmered in beer until it was swollen and done.

He had not long finished foraging for his second helping when Marian Witczak called him on the phone. "Charles, how are you? I have been meaning all day to wish you a merry Christmas, but, I don't know, somehow it has all been so busy."

Resnick pictured her, alone in the extravagant Victoriana of her house across the city, drinking Christmas toasts to long-departed Polish heroes, pale sherry in fragile crystal glasses; sitting down, perhaps, to play a little Chopin at the piano before taking some general's memoir or some book of old photographs down from the shelf.

"So, Charles, you must tell me, my presents, what did you think?"

They were still on the hall chest, neat in their snowy paper, white and red ribbon tied with bows.

"Marian, I'm sorry, thank you. Thank you very much."

"You really like them?"

"Of course."

"If only you knew how much time I spent deciding, well, I think you might be surprised. But the colors, the design, it had to be just right."

Socks? Resnick thought. A tie?

"Even so, I have kept the receipt. Should you decide to take it back and exchange …"

"Marian, no. It's lovely." A tie.

"And the other gift, Charles, what did you think of that?"

The other? He pictured a second package, square and flat, he had taken it for a card. But, no, Marian's card was in the living room, a starry night over Wenceslas Square.

"It was not too presumptuous, I trust."

"We're old friends, Marian …"

"Exactly. This is what I tell myself."

"You know me well enough …"

"So you will come?"

Come? Resnick swallowed most of a sigh. Come where?

"We will both wear, Charles, what would you say? Our dancing shoes."

The conversation over, Resnick went through to the hall. Faced with the broad expanse of the chest's wooden lid, Bud had chosen Marian's presents to curl up on. The tie was silk, a swirl of soft color, blue on blue. Inside the second package was his ticket to the Polish Club's New Year's Eve Dinner and Dance. What was it, this sudden desire of everyone to get him out on to the floor?

The same films were on the television, immovable as the Queen's Christmas Address. What he wanted was a good old-fashioned first division encounter, Southend and Grimsby, one of those. Where the long ball hoofed out of defense was deemed creative play and tackles thudded in so hard the TV set seemed to shake with the impact. What he got were daring prisoners-of-war, straw men, a sweep of hills on which, if only people would stop singing, you might hear edelweiss grow. Was it Exeter, the name smudged almost out of recognition? Exmoor? Exmouth? Resnick held up the envelope, angled against the light. Through it he saw, in veiled outline, something that might have been a coach with horses, reindeer with a sledge. *Let me tell them about the letters, Charlie. All the letters I sent you, the ones you never answered. All the times I rang up in pain and you hung up without a word.* With care, he set it back upon the shelf. *Tell them all about that, Charlie. How you helped me with everything I've been going through.*

He had not heard from Elaine for years, not since the divorce. And then they had started arriving, envelopes on which it was sometimes difficult to read his own address. Afraid of their contents he had shredded them into fragments, turned them to ash, pushed them deep to the back of the kitchen drawer. He had not wanted to know and it had taken Elaine to tell him, face to face, her voice strident and off-key, puncturing his seeming indifference with its accusations and its pain; later, in this house, this room, she had outlined with disturbing calmness her journey from miscarriage and desertion to the hospital ward, the treatments, the analyst's chair.

Resnick had felt sympathy for her then, love even, not the same but a different kind. Almost, he could have crossed the floor and held her in his arms. But guilt had numbed him. That and a sense of self-preservation too.

She had walked out of the house and he had not heard from her again.

Till now.

From the upstairs window he mourned the slow fading of the light.

Coffee, he ground fine and made strong, drank with a tumbler of whisky at its side. Sliding an Ellington album from its buckled sleeve, he set it to play. The notes on the incident at the Housing Office and Gary James' interview he had brought with him and he scanned them now, wondering again if it had been right to release him, let him return home. Injuries to a small boy consistent with what? Running smack into a door. Smack into his father's fist. One of the cats jumped into Resnick's lap, nudged his fingers with its nose, turned twice and settled, lay a paw across its eyes, and fell asleep. Jimmy Blanton's bass was rocking the whole band. Exmouth or Exeter? A coach or a sledge? Miles stared up at Resnick resentfully as he was set down on the floor. So easy, the act of sliding a finger behind the envelope's flap, tearing it open, shaking the contents down into your hand. It was a stage-coach, holly at its windows, snowflakes round its wheels; someone akin to Mr. Pickwick beamed from the driver's seat and lifted his hat. *Forgive me, Charlie?* it said inside, and then, below, the words close to falling off the bottom of the card, *Merry Christmas, Elaine.*

No love, no kiss.

Forgive me.

He heard Alice Skelton's harsh whispers. *How much proof d'you need? Catching them doing it, there in your bed?*

It had been someone else's bed, an empty house, the duvet carefully replaced, pillows slightly overlapping, not quite so. When he had lifted the duvet aside and brought his face close to the center of the sheet, there had been no denying it, the lingering warmth, the tang of recent, hurried sex. The smile upon Elaine's face when he had seen her leaving, minutes before. That smile. When Resnick brought his hand to his face, as he did now, and closed his eyes, he could taste, deep in the cracks between his fingers, that memory, salt like the sea.

Nine

Dana hadn't given much attention to the compliments being paid her at their Christmas Eve function. Not at first, anyway. The usual remarks about what she was wearing, her hair, her natural contours, the comparisons with Madonna. "Someone's giving you *Sex* for Christmas, I'll bet." "Come on, Jeremy, you can see, she's already got it." For some of them, some of the men she worked with, it came as naturally as breathing. Especially the married ones: all the things they no longer said to their wives. She didn't even think of it as sexual harassment. She didn't feel threatened, hardly ever embarrassed; it was constant, within the bounds of the generally acceptable, and even if it did become a little wearing, well, it was better than spending your time with a bunch of yobbos who were likely to break into "Get your tits out for the lads!" at the first opportunity.

The other thing was, she did like to be noticed. And by men. It wasn't that she flaunted herself in front of them, but it did please her when they knew she was there. As she'd said to Nancy, if you're never allowed a little sexual repartee, if the flower didn't attract the bee—well, how was anything ever going to happen? And she had this certain feeling: too much repression was harmful. Tiptoe around each other pretending you've got blinkers on, not a word or a glance out of place, and then, suddenly, there's this guy, can't control it any longer, hurling you down behind the color photocopier, leaving his unrequited passion all over the floor. "Mmm," Nancy had said, uncertain, "maybe there's something in between."

Well, Dana had thought, when Andrew Clarke, hand just touching her elbow, had guided her out on to the floor, maybe there was.

Andrew was a senior partner, Victorian house in the Park, all the original architraves, things like that. Family car was a BMW, but Dana had noticed recently this little Toyota MR2 in his slot in the parking lot. Red, something to run around in now the days of public school fees were coming to an end. The most provocative remark he'd ever made to her in the office was about the air-conditioning. No, he was scrupulous, correct; she'd never even caught him looking at her as she walked away, admiring her backside.

"Not very good at this, you know. Even though my daughters try to teach me at family parties."

There were so many crowded on to the small circle of polished floor, it didn't matter that Andrew Clarke's attempts to boogie resembled the final struggles of a man trapped in quicksand. In fact, there was something about the earnestness with which he went about it which Dana found almost endearing.

So, when the music switched to some old Stevie Wonder and he pulled her into some kind of smoochy waltz, she didn't object. Though she was surprised, after a while, to feel something remarkably close to an erection pushing against her thigh.

She was on the steps outside the cloakroom, after one o'clock, when she saw him again. He had on his Crombie overcoat, a little nicked up at the collar, and his car keys in his hand.

"Going home alone?"

It looked like it; Nancy, despite her earlier protestations, seemed to have found congenial company.

"Still in that place on Newcastle Drive, aren't you? On my way. Why not let me drop you off?"

The inside of the car smelt of leather polish and cologne. She was ready for the invitation to coffee when it came, had determined to say no, the exact tone rehearsed inside her head so as not to offend.

"Yes," she said. "A quick cup. All right."

The family, of course, had headed north that morning, getting an early start. "Little place off the Northumbrian coast. Had it for years. Nothing special." Dana noticed a photograph of Andrew and his sons in front of what looked like a small castle, Andrew and the eldest boy with their shotguns, smiling as they held up dead birds.

"Still ..." pressing a large glass of brandy into her hands "... their not being here, affords us a bit of privacy. Chance to get to know one another better."

When Dana limped out forty minutes later, her bra strap was round her neck, unfastened, her tights were torn, she had lost the heel from one of her shoes. Andrew's mood had switched from amorous to angry and back again and when finally she had slapped him hard, pushed him clear, and told him to grow up, he had astonished her by bursting into tears.

Back in her own flat, Christmas Day was already two hours old and no sign of Nancy. Dana only hoped she was having a better time than herself. Quickly, she undressed and showered and made herself some camomile tea. Cross-legged on the floor in front of the TV set, she raised a cup to her reflection in the blank screen. "Happy Christmas to you, too."

At some point she must have woken cold and found her way into her bed, but when she came round beneath the floral duvet at what felt like half-past six, she couldn't remember it. The digital clock on the floor read 11:07. The telephone was ringing. Dana stumbled towards the bathroom, rubbing the residue of makeup from around her eyes. On the way, she lifted the receiver from the body of the phone and set it down, unanswered. In the mirror she looked fifty years old.

Thirty minutes in the bathroom reduced that by all of five years. Great! Dana thought. Now I look like my mother just back from a fortnight on a health farm. She pulled on a T-shirt, sweater, and old jeans. There were two mandarin orange yogurts in the fridge and she ate them both, washing them down with some stale Evian. Well, Nancy, midday—must be having a pretty good time.

When she remembered the phone, a woman's recorded voice was instructing her to replace the hand set and redial. The moment she put the receiver back in place, it rang again.

"Hello?"

It was Nancy's mother, calling from Merseyside to wish her daughter a merry Christmas. From the background noises, the rest of the family were waiting to do the same.

"I'm sorry, Mrs. Phelan, she's not here now."

"But we thought she was spending Christmas Day with you. She said ..."

"She is, she is. It's just ..." It's just that she's not back yet from getting laid. "She's popped out. A walk. You know, clear her head."

"She's not ill?"

"Oh, no. No. Just last night, we went to this dinner-dance ..."

There was a silence and then, indistinctly, the sound of Mrs. Phelan reporting back to the family. "Be sure to tell Nancy I called," she said when her voice came back on the line. "I'll try again in a little while."

Which she did several times over the next few hours. And on each occasion the questions were increasingly anxious, Dana's responses increasingly vague. When she was fast running out of excuses, Mr. Phelan spoke to her himself. "Enough of this pissing about, right? I want to know what's going on."

Best as she could, Dana told him.

"Why on earth didn't you say that before?"

"I didn't want her mother to be upset."

"The minute she drags herself back in," Mr. Phelan said, "you tell her she's to call us, right?"

Right. At the far end of the line there was a sharp swerve of breath before the connection was broken.

Dana looked at the turkey taking up most of the refrigerator, the black plastic vegetable rack overloaded with several weeks' supply. She pulled a frozen broccoli lasagna, only two days past its use-by date, from the freezer and put it in the microwave. In the time it took to cook, she had looked at her watch, at the clock on the kitchen-diner wall half a dozen times. When Nancy's father next phoned, she had the directory open on her lap and was about to try the casualty department at Queen's.

"Is it like her?" Mr. Phelan asked, no attempt to disguise the anxiety he was feeling. "Not to let you know where she is?"

"I don't know."

"You're living with her, girl."

"Yes, but I mean ... Well, it's not as if there've been a lot of occasions ..."

"So being down there hasn't turned her into a tart, her mother will be pleased. Now have I to get in the car and drive down there or what? Because it seems to me you're not treating this as seriously as you should."

"I really don't think we have to worry, I'm sure she's fine."

"Yes? That's what you'd want our Nancy thinking if you were the one not come home, is it?"

A pause. "I was about to phone the hospital when you called," Dana said.

"Good. And the police, I dare say."

Ten

Christmas morning or no Christmas morning, Jack Skelton had been for his normal four-mile run, setting off while his wife was still apparently sleeping, returning, lightly bathed in sweat, to find her staring at him accusingly in the dressing-room mirror.

"Have fun last night, you two?" Kate asked disarmingly at breakfast.

Skelton pushed the back of the spoon down against his Shredded Wheat, breaking it into the bottom of his bowl; carefully, Alice poured tea into her cup.

"Like to have seen it," Kate went on into the silence, "the pair of you, dancing the light fantastic. Bet you were a regular Roy Rogers and Fred Astaire."

"It's Ginger ..." began Alice, sounding her exasperation.

"She knows," Skelton said quietly.

"Then why doesn't she ...?"

"Can't you tell when you're being wound up? It was a joke."

"Funny sort of a joke."

"Isn't that the usual kind?" Kate said, no disguising the malicious glint in her eye.

"Katie, that's enough," Skelton said.

"Your trouble, young lady," Alice said, "you're altogether too smart behind the ears."

"It's what comes of having such clever parents," Kate replied.

Half out of her chair, Alice leaned sharply forwards, about to wipe the smile from her daughter's face with the back of her hand. Kate stared back at her, daring her to do exactly that. Alice picked up her cup and saucer and left the room.

With a slow shake of his head, Skelton sighed.

"Did you have a good time last night?" Kate asked, this time as though she might have cared.

"It was all right, I suppose."

"But not great?"

Skelton almost smiled. "Not great."

"Neither was mine."

"Your party?"

"All so boring and predictable. People getting drunk as fast as they were able, chucking up all over someone else's floor."

"Tom there?"

Tom was Kate's latest, a student from the university, a bit of a high-flier; in Skelton's eyes a welcome change from the last love of her life, an unemployed goth who wore black from head to toe and claimed to be on quite good terms with the Devil.

"He was there for a bit."

"You didn't have a row?"

Kate shook her head. "He hates parties like that, says they're all a bunch of immature wankers."

Skelton managed to stop himself reacting to her choice of word; besides, it sounded as if Tom had got it pretty right. "Why on earth stay? Why not leave when he did?"

"Because he didn't ask me. And besides, they're my friends."

The same friends, Skelton was thinking, you used to take E with at all-night raves.

"I hope you're not expecting," Kate said, "me to hang round here all day. I mean, just 'cause it's Christmas."

The day wore on in silent attrition. The turkey was dry on the outside, overcooked, pink, and tinged with blood close to the bone. Alice accomplished the moves from sherry to champagne to cherry brandy without breaking stride. Kate spent an hour in the bath, as long again on the phone, and then announced she was going out, not to wait up. As it was beginning to get dark Skelton appeared at the living-room door in his navy-blue track suit, new Asics running shoes.

"In training for something, Jack?" Alice asked, glancing up. "Running away?"

Before the front door had closed, she was back with her Barbara Vine.

When Skelton returned almost an hour later, Alice was sitting with the lights out, feet up, settee pulled close to the fire. She was smoking a cigarette, a liqueur glass nearby on the floor.

"Why are you sitting in the dark?" Skelton asked.

"There was a call for you," Alice said. "From the station." And as he crossed the room. "Don't hurry. It wasn't from her."

The pavement outside the police station was littered with broken glass. Crepe paper and tinsel hung, disconsolate, from nearby railings. In the waiting area, a young woman with half her ginger hair shaved to stubble and the remainder tightly plaited, was nursing a black mongrel dog bleeding from a badly cut ear.

"What's this, the Humane Society all of a sudden?" Skelton said to the officer on desk duty.

"Every day except Christmas, sir."

When Skelton went close to the dog it barked and showed its teeth.

Upstairs in his office, door to the CID room open, Resnick was talking to a well-built woman Skelton took to be in her early to mid-thirties. Friend of the girl who'd gone missing, he assumed. Not a bad looker in a blousy sort of a way. At opposite sides of the room, Lynn Kellogg and Kevin Naylor were on the phones.

"When you've a minute, Charlie," Skelton called from the doorway, "all right?"

He was tipping ready-ground decaf into the gold filter of his new coffee machine when Resnick knocked and walked in.

"So, Charlie, where are we? Not throwing up panic signals too soon?"

Resnick waited until the superintendent had added the water, flipped the switch to on. New machine or no, he was thinking, it'll still be too weak to stand. When Skelton was back behind his desk, Resnick took a seat himself and relayed Dana Matthieson's concern over her flatmate, Nancy Phelan.

"That's not the same woman involved in that incident yesterday? Phelan?"

"At the Housing Office, yes."

"Threatened, wasn't she?"

"In a manner of speaking."

"The man responsible ..."

"Gary James, sir."

"We released him."

"Last night, yes."

"No suggestion he might have been involved?"

Resnick shook his head. "Not as far as we know."

"What happened at the Housing place, was it personal between them?"

"Not as far as we know."

"We know damn all."

"Very little, so far."

Skelton crossed to the side of the room; the coffee had all but finished dripping through.

"Black, Charlie?"

"Thanks." When the superintendent held up the glass pot of coffee, Resnick was alarmed: you could see right through it.

"You've got someone out having a word with him, James, all the same?"

"Not yet, sir."

Skelton sat back down. "Boyfriend?" he asked.

"No one special, not at the moment. Not according to her flatmate. She gave us some names, though. We've started checking them out."

"Family?"

"We're in touch."

Skelton squeezed the arms of his chair. He had never noticed before the way Alice's eyes followed him from that photograph on his desk; carefully, with forefinger and thumb, he angled her away until all she could see was the blackening brick of the city beyond the window. "How long since anyone saw her last?"

"Nineteen hours, give or take."

"Around midnight, then."

"I think, sir," Resnick said, reaching down to rest his coffee on the floor, "the last person to see her, so far as we know, it was likely me."

He had the superintendent's attention now, taking him through Nancy Phelan's unscheduled visit to the station, his chance meeting with her later in the hotel courtyard, the engine ticking over just beyond the edge of his vision, the car.

"Make? Number?"

Resnick shook his head. "Saloon, four-door probably. Standard size and shape. Astra, something close."

"Color?"

"Black, possibly. Certainly dark. Dark blue. Maroon."

"Damn it, Charlie, there's a lot of difference."

"There wasn't a lot of light."

"I know, and you had no reason to pay special attention."

Which doesn't stop me, Resnick thought, from thinking that I should.

"We can't be certain, presumably, the car was waiting for her?"

"No."

"You didn't see her get into it?"

"No."

"So she could have been going back into the hotel?"

"It's possible, but from what she said … I'd guess she was about to leave."

Skelton leaned back, locked his fingers behind his head.

"If the car, any car, had gone past me," Resnick said, "between there and the castle, I think I'd have noticed. But all he had to do was turn right instead of left, I'd never have seen him."

"He?" Skelton said.

Elbows on his knees, Resnick brushed a hand across his forehead, closed his eyes.

Eleven

Dana Matthieson was sitting on the edge of a chair in Resnick's office, trying to concentrate while he double-checked the names of people who had been at the dinner, the connections between them, making sure it had all been noted down. The door to the outer office was open a couple of inches, enough to let the overlapping conversations, occasional bursts of anger or laughter slide through. It was difficult not to keep thinking about Nancy, where she might be.

"This name here," Resnick said, "Yvonne Warden ..."

"Andrew's assistant. She'd have the list of invitations, everything would go through her."

"And Andrew is?"

"Andrew Clarke. The senior partner."

"He was there?"

Dana visualized Clarke's expression when he had asked if she wanted a lift home, did she want to pop in for coffee? The narrowing of those piggy eyes. How could she have been so naive? "Oh, yes," she said, "he was there."

Resnick wrote something on the sheet of paper. "We should talk to him, certainly."

"Yes," Dana said. "I think you should." She was wondering if there were others in the office Clarke had tried it on with. Probably, she decided. Clarke and men like him. Carrying on as if sexual harassment was a headline they passed over in the morning paper, nothing to do with them. Men in authority and middle-age. She was looking at Resnick across his desk, tie twisted inside his shirt collar, worry lines pouched deep into his face. When she had been close to tears, earlier, blaming herself for persuading Nancy to go with her, he had been sympathetic, straightforward, done his best to assure her that her friend would turn up safe and well.

"Then why are we doing all this?" Dana had asked. "Going to all this trouble?"

Resnick had smiled reassuringly with his eyes. "A precaution. In case."

Now he was standing, telling her there was nothing more. "The minute you hear from her, you'll let us know?" Dana assured him that she would.

Resnick had spoken to Nancy's parents several times within the past hour, the mother alternately tearful and bravely matter-of-fact, her father ever closer to anger, frustrated that as yet there was no one for him to aim that anger at. Resnick spelt out all that they were doing, wanting them to feel involved, not wishing that anger to be directed at him. If Nancy's disappearance proved not to be voluntary, they were going to need the parents on their side.

"Shall you not be wanting a picture? Her mother's bound to have something recent ..."

Resnick explained they were getting one from Dana, taken only a few weeks before. A detailed description had already been forwarded to all stations in the city, all officers on duty.

"And shall you put it, like, on tele? On the news?"

He had discussed this with Skelton, Skelton with the chief superintendent. They had decided not to go public for another twelve hours.

"I thought you were treating this as urgent? That's my bloody daughter ..."

"Mr. Phelan, we still think the most likely explanation is that Nancy decided at the last minute to spend Christmas Day with a friend."

"Without letting anyone know?"

"It's possible."

"Aye, and pigs might bloody fly!"

"Mr. Phelan, we have to—"

"What you've got to do is get off your arse and bloody find her!"

"Mr.—"

"Listen. Never mind your cock and bull theories. Whatever our Nancy took it into her head to do, Christmas Day she would have phoned her mother. And what about her friend, her as she lives with, she'd have got in touch, told her what she was up to, surely to God? I mean, how long's it take to make a phone call, after all?"

"The most likely assumption, the one we're working on, is that she met a man on Christmas Eve ..."

"What man?"

"We don't know the answer to that yet. We're still—"

"What bloody man? Someone she knew or what?"

"Not necessarily."

"Are you telling me my daughter's a whore?" A hundred miles or more to the northwest, a telephone receiver was slammed against the wall. Better a whore and alive, Resnick thought, than virtuous and dead.

Naylor and Divine were working through the lists that Lynn had compiled: men that Nancy had dated, those that she'd danced with, spent significant time talking to on Christmas Eve. No way had Dana been able to swear either list was complete.

There had to be easier things to do, easier times.

Receiver cradled between chin and shoulder, Divine fumbled another extra-strong mint from its pack; finishing the call, he checked off another name on his list.

"Yes, sir," Naylor was saying across the room, "Phelan. P-H-E-L-A-N. Nancy. Yes, that's right."

Deaf, Divine thought, or daft. Comatose. All those blokes having to haul themselves off the couch where they'd fallen asleep after a surfeit of mince pies and turkey. Divine hadn't surfaced till mid-afternoon himself, coming out of a bitter and Bacardi haze with a head like a rear tire in need of a retread.

"Hello, love. Yes. Can I speak with Mr. McAllister, please?"

Divine was at his desk against the rear wall, the wall where his *Sun* calendar used to hang before Lynn had lost her rag and torn it into little pieces. Pissed him off no end, that had. Kellogg getting into her hard-hat feminist routine every time her pre-menstrual cramps came visiting. Still, the one he'd bought for next year, *Page Three Lovelies*, that was already up in the bathroom at home: give himself a lift each time he stepped out of the shower.

"Hello, Mr. McAllister? DC Divine here, CID."

When Andrew Clarke's wife told him there was a police officer on the line wanting to speak with him, he had just got back from a long walk with the boys along an almost deserted beach. Gulls low over the water as the tide turned and began to roll back in. Haze of moon in the sky and the light almost gone. They had walked briskly, as briskly as one could on sand, well wrapped against the cold. Later there would be mulled wine, sandwiches, snooker, cards.

"Sure it's for me?" Clarke asked, unwinding his scarf, feeling the first signs of panic tickling his gut.

His wife had raised an eyebrow and turned back to the kitchen table.

"Hello," Clarke said, picking up the extension in the hall, "This is Andrew Clarke."

At the other end of an imperfect line, Resnick identified himself and said there were a few questions concerning the Christmas Eve dinner-dance.

Oh, Christ, Clarke thought, I was right. The stupid bitch has only gone and made a complaint to the police.

"How can I help you, Detective Inspector?" he said.

"There was a young woman," Resnick said, "one of the guests ..."

Oh God, thought Clarke, here it comes. In his mind he was erecting excuses, explanations, I'd been drinking too heavily, under severe stress at work, she led me on.

"... as far as we can tell she left at around midnight, possibly accepting a lift, and hasn't been seen since."

"Dana," Clarke said.

"Sorry?"

"The woman you're talking about, Dana Matthieson."

"No. Not Dana. Her friend."

"Friend?"

"Yes. Nancy Phelan."

Resnick clearly heard the gear change in Andrew Clarke's breathing. "You do know her then?" he asked.

"I'm afraid not, no. Dana, of course, she's been with us for quite a while. A good worker. Very good. Reliable, shows initiative ..."

"Nancy Phelan," Resnick said.

"No, not at all. That is, I may have met her. We may have been introduced. I'm afraid I can't quite remember."

"You don't remember dancing with her, for instance?"

Andrew Clarke laughed nervously, more of a bark.

"Not much of a dancer, Detective Inspector. Not my style."

"Even so, Christmas. Special occasion. I should have thought, just to show willing ..."

"I did dance, of course. Once or twice."

"And that would be with Mrs. Clarke?"

"My wife wasn't present, she ..."

"With somebody else, then?"

"Of course. You don't think I'd make a fool of myself ..."

"And this person you were dancing with, it couldn't have been Nancy?"

"No."

"You're sure?"

"Haven't I said ..."

"But if you're not certain you knew who she was, Nancy, isn't it possible she could have been ...?"

"Inspector, I know the person I was dancing with."

"And you wouldn't mind telling me, just for the ...?"

"It was Dana Matthieson, as a matter of fact."

"Dana."

"Yes."

"And at the end of the evening?"

"What do you mean?"

"As I said, to the best of our knowledge someone offered Nancy Phelan a lift in their car."

"It wasn't me, Inspector."

"You're sure of that?"

"Positive."

Resnick let him have a moment of time; not too long. "Functions like that, Christmas Eve, it's easy to forget ..."

"I assure you ..."

"I mean, at first you *said* you hadn't danced, but then, when you thought about it, you remembered that you had."

"Detective Inspector ..."

"Mr. Clarke, it's important that we compile as accurate a picture of what happened yesterday evening as possible. You realize the potential seriousness of the situation, I'm sure."

Clarke shifted his stance so that his back was towards the kitchen door. "As it happens I did give somebody a lift home ..."

"I see."

"Dana, actually."

"Dana Matthieson."

"Yes. She lives not so far away from me."

"So must Nancy then."

"I suppose so. I really don't know."

"And you didn't see her when you drove Dana home?"

"No."

"What happened exactly? I mean, did you just drop her off outside, did she invite you in, coffee maybe? What?"

The pause was too long. "Outside," Clarke said. "I dropped her off outside."

"And she'll confirm that? I mean, if necessary?"

"We didn't go directly there," Clarke said, voice lowered, "we stopped off at my place on the way."

"For coffee," Resnick said.

"A nightcap, yes."

"And then you drove her home?"

"Not exactly, no."

"Not exactly?"

"She decided to walk."

"Wasn't that, well, a little odd? I mean, having accepted a lift from you in the first place."

"Perhaps she wanted to clear her head."

"Is that what she said?"

"I can't remember."

"You can't recall what reason she gave for wanting to walk home after accepting a lift?"

"No."

"So you had, in fact, no idea that she got home all right?"

"I assumed ..."

"Of course. People do. But her friend, Nancy Phelan, seemingly didn't."

"I told you, Inspector, I know nothing about that. Nothing about that at all. I may have noticed her once or twice in the course of the evening, talking with Dana. At least, I assume it was her. But later, no. I'm sorry. I wish I could be of more help."

"When do you think you'll be back down here, sir? In the city."

"We'd planned to stay here until after the New Year."

"There are some addresses we still haven't been able to track down," Resnick said. "You've no objection if we ask your assistant for her help?"

"Yvonne? No, of course not. The firm will do anything it can."

"And you, Mr. Clarke? Yourself?"

"Of course, but I really don't see ..."

"Thank you, Mr. Clarke. Thanks for your time."

When Andrew Clarke went back through the flagstoned kitchen, seeking out some fifteen-year-old malt, his wife remarked that for some reason he seemed to be sweating, She hoped he wasn't coming down with something, a cold.

Divine's back was aching, sitting in the same position too long, asking the same questions. Naylor had been out in search of a takeaway and returned empty handed, everywhere shut tight as an old maid's arse. Even the mints had run out.

"Oh, her with the dress and the legs," a voice was saying at the other end of his phone. "You kidding? Course I remember her. What about her?"

There was a moment when Dana arrived back at the flat when she was certain Nancy would be there. It lasted only as long as it took to push the front door closed behind her, slip the catch on the lock, and feel the emptiness settle round her shoulders like a shroud.

Twelve

"Another cup of tea?"

"Say what?"

"Another cup of tea?"

Gary reached out and turned the TV down, unable to hear Michelle from the kitchen above the roar of pre-recorded laughter.

"Tea?"

By that time she was in the doorway, ski pants and sweater, and even though the sweater hung loose he could see how she was getting her figure back after Natalie. See: he knew. Strands of hair hung loose across her face. Gary wanted to give her a look, the look towards the stairs, but he knew what she would say. Karl's this minute dropped off; the baby'll be awake soon anyway.

"Gary?"

So, all right, what was wrong with down here? Least, in front of what was left of the fire, they'd keep warm.

"C'm here," he said.

"What for?"

But she knew the grin, the way it was meant to make her feel. "I've got the kettle on," she said.

"Then take it off."

"Oh, Gary, I don't know."

"Well, I do. Come on." Winking. "While it's hot."

Pushing the hair out of her eyes, Michelle went back into the kitchen and switched the kettle off. She'd been so pleased when Gary had come home, late on Christmas Eve, relieved, she would have made love to him there and then, but all he'd wanted was to carry on about the bastard coppers, the bastard law, bastards at the Housing whose fault it all was anyway. Hadn't even wanted to see the kids. Ask after Karl. Take a look at his face.

She hadn't told Gary about that. Not any of it. The social worker, visit to the doctor, none of it. It would only make more trouble. He couldn't stand it, Gary couldn't, not ever, every Tom, Dick, and Harry coming round from Social Services, barging into the place as though they owned it, telling him how to bring up his own kids.

"Get us a decent place," that was what he'd said last time. "Get us a decent place and then we'll bring 'em up decent, you see."

But what if they don't, Michelle had wanted to ask? What if we have to stay here? What then?

"Michelle? You coming or what?" When she got back into the room, he had switched off the television, turned out the light, pushed the settee closer to the fire. He was leaning back against the far end of it, legs stretched out, slightly parted. Those jeans on, no way she couldn't tell he was excited.

"Well?"

Forcing a smile on to her face, she started towards him; if only she could get the memory of him hitting Karl out of her mind, it might be all right.

He was kissing her, tongue pushing against her teeth, one hand reaching under her sweater when Lynn Kellogg knocked sharply on the door.

Lynn had talked to Dana earlier, back at the station, drinking tea and trying not to mind that the smoke from the other woman's cigarettes kept drifting into her face, irritating her eyes. What is she, Lynn thought? Six years older than me? Seven? One of those round faces, not unlike her own, in the right circumstances they were full of life; dark eyes with an energy, a glow. But sitting there, on and on about Nancy, the same details, facts, suspicions, what Dana had looked was heavy-featured, exhausted, her face flabby and pale.

"Isn't there a friend you could stay with?" Lynn had asked. "Just for tonight. Rather than being on your own."

But Dana had insisted, she had to be there, by the telephone when Nancy rang, by the door when she walked back in.

"You think she's all right, don't you?" Dana had said suddenly, clutching Lynn's arm. "You do think she's all right?

It wasn't yet twenty-four hours; there was still time for her to turn up unannounced, unharmed. A postcard. Phone call. *I just had to get away, Sorry if you were worried. Chance came along and I took it.* It happened all the time. People taking off on an impulse, a whim. Paris, London, or Rome. Those weren't the incidents Lynn had to deal with, not closely, not often. The twenty-four hours would stretch to forty-eight and if there'd been no word from her by then, no sign … Well, there was still time.

Although the lights seemed to be out, she could hear voices inside; reversing her gloved hand, she knocked again.

"Yeh?" It was Gary who finally came to the door, still pushing one side of his shirt back down into his jeans. Behind him, Michelle had switched on the light.

Lynn showed Gary her warrant card and asked if she could come in.

"What's this about then?"

"It might be easier if we talked inside."

"Easier for who?"

"Gary …" Michelle began.

"You keep out of this!"

In the center of the room, involuntarily, Michelle flinched, a spasm of fear passing across her eyes.

Lynn set one foot on the scarred boards inside the door.

"Who said you …?"

"Gary …"

"I thought I told you …"

"Better we talk here," Lynn said, "than back down at the station. Surely?" Gary's head dipped and he stepped away. "You'll not want to let too much cold in," Lynn said. "Night like this." And she pushed the front door closed.

"I was going to make tea," Michelle said.

"She'll not be here that long," Gary said. "This isn't going to take all night."

"A cup of tea would be nice," Lynn said. "Thanks." She smiled and Michelle headed off for the kitchen, glad to be out of there and leave the two of them alone.

Except that the settee had been moved, nothing seemed to have changed since Lynn was there the day before. The same squares of worn carpet, oddments of furniture that had come from Family First. Two or three Christmas streamers, held in place with pins. A few Christmas cards. Mold in the corners, damp on the walls. Despite what was left of the fire, it was cold enough for Lynn to think twice before taking off her gloves.

"Well?" Gary lit his cigarette, then dropped the spent match on the floor.

"Where were you last night?" Lynn asked.

"You know bloody well where I was last night."

"After you were released."

"Where the hell d'you think I was?"

"That's what I'm asking."

"Here, of course. Where d'you think I was going to fucking go?"

In the doorway, Michelle bit her tongue; if only Gary didn't lose his temper all the time.

"So you were here all evening?"

"Yes."

"From what time?"

"Listen, I want to know what all this's about."

"From what time were you here?"

"From right after you bastards let me out!"

"Which would be when?" Lynn said. "Eight? Half-past eight?"

"It was twenty to nine," Michelle said. "Almost exactly. I remember."

Gary looked as though he was going to tell her to keep quiet, but he scowled instead.

"And you didn't go out again?"

"Isn't that what I just said?"

"Not exactly."

"Well ..." Coming towards her now, past the edge of the settee, right up close, "... that's exactly what I'm saying now. I came in and I never went out. Not till this morning. Right?"

Lynn could smell his tobacco breath, warm on her face. Dinner. Beer.

"And Nancy Phelan?"

"Who?" But she could tell in his eyes that he knew.

"Nancy Phelan."

"What about her?"

"You do know who I mean, then?"

"Course I know."

"And did you see her?"

"When?"

"Yesterday."

"You know bloody well ..."

"Not at the Housing Office. Later."

"When?"

"Any time."

"No."

"You didn't see Nancy at any other time?"

"No."

"Not that evening? Later yesterday evening? Christmas Eve?"

"I told you, didn't I? I never went out."

Michelle was hovering in the doorway. "How d'you want your tea?" she asked.

"How d'you think she wants it? In a bastard cup."

"I mean d'you want sugar?"

"One, thanks."

Gary turned away disgusted. He's a kid, Lynn thought, younger than me. Stuck in this place with a wife and a couple of kids. Except she isn't even his wife. And what is he? Nineteen? Twenty? Twenty-one? Is it any wonder he needs to shout? And at me. If Divine had come round instead, she thought, Kevin Naylor, he wouldn't be carrying on like this. At least, not while they were here. The anger, he'd bottle it up for later.

She remembered the flinch of pain on Michelle's face. Karl's bruising.

Injuries consistent with the mother's story that he had run smack into a door.

"I'll give a hand with the tea," Lynn said.

"No need," said Gary, but he did nothing to stop her going into the kitchen.

Michelle poured in the milk first, UHT from a carton, then the tea. One tea bag, Lynn reckoned, for a large pot.

"How are the children?" Lynn asked.

"Sleeping, thank heavens. They got so excited earlier, you know, presents and everything."

"And Karl?"

Michelle paused in sugaring their teas, spoon tilting in mid-air.

"How's Karl?"

"The doctor said ..."

"I know what the doctor said."

"Well, then. That's it, isn't it? He's fine."

"He was hurt."

"It was an accident. He ..." Michelle's eyes flicked towards the door in response to a sudden noise: the television had been switched back on.

"The sugar," Lynn said.

"What?"

"You're spilling the sugar."

Lynn took the spoon from her hand and began to stir one of the mugs of weak tea.

"I never told him," Michelle said in a rushed whisper. "I never told him anything about it."

"Never told me anything about what?" Gary said from the hallway, stepping into the room.

"Here," Lynn said, handing him a mug. "Your tea."

"Never told me anything about what?" Ignoring her, staring at Michelle.

Michelle's hand went to her throat.

"When I was here yesterday ..." Lynn began.

"I never knew you was here yesterday."

"That's what Michelle meant," Lynn said.

Gary was all but ignoring her now, intent upon Michelle. "Why didn't you tell me?"

"I don't know. When you came home I was so pleased, I suppose I forgot."

"How could you forget something like that? Bloody law ..."

"It wasn't important," Lynn said. "I just dropped by, tell Michelle where you were."

Gary had put his mug down and now he snatched at it, splashing hot tea across his hand. One taste and he had dashed it down the sink. "What the hell d'you call that? Like bloody dishwater!"

"I'll make some fresh," Michelle said, reaching for the kettle.

"Don't waste your time."

Between his sullen shout and a fanfare of television sound, came a whimpering from upstairs.

"It's the baby," Michelle said, setting the kettle back down.

"When isn't it?" Gary grumbled.

"Gary, that's not fair."

Gary didn't care; he was on his way back into the living room, leaving Natalie to cry upstairs. Michelle looked at Lynn uncertainly.

"You go up," Lynn said. "I'll see to the tea."

When Lynn came in from the kitchen, three mugs of fresh tea balanced on a breadboard she was using as a tray, Michelle was sitting in an easy chair with curved wooden arms, the baby restless against her breast. Gary was on the settee, pretending to watch the TV, sulking quietly.

Lynn drank her tea, chatting to Michelle about Natalie, keeping things as light as she could. She would have liked to have gone upstairs, taken a look at Karl, but sensed that if she asked Gary would object. Better to have another word with the social worker, let them do what they were trained to do.

When she got up to leave, Michelle went with her to the door, Gary grunting something from where he slouched that could have been goodbye.

Moving past Michelle at the door, Lynn said quietly, "If you need someone to talk to, get in touch. Phone me. All right?"

Michelle stepped quickly back inside, shutting out the cold.

Later, as she lay curled away from Gary, listening to the suck and whine of his breathing, Michelle was unable to sleep, thinking about it. Not what Gary had said only minutes after Lynn had gone, about keeping things from him; not the ache in her ribs where he had punched her, low where it wouldn't be seen. Not those, but what he'd said when she'd asked him, the policewoman, if he'd gone out again that night, Christmas Eve. Why he'd lied.

Thirteen

"Kevin?"

"Shhh!"

"What time is it?"

"Early. You go back to sleep."

"The baby ..."

"I gave her a drink and she went off again."

Debbie rolled on to her side, face to the pillow. It was dark in the room, even the gap at the top of the curtains, where they refused to meet, offering no light.

"You're on an early."

"Yes." Dressed in all but his jacket, Kevin sat on the edge of the bed, close to her bare arm.

"I'm sorry, I forgot."

Lightly stroking her shoulder, Kevin smiled. "Doesn't matter."

"You used to hate that."

"What?"

Slowly lifting her face, a thin skein of spittle stretched from the pillow to the corner of her mouth until it snapped. "When I used to forget your rota, which hours you were on."

"I used to hate a lot of things." Her mouth was damp and warm and musty from sleep. "Love you," he said.

"I know," Debbie said. She brought her other arm around him, crook of her elbow tightening against his neck. One breast slipped free from the Snoopy T-shirt she wore in bed.

"I'll be late."

"I know," Debbie said.

She kissed him hard and let him go.

Pulling the front door shut and stepping out on to the street, the same, now familiar feeling closed cold around his stomach: how close he had come to losing this, all of it, letting it go.

Resnick had woken something short of four, finally got up at five. When he had opened the garden door to Dizzy, the black cat had entered with sprung step and hoisted tail as if there were nothing new in this. Below freezing outside, Dizzy's fur was sleek and tinged with frost.

Resnick warmed him milk in the pan, testing the temperature with his finger before pouring it into the dish. The cat's purrs filled the kitchen as it ate and Resnick sipped hot black coffee: a secret between them, no one else awake.

The first news of Nancy Phelan's disappearance would go out on the local news at six, would possibly rate a minor mention on the national network an hour later. Jack Skelton had called a meeting for nine. The evidence, such as it was, would be assembled, evaluated, broken down; assignments would be made, which interviews warranted following up, which gaps had still to be filled. Her father's pain and anger on the phone. Doing everything we can. He remembered the way Nancy had looked in the otherwise empty CID room, red coat unbuttoned and loose at her shoulders. Later that evening, the voice that had seemed to come from nowhere, silver of her smile, breath that had hung between them in the air.

"Very well, ladies and gents, let's come to order if you please."

The new DCI wore his Wolverhampton Polytechnic education like a thin veneer; a supercilious smugness which his Black Country vowels disavowed. Recently promoted over the pair of them, Malcolm Grafton was ten years younger than either Resnick or Reg Cossall—as Reg never failed to remark.

"Jesus, Charlie! You don't think he wore those for his interview, do you?"

As Grafton had resumed his seat on the platform, one leg had crossed high over the other, revealing a sock that looked, as Reg Cossall remarked, as if it had been dipped in a late-night curry disaster, then hung on the line to dry.

Resnick grunted and kept his own counsel, only a while back he had noticed he was wearing odd socks himself, dark blue and maroon. No wonder he hadn't pinned down the color of the car waiting to drive Nancy Phelan away.

"For the present, we're looking at three areas for the possible abductor ..." Jack Skelton was on his feet now, gesturing towards the boards to his right, "... boyfriends, men friends, call them what you will, that's for starters; guests at the hotel on Christmas Eve—initially that's those at the same architects' do as her, but ultimately anyone and everyone who used the place that evening." A groan from the assembled officers at this. "And lastly, at the moment no more than an outside chance, this man, Gary James."

Heads swiveled to where Skelton was now pointing and Gary's whippet face stared back at them, full-on, from between twin profiles, left and right.

"As most of you'll know," Skelton continued, "there was an incident at the Housing Office the same afternoon, James became violent, offered threats to various personnel, including the missing woman, Nancy Phelan, whom he kept a prisoner in her office for a time. The initial grudge he has against her seemed to stem from an argument over the housing allocated to James, his common-law wife, and their two children. Whether, as a result of anything that happened yesterday, it's gone beyond that, we don't know."

Skelton stepped back, seeking out Lynn Kellogg through the rising haze of tobacco smoke. "Lynn, you saw him yesterday, I believe."

Slightly self-conscious, buttoning, then unbuttoning the front of her jacket, Lynn got to her feet.

"I spoke with James yesterday, sir. Claims he was home the later part of the evening and his wife, Michelle Paley, that is, she supports him in that."

"You think he's telling the truth?"

"I've no reason not to think so."

"But you're not convinced."

A pause. "No, sir."

"The woman, Michelle, she'd lie to alibi him?"

Without hesitation, Lynn said, "She'd be frightened not to."

"Knocks her about, does he?"

"No direct evidence, sir. No obvious signs. But he's got a temper;

flares up out of nothing. And there are the injuries to the little boy."

"I understood we'd cleared that up?" Skelton was looking towards Resnick now. "Clean bill of health."

"According to the doctor," Resnick said, half out of his chair, "bruising and swelling tallied with the mother's story. Accidental injury."

"But you think it could be something else?"

Resnick shrugged. "Possible."

"The situation's being watched?"

"Social Services, yes."

Skelton nodded gravely, pressing the tips of his fingers tight together; Resnick lowered himself back into his seat. Lynn was still on her feet.

"Yes?" Skelton said.

"I was wondering, sir, whether that was enough. The whole situation there, I don't know, it's like something waiting to explode?"

"We've heard, Social Services are keeping an eye ..."

"Even so, overstretched the way they are ..."

"And we're not?" There was more than a touch of anger in Skelton's voice.

"But if James is a strong suspect ..."

"Is he? Is that what we're saying? He's really a viable suspect here?"

Lynn didn't answer; glanced across at Resnick for support. At the back of the room, Kevin Naylor shuffled his feet and looked embarrassed on her behalf.

"Are you saying it's possible," Malcolm Grafton put in, "that James could have been the driver of that car, waiting to whisk Nancy Phelan away?"

"We don't know that's what happened," Resnick said.

"Best bet, Charlie. Your call." Grafton leaned back and recrossed his legs, giving his socks another airing. "Got to be where we're looking, surely? Not this sorry bugger. Knocking his wife and kids about, throwing chairs at women clerks, that's his mark."

"That doesn't mean—" Lynn began, color leaping to her cheeks.

"Lynn ..." Resnick was out of his seat, faster this time.

"You're not suggesting, sir," Lynn said, gripping the chair in front of her hard, "that domestic violence ..."

"I think what the DCI means ..."

"Thank you, Charlie, but I don't need an interpreter," Grafton said.

"Just a decent pair of socks," murmured Reg Cossall.

"Our concern here is finding Nancy Phelan, what happened to her," Grafton continued. "Anything else, it gets in the way."

Slowly, Lynn sat back down.

"'Bout chuffing time!" Divine said to no one in particular. "Now we can get bloody on."

Grafton allowed himself a quick smirk.

"Nevertheless," Resnick said, "man with a record of violence, currently on probation, already subjected the missing woman to an actual assault, we wouldn't be dropping him from our inquiries entirely. Would we?"

Grafton stared down at him through narrowed eyes.

"A watching brief, Charlie, your team." Skelton was back on his feet, quick to intervene. "Not priority, though; that's Nancy Phelan's boyfriends, they're down to you. Reg ..."

"Here we bloody go!" stage-whispered Cossall

"... the guests at the hotel, if you please. Malcolm's arranging for you to have some extra bodies."

"Old ones he's done with, is that, then?"

"Sorry?"

"Nothing, sir. You're all right."

As Skelton continued, Cossall leaned towards Resnick, talking behind the back of his hand. "Ever occur to you, Charlie, if any one of us was going home to his little semi of an evening, carving up corpses and stuffing 'em into plastic bags, our Malcolm up there's your man?"

There had been fifty-seven guests at the dinner: Andrew Clarke's assistant had provided the names, almost all of the addresses. Times of departure would be ascertained and, where possible, double-checked; modes of transport, makes and types of car. When was the last time that evening they remembered seeing Nancy Phelan? Where had that been? Who had she been with?

Once that had been done, answers compared and tabulated, leads and questions followed up, the lists, still slowly being compiled, of the hotel's other clients would be waiting. Somewhere between three and four hundred in total—without casual callers at the bar.

Reg Cossall, extra bodies or no, was going to have his work cut out.

Resnick was in his office with Lynn Kellogg, Naylor, and Divine, looking at the names Dana Matthieson had supplied of the four men Nancy had recently been involved with. Patrick McAllister. Eric Capaldi. James Guillery. Robin Hidden. Divine had already talked to McAllister on the phone and was due to call on him that afternoon. Naylor had made contact with Guillery's parents, who had informed him their son was on holiday in Italy, skiing, and wasn't expected back until after the New Year. Eric Capaldi's answerphone offered some blurry piano music and not a lot else. Robin Hidden had so far remained, well, hidden.

"It's not possible," Kevin Naylor said, "there's others? I mean, that her flatmate didn't know about?"

"As far as I know," Dana had said. "This's who she'd been seeing. The only ones she talked about, anyway."

"You think there could have been someone else, then? That she never mentioned."

"It's always possible."

"Was she secretive, though? Things like that?"

"Not specially. But, you know ... there's always somebody, isn't there? Whatever reason, the one you won't talk about, not even to your best friend."

Is there? Resnick had thought.

And then—yes, of course.

Now, prompted by Naylor's question, he thought of Andrew Clarke. Was that the kind of relationship Dana had been hinting at? Older, married, somebody where she worked?

"The receptionist from the Housing Office," Resnick said.

"Penny Langridge," Lynn read from her notes.

"Have a word with her, see if there was anything between Nancy Phelan and any of her colleagues, something she might not have wanted broadcast about."

"Quick knee-trembler back of the typing pool," Divine grinned. "That the sort of thing?"

Lynn shot him a quick angry look. Any other time, Resnick thought, she would have had a sharp remark to go with it. But now part of her mind was on other things.

The minute Resnick was alone in his office the phone rang: it was Graham Millington calling from his in-laws in Taunton, just this minute heard about the missing girl on the news and wondering if they could use him back at the station.

Fourteen

Graham Milllington had met his wife in the Ladies' lavatory of Creek Road Primary School, a little after eleven in the morning and caught short in the middle of a talk to forty-seven ten-year-olds. Millington, not his wife.

One thing he hated above all others, worse than charging into the ruck of a Friday night bar-room fight with glass flying, barging into the Trent End on a Saturday afternoon to collar the smart-arse bastard who's just felled the visiting goalie with a sharpened fifty-pence piece to the head, was standing in front of a class of kids in his best suit and behavior, lecturing them on the dangers of solvent abuse and underage drinking. Knowing sneers on their scrubbed little faces.

And this particular morning, fielding the usual sporadic questions about airplane glue and which brands set to work fastest, he was overcome by a sharp sudden pain deep behind his scrotum, an urgent message that he needed to pee.

"I wonder ..." he stammered to the deputy headteacher, sitting at the corner table, filling out what suspiciously resembled a job application. "Could you ...?"

The nature of Millington's discomfort was clear for all to see.

"First right down the corridor, second left."

Millington remembered it wrong, first right, first left instead. He was just easing himself through his fly, looking wildly for the appropriate stall, when, with a swift whoosh of water, Madeleine Johnstone stepped out from the cubicle in her bottle-green Laura Ashley dress, pale green tights, sensible shoes.

"Sorry, I ..."

"Here," Madeleine said, pushing open the cubicle door, "you'd better go in here." And then, as he dived past her, slamming the door shut and fumbling the bolt across, "I'll keep watch outside."

Something wrong, she thought, out there in the corridor surrounded by all that project work on Third World hunger, a man of his age with problems of the prostate.

He had met her next in the Victoria Centre, Madeleine backing out of the Early Learning Centre, weighed down with plastic bags of presents for her sister with the twins, Millington whistling his way across to Thorntons, mind set on a quarter-pound of peppermint creams, maybe the odd Viennese Whirl.

"Sorry!" as he cannoned into her and a slew of carefully designed and educationally approved packages spilled around his feet.

He knew that she had recognized him by the way her eyes flickered downwards in the direction of his trousers, checking that he wasn't flashing at her in artificially reproduced daylight.

Millington picked up a package of brightly colored balls (eighteen months to three years) and set it in her hand. She suggested tea and led him to the coffee bar in Next, where he perched uncomfortably on a black leather stool and ate a tea cake that tasted oddly of lemon.

"It's because they use the same board," Madeleine explained, "for making the salad and buttering those."

The girl who served them was black and disdainful and her dark hair was curled like spun glass.

"She lovely, isn't she?" Madeleine said, following Millington's hopeless gaze.

Even Millington, perhaps not the most sensitive of men, understood this meant what about me? Look at me.

Madeleine was broad at the shoulders, narrow to the hips, good strong calves that suggested lots of schoolgirl hockey or netball or both. She had brown hair a few shades short of chestnut, a healthy down on her upper lip, eyes that were disconcertingly blue. A complexion like that, Millington wagered a week's wages she came from somewhere south, Sussex or Kent or farther southwest, soft winds and cream.

Some detective, it had taken him till now to check the third finger of her left hand.

"They're not for me, if that's what you're thinking." Madeleine glanced at the bags by her feet "My sister. Twins. It runs in the family."

Something inside Millington shuddered.

"It's considered old-fashioned, nowadays, isn't it?" Madeleine said. "For men to wear wedding rings."

They hadn't been able to have children. Not so far. Not for want of trying. Whatever was in the family, the genes, the almost careless fecundity of her several sisters, it wasn't there for them. They had had therapy, tests, everything short of acupuncture, the thought of which had reduced Millington's eyes to tears. "Graham, they don't put the needle there." It hadn't mattered; acupuncture was out.

Madeleine applied for promotion and was rewarded; she embarked upon a never-ending series of self-improvement classes, everything from Chinese cuisine through European languages to British Visionary art and beyond. On the kitchen wall she kept a chart, color-coded, on which she annotated the ages and birthdays of her nieces and nephews so that none would go uncelebrated, unremarked.

Christmas, in her parents' vast house in Taunton, had been a maelstrom of unrestrained young middle-class voices, each intent on clamoring its instant needs above the rest. Madeleine and her sisters had sat around the oak table that had once graced the refectory of a nearby abbey and laughed about old photographs, old jokes. And all around them, in and out and up and down, the children ran and ran, with only the occasional, "Oh, Jeremy!" "Oh, Tabetha! Now see what you've done!" to acknowledge they were there at all.

Millington had listened to her father's ideas on law and order and the breakdown of family, the lack of respect for authority and the failure of religion, the seemingly equivalent evils of the single-parent family and the admission of women priests into the Church. Even grace on Christmas Day had been accompanied by a sideswipe at leniency towards young offenders, before sinking the knife deep inside the bird.

"Are you all right?" Madeleine asked from time to time, passing him by chance.

"Me? Yes, of course. Fine."

And then she had been off again, attention tugged away by some tousled three-year-old pulling at her sleeve. "Oh, yes, Miranda, that's lovely! Let's go and show it to Granny, shall we?"

He had been seeking refuge in the bathroom when he had heard the news, trimming the ends of his moustache for want of something better to do. The small Roberts portable, dusted with talcum powder on the shelf, had been left on low. Hearing the city's name, he had turned the volume up. A young woman who had gone missing on Christmas Eve; the parents' concern; police investigations proceeding.

Millington had used the drawing-room phone. "Graham, sir. Wondering if I could be any use."

"How soon can you get here?" Resnick had said. Millington grinning as he weaved his way between small children, opening doors, looking for his wife so he could tell her sorry, but there was no alternative, he was leaving.

Fifteen

"Made a real fool of myself, didn't I?" Lynn was sharing a cemetery bench with Resnick, one of the few places near the police station it was possible to find sanctuary. In front of them, the ground dipped away steeply, paths winding between Victorian tombstones raised in loving memory of Herbert or Edith or Mary Ellen, aged two years and three months, gone to a better place. In the middle distance, beyond Waverley Street, the green of the Arboretum shone dully in midwinter sun.

Resnick finished chewing a mouthful of chicken salad sandwich. "You said what you thought needed saying."

"It wasn't the time," Lynn said. "And standing up to Grafton like that, it was stupid."

"What he said wasn't over-bright."

"But tactically ..." Lynn shook her head. "If I stopped to challenge every statement by a senior officer that was sexist or insensitive, how long d'you think I'd last in CID? Never mind promotion."

Resnick crunched down into a pickled cucumber, head dipping forward in a vain attempt to prevent vinegar splashing across his shirt.

"What would really worry me," Lynn went on, "would be if it meant Gary James didn't get taken seriously. You know, just Lynn again, riding another of her hobby horses."

Resnick grinned ruefully. "People have been saying that about me for years."

Lynn looked back at him. She didn't say and where's that got you, because she didn't have to. They both knew a younger, less experienced man had been promoted over him.

"You really fancy him for this, James? Nancy Phelan?"

"If not for that, then for something."

"The kiddie."

"Maybe."

Resnick's stomach stirred uneasily. "You've been back to Social Services?"

"Martin Wrigglesworth, yes. Well, I've tried. Left messages, but so far he's not come back to me. Off duty, bound to be."

Getting to his feet, Resnick screwed the paper bag that had held his lunch into a ball, brushed crumbs from the front of his coat. "Let's hope you don't have to wait till after the New Year."

As they were walking back through the archway towards the broad sweep of road, Lynn prompted him about Gary James' probation officer. "Pam Van Allen, I do think she'd be more likely to talk to you than me. You never know, she might throw some light."

Without any great enthusiasm, Resnick nodded. "I've got Nancy Phelan's parents in half an hour. After that, I'll see what I can do."

The holiday traffic was light enough to allow them across all four lanes and on to the central island without breaking stride. A dusty Ford Prefect with its offside door painted a different color was just turning into the car park alongside the police station: Mr. and Mrs. Phelan had arrived early.

Harry Phelan's father and grandfather had worked on the Albert Dock before it became a home for shopping boutiques and an art gallery; Harry had grown up with every intention of following in their footsteps. But by the time he was ripe to leave school, the writing had been scrawled all too clearly on the wall and he had got himself apprenticed at Raleigh making cycles and moved to the East Midlands. Now that trade, too, was virtually dead and the family had moved back to its roots.

Harry was a tall man, strongly built, with failing sandy hair, a fair moustache, and broad hands which sprouted reddish hair between the knuckles. His tie was knotted too tight and he tugged at it constantly, this way and that. His wife, Clarise, no more than a couple of inches above five foot, wide at the hip and big at the bust, was forever fidgeting with the black handbag that she held in her lap, always close to tears.

Resnick saw them with Jack Skelton, four seats pulled round in the superintendent's office, one of the uniformed PCs bringing a pot of tea from the canteen, Rich Tea biscuits overlapping on a small plate.

Increasingly agitated, Harry Phelan listened to the explanations of what steps had been taken, which directions the investigation was following. What he wanted to hear about were arrests, appeals, rewards, not computerized cross-checks, methodical questioning, the gradual elimination of people from the inquiry.

"Looks like," he said finally, "you're treating this about as serious as someone lost their second-best sodding coat!"

"Harry, don't," said Clarise, fumbling a small square handkerchief from her bag.

"One of your lot, we'd see something different, no two ways about that."

"Mr. Phelan, I can only assure you ..." Skelton began.

But Phelan was on his feet now, chair pushed back against the wall. "And I can assure you ..." jabbing a hand in the superintendent's direction, "... if someone doesn't pull his finger out here, I'll raise such a bloody stink, you'll be back on the beat and lucky for it."

"Harry," begged Clarise, "you'll not do any good."

"No? What bloody will, then?" He pointed at Skelton again, swinging his arm wide to include Resnick also. "Forty-eight hours, that's what they reckon, isn't it? Forty-eight hours. If you don't find them in that, likely they're sodding dead!"

"Oh, Harry!" Clarise Phelan covered her face with her hands and began, loudly, to cry.

Resnick was out of his chair, moving automatically to comfort her, when Harry Phelan set himself in his way. There was no avoiding the anger, bright in Phelan's eyes. For a moment Resnick held his stare; then slowly he backed away, sat back down.

"Come on," Phelan said, taking hold of his wife's arm. "We're only wasting our time here."

"When are you going back?" Skelton asked, as they walked away.

"We're not going bloody anywhere. We're staying here till this is sorted." He didn't add, one way or another.

"Is there an address, then," Skelton asked, "where we can contact you?"

Harry Phelan gave them the name of a small hotel on the Mansfield Road.

"You'll have to forgive him," Clarise said through her tears. "He's upset, that's what it is."

Harry bustled her into the corridor, slamming the door shut behind them.

Skelton and Resnick sat for some little time, avoiding each other's eye, saying nothing. Skelton tried a mouthful of tea, but it was cold. When Resnick moved, it was to look at his watch. "Little under ten hours to go."

Skelton raised an eyebrow.

"Till it's forty-eight," Resnick said.

Divine and Naylor visited Patrick McAllister together. His address was in Old Lenton, a factory that once had made fruit machines and which since had been transformed into an apartment block for upwardly mobile singles and young couples passing through. McAllister was waiting for them at the head of the stairs, khaki chinos and artificially faded check shirt, deft handshake, blokes-together smile. Happy to invite them inside.

They asked him questions as they looked around.

Sure, McAllister said, he knew Nancy Phelan. Had done. Been out with her quite a few times, matter of fact. Clubbing, you know, pictures once or twice, evening or two in the pub. Nice girl, lively, spoke her mind. Liked that about her. Couldn't stand women who sat there all night, no more than half a dozen words to their name and two of those, please and thanks.

There were photographs on the wall in the small living room, McAllister with various young women; others clamped to the front of the fridge by magnetic fruit, raspberries, pineapples, and bananas. Divine lifted one of those clear and took it towards the light.

"Here ..."

"Don't mind, do you?"

McAllister shrugged and shook his head.

"Where's this, then?" Divine asked. McAllister was sitting outside a café, somewhere warm, white shirt open over red trunks; alongside him, Nancy Phelan was smiling, holding a tall glass of something cool towards the camera. She was wearing a pale bikini top and tight shorts and she looked lithe and tanned. Divine could see why McAllister would have wanted to get involved.

"Majorca," McAllister said.

"You went on holiday together?" Naylor asked.

"Where we met. June. She was there with that pal of hers."

"Dana Matthieson?"

"That's her."

"Holiday romance, then," Naylor said.

"How it started, I suppose. Yes."

"Love at first bite," Divine said, slipping a corner of the photograph back beneath a plastic banana.

"Sorry?" McAllister said.

"Nothing."

"How long did you carry on seeing her?" Naylor asked. "Once you got home."

"Couple of months, more or less."

They were looking at him, waiting for more.

"You know," he shrugged, managing to avoid looking at either of them, "way it goes."

"She dumped you," Divine said.

"Like hell!"

"She didn't dump you."

"No."

"You dumped her."

"Not exactly."

"What exactly?" Divine was enjoying this.

Through one of the small windows, Naylor could see a man wheeling his bike beside a narrow strip of canal; an older man, almost certainly asleep, fishing,

"We just stopped seeing one another." McAllister's expression suggested they should understand, men of the world, it happened all the time.

"No reason?"

"Look ..."

"Yes?"

"I don't see the point of all these ..."

"Questions?"

"Yes. It's not as if ..."

"What?"

McAllister seemed to be getting a little warm for the time of year, but then the room was small. The cuffs of his shirt were folded back just one turn. "I saw it on the news. Christmas Eve, too, it's hard to believe. Girl like that." He looked first at Naylor and then at Divine. "I don't suppose you want—should have asked—cup of coffee? Tea?"

"What do you mean?" Naylor asked. "A girl like that?"

McAllister took his time. "You always think, don't you ... I mean, it might not be fair, but what you think, well, maybe they weren't too bright, couldn't see what was coming ... You know what I mean?"

"Who are we talking about?" Naylor said.

"These women you read about, getting themselves kidnapped, attacked, whatever. Agreeing to meet some bloke they don't know, stuff like that." He flexed his shoulders, hands in pockets. "Try getting Nancy to agree to something she didn't want to do, forget it."

Divine glanced over at Kevin Naylor and grinned.

"Where were you on Christmas Eve?" Naylor asked, notebook at the ready.

"The Cookie Club."

"You're sure?"

"Of course, I'm ..."

"All evening?"

"From—oh, what?—ten-thirty, eleven."

"And before?"

"Er, couple of drinks in the Baltimore Exchange, few more in Old Orleans, Christmas Eve, you know how it is. Fetched up at the Cookie, yes, not later than eleven. Eleven-thirty, the very outside."

"And you stayed till?"

"One. One-fifteen. Walked home. There was a line waiting for a cab on the square, hundred, hundred and fifty deep."

"You've got witnesses," Divine asked.

"Witnesses?"

"Someone who'll back up your story, swear you were where you say."

"Yes, I suppose so. I wasn't on my own, if that's what you mean. Yes, there were people, friends. Yes, of course."

"You'll give us the names?" said Naylor. "So we can check."

McAllister's mouth was dry and his eyes were starting to sting; damn central heating. "Look, I suppose you have to do this, but ..."

"When did you last see her?" asked Divine, moving in.

"Nancy?" Wetting his lips with his tongue.

"Who else?"

"Six weeks ago? No more."

"Date, was it?" Divine was close to him now, close enough to smell the heady mix of aftershave and sweat.

"Not exactly, no."

Divine smiled with his eyes and the edges of his mouth and waited.

"A quick drink, that was all. The Baltimore."

"You go there a lot."

"It's near."

Not to say overpriced, Divine thought. That's if you can get someone to serve you in the first place.

"I haven't seen her since," McAllister said. "You've got my word."

"So what d'you reckon?" Naylor asked.

They were crossing the narrow street towards the car. In front of them was the Queen's Medical Centre and Divine had a quick memory of Lesley Bruton teasing him with her offer to model underwear. Over a day now and there'd been no fresh news of poor bloody Raju, still languishing in Intensive Care.

"Well?" Naylor was standing by the nearside door.

"No doubt about it," Divine said. "She dumped him."

Sixteen

There were times, Resnick knew, what you didn't do was play Billie Holiday singing "Our Love is Here to Stay"; when it was self-pitying, not to say foolish, to listen to her jaunty meander through "They Can't Take That Away From Me" because it felt as if they already had. What was okay was Ben Webster wailing through "Cottontail," the version with Oscar Peterson kicking out on the piano; Jimmy Witherspoon assuring the Monterey Jazz Festival "Tain't Nobody's Business What I Do." Or what he set to play now, Barney Kessel's "to swing or not to swing" with its lower-case title and dictionary definitions on the cover. The tracks he liked best were up-tempo, carefree, Georgie Auld sitting in on tenor, "Moten Swing," "Indiana."

Bud cradled along one arm, he went down the steps into the kitchen and began opening fresh tins of cat food, pouring milk, surveying the interior of the fridge for the sandwich he was going to make himself later. It was true, it appeared, Reg Cossall was intent upon getting his name in the registrar's book for the third time. The woman in question was the matron at an old people's home out past Long Eaton. Bright-faced and bonny, Resnick had met her twice and she had scarcely seemed to stop laughing. "Getting set for your retirement then, Reg?" a foolhardy DC had suggested. Cossall had been all for castrating him with his reserve set of dentures.

As he ground coffee, Resnick tried to think what it was about Reg Cossall—sour, cynical, and foulmouthed—that made him such an attractive proposition. But then, Charlie, he thought, waiting for the water to come to the boil, it isn't as if you haven't had offers either.

Marian Witczak, waiting for him to step into her peculiar time-warp, careful not to broach the possibility herself, of course, relying on old friends at the Polish Club to do the hinting for her. And then there had been Claire Millinder, the estate agent engaged in the fruitless task of moving him out of this Victorian mausoleum into something compact and modern with a microwave oven and flush doors you could punch a hole through with your fist. "What does it have to be with you, Charlie? True love?" The last he had heard, Claire had gone back to New Zealand; there had been a card from the Bay of Plenty where she and her fruit-farmer lover were raising kiwi fruit and babies.

There was a small moan of complaint from near his feet as Dizzy hustled in on Bud's bowl and Resnick scooped up the big cat by its belly and put him out in the garden.

Maybe it didn't have to be true love, after all; nor love of any kind.

He poured himself a small scotch, a bottle of fifteen-year-old Springbank single malt he'd won in the CID raffle, and took it, together with his black coffee, into the front room.

Pam Van Allen's number was in the phone book. Turning down the stereo, he dialed. What had it been? Certainly less than a year ago, walking into that wine bar opposite the snooker hall, their first and last meeting: alone at a table close against the wall, an open book and a glass of wine, perfectly self-contained. He knew that calling her now was a mistake, crass, stupid, but before he could break the connection, she had answered.

"Hello?" The tightness of her voice there in just that word.

"Oh, Pam Van Allen ...?"

"Yes?"

"Charlie Resnick."

"Who?"

"Detective Inspector ..."

"What gives you the right to call me at home? And today? This is a public holiday."

"I know and I'm sorry, but if it wasn't important ..."

"Get to the point, Inspector."

"Gary James, he's one of your clients, I believe ..."

"And I'll be in my office tomorrow morning. As long as you're not trawling for information to which you have no right, you can contact me there."

And the conversation was over. Resnick eyed the receiver as though it might have been some way responsible for Pam Van Allen's anger, then placed it carefully down. Not much of a whisky man, nevertheless he downed it in one. With a mock-cheery coda, Barney Kessel's "Twelfth Street Rag" pranced to a close. In the room it was silent. Resnick stroked Pepper, knuckle of one finger behind its ear, until the cat began to purr.

He was back in the kitchen, shaving several-day-old Stilton on to a mixture of duck meat and tomato, when the phone rang.

"I'm sorry about that. You caught us in the middle of an almighty row."

The "us" resonated in Resnick's mind. "That's okay," he said.

"But then," Pam Van Allen continued, "it *is* Boxing Day."

He thought if he could see her she might almost be smiling. "Well, is it all right now, to talk, I mean? If you're in the middle of something ..."

"It's fine. Seconds are out, I think. I'm in the bedroom. Getting my second wind."

Resnick tried to picture it; tried not to.

"You wanted to say something about Gary James?"

"More ask something, really."

"Ah-huh."

"Share some information ..."

"Share?"

"Of course."

This time he heard her laugh. "A little early for New Year's resolutions, isn't it, Inspector?"

"Charlie."

"What?"

"It's my name."

"Inspector comes more easily to the tongue."

Sidestepping his best intentions, Resnick's mind hopped into the unseen bedroom. Was she really resting, pillows propped up behind her, legs stretching slimly before her? Jesus, Resnick thought! What is the matter with me?

"Share away," Pam said.

He told her about the incident at the Housing Office, about Nancy Phelan's disappearance, Lynn's suspicions about the injuries to Karl's face.

There was silence at the other end of the line, Pam Van Allen thinking. "You want to know what I think he's capable of?" she said eventually.

"I want to know anything that might be useful."

After more consideration, Pam said: "I've got time for him, Gary; he gives one kind of impression, but he's not as bad as you might think. It would have been easy for him to have left Michelle alone with those two kids, lots of men in his place would. It's not even as if they were married. But he's not like that, Gary. Not irresponsible. Not really. But the situation he's in, no work and not for lack of trying, precious little money, a house that either wants a small fortune spending on it or knocking down, it's no wonder he gets frustrated and that the frustration shows. And he has got a temper. He is physical. The education he had, it's all he can be."

She gave Resnick time for that to sink in.

"So if you're asking me, could he have struck out at that lad of his, I'd have said he could; just like being kept sitting around at Housing could get him banging the odd chair about. None of it's premeditated, though, and that's what I can't see. Gary bearing that kind of a grudge, planning something out, some kind of revenge, waiting to carry it out."

Resnick thought a few moments more, weighing up what Pam Van Allen had said. "Thanks, I appreciate that. I value your opinion. I'll pass it on to my DC."

"Glad I could help." There was another pause in which Resnick struggled for the right thing to say and he was sure she was about to say goodbye. Instead she said, "Last time we spoke, you said something about a drink or something, after work."

"Yes."

"Well?"

"You said you'd get back to me. You were going to think about it."

With a smile in her voice, she said, "I lied."

"I see."

"But I'm thinking about it now."

"And?"

"Can I call you? Next couple of days?"

"Of course."

Muffled in the background, Resnick could hear another voice raised. "Round two," Pam Van Allen said, and for the second time that evening broke the connection.

Gary's pal from up the street had knocked before nine, on his way to the corner pub. "Spent up," Gary had said, but Brian pulled a twenty-pound note from his back pocket and flourished it with a whistle. "Jammy bugger!" Gary had exclaimed. "Where d'you get that?" "Sharon's gran," Brian grinned, "sent it her for Christmas." Michelle had almost said something, but she bit her tongue instead. No sense in risking an argument. Not another. "Not be late," Gary had said, and off they'd gone, wide-eyed and laughing, a couple of great kids.

As well he left when he did, really, because within fifteen minutes Karl started screaming from upstairs, some kind of nightmare, and Michelle had to go up and comfort him, take him a drink, and sit with him awhile until he was ready to go back to sleep. It was cold in there, not as cold as the night before, but still Karl's legs were like ice under the covers and, too early to carry him downstairs for the night, she put him in their bed, hers and Gary's, and doubled the blankets round him. Natalie woke soon after and Michelle changed and fed her and sat with her down on the sofa, Natalie asleep against her breast while she watched a comedy show with Bobby Davro.

The clock said five to ten and despite what Gary had said she knew he wouldn't be back till chucking-out time. Gone. She made up her mind that by then she would have the children tucked up down here, the kettle on in case Gary fancied a last-minute cup of tea, and be ready herself for bed.

At least Gary didn't get riled up when he had a drink or two inside him, not the way it was with some. Didn't get randy, neither. She'd heard from Brian's wife about him stumbling home late, not able to get the key in his own front door, but still expecting her to do it with him the minute he got into the house. What Gary did was fall asleep. Get a bit cuddly first, he would, snuggling up to her back and mumbling away, nothing she could ever understand, and then after a while he'd roll on to his back, fast off. Sweet, he looked then, lying there with a sort of smile on his face, young, too, really young.

The news was on now, Michelle thinking she would get up and

switch it over, switch off. But little Natalie's head was just so, her breath warm close against Michelle's skin. Missing since before Christmas, the newscaster said, and there was a photograph of her there, dark hair, down past her shoulders, the woman she and Gary had been to see together at the Housing, the one who, after a lot of prodding and pushing and form-filling, had found them the place they were now. Nancy Phelan.

Michelle was on her feet, pacing, the baby whimpering a little, upset at being disturbed. All of the questions that policewoman had been asking. Have you seen her? When have you seen her? At the Housing Office? Not later? Not later?

The news had moved on to another item, a tanker aground somewhere north of Scotland, but Michelle could still hear the newscaster's words: last seen late on Christmas Eve, shortly before midnight.

Gary standing up to her, the policewoman. "I came in and I never went out. Not till morning. Right?"

Michelle's hands around the baby were clammy and cold.

"You didn't see Nancy at any other time?" the policewoman had asked.

"I told you, didn't I? I never went out."

Michelle pressed her mouth softly against Natalie's head, hair that was light as feathers and faint. "If you need someone to talk to, get in touch."

Michelle's legs were beginning to shake.

Seventeen

Robin Hidden put through a call to the police station at ten-thirty-five on Boxing Day Night. He had been sinking a pint of Boddington's in a pub in Lancaster; earlier that day he had been climbing on the east side of the Lakes and then driven back, muscles pleasantly aching, to his friend Mark's place near the university to dump their boots and change their clothes. They were sitting in the small bar, in front of them plates that had once held pie and chips and gravy, now wiped clean with doorsteps of bread and butter. The beer was going down a treat, backs of their legs just beginning to stiffen. The television set had been on in the other bar, attached to a bracket high on the wall, and Mark had chanced to glance over his shoulder as the picture of Nancy flashed on to the screen.

"Hey! Isn't that ...?"

By the time they had hobbled through into the main room, Robin fumbling with his glasses, the program had moved on and scarcely anyone they asked had paid much attention to what had gone before.

"Christ knows, pal," someone had said, "but whatever it was, it weren't good, you can bank on that."

"That lassie," the barman said, pulling a pint, "gone missing. Didn't know her, did you?"

Robin Hidden pulled a five-pound note from his trouser pocket and placed it on the counter. "Ch-change please, as m-much as you can. For the phone." The constable who took the call wouldn't give a lot of detail, only the facts, such as they were known, simple and unadorned. He listened when Robin said that he had known Nancy, known her well, wrote down his name and asked a few questions of his own.

"When would it be convenient for you to come into the station, sir?

I'm sure one of the officers dealing with the case would like to talk to you, face to face as it were, possibly make a statement."

Robin's first reaction had been to drive back down there and then; but he'd had two pints of beer, as Mark pointed out; and driving all that way in his condition, he'd be lucky not to get cramp in his legs.

"You'll fall asleep at the wheel," Mark said. "What's to be gained from that? Far better to sleep now, set the alarm for half-five, get an early start."

"Mid-morning," Robin Hidden told the officer. "I'll be there by mid-morning at the latest."

"Very well, sir. I'll be sure to pass that on. Goodnight."

Mark gave his friend's shoulder a sympathetic squeeze. Not that he wanted anything awful to have happened to Nancy, of course, but the way Robin had been mooning on about her all the time they were walking ... Besides, they'd never really been suited, anyone who knew Robin could tell that.

James Guillery's parents had tried contacting their son in Aosta, but the hotel he was supposed to be staying at denied all knowledge of him; there had been a mix-up with the travel agency, overbooking. They were given two other numbers, one of which seemed to be permanently engaged, while dialing the other resulted in a high-pitched, unbroken tone which suggested it was unobtainable. The travel agency was closed and its answering machine swallowed the Guillerys' message halfway through.

"I don't know how he met her," Mrs. Guillery said. "Nancy, that is. Wherever it was, he went out with her a few times ..."

"More than a few," Mr. Guillery put in.

"Do you think so? Yes, well, I suppose it was. Though I don't think it was ever what I'd call serious."

"He wasn't going to marry her, that's what she means," Mr. Guillery interpreted.

"No, what I mean, James seemed to like her well enough, that is, he spoke well of her, but, as I said, it never occurred to me they were what I'd call serious."

"What she doesn't understand," Mr. Guillery confided, "young people today, it's not the same. Not like it was even in our day. Young people today, they can be serious without being serious. If you see what I mean."

Eric Capaldi's neighbors in Beeston Rylands knew very little about him, beyond the fact that he was an engineer for BBC Radio Nottingham. Or was it Radio Trent? He owned a sports car, not new, one of those little jobs, close to the ground; forever stretching an old blanket and a piece of tarpaulin on the street, he was, then crawling underneath the engine.

One person thought he might have recognized Nancy Phelan from her photo as someone he'd once seen Eric with, but he couldn't swear to it. How could he? Late evening it had been and the street lights down there, all very well for the council to be saving money, but when you could hardly see a hand in front of your face without there was a moon, that couldn't be right, could it?

The woman on the switchboard at Radio Nottingham confirmed that Mr. Capaldi was on a fortnight's leave and she had no idea where he had gone. Yes, certainly, if it was important she would try to find out. Who was it calling?

Andrew Clarke kept a half-size snooker table in the room that was still called the breakfast room and he shut himself in there with a bottle of sherry and practiced running through the balls on the table, all the reds and then the colors, right up to the black. Steadying each shot, remembering to bend low, eye along the cue, right hand firm.

"You don't think, Andrew," his wife said when she found him there, "you ought to go back down?"

"Whatever for?" The brown was a fraction too close to the cushion and he chipped it back next to the D.

"Well, you are sort of involved."

"Nonsense." Better shot now, let the cue ball spin back for the green.

"It was your affair …"

"Affair?"

"Your do, that she disappeared from."

"That hardly makes me responsible."

Audrey wished he would look at her when he spoke, not keep

wandering round the blessed table all the time, squinting down at all those balls like a general poring over a battle plan. "Besides," she said, moving herself so that she was close to his eye line, "isn't she your librarian's best friend or something?"

"Dana, mm. Live together, I believe. Flat-share, not you know ..." He made his shot and the green rolled slowly towards the pocket and hovered there, close to the rim, refusing to drop out of sight.

"Not what, Andrew?"

With something of a sigh, he straightened and reached for the chalk. "I mean they're not—what-d'you-call-it?—gay."

"Really? However would you know?"

"Surely you can tell?"

"I don't know. Can you? I shouldn't have thought it was that easy. Especially nowadays."

"Likes the men, too much, Dana. You've met her, seen the way she dresses. Christmas Eve, for instance, more out of that frock or whatever it was than in."

"Andrew, I don't think all lesbians have their hair cut short and wear motorcycle suits."

For a moment, he stared at her, he didn't think he had ever heard his wife say the word lesbian before.

"Anyway," Audrey Clarke tasted the tip of her forefinger, she had been making tartlets with lemon cheese.

"It's just not like you, that's all. You're so anxious to be on top of things. As a rule."

"Audrey, if I thought my presence would make the least difference, I should be there already. As it is, I'm on holiday and I intend to enjoy it. With you."

There had been a time when Audrey Clarke had found that somewhat anxious smile of her husband's attractive, skin furrowing deep between his eyes; she supposed she must have.

"I'm popping out," she said, "stroll down by the sea."

He watched her walk away, a middle-aged woman in a long tweed skirt, a barbour jacket, and green wellington boots, a Liberty print scarf tied about her head. When she was well clear of the house, Andrew Clarke looked up Dana Matthieson's home number and dialed it from the hall.

The answerphone clicked on first and Andrew was lowering the receiver when Dana's voice broke through. "Nancy? Nancy, is that you?"

"It's Andrew," he said, more high-pitched than he had intended. "Andrew Clarke. I was just wondering how you were. I mean ..."

But Dana had hung up and he was left talking to the air.

"Bastard!" she whispered softly to herself. "Bastard!"

Dana was squatting by the low table where she had taken the call. She had been getting out of the bath when Andrew Clarke had phoned and she had two towels carelessly round her, water trickling on to the floor. Every time she looked in a mirror and saw her mascara smeared down her face again, she told herself she was through with crying, she had no more tears left. Shivering, she clasped her arms across her chest and rocked lightly heel to toe, forwards and back, crying again.

Eighteen

"So, Charlie, getting any closer, d'you think?" Skelton had both hands flat against the wall, arms straight, stretching his legs muscles till they were fully taut; last thing he wanted, running back up Derby Road, one of his hamstrings going.

Resnick shrugged. "This lad Hidden's coming in today, all accounts he was the one went out with her most recent."

"And the bloke Divine and Naylor checked out yesterday?" Skelton was lifting one leg with his hand, fingers around the toe of his running shoe, holding it so that the heel touched his buttock, right leg first and then the left.

"Got an alibi for all the relevant times. We're checking it out. But what I've heard, I don't fancy him, frankly."

"The car, Charlie, that's the key."

Resnick nodded: as if he needed reminding.

"You've not come up with anything more yourself? Not got a clearer picture?"

Stubborn as a stain, the dark blur clung to the edge of Resnick's vision, refusing to take on true color or shape, its driver a notion of a person, nothing more.

"Someone offered her a lift, Charlie, no two ways. Like as not, someone she didn't know, met that evening, fancied her, danced with her a bit, like as not. Whisked her off with his eye to the main chance. After that, who knows?"

With any luck, Cossall and his team would have pushed through their initial inquiries by the end of the day. Matching men and cars that had been present. After that, it would be a slow process of elimination. And time, they knew, was the one thing Nancy Phelan likely didn't have.

"There's a press conference at three," Skelton said. "Her parents'll be there, too. Not what I'd've wanted, but nothing I could do about it. So if you think Hidden's going to lead us anywhere, you'll let me know as soon as you can."

"Right."

Skelton turned away, jogged a few paces on the spot, lifting his knees, then set out along the pavement at a tidy pace, fumes from the incoming traffic dancing round his head.

Resnick knew it was Graham Millington in the Gents' as soon as he arrived at the door. From inside, the unmistakable sound of Millington whistling his merry way through the songs from the shows told him that his sergeant was back on duty.

"'*Phantom of the Opera*,' Graham?"

"'*Carousel*,' that," Millington said, slightly offended. "Wife and I went down to see it in London before Christmas. That Patricia Routledge—never've thought she'd have a voice like that, never."

He shook himself a few more times, just to be sure, zipped up and stepped away. "That song—what is it?—'You'll Never Walk Alone,' scarce a dry eye in the house."

"Fellow coming in this morning," Resnick said, "Nancy Phelan's boyfriend. Sit in with me on that, will you?"

"Right." Checking in the mirror, Millington brushed a few flecks of white from the shoulders of his dark suit. Dandruff best not be coming back, he thought he'd seen the last of that. "Right, I'll be there."

And he sauntered off into the corridor, reinterpreting Rodgers and Hammerstein with an atonality that would have made Schoenberg proud.

Robin Hidden was late. Three sets of roadworks on the M6, a caravan overturned on the A1M. He was perspiring beneath his sweater and corduroy trousers when he made his way into the station, stammering when he announced his name. It was something that happened when he was feeling excited or stressed. Nancy had teased him about it, how the words he called out when they were making love came in spurts.

"Robin Hidden?"

Startled, he looked round to find a man with a roundish face and trim moustache, smart suit, and neatly knotted tie. "Detective Sergeant Millington."

Robin didn't know if he were supposed to shake hands with him or not.

"If you'll just come with me."

He followed the sergeant up two steeply winding flights of stairs and right along a corridor to an open door; behind this was an empty space, nothing that you could call a room, and beyond that another door.

"Through here, sir, if you please."

This was more what he had been expecting, what he had seen on the television, the table, plain, pushed over towards the side wall, empty chairs on either side. What he'd been less sure of, the tape machine on a shelf at the rear, double recording decks, a six-pack of cassettes, cellophane-wrapped, waiting to be used.

"Mr. Hidden, this is Detective Inspector Resnick."

A large man coming towards him, holding out his hand; the grip was firm and quick and almost before it was broken, the inspector and his sergeant pulling out their chairs, sitting down. Waiting for him to follow suit.

"Should be some tea along, any minute now," said Resnick, glancing back towards the door.

"Likely need something," Millington added pleasantly. "Long drive like that."

"If you want to smoke ..." Resnick said.

"Have to be your own, though," Millington smiled. "Getting my resolutions in ahead of the New Year."

"It's all right, thanks," Robin Hidden said. "I don't."

"Wise," said Millington. "Sensible."

There was a knock on the door and a uniformed officer came in with three cups on a tray, spoons, several sachets of sugar.

"You heard about Nancy how?" Resnick asked.

"Television news, this pub in Lancaster ..."

"You'd been walking?"

"Yes, I ..."

"Alone, or ...?"

Robin shook his head. "With a friend."

"Female or ..."

"Male. Mark. He's ..."

"Oh, that doesn't matter," said Millington, reaching for his tea. "Not now."

Robin tried to tear a corner of the sugar with his fingers and failed; when he used his teeth, half of the contents spilled down his arms and across the table.

"Not to worry," Millington said. "Good for the mice."

Robin had no idea if he were joking or not.

"Nancy," Resnick said, "how was it you met her?" As if it were something he already knew but just couldn't call to mind.

"The marathon ..."

"Local?"

"The Robin Hood one, yes."

"You were both running?"

"N-no. Just me. Nancy was watching. Lenton Road, where it goes through the Park. I got a cramp. Really bad. I had to stop and, well, lie down, massage my leg till it went off. N-Nancy was there, with her friend, where I dropped out."

"You got to talking?"

"They asked me if I was okay, if I n-needed a hand."

"And did you?"

"No, but she said, Nancy's friend said ..."

"Is that Dana?"

"Y-yes. She said if ever I wanted someone to rub in Ralgex, she knew someone who'd be happy to oblige."

"Meaning herself?"

"M-meaning Nancy."

"Took her up on it, then?" Millington smiled. He was doing a lot of smiling today; glad to be back at work, away from Taunton, back in tandem with the boss, enjoying it. "Kind of offer doesn't come every day. Not when you're already down to your shorts, I dare say."

"I didn't take it seriously. Thought they were just joking, having me on, but before I got back in the race, Nancy said, 'Here,' and gave me her phone number. Corner of her Sunday paper."

"Stick it down your athletic support?" Millington wondered. "Keep warm."

Robin shook his head. "In my shoe."

Millington smiled again and looked across at Resnick, who was jotting odd words on a sheet of paper.

"Sh-shouldn't we ...?" Robin said a moment later, glancing over his shoulder at the tape machine.

"Oh, no," Millington said. "I don't think so. Just background this. An informal chat."

Why, then, Robin Hidden wondered, didn't it feel like that?

Dana had been thinking about Robin Hidden that afternoon, walking in Wollaton Park, making a series of slow circuits around the lake, scarf knotted high at her neck. His body aside—and it had seemed a good body, right from their first sight of him there had been no doubt about that—she could never see the attraction. He wasn't especially interesting, no more than run-of-the-mill, a medium-grade job with the Inland Revenue, something at Nottingham 2. Evenings out with Robin seemed to consist of a visit to the Showcase to watch *Howard's End*, then rhogon josh and a peshwari nan at the curry place on Derby Road. Better still, letting Nancy cook pork and mushroom stroganoff and eating it in front of the telly, Robin blinking behind his glasses at a program about the disappearing llamas of Peru. The only time she had seen him really come to life had been when he was planning their weekend walking in the Malvern Hills, designed to get Nancy in shape, get her prepared for the mountains to come.

Yet Nancy had seemed happy with him, content anyway, more than with the others. Eric, who, when he wasn't whisking her round motor accessory shops on a Sunday to buy bits and pieces for his car, used to drag her off to the back rooms of pubs to listen to bands with names like Megabite Disaster. Or that weirdo Guillery, who wore combat boots and woollies his mum had knitted him and persuaded Nancy to go to horror movies, where they sat in the front row and ate popcorn. Once, according to Nancy, after they'd gone to bed together—a strange experience in itself, apparently, though she wouldn't go into detail—Guillery had insisted on reading her his favorite bits from something called "Slugs" while he stroked her inner thigh with his big toe.

All of them, though, were preferable to that smartarse McAllister they'd had the misfortune to meet when she and Nancy had both been under the influence of too much sun and Campari. She'd even fancied him herself, God help her! A Paul Smith T-shirt and a subscription to *GQ*—would have been a yuppie if he'd known what it meant. A brain the size of a mangetout out of season and, though she'd never actually asked Nancy, most likely a dick to match.

A pair of Canada geese rose up from the far side of the lake, completed a lazy circle above the trees, and skidded back on to the icy water near where she stood. Hadn't she read somewhere that they'd stopped migrating and there were council workmen in some London park going out at dawn to shoot them? She couldn't recall if that were true or why it might be.

Nor why it was that Nancy, who was bright and certainly good-looking, anything but lacking in confidence, had so much trouble finding a man who was any kind of a match? By the time you got to her own age, you could start to say they had all been snapped up or they were gay, but Nancy, still in her twenties, seemed, nevertheless, to go from one near-disaster to another.

Maybe that was what had made Robin Hidden so appealing: the oddest thing about him was probably that he laced his hiking boots up the wrong way. Was that what Nancy had been doing? Cutting her losses and thinking of settling down? Babies and Wainwright's guide to the White Peak with Mr. Dependable?

"Serious, then, Robin, is it? Between the two of you, you know?"

"I—I'm not sure I do."

"Not just fooling around."

"No."

"True love, then?"

Robin Hidden blushed. There was half an inch of tea, cold, at the bottom of his cup and he drank it down. "I love her, yes."

"And does she love you?" Resnick asked.

"I don't know. I think so. But I don't know. I think she doesn't know herself."

"You'd say you were close, though?"

"Oh, yes."

"Close enough to spend holidays together, for instance?"

"Yes, I think so. C-certainly, yes. We went …"

"Not Christmas Day, though?"

"Sorry?"

"You hadn't planned to spend it together, Christmas Day?"

"No, I was going to … usually, I went to my parents', they live in Glossop, and Nancy, she wanted to keep D-Dana company. D-didn't want her to be on her own."

"You went on from Glossop up to the Lakes, then?" Millington asked. "Boxing Day?"

"Early. Yes."

"And you drove up to your parents' when? Christmas Eve?"

"No."

"Not Christmas Eve?"

Robin Hidden swallowed air. "C-Christmas D-Day."

"So you were here on Christmas Eve?" Resnick asked, leaning forward a little, not too much. "In the city?"

"Yes."

"Strange, isn't it," Millington said, almost offhandedly, "you didn't see one another, you and Nancy, Christmas Eve? Specially since you weren't going to be together Christmas Day. Close like you were."

Sweat trickled into Robin's eyes and he wiped it away. "I asked her," he said.

"To see you Christmas Eve?"

"She said no."

"Why was that?"

Robin wiped the palms of his hands along his trouser legs.

"Why did she say no, Robin?" Resnick asked again.

"We'd h-had this, well, not row exactly, discussion, I suppose you'd say, a couple of days before. She'd said, Nancy had said, let's go out to dinner, somewhere nice, special, my treat. It wasn't easy, getting a booking, you know what it's like, Christmas week, but we did, that place in Hockley, fish and vegetarian, it's called … it's called … stupid, I can't remember …"

"It doesn't matter," Resnick said quietly, "what it's called."

"I suppose I was excited," Robin said, "you know, about us. I thought she'd made up her mind. Because she hadn't seemed certain, one time to the next, like I said before, what she felt, but I was sure, since she'd made such a thing out of going there, she was going to say she felt the same as me. I w-was p-p-positive. I said let's go out again, Christmas Eve, r-really celebrate. She said she was sorry but she realized she wasn't being f-fair to me, leading me on; she didn't want to see me again, ever."

Robin Hidden lowered his face into his hands and behind them he might have been crying. Reaching out, Resnick gave his arm a squeeze. Millington winked across at Resnick and got to his feet, signaling he was going to organize more tea.

Nineteen

Robin Hidden's car was parked close against the side wall, steeply angled across from the green metal post which had the security camera bolted near the top. He had bought it nine months before, the deposit borrowed from his parents when his father's redundancy money had finally come through. The remainder he was paying off over three years at a reasonable interest.

"A bit on the large size, isn't it, son," his dad had asked, "should have thought one of them compact jobs, two doors, Fiesta or a Nova, more the kind of thing for you. More economical, too."

But Robin had fancied something comfortable for cruising along the motorway, weekends; throw your walking gear in the back and you were away. Friday nights, once the traffic had fallen off, setting out for Brecon Beacons, Dartmoor, Striding Edge. Travel back on Sunday with a minimum of stress. If a friend or two from the office fancied coming along, which occasionally they did, no problem, plenty of room.

After a little shopping around, he'd tracked this one down to a garage on Mapperley Top, one owner only, sales rep it was true, but one advantage of all that high mileage was it kept the price down within reason. "No," he had told his father, just this past couple of days, "good investment, that. No doubt about it."

Resnick and Millington saw it first on the monitor, black and white, picture vibrating a touch as the camera shivered in the wind. From just outside the rear door of the station, the vantage point of the top step, they could see the way the dirt of its recent journey had risen in waves above the car's wheels, had been smeared by inefficient wipers across the windscreen in faint curves. The aerial, partly withdrawn, was bent over near the tip. A good car, though.

Reliable. Robin Hidden's Vauxhall Cavalier, J registration, midnight blue.

They had left him alone in the interview room, door wide open. Just a few minutes, sir, if you wouldn't mind hanging on. The tea was strong and this time there were biscuits, digestives, and a chipped lemon cream. He could walk out and down the stairs and be in the street in moments. There was nothing they could do to stop him. Surely. Here of his own volition. Anyone with information ...

Footsteps approached along the corridor and, automatically, he sat straighter in his chair, brushed biscuit crumbs from his thighs. The steps carried on past.

"It's over then, is it?" his friend Mark had asked. "You and Nancy?"

Oh, yes. It was over.

"So what are you telling me, Charlie? You've got a suspect or not?"

"Early days, sir."

Skelton frowned. "Try telling that to the girl's father."

"Better than giving him false hope."

Skelton sighed, turned towards the window, checked his watch. The car that was to drive him to the Central Station and the afternoon press conference would appear at any minute, up the hill from the city.

"You're saying about the Cavalier ...?"

"It could be the one."

"Could?"

"No way I can be sure. But the shape, the color ..."

"The registration?"

Resnick shook his head.

"Jesus, Charlie!" The superintendent moved round from behind his desk, shook a clean handkerchief from his pocket, cleared his nose, glanced quickly at the contents of the handkerchief before slipping it back.

"How about—a friend of the missing woman, providing useful background information?"

"Say that and it's like breathing murder suspect down the back of their necks. They'll have his picture on the front pages by tomorrow's first editions."

Skelton sighed again. "You're right. Better to say nothing. Let them think we're bumbling around, slow and steady, chasing our tails. Till we've got something more."

Resnick nodded, headed for the door.

"Gut feeling, Charlie?"

"Ditching him the way she did, she hurt him more than he's letting show."

"Enough to want to cause her harm?"

"Sometimes," Resnick said, "it's the only way people think they've got of making the pain stop."

"I don't want to say it," Mark had said. They were out on a ledge overhanging a valley swathed in mist. Mars bars and a thermos of coffee laced with scotch. Careful not to stop for too long and let the muscles seize up.

"Then don't," Robin had said.

"You should never have got mixed up with her in the first place."

"Mark, come on ..."

"Well, she wasn't exactly your type."

"Exactly."

"Exactly what?"

"That was why, wasn't it. Because she wasn't some Ramblers Association groupie who couldn't see beyond the next youth hostelling weekend in the Wrekin, She wasn't like anyone I'd ever been with before and I'm not likely to find someone like that again."

Mark tipped the flask high over the cup, shaking out every last drop. "Girls like her, two a penny."

The way Robin had looked at him then, rearing up, for all the world as if he might have thrust out an arm, sent his friend hurtling from the ledge.

"Hey!" Mark had shouted, swinging back, alarmed. "Don't take it out on me. I'm not the one led you on and then said, thanks very much, goodbye. That was her. Remember? If you want to take out your anger on someone, take it out on her."

And Robin had stood close to the edge, very close, staring down. "I'm not angry with Nancy. What right have I got to be angry with her?"

"Mr. Hidden?" Millington said. "Robin?" He'd been so bound up in what he was thinking, remembering, he hadn't noticed the sergeant coming back into the room. "There are just a few points we'd like to clarify," Millington said. "If you can spare us the time."

Robin Hidden barely nodded, blinked, and turned his chair back in towards the table. Millington closed the door and waited for Resnick to sit down before crossing to the tape machine.

"I thought this was the same as before? Just a few things, you said."

"So it is," Resnick said.

Millington took hold of the tab between forefinger and thumb and pulled, freeing the tape from its wrapping, did the same with a second, slotted them both into place. Twin decks.

"For your protection," Resnick said. "An accurate record of what you've said."

"Is that what I need?" Robin asked. "Protection?"

"This interview," Millington began, sitting down, "is being recorded on the twenty-seventh of December at ..." Checking his watch, "... eleven minutes past two. Present are Robin Hidden, Detective Inspector Resnick, and Detective Sergeant Millington."

"What we're interested in, Robin," Resnick said, "is where you were, late on Christmas Eve."

It was a slow day in Fleet Street. No coded messages from the IRA to Samaritans' offices, giving details of bombs left outside army barracks or in shopping centers; no cabinet ministers with their fingers caught in the Treasury till or the knickers of women other than their wives; no photographs of starving children newsworthy enough after the Christmas overkill; no gays to bash, no foreigners to trash, no sex, no drugs, no rock 'n' roll.

So it wasn't only the local Midlands press who were there at the news conference, nor had the Nationals sent their stringers merely; these were the big boys, men and women with serious expense accounts and bylines, the real McCoy. Both Central TV and the BBC had their cameras loaded and ready, each had earmarked Skelton for separate interviews later, one on one. A researcher from *Crimewatch* was there with rubber-covered notebook and mobile phone.

Four papers, two dailies and two Sundays, were primed to speak with the Phelans afterwards, sound them out about an exclusive contract—"Our Daughter Nancy"—in the tragic eventuality that when she was found she was dead.

—"So are you saying, Superintendent, that after all of this activity, the police have no leads at all? Either as to the whereabouts of the girl or the possible identity of her abductor?"

—"Would you tell us, Mrs. Phelan, just what you're feeling about your daughter's disappearance?"

—"Mr. Phelan, would you care to comment on the way in which the police investigation has been conducted so far?"

"So you went back out at around ten then, Robin?"

"Yes."

"Nothing special in mind?"

"No."

"No plan, no destination?"

"No."

"And you were in the car?"

"Yes."

"The Cavalier?"

"Yes."

"And you just drove?"

"Yes."

"Around the city?"

"Yes."

"Round and round?"

"Y-yes."

"You never stopped once?"

Robin Hidden nodded his head.

"Does that indicate yes or no?" Millington asked.

"Y-yes."

"You stopped the car?" Resnick said.

"Once or tw-twice, yes."

"Where was this?"

"I d-don't remember."

"Try."

The whirr of the tape machine faint in the background.

"Once by the square."

"Which side of the square?"

"Outside Halfords."

"Where else?"

"King Street."

"What for?"

"S-sorry?"

"Why did you stop on King Street?"

"I was hungry. I wanted something to eat. A burger, cheeseburger. Chips, you know, fries."

"Where from?"

"Burger King."

"And you parked on King Street?"

"It was the nearest I could get."

"Nancy," Resnick said, "you knew where she was spending Christmas Eve?"

"With Dana, yes. At this stupid dance."

"But you knew where?"

"Where what?"

"Where it was being held," Resnick said.

"This stupid dance," Millington smiled.

"Robin, you knew where it was, the dinner-dance? Dana's firm's function, you knew where ...?"

"Yes, of course ..."

"Where Nancy was?"

"Yes."

"And you drove round all that time—what?—two hours, give or take. Round and around the center and you never went, never once went near where you knew she would be?"

Robin Hidden's body had half-turned in his chair and he was staring at the floor; it looked as far off, as hazy and unclear as a valley viewed from some high place. "If you want to take out your anger on someone," Mark had said, "take it out on her."

"Not on the off-chance," Millington said, leaning in a little closer, "that you might bump into her?"

"Catch a glimpse?" Resnick said.

"All r-r-right, so what if I did? So what if I went by there, by the stupid bloody hotel, all those idiots dressed up like clowns, prancing about and flashing off their money, so what if I did?"

"You did go to the hotel then, Robin? That night?"

"Isn't that what I just said?"

"Did you drive past outside or did you turn into the courtyard, by the main doors?"

"The courtyard."

"I'm sorry, could you say that more clearly."

"The courtyard. I d-drove into the courtyard."

"And parked?"

"Yes."

"What time was this?"

"About ... about ... it must've been j-just before twelve."

"And that was when you saw Nancy? When you were parked in the hotel courtyard a little before midnight on Christmas Eve?"

"Yes," Robin said. "That's right." His voice seemed to come from a long way off.

Twenty

Dana had spent the first hour that morning sorting out her room, tidying away things she'd long forgotten existed. By the time that particular task was over she had filled four plastic bin bags with clothes, three of which would be passed on either to Oxfam or Cancer Research, the other—mostly things which were too worn, too soiled, or simply beyond repair—she would put out for the bin men.

That done, she defrosted the freezer, cleaned the cooker—the surface, not the oven, she wasn't that much in need of distraction—wiped round the bath. She was on her knees, rubbing a Jif-laden J-cloth around the inside of the toilet bowl when she remembered a scene from a film she'd seen recently: a young woman—that actress, the one from *Single White Female*, not her, the other one—giving the inside of the lavatory bowl a shine with the blue T-shirt some man had left behind.

What she would have liked to have done with Andrew Clarke was push his head down till his nose reached the U-bend and hold him there while she flushed the chain.

What she might do, Dana thought, up on her feet with a new spring to her step, was sue the bastard for sexual harassment in the workplace. See what that did for his senior partnership, his place in the country, his snazzy little sports car.

She switched on the radio, a few minutes of Suede and she clicked it back off; fumbling through her tapes for Rod Stewart, she hesitated over Eric Clapton or Dire Straits, finally found what she was looking for inside the cassette box labeled Elton John. This was more like it. Old Rod. "Maggie May"; "Hot legs." Forget the new haircut, remember the bum. Listlessly she flicked through the pages of *Vanity Fair*. One more thing, sort through the drawers of her dressing table, and then she'd get out to the shops, buy herself something she didn't really need in the sales.

Her mood lasted as long as finding one of Nancy's earrings jumbled amongst her own: it came back to her then like cold wind, chilling her where she stood; she didn't think she would ever see Nancy again.

Kevin Naylor had taken the call from the hospital, listened a moment, before holding out the receiver towards Divine. "For you."

"This is Staff Nurse Bruton, it's about Mr. Raju."

Poor sod's bought it, Divine thought.

"He's been making a good recovery, and he's certainly well enough now to be able to talk to you."

"Well," Divine said, "the thing is, something big's come up here, this woman that's gone missing, and I really don't know ..."

"He could have died," Lesley Bruton said.

"Sorry?"

"Mr. Raju, what those youths did to him, he could have died."

"I know, I'm sorry and ..."

"And it doesn't matter?"

"Look, I should have thought you'd have been pleased. I mean, this is a woman this has happened to and ..."

"And this is only an Asian man."

Oh, Christ, Divine thought, here we go.

"I'll tell him you're too busy, then, shall I?"

"No," Divine said.

"Perhaps you could send somebody else?"

"No, it's okay ..." Looking at his watch, "... I could be there in forty minutes, give or take. How'd that be?"

"If he has a relapse," Lesley Bruton said, "I'll try to let you know."

The queue just to get into Next was right across the pavement outside Yates's and curled, four-deep, around the corner and up Market Street as high as Guava Records. Warehouse was hip to hip with customers eager for the twenty-five to fifty percent markdowns and Monsoon was crammed with well-bred women over thirty-five wearing what they'd bought at last year's sale.

Dana walked up past the futon shop into Hockley and considered treating herself to lunch in Sonny's; discretion sent her down Goose Gate to Browne's Wine Bar, a glass of dry house white and a chicken salad baguette. One glass became two and then three and from there it was a short, less than steady walk to the architects' office where she worked.

"Closed till January 3rd," read the card in neat black italic calligraphy taped to the center of the door.

She had the keys in her bag.

For a while, she wandered from room to room, past the drawing boards and the intricately made models and into the library where she worked amidst carefully cross-catalogued collections of slides and plans.

She walked back to Andrew Clarke's office. Only gradually, sitting on the corner of his matt-black executive desk, toying with the lipstick she had bought that morning at Debenhams, did the idea form, in Moroccan Scarlet, in her mind.

For all that Raju was out of the woods, Divine thought, he still had one hell of a lot of British taxpayers' money hooked up to him, one way and another. It was all he could do to maneuver a place to park his chair amongst all those stands and tubes and dials.

But old Raju, now he was propped up and looking perky, he came up with the goods as far as descriptions were concerned. One of the youths, the one who had done all the talking, the one who'd tapped on his window for him to stop, he had a small scar, the shape of a half-moon, there, underneath his right eye. And fair hair. Very, very fair. Divine knew full well none of the other witnesses had said anything about fair hair.

"You're positive," he said, "about the hair?"

"Oh, yes. Indeed."

More than likely, the bugger's still a bit delirious, Divine thought.

The second youth, the one who had hit him from behind, Raju was sure that he had several tattoos along his arms. Some kind of strange creature on one of them, a serpent maybe, something like that. Someone on a horse. A knight? Yes, he supposed that was right. And a Union Jack. No confusion about that. But left arm or right—no, sorry, he couldn't say.

"Age?" Divine asked.

"The age you would expect. Young men. Sixteen or seventeen."

"No older?"

Raju shook his head and the movement made him draw a sharp breath. "A year or two, perhaps. No more."

Divine closed his notebook and eased back his chair.

"You will be able to catch them now?"

"Oh, yes. Now we're armed with this. Two shakes of a dog's tail."

Leaning back against his pillows, Raju, smiling, closed his eyes.

Lesley Bruton was talking into the telephone at the nurses' station and Divine had to bide his time until she was through. "Thanks a lot," he said. "Raju, there. Tipping me the wink."

She looked back at him, saying nothing, waiting.

"Look," Divine said, "I was thinking. You wouldn't fancy coming out for a drink sometime?"

"This is," Lesley Bruton said, "some kind of a joke? Right?" And she brushed past Divine so close he had to step out of the way; it was three-fifteen and she had an enema to organize.

"Have you got a solicitor, Mr. Hidden?" Graham Millington asked.

They were in the corridor outside the interview room. After his second session, Robin had been decidedly shaky and they had suggested he walk up and down for a bit, make sure the windows were open, get some fresh air. Voices rose and fell along the stairways at either end. Someone's personal radio flared to life, overloud. Behind doors, the muted clamor of telephones.

"No, why? 1 don't see ..."

"It might be as well if you contacted one. If there isn't anyone you know personally, there's a list we can provide."

Robin Hidden stared into the sergeant's face, the brown, unblinking eyes, curl of the mouth beneath a moustache so perfect it could have been a fake.

"I thought once I'd answered all of your questions, it would be all right for me to leave," he said.

The mouth widened to a smile. "Oh, no, I don't think so, Mr. Hidden. Not quite yet. Not now."

Twenty-one

The solicitor appointed to represent Robin Hidden was David Welch, a forty-nine-year-old bachelor with two small Jack Russells, which he left in the back of his BMW, with a request to the officer on the desk that they be let out to do their business after a couple of hours.

Welch was experienced but lazy; some years before, he had realized that he lacked certain requisites for a really successful career. He lacked a wife, but clearly he wasn't gay; he was neither a Mason, nor a Rotarian, nor the possessor of the right stripe of school or college tie; not driven by burning ambition, he had never successfully cultivated the appearance of someone sure to succeed. Poor David, he didn't play bridge or poker, he didn't even play golf. He had looked around and understood the score. It would have been possible to move to another practice, another city, start again; he could have sought a new career—what he had settled for was an easy life.

"Your client's waiting, Mr. Welch," Millington said. "Along the corridor, third on the left."

"I suppose you've been allowing him all the proper breaks? Rest periods? A decent meal?"

"Cod and chips," Millington said chirpily. "Tea. No slices of bread and butter. Turned down the syrup sponge and custard." Millington patted his own stomach. "Not want to be putting on weight, like as not."

"I'd like a good half hour," Welch said.

"All the time you want," said Millington. They both knew it was a lie.

Divine was at his desk in the CID room, talking to a young woman who, two hours before, had had her handbag and two carriers of new purchases stolen from her in the middle of the city. Late lunchtime.

Sandra Drexler had been walking through the underpass below Maid Marian Way, the one with the news kiosk at its center, close to the Robin Hood Experience. Several families had been passing through at the time, children wearing Lincoln-green hats made from felt and waving bows and arrows in the air. Two youths in jeans and shirt sleeves had come running down the steps from the entrance nearest to St. James Street, caught hold of Sandra Drexler's arms, and swung her round in what had seemed, at first, like a drunken game. A couple of six-year-olds had pointed and laughed and their mother had shushed them on their way. But the youths had pushed Sandra hard against the tiled wall and torn the bags from her hands, her bag from her shoulder. They had gone running past the kiosk and along the tunnel towards Friar Lane and the castle, leaving Sandra on her knees, shocked and in tears, people walking wide to avoid her. Five minutes in which she had limped slowly towards the street, before an elderly woman had stopped to ask if she was all right.

"These tattoos," Divine said, interrupting her account. Sandra was in her second year of an Art and Design course at South Notts College. She took a sheet of A4 and a pencil and sketched them within minutes, the Union Jack, St. George and the Dragon.

"Sixteen, seventeen, you say?"

"That's right."

"And you're sure about the hair?"

"Yes, quite sure. Sort of washed-out sandy color. Really fair."

Divine thanked her for her trouble and gave her his second-best smile; if he weren't so full of himself and wearing that awful suit, Sandra thought, he might be almost good looking.

Resnick was weary. The muscles at the back of his neck were beginning to ache and he had drunk so much canteen tea it felt as if there was a coating of tannin furring his tongue. Across the table, Robin Hidden, with his solicitor's encouragement, had withdrawn into his shell. Saying as little as possible, giving nothing away.

"Robin," Resnick said, "don't you think we're making this more difficult than it has to be?"

Robin didn't respond; pointedly, David Welch looked at his watch.

Inside the machine, the twin tapes wound almost silently on.

At any moment, Resnick knew, Hidden was going to exercise his right to get up and go. Any solicitor other than Welch would surely have advised him to do so already.

"All right," Graham Millington said, business-like, "let's get it clear once and for all."

"Is it necessary to go through this again?" Welch asked.

"You arrived at the hotel between half-eleven and a quarter to twelve," Millington went on, ignoring him. "Parked the car at the edge of the courtyard and took a quick look in the main bar, hung around for a while, no more than five, ten minutes, then got back in the car. You drove round the block a few times, came back to the hotel ..."

"By then it must have been close to midnight," Resnick said.

"Almost midnight," Millington said.

"And that was when you saw Nancy." Resnick looked at Robin Hidden squarely and Robin blinked and stammered yes.

"And she saw you?"

"No."

"No?"

"I don't know."

"She saw the car?"

"I d-don't know. How could I know?"

"You can't expect my client to speculate ..."

"Nancy did know your car, though," Resnick said, leaning back, softening his tone. "She must have been in it a number of times? Associated it with you."

"I suppose so, but ..."

"Detective Inspector ..."

"But on this occasion, either she didn't make the connection or if she did, chose to ignore it. Ignore you."

Robin Hidden closed his eyes.

"And you did nothing? Stayed in the car and did nothing, no move to attract her attention, you didn't call her over, get out of the car, you didn't do anything—is that what you're saying?"

"Yes, I've told you. H-haven't I t-told you already?"

"Inspector ..."

"All right, Robin, listen ..." Reaching forward, Resnick, for a moment, rested his fingers on the back of Robin Hidden's hand. "Listen. I don't want to make a mistake here. You were upset about not seeing Nancy, upset at the way things were going, the way they seemed to be falling apart. You were out on your own, driving around, thinking about her. Is that right?"

Robin nodded. Resnick's hand was still close to his, close on the table's scarred surface. His voice was deep and quiet in the still room.

"You thought that if you could only talk to her, you might be able to sort things out, put them right."

Robin looked at the table, the marks, his hand, how small his own fingers seemed, narrow and thin; his breathing was more agitated, louder.

"And when you went back to the hotel the second time, there she was. Walking across the courtyard towards you. On her own." Resnick waited until Robin Hidden's eyes met his. "You had to talk to her. That was why you were there? You did talk to her, didn't you? Nancy. Either you got out of the car or she came to you, but you did talk to her?"

"No."

"Robin ..."

"N-no."

"Why ever not?"

Head in his hands, the words were indistinct and Millington would ask him to repeat them for clarification. "Because I was frightened. Because I knew what sh-she'd say. She'd tell m-me she d-didn't ever w-want to see me any more. N-not ever. And I c-couldn't, I couldn't s-stand that. So I w-waited u-un-til she'd gone past and then I drove away."

The tears came then without restraint and David Welch was on his feet to protest, but Resnick had already turned aside, Millington was looking at the ceiling, embarrassed, and for all intents and purposes the interview was over. Five thirty-seven p.m.

Twenty-two

"Struck lucky, then, Charlie. Took the old golden bollocks out of their case and give 'em a bit of a shine." Reg Cossall was leaning against the open door of Resnick's office, leering his lop-sided grin.

Resnick came close to sighing; he'd like to think Cossall was right.

"What? Boyfriend told to go walkies. The night before Christmas. Jesus, Charlie, don't have to be much of a wise man to work out that one."

"Too easy, Reg."

Cossall looked for somewhere on Resnick's desk to stub out his cigarette; made do with the heel of his shoe. "Never too easy. Blokes like that. Make 'em cough, bang 'em up, get yourself over the pub by opening time." As a philosophy of police work it remained, in Cossall's mind, undented by the fact that most pubs now stayed open all day. It also depended, from time to time, on not being fazed by the exact truth.

"Still a way to go, Reg," Resnick said.

Cossall tapped another Silk Cut from its pack. "Least you and Graham've got a live one to get your teeth into. I'm still halfway up the arse in computer printout and sodding cross-reference." When his lighter refused to work, he fumbled out a box of matches from his jacket; the spent match he snapped between finger and thumb and dropped back down into his pocket. "Meeting up with Rose in the Borlace, likely go for a bite later on," he released gray-blue smoke through his nose, "fancy joining us?"

Resnick shook his head. "Thanks, Reg. Things to do."

Cossall nodded, "Some other time, then."

"Maybe."

"Partial to you, you know, Rose is. Reckoned as how you've got a sense of humor. Told her she must be getting you mixed up with someone else."

"G'night, Reg."

Cossall laughed and walked away.

Was it too easy, Resnick thought? Too simple? He conjured up the look on Robin Hidden's face when the young man had talked about his last evening with Nancy, their last meal together, all those expectations dashed. The lie about seeing her outside the hoteL How much anger did it take? How much hurt? Pain like a vivid line, drawn through Robin Hidden's eyes. How many other lies?

"How d'you want to play it?" Skelton had asked. "Hold him overnight? Keep pushing hard?"

Resnick's sense was that, for now, Hidden had been pushed as far as he could usefully go. Shocked by his own admission he had closed in on himself fast and even David Welch was on the ball enough to encourage him in his silence. So they had let him go home to the flat in West Bridgford, Musters Road, second floor of a detached house with a car port and an entryphone. Home to his microwave and his OS maps and his thoughts. "We'll be wanting to talk to your client again," Millington had smiled benevolently at the door.

Resnick stood up, rubbed the heels of both hands against his eyes. Through the window the shapes of the buildings were wrapped in purple light.

Lynn's flat was in a small housing association complex in the Lace Market, balconies facing in on a partly cobbled courtyard. The rooms were large enough that she didn't fall over her own feet, not so big they encouraged her to own a lot of stuff. The floors she hoovered or mopped about once a week, the surfaces she dusted when there was a chance someone might call. A film of soft gray attached itself to her fingertip as she drew it along the tiled shelf above the gas fire. A gentleman caller, where had she heard that expression? She tried to blow the dust away but it stuck to her skin and she wiped it down the side of her skirt as she bent low, turning the circular switch alongside the fire to ignition. She remembered now, a film she had seen on television, *Glass* something, *The Glass Menagerie*, that was it. This young woman with a limp, not so young actually, that was part of it, surrounding herself with these little glass animals, waiting all the while for her gentleman caller to arrive at her door.

The radio was in the kitchen and Lynn switched it on before half-filling the kettle; a singer she failed to recognize was singing an Irish song. The voice was soft and warm and for no good reason it made her think of home. Swishing warm water around the inside of the pot, then emptying it into the sink, she saw her mother, year on year, doing exactly the same. She clicked the radio off, dropped a single teabag into the pot. How long had it been, Lynn asked herself, since she had stopped waiting for gentlemen callers herself? Before the tea had time to brew, the telephone rang.

"I've been calling you all day," her mother said.

"I've only this minute got in from work," Lynn said, shorter-tempered than she'd intended.

"I tried the station once. The line was busy."

"I'm not surprised. It's the holidays, we're more understrength than usual. And you know there's a girl gone missing."

Most often, any such remark would have brought forth from her mother a warning about being extra careful, bolting the door top and bottom, checking the window locks before going to bed; to her mother, any city bigger than Norwich was a place of constant danger, the worst she'd read about New York and New Orleans combined. But now there was nothing, a dull silence. Then, out in the courtyard, the sound, muffled, of a car starting up, misfiring. Lynn wondered if she could excuse herself a moment, pour the tea, bring it back to the phone.

"Lynnie, I think you should come home."

"Mum …"

"I need you here."

"I was there just a couple of days ago."

"I'm at my wits' end."

Lynn suppressed most of a sigh.

"It's your dad."

"Oh, Mum …"

"You know he was going to the hospital …"

"That's tomorrow."

"It was changed, the appointment was changed. They rang to tell him. He's been already. Yesterday."

"And?"

In the hesitation she heard the worst, then heard it again in her mother's words. "He's got to go back. Another test." I don't want to know this, Lynn thought. "To check, that's all it is, the doctor explained. Only to make sure that he hasn't got ... well, what they thought, you know, he'd got, he ..."

"Mum."

"They thought, all this trouble he was having, his eating, going to the lavatory and that, it might be a growth, there, you know, in the, the bowel."

"And it's not?"

"What?"

"It's not a growth, is that what they're saying? Or are they still not sure?"

"That's why he's got to go back."

"So they're not sure?"

"Lynnie, I don't know what to do."

"There's nothing you can do. Not until we know for sure."

"Can't you come?"

"What do you mean? You mean now?"

"Lynnie, he won't sit, he won't eat, he won't as much as look me in the eye. At least if you were here ..."

"Mum, I was there. Just days ago. He hardly spoke to me either."

"You won't come then?"

"I don't see how I can."

"He needs you, Lynnie. I need you."

"Mum, I'm sorry, but it's a difficult time."

"You think this is easy?"

"I didn't say that."

"Your poor dad's not important enough, that's what you said." She was close to tears, Lynn knew.

"You know that's not true," Lynn said.

"Then go with him to the hospital."

Lynn rested the top of the receiver against her forehead.

"Lynnie ...?"

"I'll see if I can. I promise. But you know what hospitals are like, that won't be for ages yet."

"No, it's soon. The man your dad saw, the consultant, he said he wanted him in as soon as possible. The next few days."

Then it is serious, Lynn thought. "This consultant," she said, "you can't remember his name, I suppose?"

"It'll be written down somewhere, I don't know, I'll just see if I can find it if you'll ..."

She heard her mother scrabbling about among all the scraps of paper that were kept by the phone. "Mum, call me back, okay? When you've found it? All right. Talk to you in a minute. Bye."

The skin along the tops of Lynn's arms was cold and her face was unusually drained of color. The small medical primer she kept with her dictionary and handful of paperbacks almost fell open at the page she wanted: the alternative name for cancer of the bowel was colorectal cancer. Its highest incidence was in males in the sixty to seventy-nine age group. Fifty percent of colorectal cancers are in the rectum. She let the book fall from her fingers to the floor. In the kitchen, she tipped away the remains of a carton of milk that smelled sour and struggled to open another without splashing too much over her hands. She put one spoonful of sugar in the mug and then another. Stirred. Two sips and she carried the mug back to the telephone.

When her mother rang back, she was crying at the other end of the line.

Lynn let her sob a little and then asked her if she'd found the name. She got her to repeat it twice, spelling it out as she wrote it down.

"Is Dad there?" Lynn said.

"Yes."

"Let me talk to him."

"He's out in the sheds."

"Call him in."

There was a clunk as the phone was set awkwardly down; Lynn drank her tea and listened to the voices of youths in the street at the rear of the flat, raised half-heartedly in anger. One of her neighbors was listening to opera, a young man who wore black turtlenecks and ignored her when they passed on the stairs.

"I can't get him to come in," her mother said.

"Did you tell him it was me?"

"Of course I did."

Her upstairs neighbor was not only singing along, now he was stamping his feet in time with the chorus. "I'm going to get in touch with this consultant," Lynn said, "see if I can find out when Dad's likely to be in. Then I'll see if I can get leave. Okay?"

She listened to her mother a few minutes more, reassuring her as much as she could. She tipped away what was left of her tea and poured herself a second cup. Turning on the hot tap in the bathroom, she sprinkled some herbal bubble bath into the stream of water. Only when she lowered herself into the steamy warmth did she begin to relax and the pictures she had begun to conjure up of her father begin to fade, at least for the time being, from her mind.

Twenty-three

Resnick had fed the cats, made himself coffee, squeezed half a lemon on to a piece of chicken he'd rubbed with garlic, and set it under the grill. While that was cooking, he'd opened a bottle of Czech pilsner and drank half of it in the living room, reading an obituary of Bob Crosby. One of the 78s his uncle the tailor had prized had been "Big Noise from Winnetka" by the Bobcats. Bob Haggart and Ray Bauduc, bass and drums and a lot of whistling. If Graham Millington ever came across it, the whole station would be in peril.

Back in the kitchen he turned the chicken and poured some of the juice back over it with a spoon. The last half of a beef tomato he cut into chunks and added to some wilting spinach and a piece of chicory on its last legs; these he tipped into a bowl and dressed with a trickle of raspberry vinegar and a teaspoon of tarragon mustard, a liberal splash of olive oil.

He ate at the kitchen table, feeding Bud with oddments of the chicken, washing it all down with the rest of the beer. There was something nagging at him, the impression he had got of Robin Hidden that afternoon, and the idea of a man attractive and lively enough for Nancy Phelan to take willingly to her bed—two sides of a puzzle that refused to come together.

He cut the last of the chicken into two and shared them with the cat; licking his fingers, he went towards the phone.

"Hello, is that Dana Matthieson?" Hearing the voice, Resnick remembered a biggish woman, lots of hair, round faced. Not unlike Lynn, he supposed, but more so. Colorful clothes. "Yes, this is Inspector Resnick. We talked ... I was just wondering, if you're not too busy, if you could spare me a little of your time? Say, half an hour? ... Yes, okay, thanks. Yes, I know where it is ... Yes, bye."

✦✦✦

Dana had been ironing some several-days-old laundry until she had got bored and now blouses and cotton tops and brightly colored trousers lay across the backs and arms of chairs and in a loose pile on the ironing board. The television was on with the sound at a whisper, a film with James Belushi, a great many car chases, and at least one large dog. All five attempts at writing her letter of resignation to Andrew Clarke and Associates, Architects, had been torn in half and half again and were now spread, unfinished, over the glass-topped table.

She had been well into a bottle of Shingle Peak New Zealand Riesling when Resnick had phoned and there was just a glass left to offer him when the door bell rang. If it came to it, Dana thought, not that she could see why it should, she could always open another.

Resnick shook off his coat, exchanged a few pleasantries, and took the offered seat. Dana's face was fuller than he had pictured it, swollen around the eyes, from drinking or crying he couldn't tell.

She held the bottle out towards him and he shook his head, so she emptied the contents into her own glass.

"There's no news," she said, scarcely a question.

Resnick shook his head.

Dana poked at the hem of an orange top that was either half inside her belt or half out. "I didn't think so or you would have said. On the phone." She tilted the glass back and drank. "Unless the news was bad."

He looked up at her steadily.

"Oh, God," Dana said, "she's dead, isn't she? She's got to be."

Resnick reacted in time to catch the glass as it fell from her fingers, what was left of the wine splashing across his sleeve. With his other arm he steadied her, fingers spread high behind her waist so that she fell heavily against him. Eyes closed, her face was close to his; he could feel her breath on his skin.

"That's not what I came here to say."

"Isn't it?"

"No. No, it's not."

Through the soft material of her clothing he could feel her breast against his chest, hip hard against his thigh.

"It's all right."

She opened her eyes. "Is it?"

He was more aware of her body than he wanted to be. "Yes," he said.

Just a simple movement, the way she raised her mouth towards his. A moment when something tried to warn him this was wrong. Her breath was warm and she tasted of wine. Their teeth clashed and then they didn't. He could scarcely believe the inside of her mouth was so soft. Gently, she took his bottom lip between her teeth.

Without Resnick knowing exactly how, they were on the floor beside the settee. The sleeve of his jacket, the cuff of his shirt were dark from the wine.

"I've ruined your clothes," Dana said.

They managed to get his jacket half off; one at a time, she licked his fingers clean.

"I don't know your name," she said. "Your first name."

He touched her breast and the nipple was so hard against the soft flesh of his finger that he gasped. Dana moved beneath him so that one of his legs was between her own. She took his face in her hands; she didn't think he could have kissed anyone in a long while.

"Charlie," he said.

"What?" Her voice soft and loud, tip of her tongue flicking the lobe of his ear.

"My name. Charlie."

Face pressed into the softness of his shoulder, she began to laugh.

"What?"

"I can't believe …"

"What?"

"I'm about to make love to a policeman called Charlie."

He moved his leg and rolled away but she rolled with him and as she leaned over him her hair fell loose about her face and the laugh was now a smile.

"Charlie," she said.

The look of shock was still there in his eyes.

Taking his hands again, she brought them to her breasts. "Careful," she said. "Careful, Charlie. Take your time."

✦✦✦

"Charlie, are you all right?"

They were in Dana's big bed beneath a duvet cover awash with purple and orange flowers. The room smelled of potpourri and sweat and sex and, faintly, Chanel Nº 5. Dana had opened another bottle of wine and before bringing it back she had put music on the stereo; through the partly open door, Rod Stewart was singing "I Don't Want to Talk About It"; inside Resnick's head Ben Webster was playing "Someone to Watch Over Me," "Our Love is Here to Stay."

"I'm fine," he said. "Just fine." Aside from the obvious, he had no idea what was happening and for now he was happy to keep it that way.

"Quiet, though," Dana said. He looked to see if she was smiling; she was.

"Hungry?" she asked.

"Probably."

Kissing him on the side of the mouth, she pushed herself off the bed and took her time about leaving the room. It amazed him that she was so unselfconscious about her body; when he had needed to go to the bathroom, he had fished his boxer shorts from the bottom of the bed with his toes and pulled them back on.

Dana had taken off Resnick's watch because it was scratching her skin and now he lifted it from the bedside table: eleven-seventeen. Cupping both hands behind his head he closed his eyes.

Without meaning to, he dozed.

When he came to, Dana was walking back into the room with a tray containing two cold turkey wings, one leg, several slices of white breast meat, a chunk of Blue Stilton, plastic pots of hummous and taramasalata two-thirds empty, a small bunch of grapes browning against their stems, one mug of coffee, and another of orange and hibiscus tea.

"Budge up," she grinned, settling the tray in the center of the bed and then sliding in behind it. "We haven't," she said, "a slice of bread or a biscuit in the place."

Slowly, she slid her forefinger down into the pink taramasalata and brought it, laden, to his mouth.

"When you rang, asked to come round," she said, "is this what you had in mind?"

Resnick shook his head.

"Honestly?"

"Of course not."

Dana sipped her tea. "Why, of course?"

Resnick didn't know how he was supposed to respond, what to say. "I just didn't … I mean, I wouldn't …"

"Wouldn't?"

"No."

She arched an eyebrow. "Clean in thought, word and deed, the policeman's code."

"That isn't what I mean."

"What you mean is, you didn't find me attractive."

"No."

"No, you didn't, or no, you did?"

"No, that isn't what I mean."

"What is then?"

To give himself time, he tried the coffee; it was almost certainly instant, certainly too weak. "I meant I knew you were an attractive woman, but I hadn't thought about you in this … like this, I mean, sexually, and if I had I probably wouldn't have called up like that and invited myself round so as to …"

"Why not?"

He put the mug back down. "I don't know."

"You're involved with somebody else?"

"No."

"Then why not?"

Not knowing why this was so embarrassing, nonetheless he looked away. "It wouldn't have seemed right."

"Oh."

"And besides …"

"Yes?"

"I'd never have thought you'd be interested."

"In sex?"

"In me."

"Oh, Charlie," touching the side of his face with her hand.

"What?"

"Don't you know you're an attractive man?"

"No," he said. "No, I don't."

Smiling she let her hand slide around to the back of his neck as she leaned towards him for a kiss. "Of course," she said, "that's one of the most attractive things about you." And then, "But you are pleased to be here?"

He didn't have to answer; she could see that he was.

"Before it's too late," she said, "why don't we just move this tray?"

She was stretching to set it on the floor when Resnick ran his hands down her back on to her buttocks, then, more slowly, out along her thighs. He heard her breathing change.

"Dana," he said.

"Mmm?"

"Nothing." He had just wanted to hear how it sounded when he spoke her name.

It was after one. The second mug of coffee had been stronger and black. The same Rod Stewart selection was playing, more quietly, in the next room. Resnick lay on his stomach, Dana with one leg and arm carelessly across him. This time she had been the one to fall asleep, but now she was sleepily awake.

"You know, I saw him once," Resnick said.

"Who?"

"Rod Stewart. That's who it is, isn't it?"

"Mm."

"Years ago. He was with the Steam Packet. Club down by the Trent. Almost couldn't get through the doors."

"Not surprising."

Resnick smiled over his shoulder. "Could've counted on one hand, most likely, those who'd as much as heard of him then, never mind gone specially to see him. Long John Baldry, he was the one they were there for."

Dana shook her head, she hadn't heard of him.

"Him and Julie Driscoll, they were the main singers with the band. Stewart came on first, did a few numbers at the start of the set. Skinny kid with a harmonica. Rod the Mod, that's what he was being called."

"Good, though, was he?"

Resnick laughed. "Terrible."

"Now you're having me on."

"No, I'm not. He was dreadful. Appalling."

Dana's face went serious. "You're not, are you, Charlie?"

"What?"

"Having me on? Messing me around?"

Resnick pushed himself around, sat up. "I don't think so."

"Cause I've had enough of that. One night stands."

She had turned away from him, shoulder slumped forward, and although he could neither see nor hear, Resnick knew she was crying. He didn't know what to do; he left her alone and let her cry and then he moved close and kissed the top of her back, just below the dark line of her hair, and she turned into his arms.

"Oh God!" she said. "It doesn't seem right. Doing this. Feeling this good. After what's happened to Nancy. You know what I mean?"

Her tears had smeared what little makeup remained on her face.

"We don't know," Resnick said, "what's happened to Nancy. Not for sure."

Though in their hearts, they were certain, both of them, that they did.

"What time is it?" Dana said. In the darkness of the room, she could see that Resnick, between the end of the bed and the door, was fully dressed.

"A little after two."

"And you're leaving?"

"I have to."

She sat up in bed, the edge of the duvet covering one breast. "Without telling me?"

"I didn't want to wake you."

Dana stretched out an arm and Resnick sat on the side of the bed, holding her hand. She stitched her fingers between his.

"You never did tell me," she said, "why it was you wanted to see me."

"I know. I thought maybe I should leave it to another time."

"What was it, though?" She brought his hand to her face and rubbed his knuckles against her cheek.

"Robin Hidden ..."

"What about him?"

"I wanted to ask you about him."

Dana released his hand and leaned away. "Surely you don't suspect Robin?"

Resnick didn't answer. She could see little more than the outline of his face; impossible to read the expression in his eyes, tell what he was thinking.

"You do, don't you?"

"You know what had happened between them?"

"Nancy had chucked him, yes. But that doesn't mean ..."

"He saw her that evening, Christmas Eve ..."

"He couldn't have."

"He went to the hotel, looking for her, just before midnight."

"And?"

Resnick didn't immediately reply; had said already more than probably he should.

"And?" Dana said again, touching his hand.

"Nothing. He saw her and drove away."

"Without talking to her?"

Resnick shrugged. "That's what he says."

"But you don't believe him?"

"I don't know."

"You think there was some kind of awful row, Robin lost his temper, and ..." Dana had raised her hands as she was talking and now let them fall to her sides.

"It's possible," Resnick said.

Dana leaned towards him. "You've spoken to Robin, though? Talked to him?"

"Yes?"

"And you still think he could do something like that? Hurt her? Harm her?"

"Like I said, it's possible. It's ..."

"He wouldn't do that. He couldn't. He's just not the type. And besides, if you'd seen him with Nancy, you'd know. Whatever she thought of him, he really loved her."

Exactly, Resnick thought. "Sometimes," he said, "that's enough."

"God!" Dana pulled at the duvet and moved away, swiftly to the far side of the bed. "I suppose it's no surprise, doing what you do, you should be as cynical as you are." Barefoot, she took a robe from where it was hanging on the open wardrobe door and slipped it around her.

"Cynical," Resnick said, "is that what it is? Loving somebody so much you lose all perspective."

"Enough to want to hurt them? Or worse? That's not cynical, it's sick."

"It's what happens," said Resnick. "Time and again. It's what I have to deal with." He was talking to the open door.

Dana took a sachet of herbal tea from the packet and hung it over the edge of a freshly rinsed mug. When she pointed at the jar of Gold Blend, Resnick shook his head. "I'll wait till I get home."

"Suit yourself." Sitting at the table, Dana toyed with a spoon, avoiding Resnick's eye.

Resnick was starting to feel more than uncomfortable; he wished he were no longer there, but couldn't quite bring himself to go. "I didn't mean to upset you," he said.

"I was already upset. What happened, it made me forget it for a while, that's all."

On the narrow shelf, the kettle was coming noisily to the boil. She was still refusing to look at him and still he hovered near the doorway, reluctant to leave. "Their relationship, Nancy and Robin, it was, well, as far as you know, it was sexual?"

Dana laughed, without humor, more a simple expelling of air than a laugh. "Did I hear the usual groans and gasps through the wall? Why not? She's an attractive woman; Robin's athletic, a good body whatever else."

"It was passionate, then, between them?"

She was staring at him now, open faced. "Is that all the proof you need, Charlie? That someone's capable of passion? Is that enough to tip the scales?"

"I'll call you," Resnick said, stepping back into the hallway.

If Dana heard him, jinking the sachet in and out of her tea, she gave no sign. Mindful of the hour, Resnick closed the door firmly yet quietly behind him.

Twenty-four

What little had been seen of the season of goodwill was soon lost in a fog of malevolence and discontent. Uniformed officers summoned to a night club in the city, after receiving an emergency call claiming that a man had been knifed, walked into a blitz of bottles and bricks, and one hastily assembled petrol bomb was rolled beneath their car. A firefighting team arriving to tackle a blaze in the upper stories of a terraced house two streets away from Gary and Michelle found themselves pelted with rubbish and abuse by a gang of white youths, one of their hoses split by an ax, the tires of an engine slashed. The family living in the house, two of whom suffered broken limbs jumping to the ground while others, children between five years and eighteen months, suffered severe burns, were from Bangladesh.

At something short of five one morning, a young woman with a Glasgow accent stumbled into the police station at Canning Circus with blood running freely from a wound to the side of her head and one eye tightly closed. She and her boyfriend, a twenty-nine-year-old known to be a small-time dealer, had been smoking crack cocaine in an abandoned house near the Forest; she had drifted off and been woken by the sound of his fists pummeling her face. Medical examination in casualty revealed a fractured cheekbone and a detached retina in the eye.

The driver of the last bus from the Old Market Square to Bestwood Estate refused to accept the fare of a clearly drunken man who had been offering him verbal abuse and had a piece of masonry thrown at his windscreen, splintering it across. Another taxi driver was attacked, this time with a baseball bat.

A memo was passed round, offering overtime for officers willing to be drafted in to assist the Mansfield division in policing a concert by right-wing skinhead rock groups to be held in the old Palais de Dance. The event had been advertised in fascist magazines all over Europe and at least two coachloads were expected from Germany and Holland.

"Sounds like just the thing for our Mark," Kevin Naylor remarked, passing the memo across the CID room.

"Knowing him," Lynn said, "he'll have his ticket already. Front row."

Nancy Phelan's parents made a ritual of visiting the station twice, sometimes three times a day, demanding to speak with either Resnick or Skelton to find out what progress had been made. Between times, they turned up on one or other of the local radio programs, wrote to the *Post*, the free papers, the nationals, petitioned the Lord Mayor and the city's M.P. Clarise Phelan took to standing in front of the stone columns of the Council House at one end of the Market Square with a placard bearing a blown-up photograph of Nancy and underneath, *My lovely daughter—missing and nobody cares.*

After forty-eight hours when the temperature had risen high enough for Resnick to discard both scarf and gloves, the weather bit back. It hit freezing and stayed. Trains were cancelled, buses curtailed; cars slid into slow, unstoppable collisions which blocked the roads for hours. Understaffed, close to overwhelmed, Skelton and Resnick struggled to delegate, prioritize, keep their feet from slipping under them.

Both of Nancy Phelan's missing boyfriends returned, shocked by what had happened, but unable to shed any light on how or why. James Guillery was stretchered off the plane at Luton Airport with a broken leg, victim not of the snow but an accident involving the chairlift and a snapped bolt. Eric Capaldi had sped in his low-slung sports car to the outskirts of Copenhagen and back. His aim had been to interview, for a potential radio slot of his own, a fifty-two-year-old percussionist who had been a counter-culture star for fifteen minutes in the late sixties and was now composing minimalist religious music for trans-European radio. After the interview and most of a bottle of brandy and to Eric's abiding confusion, he had ended up in the percussionist's arms and then his bed.

Robin Hidden continued to maintain that he had driven away that night without speaking to Nancy Phelan and had finally issued a statement through his solicitor saying that, as far as that particular subject went, he had nothing more to say.

As David Welch, smiling for once, had expressed it, handing Graham Millington the envelope, "Put up or shut up, you know what I mean?"

"Cocky so-and-so," Millington thought. "Well above himself." But he and Resnick knew only too well Welch was right. Arrest Hidden as things stood and within twenty-four hours, thirty-six at most, he would be back out on the street again and what would have been gained?

What did happen, inevitably, was that Harry Phelan got wind of what was going on. A new-found friend of a friend, drinking late one night in his Mansfield Road hotel, had told him one place to find the crime reporter for the *Post* was in the Blue Bell of a lunchtime, swopping yarns and enjoying a peaceful couple of pints. Next day Harry went along and stood around and by the time he'd bought his round, had heard about the young man the police had been questioning.

"Where is the bastard?" Harry Phelan had yelled later, catching Skelton coming back from one of his runs to the station. "Why haven't you bleedin' arrested him? Just wait till I get my hands on him, that's all. Just wait."

Skelton calmed him down and invited him to his office, tried to explain. "Mr. Phelan, I assure you ..."

"Don't insult me with that," Harry Phelan said. "Assure. Look at you. Out there friggin' about in that poncey gear, joggin', instead of saving my poor bleedin' kid! You—you couldn't assure me of shit!"

Meanwhile, Reg Cossall and his team had interviewed one hundred and thirty-nine men and forty-three women, thirty-seven of whom had a clear recollection of seeing Nancy on Christmas Eve. Five of the women had spoken to her, eight in all remembered what she had been wearing. Seven of the men, had spoken to her, five had danced with her, two had asked her if they could give her a lift home. She had said no to them both. And both had gone home with someone else.

As police work went it was painstaking and thorough and it didn't seem to be going anywhere. "Like farting down an open sewer," Cossall said, disgusted. "Not worth parting your bloody cheeks."

By the time Resnick had arrived home after his night with Dana Matthieson, walking all the way across the city, down beside the cemetery to the gates of the Arboretum, through towards the site of the old Victoria railway station and up past the Muslim temple on the Woodborough Road, he had convinced himself that it had all been a mistake. Enjoyable, yes, exciting even, but certainly a mistake. On both sides.

Naturally, he reasoned, after what had happened to her flatmate, Dana had been upset, disorientated, looking for comfort and distraction. As for himself—Jesus, Charlie, he said to the empty streets, how long is it since you went with a woman?

Is that what it had been, then? Only that? Going with a woman?

Suddenly chilled, he had pulled up his coat collar and shivered, remembering the warmth of Dana's body.

And of course, he hadn't done as he had said, he hadn't called. For the first couple of days, whenever the phone rang in his office or at home, he had lifted the receiver with the same strange mix of anxiety and anticipation. But it was never her. Easy to stop waiting for it to happen.

When, finally, three days later, Dana did call, Resnick was talking to Lynn Kellogg about her application for leave, a day accompanying her father to the outpatient department of the Norfolk and Norwich.

"An endoscopy," Lynn said, the word unfamiliar on her tongue.

Resnick looked at her inquiringly.

"An internal examination. As far as I can tell they pass this thing, this endoscope up into his bowels."

Resnick shuddered at the thought.

Lynn breathed uneasily. "If they suspect cancer, most likely they'll take a biopsy."

"And if it is," Resnick asked, "what kind of treatment ...?"

"Surgery," Lynn said. "They cut it out."

"I'm sorry," Resnick said. There were tears, suddenly, at the corners of Lynn's eyes. "Really sorry." Part way round his desk towards her he stopped. He wanted to take her in his arms, reassure her with a hug.

"It's all right." Lynn found a tissue and blew her nose, leaving Resnick stranded where he was. Thank God for the phone.

"Charlie?" said the voice at the other end of the line.

"Hello?"

"It's me, Dana."

By then he knew.

"You didn't call."

"No, I'm sorry. Things have been, well, hectic." Without meaning to, he caught Lynn's eye.

"I've been thinking about you," Dana said.

Resnick transferred the receiver from one hand to another, studied the floor.

"Do you want me to wait outside?" Lynn said.

Resnick shook his head.

"I've been thinking about your body," Dana said.

Resnick, found that hard to believe. He thought about his own body as little as he could and when he did it was usually with dismay.

"I want to see you, that's all," Dana said. "No big deal."

"Look," Lynn was almost at the door, "I can come back later."

"Is this a bad time?" Dana said. "Is it difficult for you to talk?"

"No, it's fine," Resnick said, waving Lynn back into the room.

"When can I see you?" Dana asked.

"Why don't we meet for a drink?" Resnick said, as much as anything to get her off the phone.

"Tomorrow?"

Resnick couldn't think. "All right," he said.

"Good. Eight o'clock?"

"Fine."

"Why don't you come here? We can go on somewhere else if you want."

"All right. See you then. Bye." By the time he put down the phone he had started to sweat.

"First-footing," Lynn said.

"What?"

"You know, tall stranger crosses the threshold with a lump of coal."

"Oh, God!"

"Problem?"

Only that he'd forgotten it was New Year's Eve. And now Marian Witczak's voice came instantly back to him: "We will both wear, Charles, what would you say? Our dancing shoes."

"Double-booked?" Lynn asked.

"Something like that."

"I'm sorry I shouldn't be laughing." She didn't seem to be laughing at all.

"This day's leave," Resnick said, "it'll be tight, but no question you must go. We'll cover somehow."

"Thanks. And good luck."

"What?"

"Tomorrow."

Dana lit another cigarette, poured herself another drink. She had already had several, finding the courage to phone him when he hadn't phoned her. And at work. Probably she shouldn't have done that, probably that had been a mistake. Except he had said yes, hadn't he? Agreed to come round for a drink. She smiled, raising her glass: he was worth a little seeking out, a little chasing after. She liked him, the memory of him: big, there was something, she thought, about a man who was big. And she laughed.

Twenty-five

Gary was sprawled across the settee wearing his County goalkeeper's shirt over the top of two pullovers in an attempt to keep warm. He was watching a program about Indonesian cookery and Michelle couldn't for the life of her see why. The extent of Gary's cooking in the past few months had been opening a tin of beans and, five minutes later, slopping the contents, lukewarm, over burned toast and then yelling at Karl because he wouldn't eat it. Beyond that, all Gary knew about cookery was "What's for dinner?" and "Where's me tea?"

Michelle didn't say anything; knew well enough to let him be.

Brian's wife, Josie, had offered to take Karl down to the Forest along with her two and Michelle had leaped at the chance. Natalie had lain, alternately cooing and crying in her cot, some twenty minutes after feeding but now she was quiet. Michelle had wiped round the sink in the kitchen, taken the rubbish out to the bin; for once in his life, Gary had grunted no instead of yes to the offer of a cup of tea and she'd taken her own upstairs to have a sort out, tidy round.

There were balls of dust collecting at the corners of the stairs.

In the small room at the back, Natalie was sleeping with her thumb in her mouth and one leg poking through the bars of the cot; Michelle took the tiny foot in her hand and slipped it back beneath the covers. So cold! Gently, she touched her lips to the baby's cheek and that was warm, at least. Leaving the door ajar, she crossed to the other bedroom and shivered: it was like an icewell in there.

There were two pairs of tights hanging from the end of the bed, one of them laddered almost beyond repair. Gary seemed to have dumped bits and pieces of clothing everywhere, a shirt, pair of boxer shorts, one sock. From the state of the collar, the shirt could just about last out another day, so she hung it back inside the chipboard wardrobe they had got from Family First. Gary's zip-up jacket, his favorite, stuffed down there on top of the shoes, getting all creased—Michelle bent down to pick it up and that was when the knife fell out.

She jumped and thought she must have cried out loud, but nothing happened; the baby didn't wake, Gary didn't call up from downstairs. The television commentary continued in a blur from which she was unable to distinguish the words.

The handle of the knife was rounded, wrapped around with tape; the blade, close to six inches long, curved out then in, tapering to a point. Near to the tip, a piece of the blade had broken away, as if it had been struck against something resisting and hard.

It lay against her one decent pair of heels, daring her to pick it up.

"You didn't see Nancy that evening? Later that evening? Christmas Eve?"

"I told you, didn't I? I never went out."

Slowly, not wanting to, Michelle bent down towards the knife. Tried to imagine it being raised in anger in a man's hand.

"'Chelle? Michelle?"

A second before the voice, she heard the board, loose along the landing, squeak. Breath caught hard in her mouth, she pulled the jacket back across the knife, pushed both with her foot further back inside, shut the wardrobe door.

"Here you are." Smiling that way with his mouth, parted just a little, twisted down. "Wondered where you were."

She was certain, the way it was pumping, he must hear her heart.

"What's up?"

Afraid to speak, Michelle shook her head from side to side.

"That cooking," he nodded back downstairs, "all it is, chop everything up small, meat and that, stick it in a jar of peanut butter." He winked. "Reckon we could try that."

Michelle had steadied her breathing enough to move away from the wardrobe door.

"Natalie sleeping is she?"

"I'll just see ..."

Gary caught her arm as she went past. Something had got stuck in the fine straggle of hairs beside his lip.

"Wondered what you'd come up here for."

"I was just tidying round. Those things …"

"Oh, yeh? Thought you might've had other ideas. You know …" His eyes grazed the bed. "… Karl out the way for a change."

"They'll be back …" Michelle began.

One hand reaching for the belt to her jeans, Gary laughed. "Oh no, they won't."

All the while they lay there, blessed by the squeak and roll of the wire mattress, Michelle thought about the knife. Gary above her, thrusting down, eyes clamped tight, mouth opening only to call her that name she hated, over and over, finally to cry out; through it all she could only see the swelling of the blade, feel its point.

When he had collapsed sideways, pulled away from her, face down into the sheet, she felt gingerly down there, certain amongst all that wetness there would be blood.

"Michelle?"

"Yes?"

"Be a sweetheart, make us a cup of tea."

She was on her way downstairs, sweater and jeans, hair uncombed, when Josie arrived back with the kids.

"Jesus, girl! Look like you been pulled through a hedge backwards." And, leaning close enough to whisper in her ear, "Not been knocking you around again, has he?"

Michelle shook her head. "Not the way you mean."

Josie rolled her eyes. "Oh, that! You know, when I was—what?—seventeen, eighteen, I used to reckon if I didn't have some bloke poking away at me every night the world was going to come to a sodding end. Now …," she shook her head and looked at Michelle knowingly, "… most of the time I couldn't give a toss. 'Fact, far as Brian's concerned, sometimes that's all I will give."

She was laughing so much now she had to grab hold of Michelle so as not to lose her balance. Josie. By Michelle's reckoning, she was all of twenty-one.

Twenty-six

Lynn woke slippery with sweat and it was too many moments before she realized she had been dreaming. The blanket she had pulled on to the duvet in the night to combat the cold was wound, tight like a rope, between her legs; the duvet itself had been thrown to the floor. T-shirt, knickers, socks, all were drenched. Coils of dark hair clung fast to her head.

In her dream she had been between the henhouses, walking in a nightgown she had never owned, long and stiff and white like something from *Rebecca* or *Jane Eyre*, when she had heard the sound.

As she ran, moonlight threw shadows against the packed earth, the worn boards of the henhouse walls. A cry, high and shrill, like the mating of feral cats: except it wasn't that. At first she thought the high, wooden door was locked, but as she threw her weight against it, she realized it was only jammed fast. Little by little it gave, then sprang suddenly backwards and she stumbled in.

Through the high, meshed windows the moon shone with a muted fall. Her father had climbed to the high conveyor and now he hung there, attached by the neck; his throat had been cut. Spurred by the silence, flies thrummed their wings, blue, and busied themselves in the dark and drying blood.

As Lynn fell fast against his legs, the body tore and tipped and spilled against her. His feet and hands were bony and cold and hard and when his eyes met hers they smiled.

She screamed herself awake. The sheet and pillow were soaked. Lynn stripped them from the bed and dropped them to the floor beside the blanket and her clothes. For several moments she stood with her head bent towards her knees, steadying her breath. It was twenty-five past three. Against all her judgment, what she wanted most of all was to phone home, make sure her father was all right. She pulled on her dressing gown and tied it tight, filled the kettle and switched it on, brought a towel from the bathroom and vigorously rubbed at her hair.

If anything had happened, her mother would have rung her. And she had worries enough already, without picking up the pieces of Lynn's dreams.

Lynn could remember her, inevitable apron smudged with flour, sitting on the side of the narrow bed Lynn had shared with a family of somewhat disabled dolls and a ragged panda, patting her hand and shushing, "Just a dream, my petal. All it was, a silly old dream."

Lynn had forgotten to buy any milk on the way home and so she drank half a cup of tea, black, before going back into the bathroom and standing under the shower. It was only then, hot water cascading from her head and shoulders, that she began to cry.

Worried about the lack of progress over Nancy Phelan, worried by the unfamiliar drawn expression he had noted on Lynn Kellogg's face, the dark shadows beneath her eyes, worried by his seemingly unresolvable predicament over New Year's Eve, Resnick had gone to bed convinced that he would never be able to sleep and had slept like the proverbial log. It had taken Dizzy's insistence to spin him awake, the cat's paws working rhythmically into his pillow with something close to desperation. It was a few minutes short of six o'clock, but Resnick felt as if he had overslept, head coddled in cotton wool.

Dizzy waited outside the bathroom while Resnick showered, sharpening his claws against the frame of the door. The other cats were in the kitchen, waiting to greet him, Pepper purring with anticipation from inside an old colander he had commandeered as his favored sleeping quarters.

Coffee brewing, cat food distributed into colored bowls, Resnick concentrated on layering alternate slices of smoked ham and Jarlsberg on to half-toasted rye bread. He was adding a touch of Dijon mustard when Lynn phoned, saying she needed to talk.

"Something about Gary James?" Resnick asked.

"No, it's personal," she said.

"All right," Resnick said, "give me half an hour."

He pressed the pieces of toast together into a sandwich and cut them in two, poured the coffee, took both back upstairs to finish getting dressed. Before leaving the house, he called Millington at home.

"Graham, wasn't sure if I'd catch you."

"Only just." Millington had been sitting at the circular table in the kitchen, chewing his way through an assortment of bran and wheatgerm that was about as appealing as the floor of his old nan's budgie's cage.

"At your age, Graham," his wife insisted, "it doesn't pay to take chances. You have to keep your arteries open." She'd been browsing through those leaflets she brought back from the well-woman clinic again, Millington had thought.

"Looks like I shall be a few minutes late," Resnick said. "Hold the fort for me, will you?"

Millington, of course, was only too pleased. Much of his sergeant's life, Resnick suspected, was spent waiting for some unforeseen and appalling accident to befall his superiors. At which time, only he, Graham Millington, mind alert, shoes buffed, and hair gleaming, would be ready to step into the breech. His moment of glory. What was it the dance director said to little Ruby Keeler in *42nd Street*? "You're coming out of that dressing room a nobody, but you're coming back a star."

The postman was at the end of the drive when Resnick left, sorting through a vast bundle of mail.

"Not all for me, I hope?" Resnick said, scarcely breaking his stride.

The postman shook his head. "Just the usual. *Readers' Digest*, Halifax, the AA, and free garlic bread if you order one large or two medium pizzas."

Resnick raised a hand in thanks. Exactly the kind of postal worker there should be more of, sifted through the junk mail for you so all you had to do was transfer it directly to the bin.

Lynn was waiting for him at the door, had heard his footsteps, heavy across the courtyard and turned up the flame under the Italian coffee pot she had recently bought. The coffee you put, ground, into a small perforated container which stood over cold water in the bottom section; light the gas and not so many minutes later the water had somehow pumped up and there was your coffee, strong and black and ready to pour. In truth, she doubted she'd used it more than a few times since buying it in the autumn. She hoped the coffee was strong enough; she hoped it didn't taste stewed.

"Good smell," Resnick said as soon as he was inside.

"You want some toast? I'm going to have toast."

"No, thanks," looking for somewhere to put his coat, "I've eaten already." And then, "All right, why not? Just one."

"Here, give me that," Lynn said, and hung his raincoat from one of the hooks just inside the door.

The radio was playing quietly in a corner of the room, not quite tuned. Trent-FM. "Let me turn that off."

"No, it's okay."

She switched it off anyway and Resnick mooched around the room while she was in the small kitchen, reading the titles of the books on the shelf, glancing at an old copy of the *Mail*, the back page with the headline, *FOREST FOR THE DROP?* Among the photographs above the fireplace was one of a happy Lynn, chubby and smiling, in her father's arms. Five years old? The pictures of her former boyfriend, the cyclist, seemed to have pedaled off into the dustbin.

"Butter or marge?"

"Sorry?"

"On the toast, butter or …"

"Oh, butter."

Resnick settled himself in the center of the two-seater settee, Lynn at an angle on a chair.

"How's the coffee?"

"Fine."

"Sure it's strong enough?"

"Why don't you tell me what's worrying you, what's happened?"

She told him about her dream. Neither spoke for a little while.

"You're bound to be frightened," he eventually said. "For yourself as well as for him. It's a difficult time."

Lynn pulled her legs towards her chest, wrapped her arms around her knees. "If it is cancer," Resnick said, "what are his chances?"

"They won't really say."

"And treatment? Chemotherapy?"

She shook her head. "I don't think so." She was focusing on a spot on the side wall, anything rather than look at him directly. "They cut it out. As much as they can. He'll probably have to have a colostomy. That's a ..."

"I know what it is."

"I can't imagine ... he'll never cope with that, he never will. He ..."

"Better that than the other thing."

"I don't even know if that's true." Her knee banged against the chair as she got up. She wasn't going to cry in front of him, she wasn't. Fingers digging into the flesh of her hands, she stood by the small window, staring out.

"I remember," Resnick went on, "when my father went into hospital. Trouble with his breathing, his lungs. Half a dozen stairs and he sounded like one of those old engines, winding down. He went into the City for tests, treatment, a rest. They gave him, I don't know, some kind of antibiotics. Physiotherapy. I'd go in sometimes to visit, I might just have been over that way, you know, passing, and this woman would be there, white tunic and trousers, pleasant but serious, deadly serious. 'Come on now, Mr. Resnick, we have to teach you to breathe.' 'What does she think I've been doing, Charlie, these past sixty years if it's not breathing?' he used to say as soon as she'd gone." He sighed. "I suppose they did what they could, but he hadn't made anything easy. Even as a kid, I can scarcely picture him without a cigarette in his hand." Resnick looked across at her. "But they did what they could. Got him so he was able to come out of hospital, come home for another few months."

Lynn turned sharply. "And you think it was worth it?"

"Yes, on balance I do."

"Did he?"

Resnick hesitated. "I think so. But truly, no, I don't know."

"He didn't say."

"Oh, he moaned. Complained. I won't lie to you, there were days when he said he wished they'd let him die; he wished he were dead."

"And yet you can still say it was right? For him to go through all that discomfort, the pain, the ... loss of dignity, all for what? A few extra months?"

Resnick drank some more coffee, giving himself time. "There were things he was able to say, we were able to say to one another, I think they were important."

"To you, yes?"

"Lynn, listen, you've got to realize, hard as it might be, this isn't just about him. About your dad. It's about you too. Your life. If he … if he dies, whenever he dies, one way or another you've got to find a way of living with that. And you will."

She let herself cry now and he stood close to her, a hand on her shoulder and for a short while she rested her head sideways against his arm, so that her face lay on his wrist and hand.

"Thanks," she said then and got to her feet and blew her nose and wiped her eyes and carried the empty cups and the plates back into the kitchen and rinsed them under the sink. "We'd better be going," she said. "It's not as if there's nothing to do."

Cossall was pacing the corridor, drawing heavily on his fifth or sixth cigarette of the morning. "Charlie, in here. You've got to hear this."

Resnick checked with Millington that everything was proceeding smoothly, then followed Cossall to the interview room, getting the details on the way.

Miriam Richards had been employed at the hotel on Christmas Eve, casual work as a waitress with which she augmented her student grant. On this particular evening she had been assigned to one of the larger banqueting rooms, shared for the occasion by the senior management of one of the larger department stores and an ad-hoc group of dentists, dental nurses, and technicians. At a little after half past eleven, Miriam had been clearing away the last of the coffee cups when a man had slid his hand between her legs, pushing the black skirt she was forced to wear hard between her thighs. No way it was any kind of an accident. Miriam had swung round, told him to keep his hands to himself, and slapped her right hand across his face. There was a cup and saucer in it at the time. The man screamed and landed with a jarring thump on his knees; amidst a lot of blood were the fragments of not one, but two broken teeth. Miriam thought there was poetic justice in this, until she found out the man worked not with fillings but furniture.

Of course, at first he denied as much as touching Miriam, never mind goosing her; all he would eventually admit as a possibility was that, being a little the worse for wear for drink, he had lost his footing getting up and reached out to steady himself.

"Bullshit!" Miriam declared resolutely, the term sounding somewhat at odds with her Cheshire accent. But she was doing American Studies and took the aculturation seriously.

When the member of the hotel's management team instructed her to apologize, she told him in no uncertain terms where to put his skirt and apron. She was on her way out of the hotel, irritable and prepared to walk back to her digs in Lenton, when she saw a car pull up beside a woman just in front of her. The driver shouted a name out of the window, jumped out when the woman didn't stop, ran after her, and grabbed her arm.

Miriam had held back for a while, worried in case what had just happened to her was about to happen to someone else. But after a few minutes of raised voices, mostly his, a little arm tugging, the woman shrugged her shoulders and seemed to change her mind. Anyway, she walked around to the passenger side of the car and got in, the driver followed suit, and they drove off, turning left down the hill.

"Descriptions?" Resnick asked.

Cossall grinned. "Talk to her yourself."

Miriam was wearing a blue denim jacket with a button reading *Spinsters on the Rampage* on one lapel, a larger one, *Hillary for President*, on the other. She wore a faded denim shirt and a yellow rollneck under the jacket, black wool leggings, and Doc Martens. She greeted Resnick with a wary half-grin.

"I'm sorry to ask you all this again ..."

"S'okay."

"But this woman, the one you saw get into the car, how old would you say she was?"

Miriam rolled her tongue and Resnick realized she was chewing gum. "Could have been a couple of years older than me, not a lot more."

"Early twenties, then?"

"Yes."

"And she was wearing?"

Miriam glanced over at Cossall before she answered. "Like I said, silvery top, matching tights, short black skirt; she had this red coat across her shoulders. Bit posey, I thought. Still ..." She looked from Resnick to Cossall and back again. "It's her, isn't it? The one who's missing. Jesus Christ, I could have done something, stopped it."

"I doubt you could have done anything," Resnick said. "You waited to see what was going to happen, that's more than most people would have done. But she got into the car of her own accord. There was no reason for you to interfere."

"But when I heard about it, on the news, back home, you know, over the holiday—I'm so stupid!—I never as much as thought."

"It's okay, love," Cossall said. "Don't get so worked up."

"Tell me," Resnick said, "about the car."

"Four-door saloon, blue, dark blue. Course, if I'd had any sense, if I hadn't been so worked out about that wanker … that idiot at the hotel, I would have thought to write down the number, just, you know, in case. But it was J reg., I'm sure of that."

"The make?"

"Can't say for certain. I could probably recognize it, though, if I had the chance."

"Tell him about the driver," Cossall said. "What he looked like."

Miriam described Robin Hidden—his height, slightly stooped posture, wiriness, spectacles—to a T. Everything except the stammer.

"Knew he was lying," Millington said. "Just bloody knew it."

"Felt it in your water, Graham?" Cossall grinned.

They were back in Resnick's office, while Lynn Kellogg gave Miriam a brief tour of the station, offered her a cup of tea, asked what exactly was American Studies.

"Let's do it carefully," Resnick said. "No slip ups now."

"You'll want an identity parade," Cossall said, one leg cocked over the corner of Resnick's desk. "Best have a word with Paddy Fitzgerald, see if he can't fix that. Graham here could probably make sure young Hidden doesn't do a runner."

Right, Millington thought, thanks a lot!

"At least that hasn't been handed over to a bunch of private cowboys yet. We catch 'em, get them into court and some half-assed security guard lets them go."

"It'll take more time organizing the cars," Resnick said. Since the Police and Criminal Evidence Act, there had to be a minimum of twelve vehicles of a similar type presented to the witness.

Cossall nodded. "Best get the car established though, hold off on pulling Hidden in for the ID; then if both come up positive, we can collar him while he's on the premises."

Resnick nodded. "Let's be about it."

"Talked to Jolly Jack?" Cossall asked over his shoulder, heading for the door.

"Next thing," Resnick said. And then, "Graham, when you go out for Hidden, under wraps as much as you can. We're right here, this'll be enough of a circus as it is."

Twenty-seven

Dana had gone to bed full of good intentions. The alarm set for seven-thirty, she was going to make an early start, get in a full day; attend to all of those things she claimed there was no time for due to her job. Well, now was her chance; she would get down to it first thing, shower, clear her head, make a list.

Idling through her wardrobe, she wondered about buying something special for tonight. Detective Inspector Charles Resnick, investigating officer, making a personal call at eight sharp. Charles. Charlie. Her hands ran down the sleeve of a silk shirt, apple green, smooth to the touch. Dana smiled, recalling how gentle he had been. A surprise. Lifting the shirt clear on its hanger, she thought about his hands against the softness of the material. Large hands. When she thought about it, now and since, it surprised her, the extent to which his initial clumsiness had disappeared. Yes, she thought, laying the shirt out on the bed. Apple green. Good. She would run the iron over it later, wear that.

In the shower she wondered if it had been right to phone him at work; not the best of times, either, from the way he had answered, a mixture of circumspect and abrupt. With some men, though, it was what you had to do. Make it clear that you were interested, what was what.

Slowly, savoring it, Dana soaped her shoulders, sides, what she could reach of her back; better to be positive, she thought, than yield the initiative from the start.

Miriam sat reading, alternating between *Light in August* and the *New Musical Express*; the earphones from her Walkman were leaking a little Chris Isaak into the CID room. At the other side of the desk, Lynn

Kellogg struggled to catch up with the never-ending demands of paperwork; tried not to think about her father, just below the level of consciousness, always waiting for the phone to ring, her mother's voice, "Oh, Lynnie ..."

Divine and Naylor returned, bullish, from the Meadows. Raju had looked at the sketches drawn by Sandra Drexler and confirmed they closely matched those he had seen on one of his attackers.

"Hey up," Divine said none too quietly, pointing across the room at Miriam. "What d'you reckon to that?"

Miriam let him know that she had heard; staring him down, she cranked up her Walkman and turned the page of the *NME*. Finish the singles reviews and then she'd get back to Faulkner. A seminar tomorrow about shifting points of view.

Lynn explained the process more assiduously than Miriam considered strictly necessary; but then, she told herself, quite a few of the people they had to deal with, the police, probably they weren't any too bright.

The vehicles had been arranged in two lines, facing, and Miriam was left to walk, taking her time, between. At one point she came close to giggling, feeling suddenly like the Queen, inspecting her loyal troops in some Godforsaken scrap of land. What a farce! The more that came to light, the more you realized that life among the Royals was a cross between *Northern Exposure* and *Twin Peaks*. Without a moment's hesitation she picked out the car. A midnight blue Vauxhall Cavalier.

Robin Hidden heard them draw up outside and almost before they had approached the house, realized who they were. Millington he recognized by name, the dapper suit, the smug smile when Robin opened the street door.

Two other officers waited behind him on the path, also plain clothes; the expression on one of them slightly mocking, as if faintly hopeful that he would panic, cut some kind of a dash, provide an excuse for a chase, a bit of action.

It was all little more than a formality, Millington explained. A witness to confirm you were where you said you were, the night your

Nancy disappeared. Nothing to worry about, as long as you were telling the truth.

Harry Phelan was in the station entrance when the car arrived bringing Robin Hidden in. Two and two had rarely come together so fast to make four. Phelan managed to hold himself in check until Hidden was level with him, then launched himself forwards, landing a two-fisted blow to the back of the head, just behind the ear. Millington moved quickly, setting himself between the two of them, Phelan's boot deflecting off his shin and catching Robin Hidden's thigh as he fell.

Before he could do any more damage, Millington took a choke hold around Harry Phelan's neck and dragged him back towards the uniformed officer who had run round from behind the desk, handcuffs at the ready.

"Enough!" Millington shouted just in time. "It's okay."

Opportunely, Divine had chosen this moment to appear. He seized Harry Phelan's shirt with one hand, the other, bunched into a fist, raised above his face.

"Mark," Millington said, "Let it be."

Divine stepped back and Phelan was swung round hard and pushed against the wall, feet kicked wide, arms stretched out straight behind, cuffs clicked tightly into place.

"Inside and book him," Millington said, straightening his tie. "And now we've done our job of protecting Mr. Hidden here," Millington smiled, "let's escort him safely inside."

Robin Hidden looked at the seven men standing still in a haphazard sort of a line. For some reason, he had expected to have come face to face, if not with carbon copies, then people who bore more than a passing resemblance to himself. But these—about the same height, certainly, none of them fat, roughly of similar age—in reality he looked nothing like them. He supposed that was part of the point.

"Like I said," the officer in charge of the parade said, "pick your own place in the line."

Seven, Robin thought, that's the number most people choose all the time. He went over and stood between a man whose hair was more gingery than fair and another slightly taller than himself.

Number four.

"Spectacles on first, gentlemen, please."

As Robin Hidden fumbled his glasses from their case, he observed, as if in some kind of joke, all of the other men taking out the pairs of glasses they had been given and putting them on.

Miriam took her time. Up and down the row twice as required, hesitating, asking if she might walk the line a third time. Silent as everyone waited, the officers, the solicitor watching her, the men staring straight ahead, blinking, some of them, behind unfamiliar glasses. Silent, save for the breath of the man she knew already she would choose. She had done since practically the first moment; but she was enjoying it, the drama of it, acting it out.

"Is the man you saw on the Christmas Eve present in the parade?" the investigating officer asked when, finally, she stood in front of him.

Nervous now, despite herself, Miriam nodded. "And will you indicate, please, the number of that person?"

"N-number four," Miriam said, stammering for perhaps the first time in her life.

Twenty-eight

The blinds in Skelton's office were drawn, closing out what was left of the winter light. Skelton's earlier conversation with the assistant chief had made him sweat. The afternoon editions of the *Post* had headlined Harry Phelan's arrest at the police station, featured a photograph of him angrily descending the steps to the street after being released. Another quotable diatribe about police incompetence, sloth. "Only time they put themselves out nowadays, something political or if it's one of their own."

"Questions being asked, Jack," the assistant chief had said. "What in God's name's going on on your patch? You used to run such a tight ship, everything battened down. Trouble with a reputation like yours, things start to get out of control, out of hand, people notice. They want to know the reasons why. Oh, and Jack, give my best to Alice, right?"

Resnick had noticed, this past week or so, that the photographs of Alice and Kate, so prominent and exact on Jack Skelton's desk in the past, had disappeared from sight. He was in Skelton's office now while Robin Hidden took his statutory break, getting the superintendent up to speed.

"Robin," Resnick had said, his voice reasonable, soothing, "no one's accusing you of lying, deliberately lying. We know this has been a difficult time for you, emotionally. What was happening, the rejection, you were bound to be upset. After all, this was somebody you loved and who you thought had loved you. Any of us would find that hard to cope with, hard to handle. And there you'd been, driving round all evening, desperate to see her, going over all the things you wanted to say inside your head. And then, suddenly, there she was."

Resnick had held his moment; waited until Robin Hidden was looking back into his eyes. "Like I say, we'd any of us, situation like that, we'd find it hard to know how to react. Hard to remember, afterwards, exactly what we did or said."

Hidden's head went down. It wasn't clear whether or not he was crying.

David Welch had leaned forward from the edge of his chair. "I think my client ..."

"Not now," Millington had said quietly.

"My client ..."

"Not," repeated Millington, "now."

And not for one moment did Resnick allow his gaze to shift away, waiting for Robin Hidden's head to come back up, blinking at him through a gauze of tears. "She t-told me," he said, "she thought I was being s-st-stupid, p-p-pathetic. She didn't want to talk to me. Not ever. S-she wished she'd never had anything to do with m-me, n-never seen me at all."

Skelton was sitting bolt upright, fingertips touching, forearms resting on the edge of his desk. "And the boy, how did he respond?"

"Admits to getting angry, losing his temper."

"He did hit her?"

"Not hit exactly, no."

"Semantics, Charlie?"

Resnick glanced at the floor; from somewhere a splash of brown, dark and drying, had earlier attached itself to the side of his left shoe. "He says that he took a hold of her, both arms. I imagine he's got quite a grip. Shook her around a bit, trying to get her to change her mind. That's when she agreed to get into the car."

Skelton sighed, swiveled his chair sideways, waited.

"They drove down towards the Castle, on into the Park. Stopped by the first roundabout on Lenton Road. What he wanted was to get her to talk about what was going on." Resnick shifted on his seat, less than comfortable. "What he wanted, of course, was for her to change her mind, agree to keep seeing him. Anything as long as she didn't carry on with what she was doing. Shutting him right out of her life."

"I love you," Robin said. Against her will, he was holding her hand.

Nancy looked through the side window of the car, up along the steadily sloping street, shadows from the gas lamps faint and blurred. Frost along the privet hedge. "I'm sorry, Robin, but I don't love you."

"A shame she couldn't have lied," Skelton said.

"She pulled her hand away and he did nothing to stop her. Got out of the car and walked back down Lenton Road; turned off right, down towards the Boulevard."

"And he just sat there?"

"Watching her in the mirror."

"Nothing more?"

"Never saw her again."

"He says."

Resnick nodded.

Skelton was back on his feet, desk to wall, wall to window, window to desk, pacing it out. "She's gone without trace, Charlie. Good looking young woman. You know what it's like, cases like this. Spend more time than you can afford checking on sightings by every loony and short-sighted granny from Ilkeston to Arbroath. This time it's like a desert out there. No bugger's seen a thing."

Back by his desk, Skelton picked up his fountain pen and unscrewed the cap, glanced at the nib, replaced the cap, put the pen back down. Resnick shuffled around on his seat, clasped and unclasped his hands.

"Nine times out of ten, Charlie, it's not some wandering nutter, spends his hours poring over true-life stories of serial killers like they're the lives of the saints. You know that as well as me. It's the husbands, boyfriends, the frustrated wives."

The drawer to which the pictures of Alice had been consigned was close to Skelton's right hand.

"You're right to tread careful, Charlie, God knows. But let's not let him get the upper hand, think he can play with us as he likes, little here, little there. We've got him this far, Charlie, let's not let him slip away."

Twenty-nine

Dana had spent the best part of the day shopping and had stopped off at the Potter's House for a coffee on her way home. Liza, her neighbor from the flat above, Liza of the pinched laugh and squeaky bed, was sitting at a table upstairs. She had been for a tan and wax session and was recovering with a pot of Earl Grey and a slice of coffee and walnut cake. A magistrate's clerk, Liza was filling in time before it was safe to go round to the house of the sixty-four-year-old chairman of the bench with whom she was having a furtive affair. When he had called on Liza once and Dana had opened the house door to him by mistake, she had thought he was collecting for Help the Aged. Now whenever the bed creaked over her head, Dana held her breath and waited for the call to emergency services, the sound of the ambulance siren approaching.

Dana persuaded Liza to order a fresh pot of tea and joined her in a relaxing gossip about winter cruises to warmer climes and the painful necessity of maintaining a neat bikini line. By the time they parted, Liza to visit her clandestine lover and Dana to lug her bags of shopping the remainder of the way back to Newcastle Drive, it was almost six o'clock.

Dana had opened her packages, put her new blouse carefully away, folded her new Next underwear inside the appropriate drawer, slipped the Sting CD on to the machine and started it playing. Poor old Sting, she wished he could stop worrying about the world and write another song like "Every Breath You Take."

The bottle of chardonnay she was saving for later safe in the fridge, she opened a Bulgarian country white she had bought at Safeway, fancying a little something to take the edge off the waiting. One mouthful made her realize that she should have something to eat as well. Tipping the contents of a carton of potato and watercress soup into a pan to heat through, she found the last of the Tesco muffins at the back of the freezer and sliced it in two ready to toast.

She ate the soup in the kitchen, thumbing through some old travel brochures; before she had finished her second glass of wine she had got as far in the quick crossword as three across, nine down and it was still well short of seven o'clock. Over an hour to go and that was if he arrived on time. In desperation, she phoned her mother, who, thank heavens, was out. Oh well, Dana thought, when all else fails, run a bath.

Undressed, she picked up the Joanna Trollope paperback a friend had given her for Christmas, the gift tag poking out so she could remember who to thank. The mirrors were already hazed in steam as, with a gasp of pleasure, Dana settled herself in. She read a chapter of the book, scarcely taking it in, dropped it over the side, and closed her eyes. Charlie, she decided, was almost certainly a figment of her imagination. At least, the Charlie she had rolled around with, cuddled up to in her bed, the one who had stared at her with shocked and startled eyes the moment before he came.

It was half-past seven by the time she climbed out and began to dry herself. In the circle she had cleared with her towel in the glass, Dana caught herself wishing, not for the first time, that she could lose six or eight pounds.

When she tried it on with her new skirt that buttoned down the side, the apple green shirt looked exactly right. What it needed, of course, was a different pair of tights. Nancy had a pair, she remembered, dove gray, that would be perfect. Well, of course, had she been there she would have said go ahead.

She lifted Sting off the stereo, settled Dire Straits in his place, and crossed to Nancy's room. When she opened the door, the silver crochet top that Nancy had been wearing Christmas Eve was on a hanger hooked outside the wardrobe door, the short black skirt had been folded neatly across the back of a chair, her silver-gray tights were draped over the wardrobe mirror, and her leather boots were in the middle of the floor.

Cold clung to Dana's arms and neck like a second skin.

Thirty

There was a clean suit he'd found, charcoal gray with a narrow red stripe, still in its plastic cover from the cleaner's; a light blue shirt that didn't need too much ironing and missing only one button from its cuffs. Near the back of the drawer Resnick found the dark blue tie that Marian had given him in desperation for a similar function two years before. Maybe three. When Resnick held it under the light there were faint spatterings of what was probably bortsch, dried into the fabric, and he scraped at these, more or less successfully, with his thumb.

Already it was ten past eight and the cab he'd ordered for a quarter to still hadn't arrived: New Year's Eve. Bud was nudging round his feet and he bent to scoop the small cat into the air and carried it across the room, nuzzled against his cheek. The battered album cover on the table showed a smiling Thelonious Monk waving from the back of a San Francisco tram. Scratched and worn, the pianist was noodling his way through "You Took the Words Right Out of My Heart." Resnick remembered buying it on the way back from watching County lose a two-goal lead in the last five minutes of a game; winter it had been, frost that had never left the railings, and cups of Bovril at half-time, gripped tight to let the warmth seep into his hands. Sixty-nine? Seventy? Resnick had taken it home and played it, both sides, beginning to end, then through again, fascinated. Only the second or third Monk LP that he had owned.

He was about to call the cab company and complain when he heard the taxi draw up outside; he switched off the stereo, switched off the light, picked up his topcoat in the hail, patted his pocket for his keys. One foot into the chill night and the phone was calling him back.

"When?" he asked, interrupting abruptly. "When was this?"

The duty officer told him what she knew.

"All right," Resnick said, interrupting again. "Make sure scene of crime have been alerted. Contact Graham Millington, tell him to meet me there. I'm on my way."

Dana's first instinct, after phoning the police, had been to run. Get herself out of the flat, anywhere outside, lock the doors, and wait. She had asked first for Resnick by name; being told that he was no longer there, she had explained as carefully as she could; no ordinary intrusion, no ordinary burglary. Fortunately, the officer she had spoken to had been sufficiently quick-witted to make the connections Dana left implicit.

"Please, whatever you do," the officer had said, trying not to alarm Dana any more than she was already, "don't touch anything."

She felt foolish standing out in the hall, exposed in the street; after no more than a few minutes, she let herself back into the flat and tried not to keep staring at the clock. She had touched the wine bottle and her glass enough times already and, anyway, she didn't think the police would be interested in those; pouring herself a drink, for the first time in ages she found herself craving a cigarette. Her hand shook as she brought the glass to her mouth and wine tipped over wrist and fingers, darkened the sleeve of her apple green shirt.

"God," she said to the wails, "now I'm becoming a sloppy drunk."

And all, she thought, well before my fortieth birthday. Reaching out to steady herself, she sat carefully down. Nancy was as many years short of thirty. Dana sighed. She had struggled to understand the implications of what had happened and then she had struggled not to. She put down the wine and looked at her watch.

There were two police cars there when Resnick arrived, successfully blocking his cab's progress along Newcastle Drive. He wasted no time telling them to repark, ordered the one whose lights were still flashing to turn them off. Millington had got there a few minutes before him and was standing close against the entrance to the flat, earnestly talking to the officer in charge of the scene of crime team. Leaving them to it, Resnick walked quickly past.

Dana was in the center of the living room, standing, hands down by her sides. As soon as she saw Resnick she pitched against him and he caught her like he had before, only this time the circumstances were different; there were three plain-clothes men in the room readying cameras and other equipment, and all Resnick could do was hold her while she cried. Two of the men winked at one another and then they kept their eyes averted and got on with their job. The items of clothing that had reappeared would be photographed in place and then tagged and bagged for special attention, after which the rest of the flat would be dusted for prints, pored over for fibers, anything which didn't belong. Nancy's room and the door to the flat were prime targets, entrance and exit; however careful people tried to be, it was unusual to leave no trace. The problem would be making that trace count.

"Want me to give Lynn a ring?" Millington said at Resnick's shoulder, eyeing the way Dana was continuing to clutch hold of him. "Bring her in to give a hand?"

"No need," Resnick said. "Not now. She's enough on her plate as it is."

He spoke quietly to Dana, mouth close against her hair, and when she lifted her face towards him, he led her into the kitchen and helped her to sit down.

"Will you be okay for a minute? I ought to take a look."

She fashioned a smile and nodded.

"I'll be right back," Resnick said.

He left her there and joined Millington in the doorway to Nancy's room. From where it was still hanging outside the wardrobe, the silver top caught the flash from a camera and spun it back into Resnick's eyes.

"How's it been? You been having a good time?"

Long legs, a sequined silver bag, a smile.

"Well, Merry Christmas, once again. Happy New Year."

Skirt, top, boots, tights. The skin along Resnick's arms burned cold. "Any sign of a bag?" he asked.

"What kind?"

"So big." He made a shape, the size of a hardback book, with his hands. "Not everyday, fancy. Silver sequins on both sides."

"Dress bag, then."

"If that's what they're called."

"Matching the top."

“More or less, yes.”

The scene of crime officer shook his head. “Not so far.”

Resnick asked Dana if she’d seen Nancy’s bag and she said no. The flat would have to be searched anyway, wall to wall, floor to ceiling, and if it were anywhere it would be found.

“I’m going to get changed out of this,” Dana said, indicating the button-through skirt, the shiny green shirt. “I feel stupid.”

“You look fine.”

“I’m going to change anyway.”

She came back out of the bedroom wearing blue jeans and a loose white sweater, blue canvas shoes on her feet. Her hair she’d tied back with a strip of patterned cloth.

“It couldn’t have been Nancy, could it?” she asked. “Brought them back herself?”

“It’s not impossible.”

“Not likely.”

“No.”

“Then it was him.”

Resnick looked at her.

“Whoever she went off with. Whoever took her away. He was here in this flat.” Fear shivered, alive, across her eyes.

One of the scene of crime team came towards them and Resnick turned aside to speak to him.

“No sign of forced entry. Not anywhere. Most likely used a key.”

Resnick nodded. Nancy’s key would have been in the missing bag.

“Why would he do this?” Dana asked, as the officer walked away. “Why go to all this trouble? What’s the point?”

“I don’t know,” Resnick said. “Not yet. Not for certain.”

“He’s showing off, isn’t he? Being clever. That’s what it is.” Dana folded her arms across her chest, fingers clenched tight. “Bastard!’

Outside, officers were knocking on doors, ringing bells, beginning to talk to neighbors, those who were still home, asking if they had noticed anything unusual, seen anyone they hadn’t recognized coming into the building, hanging about outside. Dana had been out of the flat from mid-morning until early evening; whoever had brought Nancy’s things into the flat could have done so at any point during that time. Not so far short of eight hours.

Resnick was thinking again about Nancy's clothing, what had been returned. "How about underwear," he said. "I don't suppose you've any idea what she might have been wearing?"

"You mean, exactly?"

"Yes."

Dana shook her head. "Not really." She shrugged. "Something nice."

"When they're through in there, would you mind taking a look? Through the drawers. Wherever she kept things like that. You might just notice something, you never know."

"Of course."

"Is it okay," Resnick asked, "if I use your phone?"

"Go ahead."

As he dialed the number he looked back to where Dana was now sitting on the arm of the settee, hands on her thighs, wide pale face close again to tears.

Alice Skelton had been waging a silent war of attrition throughout the evening, pointedly ignoring her husband in front of the two couples who were their guests. By the start of the main course, she was well on the way to being drunk and had taken to insulting him openly.

"Jack, here," she proclaimed, passing the redcurrant jelly, "was the man for whom the term anally retentive was invented."

Skelton disappeared to fetch some more wine. His guests wished they could do the same.

When the phone rang a little while later, Skelton was on his feet before the second ring, praying it was for him.

"It's probably her," Alice's taunt chased him from the room. "The ice maiden. Wishing you a happy New Year."

It wasn't; it was Resnick. Skelton listened for long enough, then told Resnick to meet him at the station as soon as he could finish up where he was.

"Something urgent?" Alice mocked. "Something they can't possibly handle without you?"

Skelton apologized to their guests and headed for the door.

"Give her my love," Alice shouted after him. And quietly, into the aubergine parmigiana, "The stuck-up bitch!"

✦✦✦

"Is there anywhere you can stay?" Resnick asked. "For tonight, at least."

"You don't think he'll come back?"

"No. No reason to think so, none at all. If you were really worried we could leave a man outside. I just thought you'd feel more comfortable somewhere else, that was all."

Dana was leaning forward slightly, looking into his eyes. "I couldn't stay with you?"

Resnick glanced around the room to see if anyone had overheard. "In the circumstances, best not."

"All right," Dana said. Clearly, it was not.

"Surely there's a friend you could go to?"

"If I did stay here," Dana persisted, "would you come back? Later?"

Resnick thought about Marian at the Polish Club, counting down the hours till midnight; thought about other things. "I don't know," he said. "I couldn't promise. Probably not."

Dana reached for the address book near to the phone. "I'll find someone," she said. "You don't have to worry."

"D'you want to let me have the number?" Resnick asked. "Where you'll be."

"There isn't a lot of point, is there?" Dana said. He touched her arm, just below the sleeve of her sweater, and goosebumps rose to meet his fingers. "I'm sorry," he said, "it's worked out like this."

She was just smiling, grudging, wary, as Millington approached.

"Hang on here, Graham," Resnick said. "Make sure nothing gets missed. And see Miss Matthieson's taken wherever she wants to go. I'm off in to see the old man."

He paused in the doorway and glanced back inside the flat, but Dana had already moved from sight, back into her room.

Thirty-one

The station was different at night, quieter yet more intense. The blood that had been splashed across the steps and the entrance hall was fresh blood, so bright beneath the overhead lights that it glowed. A sudden shout from the cells aside, voices were muted; footsteps along the corridors, up and down the stairs, were muffled. Only the telephones, sharp and demanding, retained their shrillness.

Skelton surprised Resnick by not being in his own office, but in the CID room, standing over by the far wall in front of the large map of the city. He was wearing a dark blazer and light-gray trousers instead of the normal suit. Unusually, the top button of his shirt had been unfastened above the knot of his tie. He didn't speak as Resnick walked in and when he did, instead of making a remark about what had happened, he said, "Since you and Elaine were divorced, Charlie, d'you ever catch yourself wishing you'd married again?"

Taken aback, uncertain how to respond, Resnick went over to where the kettle stood on a tray, lifted it up to check there was enough water inside, and switched it on at the wall.

Skelton was looking at him still, waiting for an answer.

"Sometimes," Resnick finally said.

"I'll be honest," Skelton said. "Living the way you do, on your own, I thought you were a miserable bugger. Night after night, going back to that place alone. Last thing I reckoned I'd want to be, living like that."

"Tea?" Resnick said.

Skelton shook his head and Resnick dropped a single tea bag into the least stained of the mugs.

"You get used to it, I suppose," Skelton said. "Accommodate. Learn to appreciate the advantages. After a while, it must be difficult to live any other way."

There were footsteps in the corridor outside and Resnick turned to watch Helen Siddons push open the door and walk in. Whichever occasion she had been called from had scarcely been informal. Her hair had been pinned up high and she was wearing a dress not unlike the one Resnick remembered from Christmas Eve, except this was blue, so pale it seemed almost all the color had leaked out of it. Somewhere along the way she had changed into flat shoes and the raincoat round her shoulders could have been a man's.

"I asked Helen to join us," Skelton said. "Her experience might be useful here."

What experience? Resnick caught himself thinking. "Kettle just this second boiled," he said. "If you want some tea."

"When Helen was on secondment to Bristol and Avon she was involved in that Susan Rogel business, you remember?"

Something about a woman whose car was found abandoned on the Mendip Hills, somewhere between Bath and Wells. No signs of a struggle, no note, nothing to explain the disappearance; if there had been foul play, no body had been found to substantiate it, no evidence either.

"I thought the suggestion was she'd taken off of her own accord," Resnick said. "Wasn't there some kind of affair that had got out of hand?"

Helen Siddons drew a chair out from one of the desks and Skelton moved to help with her coat. "She'd become involved with her husband's business partner," Helen said. "They ran an antiques business, branches all over the south west." She took a cigarette from a case in her bag and Resnick half expected Skelton to lean over and offer her a light but he allowed her to do it for herself. "Seems that the husband knew what was going on, had done for some while, but hadn't said anything as the business was in a pretty shaky state and he didn't want to rock the boat any more than it was already." She arched back her long neck and released smoke towards the ceiling. Skelton was staring at her like a man transfixed. "When it became clear they were going to go bust anyway, he gave his wife an ultimatum. Stop seeing him or I want a divorce. The wife, Susan, she would have been happy to jump the other way but faced with the possibility her lover backed off. Preferred to carry on sneaking around, didn't want to get married and make it all respectable, settle down." It was the slightest of glances towards Skelton, probably no more than coincidental. "All this had made Susan ill, she'd seen a doctor, was taking all kinds of pills for stress, depression, whatever. There's a suggestion, unproven, that she made at least one attempt on her own life. We do know that on more than one occasion she told a girl friend that she couldn't be doing with either man any more. She just wanted to get out."

"So she staged this business with the car as a red herring and headed for Spain or wherever?" Resnick asked. "That's the assumption?"

Helen tapped ash into the metal waste-bin near her feet. "A lot of the evidence pointed that way. There was a suitcase and clothes missing from home and her passport wasn't found. But I never believed it."

"Why not?"

Behind blue-gray smoke, Helen Siddons smiled. "Because of the ransom demand."

If she hadn't had all of Resnick's interest before, she had it now. "I don't remember anything about a ransom," he said.

"We asked for a media blackout and got it."

"And you think that's what's happening here?" Resnick asked. "With Nancy Phelan? Ransom?"

Helen Siddons took her time. "Of course," she said. "Don't you?"

Half an hour had passed. More. From somewhere Jack Skelton had magicked a half-bottle of Teacher's and they were drinking it from thick china mugs. Somehow the clock slipped past midnight without any of them noticing and no toasts were offered up. Ash sprinkled here and there down the pale blue of Helen Siddons' dress as she talked.

Painstakingly, she took them through the Rogel case, stage by stage. When the first ransom note had been delivered, pushed through the door of the missing woman's parents' house in the early hours of the morning, it had gone unnoticed for the best part of a day, the envelope pushed between a pile of old newspapers and unsolicited catalogs. When a follow-up phone call was made, at four o'clock that afternoon, Susan Rogel's mother had had no idea what it was referring to, took it as some kind of sick joke and hung up. By the time the second call came through, though, they'd found the note. It was asking for twenty thousand pounds in used notes.

Rogel's father was a retired army colonel, not someone to be toyed with. He made it clear they wouldn't as much as think of handing over a penny without proof. He also immediately contacted the police.

Nothing happened for three days.

On the fourth, the Rogels drove to the nearest supermarket to do their weekly shopping and when they returned, someone had jimmied open one of the small windows at the rear of the house. Naturally, they thought they'd been burgled, looked anxiously round but found nothing obviously missing. What they did find, folded neatly inside tissue paper in one of the drawers in the spare bedroom, the room that had been Susan's when she had lived at home, was one of her blouses, the one she had been wearing when she was last seen, filling her car with petrol at a garage on the Wells road.

The family wanted to pay the ransom, asked for time to find the money; they were given another three days. Instructions were given about leaving it in the courtyard of a pub high on the Mendips. All of this information was passed immediately to the police. On the morning the drop was to be made, the location was carefully staked out, it would have been difficult to be more discreet.

"What happened?" Resnick asked.

"Nothing. The money was left in a duffel bag by the outside toilet of the pub. No one came near it. Not many vehicles came over the tops that day and all that did were checked. Nobody suspicious."

"He got scared then? What?"

"There was one final call to the Rogels the following day. Angry with them for trying to trick him, get him caught, going to the police. There was no attempt at contact after that."

"And Susan Rogel?"

Helen Siddons was standing against the window, outlined against the white strips of blind. "No sign. No word. If she did simply run off, if the ransom note was somebody's bluff, she's never resurfaced, never been back in touch with anyone in her previous life. Husband, lover, parents, not anyone."

"And if it was real?"

Helen smoothed one hand down the leg of her dress. "This was almost two years ago. If someone kidnapped her, it's difficult to believe she's alive now."

"You double-checked everyone in the area of the pub that day?" Skelton asked.

"Double, triple." Helen shook her head. "No way we could connect any of them with Susan Rogel or the way she disappeared."

"How easy would it have been for this person to find out you and her parents were hand in glove?"

Helen Siddons lit another cigarette. "I was the liaison officer. Any meetings we had were well out of the way, never the same location. Phone calls call box to call box, never to their house or the station. No mobile phones used because they're more susceptible to being tapped. If he found out, rather than guessed, that wasn't the weak link."

"Have you any idea what was?"

She gave a quick shake of the head. "No."

"Near enough two years back," Skelton said, looking at Resnick. "Time to lay low, move maybe, try again."

"Blouse aside," Resnick said, "there's not much says this case is the same."

"Not yet, Charlie."

"Wait till Nancy Phelan's parents get the morning post," Helen said. "Special delivery."

"And if they don't?"

Helen blinked and looked away.

Skelton tipped the last of the bottle into the three mugs. "So, Charlie, what d'you think? If this is a runner, where does that leave young Hidden in the scheme of things?"

"Between Dana Matthieson leaving the flat and our bringing Robin Hidden in for questioning, he had time and plenty to get round there and leave those clothes. And he knew the layout of the flat well, remember, in and out in no time."

"I thought you had your doubts about Hidden for this," Skelton said. "That was the feeling you gave. Now you want to keep him tied in."

"One way or another, he already is."

Skelton looked thoughtful, sipped his scotch. "Helen?" Skelton said.

"I think we should make good and sure," she said, "the minute anyone contacts the Phelans, we know about it. And by the time they do, we know how we're going to respond."

"Charlie?" Skelton said.

"That only makes sense," Resnick said. He was uncomfortable with the knowledge that he was bridling inside every time Helen Siddons said we, at the way she seemed to be edging herself more and more into the heart of things.

"I'll give you a lift then, Helen," Skelton said, hopefully holding her coat.

Resnick knocked back the last half-inch of whisky, rinsed out the mug from which he had been drinking, and wished them both goodnight; whatever was going on there, as long as it didn't get in the way of the task in hand, it didn't have to concern him.

"Night, sir. Happy New Year, sir," said the young constable at the desk.

Resnick nodded in reply and stepped out on to the street; it wasn't clear if someone had wiped the blood away or whether it had been trodden clean by a succession of passing feet. Above, the sky had cleared and there were stars, clustering close to the moon.

In little more than minutes he was standing at the far end of Newcastle Drive, hands in pockets, looking up at the blank windows to Dana's flat. If she had decided to stay, he hoped by now she would be safely asleep. For several long moments he allowed himself to recall the warmth of her body, generous beside him in her bed.

"If I did stay here, would you come back? Later?"

By the time he had crossed town, avoiding the raucous celebrations continuing in and around the fountains of the Old Market Square, and arrived at the Polish Club, almost the last of the cars was turning out of the car park, exhaust fumes heavy in the air. Those that remained belonged to the staff. There was a taxi idling at the far side of the street, but Resnick didn't linger to see who it was waiting for. He would call Marian tomorrow, make his apologies with a clear head.

Dizzy was sitting on the stone wall at the front of the house when Resnick arrived, stretching his legs and trotting along the top of the wall beside him, tail arched high in greeting.

Happy New Year.

Thirty-two

Michelle opened her eyes to see Karl staring down at her, his face close enough to hers for her to feel the faint warmth of his breath. How long he had been standing there she didn't know. Through the gap at the top of the curtains, the street light shone a muted orange. Karl started to speak but she shushed him and smiled and pressed her finger lightly against first his lips and then her own. As usual, Gary had fetched up close beside her in the bed and Michelle eased herself sideways, slipping out from beneath the weight of his arm and leg.

"I not sleep," said Karl on the stairs. "Cold."

Michelle tousled the tangle of hair on his head and shooed him into the living room. Natalie had bunched herself sideways along the top of her cot. When Michelle reached under the covers to move her she was shocked by the child's coldness. Natalie stirred, whimpered, fell back to sleep.

"Come on," she whispered to Karl, "let's go and make the tea."

Even with slippers and two pairs of socks, the damp seemed to seep up through the kitchen floor. While she watched, Karl took two slices from the packet of sliced bread and placed them on the grill to toast; once she had swilled almost boiling water around the pot and emptied it down the sink, he lifted two tea bags from the box and dropped them inside.

"Good boy," Michelle said encouragingly.

"'ood boy."

"Soon be able to do all this by yourself. Bring me and Gary breakfast in bed."

Karl looked uncertain. The swelling at the side of his face had mostly gone down and even the bruise was beginning to fade.

Michelle caught herself yawning and when she moved her hand to her mouth she realized she was nursing a headache. She and Gary had been to the pub last night, along with Brian and Josie. Where Brian got the money from to spend on drink she couldn't imagine, didn't want to know. Generous, though, she'd say that for him. Even if, when he'd had his fair share, he wasn't above pushing his leg against hers under the table, once or twice sliding his hand along her thigh. Michelle had mentioned it to Josie when they were on their own and Josie had just laughed. Brian having a bit of fun. Gary wouldn't laugh, not if he knew, she was certain of that. Gary saw him as much as put his little finger on her and he'd kill him for it.

She pulled out the grill pan just in time before the toast started burning. "You're supposed to be watching that," she said. "What d'you want? Marmalade or some of that strawberry jam?"

Pam Van Allen was at work early, earlier than usual; only her senior's Escort was in the car park ahead of her, right-on slogans occupying a goodly proportion of its rear window. Although no more than thirty yards from the entrance Pam wrapped her scarf around her neck before reaching to the rear seat for her briefcase and *Guardian*, and locking the car door. Chilly again this morning, but at least it was bright.

Neil Park was in his office, leafing through reports on green and yellow paper, sipping at the first of many cups of Maxwell House. He called a greeting as Pam walked past reception and while she was making coffee for herself, he came out and joined her.

"Some offices," Pam said, "have a decent coffee machine. Real coffee."

"But we have biscuits," Neil said, offering her the tin. Inside were a couple of plain digestives, the wrong half of a coconut cream, a Rich Tea, and a lot of crumbs.

"Good night last night?" Pam asked, opting for one of the digestives.

"Terrific, Mel and I fell asleep in front of the TV. Woke up and it was next year."

Pam smiled. After failing to interest any of her friends in joining her in a search for something to eat, she had settled for a chicken and black-bean takeaway and the remains of a bottle of white wine. It had been the ideal opportunity for watching those programs she'd taped about the lives of women between the wars. These were so depressing, she had found a documentary about the Sequoia National Park and watched it through twice.

"Who've you got today?" Neil asked. "Anyone interesting?"

"Gary James, first thing."

"Oh, well," Neil said, wandering off with the last half of coconut cream, "start as you mean to go on."

Gary was close to fifteen minutes late, par for the course in his case, though less than desirable. Old Ethel Chadbond was out there already, spilling herself and her belongings across three seats in the waiting area and already imbuing everything with a healthy smell of methylated spirits and Lysol.

Pam restrained herself from looking too pointedly at her watch. "Gary, take a seat."

He slouched sideways, soccer shirt, jumper, jeans jacket, jeans. Gave her that look that said, so, what do we do now?

"That interview I arranged for you, at the training center." Pam picked up the sheet of notepaper as if it were relevant. "You didn't go."

"No."

"You mind me asking why?"

On and on for a further fifteen minutes, Pam's questions, remarks, suggestions, all of them fielded with the same sullen indifference; part of a ritual both knew they had to go through. God! Pam thought, sliding open a drawer for something to do, coming close to slamming it shut, was this the first day of a new year? Another three hundred and sixty four days of this?

"Gary!"

"What?" He sat bolt upright, eyes wide open and she realized she had shouted, startling him.

"Nothing, I'm sorry. It's just ..."

It's just you're getting your monthlies, Gary thought.

"It's just we seem to be going over the same ground, you know. Over and over."

He breathed heavily and leaned back in his chair: what d'you expect me to do about that?

"The house," Pam asked, "have you made any more progress finding somewhere else?" She knew as soon as the words were out of her mouth it was the wrong thing to say.

"That poxy fucking place," Gary said. "Ought to be against the fucking law bringing up kids in there."

"Gary …"

"You know how cold it was this morning when I got out of bed? D'you know? Put my hand on the baby's face and I thought she was fucking dead! That's how cold it was."

"Gary," Pam said, "I'm sorry, but I've told you before, that's not really my province. That's the Housing department's responsibility, it's not …"

He was on his feet so fast, the chair skittered backwards beneath him and collided with the wall. His fists were so close to her face, Pam let out an involuntary shriek and covered herself with her hands.

"You know what fucking happened when I went to the fucking Housing. You know about that, don't you? Eh? One of these bits of bloody paper'll've told you all about that." With a sweep of his arms, he cleared everything from the desk: pens, paper, diary, telephone, paper-clips. Pam was on her feet, backing away, staring at him. There was a panic button underneath the ledge of her desk, but no way now could she reach it. "You and that tart up at Housing, that dirty cow as used to spread her legs for my brother's mates every chance she got, you think you can shit on me like I'm nothing, don't you? Eh?" He walked on into the table and it jarred sideways off his thigh. "Nice Gary, good Gary, here Gary, good dog, Gary."

He snorted at her in his anger, took another step towards her before moving suddenly sideways to the door. "You wouldn't treat one of your pets the way you treat 'Chelle an' me." He wrenched at the handle and pulled the door wide open. Neil Park was standing anxiously outside, wondering whether he should intervene. "None of you."

Neil Park had to step back quickly to get out of Gary's way.

"You all right?" he said finally, walking into Pam's room.

"Terrific."

"Here, let me give you a hand with this," he said, taking hold of one end of the desk.

"Tell Ethel Chadbond I might need a few more minutes," Pam said, when most things had been rescued from the floor.

"You want me to see her?"

"No, it's okay. Thanks."

Once Neil had gone and she had closed the door, Pam sat for some little while thinking about the abrupt violence of Gary's anger, the nature of the remarks he'd made about Nancy Phelan, that tart, that dirty cow, wondering whether or not she should telephone Resnick, tell him about this latest outburst.

Thirty-three

Resnick had woken full of good intentions. He would write a note to Marian, apologizing for last night, wishing her all the best for the New Year. On his way to work, drop in at the market and order some flowers, arrange for them to be delivered. Three attempts at the brief letter and when he'd almost got it right, a thick splodge of apricot jam slid between the cream cheese of his breakfast bagel and obliterated Marian's name and half the first sentence. Sitting at the coffee stall later, he changed his mind about the flowers; a bouquet, over-dramatic, open to misinterpretation. Besides—sipping his second espresso—flowers arranged in that way always made him think of his father's funeral. The coffin laden with them: and afterwards, laid out near the rose garden at the back of the crematorium. "Don't let them do that to me, Charles. A priest and a requiem mass. A coffin for my ashes to wither away in." At the end, when so many people come to God, his father had lost his faith. "A bit of fertilizer, let me do that much good at least."

Resnick walked away from the market with a heavy heart and indigestion. He would give Marian a quick call from the office, maybe later in the day. Or tomorrow.

Divine's fascist night out had been a shade disappointing. No major rucks, no riots, not even many arrests. Most of the evening, bad music and easily shepherded bands of youths wearing BNP badges and off-the-peg Nazi regalia; the worst Divine had thrown at him, taunts and a half of warm lager. On the plus side, be had found himself cheek by jowl with a couple who answered the descriptions of Raju's and Sandra Drexler's attackers to a T: fair, sandyish hair, St. George and the Dragon tattoo.

Along with six or so other officers and a couple of dogs, Divine had stopped a dozen or so likely lads passing by outside the Town ground and ordered them back against the wall to be searched. Three blades, two lengths of chain, a piece of two-by-four with a nail protruding from it, one manky sock stuffed with sand, a handful of pills. Nothing spectacular.

The youth with the tattoo had been in the middle of the group, combat trousers and jeans jacket, mouthing off about police harassment. Divine had chanced to kick him in the back of the calf, pure accident. Instinctively, the youth had rounded on him, fist raised.

Bingo!

The noble St. George, lance at the ready, right before Divine's delighted eyes. Not enough to prove anything on its own. But when, at Divine's polite inquiry as to whether he'd taken any good taxi rides lately, the youth and his mate panicked and tried to do a runner, well, dead giveaway, wasn't it?

Shame was, in the ensuing scuffle, Divine didn't get to land as much as a solid punch. The lads, though, had spent a mournful night in Mansfield nick and were on their way down to the city that morning. Positive identification and they'd be up in front of the magistrate without a leg to stand on. Trouble was, instead of getting banged up, doing some real time, more than likely some soft sod on the bench would give them all of six months' community service, a supervision order, be good boys and talk politely once a week to your probation officer.

Made you wonder, sometimes, why you bothered.

Divine wished he'd given the little shits a good thumping while he'd had half a chance.

There were several reasons for liking Jallans at lunchtime, not least they did a chicken club sandwich which easily outstripped anywhere else in the city. Not only that, on a good day you might go from Miles Davis to Mose Allison to Billie Holiday, one CD after another slipping on to the player behind the bar. Resnick thought he was there before her, but no sooner had he picked out a table over by the far wall than he saw Pam Van Allen making her way between the tables from the other side of the room.

"Is this okay?" Resnick asked.

"Fine," Pam said, pulling out a chair. "Fine."

"I didn't see you ..."

"I was in the Ladies'."

She was looking, Resnick thought, more than a little strained. Smart enough in her striped wool jacket and gray skirt, well-cut silver-gray hair, but the makeup she discreetly wore failed to lessen the tiredness, disguise the jumpiness around her eyes.

"I already ordered," Resnick said, "at the bar."

"Me too."

"You said you wanted to talk about Gary James," Resnick said. "You've seen him again?"

She held Resnick's gaze before answering. "And how," she said.

The waitress brought over Resnick's chicken club with salad and for Pam a jacket potato with prawns; Resnick asked her if she wanted anything to drink and she shook her head. He was drinking black filter coffee himself.

"That stunt he pulled at the Housing Office," Pam said, spreading a little extra butter over her potato, "he came close to doing the same with me."

Resnick listened as she took him through what had happened, picking up half of his sandwich every now and then and trying not to let too much of the filling spill down his sleeves. "And this anger," Resnick said when she was through, "d'you think it would disappear almost as suddenly as it came? Or was it the kind he'd cling on to?"

"Like a grudge, you mean?"

He nodded and she took his meaning, knew what he was thinking: the anger he felt towards Nancy Phelan, could he have held on to that for close to ten hours, harbored it long enough to go out and find her, let that anger out?

Pam took her time. A group of women from the Victoria Street branch of the Midland Bank, all wearing their uniform blouses under their coats, settled at the long table behind them. "I don't know," she said. "I really don't know."

Resnick had a refill of coffee and finished the demolition job on his sandwich; more than half of Pam's baked potato was still inside its jacket, but she had already pushed the plate away.

"You like that, don't you?" she said.

"The chicken club? It's …"

"Eating," she smiled. "Just eating. That's all."

"I suppose," Resnick said, mouth quarter-full, "I suppose I do."

She waited till he'd finished before fetching a book of matches from the counter and lighting a cigarette. Resnick didn't know why, but he'd assumed she didn't smoke.

"Stress," she said wryly, reading his thoughts. And then, "Something's happened, hasn't it?"

"In the investigation?"

Blowing smoke down her nose, she gave a slight shake of the head. "To you."

"Has it? How?"

"Before, when we've met, spoken on the phone, whatever, you were always interested in me."

Resnick was looking at the table, the few stray filaments of cress green upon the plate, not at her.

"Don't misunderstand me, not some great passion, but, well, like I say, interested." She shrugged. "Now overnight you're not."

"Overnight?"

The smile was warmer and crinkled the lines either side of her mouth. "I presume it was overnight."

Resnick gave her a little of the smile back with his eyes.

"Congratulations. Who's the lucky woman? Anyone I'm likely to know?"

"I shouldn't think so, no."

"And are you happy? Is it going well?"

Does it ever, Resnick thought, go well. He would have let it drop there, but Pam was looking at him, waiting for an answer. "It isn't that kind of a thing, not … I mean, what you said made it sound like a proper relationship …"

"Improper would do."

"… and I don't think it is that. At least, not yet."

"Not ever?"

Aside from the not inconsiderable complication of Dana being closely involved in the case he was working on, Resnick could see a number of other obstacles. Her flamboyance, her drinking—sex aside what could they hope to find in common?

"Probably not," he said.

Pam Van Allen laughed: "Spoken like a true man," she said.

"Let me get this," said Resnick, reaching for the bill. "Or is that acting like a true man again?"

"Not nowadays," Pam smiled.

"You realize," Pam said, "that if Gary finds out I went running straight to you and told you about this morning, I'll forfeit whatever small amount of trust I've built up?"

"Don't worry. There's no need for him to know."

They were walking towards Holy Cross and the spot where Pam had parked her car. It was cold enough for them both to be wearing gloves.

"You're keeping an eye on him, though?"

"Not me personally, but yes. DC Kellogg, I don't know if you know her?"

Pam nodded. "By reputation. Maureen Madden thinks a lot of her."

"So do I."

They were level with Pam's car. "Good luck," she said. "With all of it."

Resnick thanked her and walked away, off in the direction of Low Pavement. Key in the car door, Pam stood a while, watching him go. She hadn't been at all sure what she'd thought of him before, didn't think she liked him but now she thought probably she did; she could. Old-fashioned as it seemed, he was what you'd end up calling, for want of a better term, a nice man.

She opened up and slid behind the wheel.

Timing, she thought, somewhat ruefully: that's where it lay, in the timing.

Thirty-four

Helen Siddons had chosen her clothes with care. Alienating Nancy Phelan's parents further was the last thing she could afford. So nothing that might be considered expensive, nothing too stylish, but neither was she going to go marching in with shoulder pads and heels and a suit that shouted authority. She wore a mid-length skirt and jacket in neutral colors, a woolen scarf, and flat shoes. Her hair was neat and orderly, makeup discreet to the point of nonexistence. No perfume.

She sat with Harry and Clarise in the small lounge of their hotel, the three of them leaning awkwardly forward in worn red and gold armchairs. Clarise poured tea from a metal pot and offered round a plate of brittle biscuits. Helen, polite, deflected, as best she could, Harry Phelan's aggression, his assertion that the police were only going through the motions. The room was heavy with the scent of furniture polish and stale tobacco smoke. Helen declined Harry Phelan's grudging offer of a cigarette and lit one of her own. "There's been a development," she said.

If Resnick had been expecting a great deal from Forensic, he would have been disappointed. "What we want here," the lab man had said, "is your average sicko. Can't wait to toss himself off over the lot. Give me that and a little time, I could let you have more than his blood group, I could give you his telephone number. As it is …"

The best he had been able to come up with was a grease mark high on the side of Nancy's silver top, close to the arm; some kind of oil mixed with human sweat. The sweat, of course, was most likely Nancy's own, but they didn't know that yet for a fact. They were doing more tests.

There had been no prints on the doors, none in Nancy's bedroom, none anywhere. Resnick stalked the corridors of the station, waiting for something to happen.

Dana had woken in the night more times than she cared to remember, alerted by every sound. The slamming of a car door in the street outside, creak of the bed overhead, each had her gripping the edge of the duvet, adrenaline flooding her veins. By the time she climbed into her morning bath, she felt a wreck.

She was drinking herbal tea, trying to concentrate on whatever they were saying on Radio Four, when the phone broke into her already jagged thoughts.

"It's Andrew," Yvonne Warden said, "he's found your little surprise package. I think signing it might have been a mistake."

With all that had recently happened, Dana had managed to forget the tipsy message she had left for her boss on his office wall, lipsticked graffiti graphically testifying to his failed attempt at seduction.

"Oh, shit!" Dana said.

"Exactly."

Dana was at a loss for what to say.

"I think you should give him an hour to climb down off the ceiling," Yvonne said, "then put in an appearance. I imagine he'll want a word with you by then."

"I can guess which one it is."

"Between ourselves," Yvonne said, "showing him up for what he is, it's not before time."

"Christ," Dana said, "don't tell me he's had a go at you, too?"

"What time," Yvonne said, "shall I say you'll be in? Ten? Ten-thirty?"

Dana sat for several minutes, staring at the phone. Then she pulled herself together, put on her good black trouser suit with a scarlet silk shirt, paid even more than usual attention to her hair and makeup, drank two strong cups of coffee, the second laced with brandy, and she was on her way.

"You're looking surprisingly good," Yvonne Warden said admiringly. "In the circumstances."

"Don't," Dana said, "let the bastards grind you down."

"He's expecting you," Yvonne said.

Dana smiled and breezed on through.

There was a smell of fresh paint which grew appreciably stronger when Dana opened the door. Andrew Clarke was speaking to somebody on the phone, but as soon as Dana entered he lowered the receiver and rose to his feet. Behind him a workman in blue-gray overalls was repainting the rear wall where Dana had lipsticked her graphic version of her Christmas Eve struggle with her employer. The final picture, just visible through the first coat, had a distraught Andrew, sweat flying, running down the street after her, flies agape, penis swaying limply in the wind.

"I suppose you think this is funny?"

"Don't you?"

Behind them, the painter sniggered.

"Outside!" Clarke snapped.

"But I haven't …"

"Out. You can finish it later."

The painter edged past Dana wearing the smuggest of grins and left them together.

"You realize you've left me no alternative other than dismissal," Andrew Clarke said.

"Resignation?"

He coughed into the back of his hand. "Very well, if that's what you want."

"I was thinking of yours, not mine."

"Then you're deluded."

Dana smiled. "Dismiss me and I'll bring charges of harassment and sexual assault. Be patient while I apply for another job, give me a good reference and a bonus, something equivalent to six months' salary, say, and I won't even post the letter I've got here in my bag addressed to your wife. Think about it, Andrew, think about exactly what Audrey might say and do. When you've made up your mind I'll be in the library. There's a new batch of slides that want cataloging."

Outside the door she winked at the workman. "I think you can go back in now."

✦✦✦

The envelope had arrived second delivery, addressed to Superintendent Jack Skelton and marked personal. It had stayed downstairs until mid-afternoon, when the duty officer had sent it up to the superintendent's office, along with a bundle of papers and other mail. There it remained on the side of his desk until a little before five, when Skelton pulled it out from between two Home Office circulars, and gave it a preliminary shake. The flap had been secured with two staples before being Sellotaped round. Skelton cut the tape at the edges, then pulled the staples free; when he held the envelope over his desk, the cassette slipped down into his hand.

Thirty-five

A low hiss lasting several seconds, broken by two clicks, evenly spaced. A quarter-second's silence, almost imperceptible, before the voice.

Hello, this is me. Nancy. I have to tell you that I'm all right. I'm well and nothing … nothing bad has happened to me, so I don't want you to worry …

There is a slight fade as the voice disappears, the briefest of pauses during which the familiar background hiss can just be heard. The voice itself is pitched low but quite strong, perhaps surprisingly so; there is only a faint tremor at the end of certain words.

I am a prisoner, though, I'm not staying away because I want to but I don't … because I don't have any choice …

Most of the time I'm kept tied up, tied up and chained and I have … I have to squat down or lean against the wall or lie on the floor and I wish I could have more …

I am given water to wash with and a bucket to use as a toilet and I'm not hungry, there's food and water to drink and once a day I get a cup of tea and …

What I want to say to you is this—Mum, Dad, whoever hears this— the person who's keeping me here; making me do this, you should believe what he says, do what he says. He's clever, yes, clever, and please, please, if you want to see me again, do whatever he says.

The click of the machine being switched off. Several seconds of constant hiss. The experts who listen to copies of the tape will disagree in their interpretation of the speaker's state of mind here, one placing her near to the end of her tether, another suggesting a resilience that goes unimpaired. What they agree upon is that Nancy is speaking under duress, that although she does not seem to be reading from something previously prepared, nonetheless she has been fairly carefully rehearsed. Considerable significance is found in the detailed description of her routine as a prisoner, her subservience to her captor, her enforced regression to an almost fully dependent childlike state.

The break in the sound is followed by another double click, similar to before. The man's voice is slightly distorted, slowed somehow in the process of recording, slurred. And the accent is regional, without being strongly so; enough, just, to blur the edges of received pronunciation. First attempts to place it centered on the northwest, not Manchester exactly but close, a touch softer and less well-defined. Somewhere, perhaps, to the south, towards the Welsh border. There seemed a strong possibility of one naturally absorbed mode of speech merging with another.

I do hope you will pay attention to that advice and listen to me carefully. Of course, I'm sure you will; I'm sure you are, right now, listening to me with such special care, playing my voice backwards and forwards and backwards again, shaking it upside down and inside out to see if you can shake me out.

But you can't.

Nancy, you see; she's right. About me, I mean. Oh, not that I'm clever, really clever, that's not me. I'm not one of those geniuses who go to Oxford at twelve and thirteen to get a degree in Mathematics, no, I wasn't even especially clever at school, but that's only because I was never given the right chance. Because no one, you see, ever listened to me, really listened to what I had to say.

And now you will.

Close to the microphone, a laugh, low and generous, drawing the listener in.

I'm sorry, it's just that I can see you now, excited, thinking, ah, he's given himself away, told us more than we should know. But, no. It isn't true and if it were it wouldn't really matter. I could tell you my date of birth, size of shoe, the color of my eyes. Even Nancy could tell you the color of my eyes. She could tell you that much. But it wouldn't matter. There still wouldn't be time.

So listen very carefully. Don't make any mistakes. Do as I say to the letter and Nancy can return, free and unharmed, to where she came from.

The day after you receive this tape you are to take two identical bags, each containing twenty-five thousand pounds, to two locations. The bags must be duffel bags, plain black, no markings, and the money must be in used notes, fifties and twenties only. The first location is the Little Chef at the intersection of the A15 and the A631 at Normanby. The second is the Little Chef on the A17 south of Boston. The bags are to be driven to the restaurants in unmarked cars, one driver and one passenger only, neither in uniform. The cars must both arrive at their destinations at a quarter to five in the evening. Park outside and leave the engine running while the passenger takes the bag into the Gents' toilet and leaves it on the floor beneath the hand dryer. As soon as that has been done, that person must get straight back into the car and the car must drive off. There's no reason this should take any more than two minutes and if it does the deal is off. If there are any other police cars in the area, marked or unmarked, the deal is off. If the locations are visited earlier in the day for the purpose of setting up microphones or hidden cameras, the deal's off. Anything, any attempt to detain me, and the agreement is null and void.

So, remember, nothing bad has to happen here and if it does it will be at your door, your fault—and I'm sure you don't want to live with that. Especially if it means somebody else is not.

The same low laugh, and then a click, louder than before. Silence. How he loves this, the experts will say, the psychologists, the precision of his orders, the control, like someone moving counters around a board. A man seizing the chance to laugh at others where previously others have laughed at him. About his apparent self-confidence there is a division; to one it is assumed, a delusion to be easily shattered, to another it is real—the confidence of someone in the process of constructing a world in which he is master, believing this more and more.

But this will come later.

Now, in the room where they have been listening—Skelton, Resnick, Helen Siddons, Millington—no one moves, speaks, swivels in their chair, cares, for several moments, to look anywhere other than at the floor. Nothing bad has to happen here and if it does it will be at your door, your fault. Finally, it is Millington who clears his throat, crosses and recrosses his legs; Helen Siddons who reaches inside her bag for cigarettes. Skelton and Resnick look one another in the eye: a quarter to five tomorrow. Give or take a few minutes, it is a quarter to five today.

Thirty-six

Through the slatted blinds of Resnick's office, the city folded in upon itself in pools of orange light softly washed by rain. He knew all too well the results of profiling in this type of crime, studies carried out initially by the FBI and confirmed here at the Institute of Psychiatry. Four basic types: those needing to compensate for their own feelings of sexual inadequacy; those who experience excitement and pleasure as a direct response to their victim's suffering; the assertive with a need to express more fully their sense of domination; those whose hostility is a reaction to deep-seated anger.

He was also aware that a high proportion of sexually motivated criminals, those who sought to exercise power over their victims, were also obsessed with the police. They read books and articles, followed cases, watched trials, collected anything and everything, from warrant cards to uniforms, they could lay their hands on. As far as Resnick knew, they were fully paid-up subscribers to *Police Review.*

He knew all that, the theory of it, and at that moment it was little help. Twenty-four hours. *It wouldn't really matter … There still wouldn't be time.* And they still had to make sure the voice on the tape was genuine, Nancy's voice.

Resnick turned away from the window towards the telephone.

As soon as she recognized his voice, Dana's face broke into a smile which as abruptly disappeared. "I'm sorry to have to ask you this," Resnick said, "but if we can avoid it, we'd prefer not to inform her parents before we must."

All assurances aside, Dana came into the CID room wearing the expression of someone asked to identify a body. She sat in Resnick's office, the tape player between them on the desk, and it was as if the two of them had scarcely met, never touched.

At the first sounds of Nancy's voice, a gasp tore from Dana's body and she began to shake. Resnick paused the tape so that she could regain control. He signaled through the glass and Naylor brought in a mug of tea which sat in front of her, ignored. When he played the tape again, she listened in silence, the tears falling slowly down her face.

"You're sure, then?" Resnick asked.

"Aren't you?"

"It is her voice, there isn't any doubt?"

"No, for God's sake. No. What's the matter with you?"

"Do you want someone to drive you home?" Resnick said from the door.

"It's all right. I'll be fine." And then, "At least, she's still alive."

"Yes. That's right." But the pause before he spoke was too long to allow anything but cold comfort.

Helen Siddons was finishing off a takeaway chicken tandoori, chasing the rice around the foil container with a plastic fork. The ends of her fingers were stained orange-red from where she had used her hands. A bottle of mineral water was almost empty beside the ashtray. Helen had been on the phone to her old headquarters, ordering up the available paperwork relating to Susan Rogel. The copy of the ransom note had already been faxed. *Obey my instructions to the letter.* She could still remember the scorn on the faces of some of her so-called colleagues. Overstepped the mark on this one, hadn't she? Standing beside her car with the wind coming hard off the tops and nothing to show but cracked lips and cold and empty hands.

"You want it to be him, don't you?" Resnick spoke from the doorway. "The same man."

"I want him to be caught, whoever."

"But if it turned out that way ..."

"Then, yes. Great. But you don't have to worry, I'm not about to develop tunnel vision."

"Am I worried?" Resnick said.

"I don't know you well enough to say. Perhaps you always act like this."

"Which is?"

Helen made a small shrugging movement with her shoulders. "Suspicious. Resentful. Almost hostile."

"And that's what I'm being?"

"Where I'm concerned, yes."

"I don't think so."

Helen smiled. "Naturally." There was nothing warm about the smile.

"Those calls that were made to Susan Rogel's parents," Resnick said. "I don't suppose any of them were taped?"

Helen shook her head. "There's someone coming in first thing. Loughborough University. Make a comparison between the Rogel note and the voice on the cassette. Vocabulary, phraseology, whatever."

Resnick nodded. The lingering smell of chicken was making him realize he was hungry. Part of his mind was sorting through the contents of the food cupboard, the refrigerator: a snack at bedtime. "See you in the morning, then. Early start."

"I think I'll stay here," she said. "Catch an hour in the chair."

Resnick said goodnight and walked towards the stairs. Outside, he noticed that Skelton's car was still backed up against the fence.

Thirty-seven

Lynn had decided to drive over the night before. She hadn't had too bad a day, a couple of burglaries to check out, both of them big places in the Park, carriage lamps bolted either side of the front door and enough personal jewelry in the main bedroom to take a dozen homeless off the streets full-time. One woman had been pleasant, matter-of-fact, had offered her tea and walnut cake and even made some nice remark about Lynn's hair. At the second house she had spoken to a man, a fleshy-faced barrister who smoked small cigars and made half-hearted attempts to look up Lynn's skirt when she crossed her legs. She could tell from the way he answered her questions about what was missing that the list which finally reached his insurance company was going to be fifty percent speculation.

Oh, and she had called in to see Martin Wrigglesworth, caught him between clients and talked a little about Gary James and his latest outburst. Wrigglesworth had been guarded, looking anxiously over his shoulder like all social workers now, worried that if he intervened too soon and with too little cause, he was likely to end up on the wrong side of a public inquiry. "But what about the kids?" Lynn had asked. Wrigglesworth had fidgeted with the stray hairs of his moustache: "We've taken the boy to the doctor once and he's been cleared. We're going to need something more before we can do that again." How much more than a badly bruised two-year-old face did you need? Lynn had thought. "You don't think you could find an excuse for dropping by, some time in the next few days?" Martin Wrigglesworth had said he would try. Lynn left, knowing that was the best she was going to get; hopeful still that what would happen was, Michelle Paley would use the number Lynn had left her, make her call.

Lynn had not really been hungry before she left, but neither did she want to break her journey. Unwilling to be more imaginative, she drove out to the McDonald's near the new Sainsbury's, not so new any longer, and sat in the window, looking out into the lights of the passing traffic and trying not to think too hard about the fillet of fish she was eating. Twenty-nine percent fresh fish, the advertisements boasted. What was the rest?

She had been aware of a new excitement in the Nancy Phelan business back at the station, out on the fringe of it though, not yet party to what was going on. They'd found a body, someone had said, in the canal by Beeston Lock. She hadn't heard anything to corroborate that. Kevin Naylor had been tying up his paperwork in the CID room and she had asked him. "There's been contact from the bloke who took her, some kind of ransom note, that's all I know." She had been at her desk when Dana Matthieson had left Resnick's office, pasty-faced and close to crying; something about the way she had looked back at Resnick from the door, as if, Lynn had caught herself thinking, there might be something more between them. Well, biting down into the batter of her fillet of fish, so what if there was? What business was it of hers? Five minutes later, she was on the road.

For a moment, as she turned off the road and her headlights swept across the pebble-dashed exterior, Lynn thought the house was in darkness. But there was a light burning in the kitchen and her mother threw open the back door and smothered Lynn in her arms.

"How is he?" Lynn asked as she released herself.

"Oh, Lynnie, it's just awful."

Her father was in the room at the front of the house, the one that was kept for occasional Sunday teas and special occasions; the last time Lynn could recall seeing her father in there was after her Auntie Cissie's funeral, awkward in his red hands and black suit, anxious to be away from the polite grieving and the sausage rolls, back among his hens.

Now he was sitting, stiff and straight, on a hard mahogany chair, the seat of which he had padded with two cushions.

"Dad, why don't you rest on the settee?"

His eyes looked at her from gray channels of pain. "You know," he said, wincing a little as he turned towards her, "them buggers won't let me have as much as a glass of milk."

He had been on a semi-solid diet for two days, this last day allowed only clear fluids, nothing more. Lynn sat on the arm of the settee and reached for his hand. The purgative the doctor had given seemed to have sucked all the life out of him. When she bent to brush her lips against his cheek, it was sallow and cold.

"What's going to happen to your mother?" he said.

"What d'you mean, happen to her? Nothing's going to happen to her."

"After I'm gone."

"Oh, Dad, for heaven's sake. It's only an examination, a precaution. You'll be fine, you see."

The veins on the back of his hand were like maps.

"Dad."

She took one of the hands and held it against her mouth and his fingers smelled of waste and decay.

"What's going to happen," he said, "to your mother?"

The hospital was close to the city center and from a distance seemed to have been made from sections of Lego by an unimaginative child. The interior was low-ceilinged and lit by strip-lighting from overhead. Staff walked briskly along corridors, while visitors stopped to peer at the neatly engraved directions, white and green. They shared the lift with an elderly woman sleeping on a trolley, tubes running from a pair of portable drips into her wrist. The porter whistled "Mr. Tambourine Man" and smiled at Lynn with his eyes.

The nurse would have made two of Lynn and left room to spare. She called Lynn's father pet and told him she'd look after him, promised him a nice cup of tea when it was over. "If you'd like to have a word with Mr. Rodgers about the endoscopy," she said to Lynn.

There were flowers on the desk and a wooden bowl, polished and stained to bring out the natural grain. The abdominal registrar wore a white coat and suit trousers and tennis shoes on his feet; he had octagonal rimless glasses and an accent that had never shaken seven years of public school. He greeted Lynn with a firm handshake and a glance at his watch. "Please," he said, "sit down."

Lynn opted to stand.

"What we're about to do," the registrar said, "is take a little look inside your father's colon. We do this by means of a fibreoptic tube, an endoscope, which is passed along the bowel." Lynn felt her stomach clenching at the thought. "As procedures go, it can be a trifle uncomfortable, but it need not necessarily be painful. So much depends upon your father's attitude. And yours."

"He's terrified," Lynn said.

"Ah."

"He's convinced he's dying."

"Then it's up to you to convince him this is not so. Be strong for him."

"If you do find something," Lynn asked, "what happens next?"

Another glance towards the watch. "If we do come across what appears to be a growth, then we may decide to take a biopsy, have a closer look. After that we'll know more."

"And if it's cancer?"

"Then we'll treat it."

He was wearing a white overall that tied at the back, sedated but awake.

"Don't fret," the nurse said, "I'll hold his hand all the way through it." She laughed. "There's a TV screen in there, he can watch what's happening if he wants."

Lynn thought it was unlikely: her father wouldn't even sit with her mum and watch *Blockbusters*. She went downstairs and sat in the WRVS canteen, chatting about the weather with a middle-aged volunteer who assured her that the jam tarts were homemade. Lynn bought two, cherry and apricot, and a cup of tea. The walls were decorated with paintings done by the children from the local First School, bright as hope and full of life. The pastry might have been home made, but the fillings were out of a tin. She was wondering, if anything did happen to her father, how they would ever manage. Accumulating all the reasons why, whatever happened, she shouldn't apply for a transfer, return home.

"Your father's fine," the registrar said, back in his office. "Complaining a little of the discomfort, but otherwise, absolutely fine. A character."

Lynn gulped down air: it was going to be all right.

"There is a blockage, however. A small growth."

"But …"

"We've taken a biopsy while we had the chance."

"You said …"

"One definite thing in his favor, if it does turn out to be cancerous, it is pretty high up in the bowel. Easier, once we've snipped out the offending part to join the rest together and leave things functioning pretty much as normal." He looked at Lynn to see if she were following. "No call for a colostomy, you see."

All the way home, her father stared through the window at the edges of buildings blending with the gathering darkness, memories of fields. Several times Lynn spoke but got no answer, secretly pleased, not wanting to discuss what sat heavy between them, waiting to be discussed. The car radio drifted through talk of the recession and ethnic cleansing and the rise of the German Right. Lynn switched it off and stared along the tracks her lights made in the lightly falling rain.

Her mother had made a meal, cold ham and salad, halves of boiled egg, each with a teaspoon of mayonnaise on top, thick slices of white bread and butter. Tea.

"Stay the night, love."

"Sorry, Mum, I can't. Early call."

At the door she held her father close till she was sure of the beat of his heart.

Rain fell more heavily, bouncing back from the black shine of tarmac, swishing across her windscreen in a wave whenever another vehicle sailed past and suddenly she was crying. From nowhere, tears ransacked her face and she began to shake. Clutching the wheel, she leaned forward, peering out. A lorry swung out behind her and as it passed the slipstream dragged her wide. Her mirror blazed with the glare of headlights and a car horn screamed. Blinded, Lynn struggled to regain her lane as the wind gusted into her broadside. Mouth open, sobbing hard, she felt the car begin to skid and when her foot tried to find the brake it slid away. With a jarring thump, the nearside struck something solid and cannoned forward, Lynn's seatbelt saving her from the windscreen but not the steering wheel, blood and tears now stinging her eyes.

Thirty-eight

One of the good things about Blue Stilton, Resnick was thinking, ripe enough it had a flavor that would survive no matter the company. This particular piece, the last of a chunk he had brought back from the market the other side of Christmas, he mashed down into a slice of dark rye bread before layering it with narrow strips of sun-dried tomato, half a dozen circles of pepper salami, a piece of ham, a handful of black olives cut into halves; a second slice of bread he rubbed with garlic before buttering and setting it on top. There were tomatoes in the salad box, a nub of cucumber, several ailing radishes, the last of an iceberg lettuce which he shredded with a knife. Somehow he'd allowed his stock of Czech Budweiser to run out, but near the back of the fridge he knew was a Worthington's White Shield in its new-shaped bottle. In fact, there were two.

Of course, he had still not bought the CD player and the Billie Holiday box set sat on the living-room mantelpiece gathering dust, an expensive rebuke. Resnick placed his sandwich on the table near his chair, watchful that one of the more adventurous cats, Dizzy or Miles, didn't jump up and start nibbling round the edges. He pulled one of his favorites, the Clifford Brown Memorial album, from the crowded shelf and slipped it from its battered sleeve. Music playing, he poured his beer, careful not to let the sediment slip down into the glass. Half of the sandwich he lifted towards his mouth with both hands, catching the oil from the sun-dried tomatoes on his tongue.

The Penguin Guide to Jazz was proving good reading, fine for dipping into, interesting as much for who was left out as who was included. Branford, Ellis, and Wynton Marsalis, but not Delfeayo. Endless sections devoted to European avant-gardists who recorded hard-to-get cassettes in Scandinavia, but no room for Tim Whitehead, whose quartet Resnick had seen recently in Birmingham, nor the altoist Ed Silver, so much a part of the early British bop scene and Resnick's friend.

Resnick set down the book and reached for his glass. A couple of years back, he had talked Ed Silver out of severing his own foot from his body with an ax, taken him into his home, and kept him company long into a succession of nights. Resnick listening to Silver's reminiscences about gigs he had played, recordings he had made, promoters and agents who had cheated him out of what was rightly his. The day, speechless, he came face to face with Charlie Parker in New York; the night he almost sat in with Coltrane. All the while easing him off the booze, encouraging him to regain a grip on his life.

As suddenly as he had materialized, Ed had disappeared. Eight months later, a card from London: *Charlie back in the Smoke. Somehow they don't want me at the Jazz Café, but I've got this little gig at the Brahms & Liszt in Covent Garden, Friday nights. Come down and give a listen. Ed.* Somehow, Resnick had never been down.

By the time he walked into the kitchen for his second White Shield, Resnick's mind had been reclaimed by other things: Harry and Clarise Phelan, awake in bed in their hotel, waiting to hear if their daughter were still alive; Lynn, driving back from Norfolk after taking her father to the hospital, alone in the night with what news?

Michelle was halfway down the stairs when she heard Gary outside. At least, she presumed it was Gary. All she could make out at first were voices raised in anger, muffled and harsh. She hugged the baby to her and Natalie whimpered; lowering her face into the fine wispy hair, Michelle shushed her and hurried towards her cot. She was sure it was Gary now. Brian, too. What on earth was going on? Gary and Brian, best mates for years.

She was tucking Natalie's blanket around her when Gary lurched through the door.

"Gary, I wondered what was ..."

At the sight of the blood, she stopped. A line of it, bright, like a Christmas streamer on the side of Gary's face.

"Gary, what's ...?"

With the back of his arm, he pushed her away.

"Gary, you're bleeding."

"Think I don't fucking know that?"

At the sound of their raised voices, Karl rolled over in his makeshift bed on the settee, Natalie began to cry. Michelle followed Gary to the bathroom and stood in the doorway, watching.

"Bastard!" Gary said, as he looked in the mirror. "Bastard!" wincing as he touched his cheek.

"Gary, let me ..."

With a snarl, he slammed the door in her face.

She lay in bed, listening to the sound of the rain, clipping off the loose slates on the roof; the sound of her own breathing. Outside on the landing, where the water was coming through, it dripped in rhythm into a plastic pail. Natalie had gone off again and Karl, thank God, had never really woken. After he'd finished in the bathroom, she'd heard Gary banging around in the kitchen, presumably making a cup of tea. She thought he might switch on the tele, curl up next to Karl, and fall asleep, until she heard his footsteps on the stairs.

"Michelle?"

Soft thump of his jeans on the threadbare square of carpet, lighter fall of his sweater and shirt.

"'Chelle?"

His hand on her shoulder was cold and she jumped.

"I'm sorry. I am, you know."

Face against her back, his fingers reached round and found her breast.

"Shouldn't 've lost my temper, not with you. Weren't nothing to do with you."

Michelle rolled away, freeing herself from his hand. "What happened then? Tell me."

"It wasn't nothing. Really. Just me and Brian, messing around."

"It didn't sound like you was messing around. And this ..." He flinched as she stretched towards him, but allowed her to touch the place just below the hairline where he had been cut.

"We was just foolin' about, that's all. Got a bit silly. You know what Brian's like after a few pints."

Again Michelle stopped herself from asking, whereabouts is he getting all this money?

"Still," Gary said, "over now, eh? What'd my mum say? Spilt milk." He lifted his hand back to Michelle's breast, shocking her with his gentleness, stroking her lightly until, through the thin cotton of the T-shirt, he felt her nipple harden against his thumb.

Thirty-nine

How long someone had been tapping on the window, Lynn didn't know. Opening her eyes, she groaned, gritted her teeth, and looked out. The car had come to rest close against a farm fence, the nearside wing buckled by a concrete post. Gloved, the hand knocked again. Oh, shit! thought Lynn. My head hurts! In the rearview mirror, she could see the sidelights of the car that had pulled in behind her, faint through the blur of rain. A man's face now, bending close to the glass, words she could read without hearing: "Are you all right? Is there anything I can do to help?"

Traffic continued to swish by, unconcerned.

She turned the key in the ignition and the engine sputtered momentarily and died.

He looked to be in his forties, clean-shaven, hair plastered dark to his head by the rain. The shoulders and arms of his jacket were soaked through and Lynn wondered how long he had been standing there, anxious to help. She wound the window down a few inches, enough to be able to talk.

"I saw you come off the road, ahead of me. Wanted to make sure you were all right."

"Thanks. I think I'm fine."

The right side of her mouth was numb and when she touched the tip of her tongue to her lip she could tell it was swollen. Wiping away steam from the mirror, she could see a swelling over her left eye, already the size of a small egg and growing.

"You were lucky."

"Yes, thanks."

Lynn knew she should get out and look at the car, examine the extent of the damage. Even supposing she did get the engine to start, it might not be possible for her to drive away. The man, standing there, kept her where she was.

"You haven't got a phone in your car?"

"Afraid not."

Neither, in this car, did she.

"Look," Lynn said, winding down the window a little farther. "It was good of you to stop, but, really, I'll be all right now."

He smiled and began to back slowly away. Lynn took a deep breath and got out into the rain. The rear of the car seemed to have collided with a pile of gravel as it left the road, then spun forward into the gate. Somewhere, out in the semi-dark, were the shapes of cattle, hedges converging. Lynn pulled up her collar and squatted near the front wheel. The metal of the wing had been forced back sharp against the tire and the tire was flat. The headlight was a tangle of silvered metal and broken glass. Maybe she could pull the metal out and change the wheel, but even then she doubted if she'd get far.

"Why don't you let me give you a lift?" He had come back and was standing back beyond her left shoulder, looking on. The wind had relented a little but not much. "Just as far as the nearest garage."

Lynn shook her head; she wasn't about to compound one stupidity with another.

"There's one six or seven miles down the road. I think it's open twenty-four hours."

Lynn looked directly at his face, forcing herself to make judgments. In the circumstances, she thought, what else was she going to do? Walk and risk getting sideswiped by a passing car? Stick out her thumb and hope for the best?

"All right," she said. "Just as far as the garage. Thanks." Rain brushing his face, he smiled. "Fine."

Lynn retrieved her handbag, locked the offside door, and, hurrying to the man's car, got into the back seat.

"Michael," he said over his shoulder. "Michael Best. My friends call me Pat."

Lynn smiled, more of a grimace than a smile. "Lynn Kellogg, it was good of you to stop. Really."

"Brownie points up there, I suspect," smiling back at her, nodding towards the roof of the car. "Few good ones to set against the bad."

Clicking on the indicator, he waited until there was a clear gap before swinging out into the traffic, not wishing to take unnecessary chances now.

The signs were not good. Michael turned into the forecourt and parked behind the pumps, but the main lights inside the adjoining building stubbornly refused to come on. Only the safety light burned, illuminating faintly the usual collection of motoring maps and engine oils, packaged food and confectionery, on sale audio cassettes by forgotten groups, and a special offer in troll dolls with purple hair.

"I'm sorry," Michael said. "I could have sworn this place stayed open all night."

"Not to worry," Lynn said. "It's not your fault."

"I travel this road quite a lot, though. I should know."

"Me, too. I had half an idea you were right."

"Perhaps it closes at twelve?"

"Perhaps."

Lynn felt a little stupid now, sitting in the back the way she had. There was this man, perfectly nice, out of his way to help her, and there she was sitting in the back like Lady Muck.

"So what ...?"

"What ...?"

Their words collided and simultaneously they laughed.

"Had I best run you back to your car, then?" Michael asked.

"Looks like it."

"Unless ..."

"Unless what?"

"Unless you're heading for Derby."

"Nottingham?"

"Fine."

Lynn leaned back in her seat. "Thanks," she said.

It was warm in the car, cocooned from the cold and rain. For a time, Michael chatted about this and that, his words half lost in the swish of other wheels, the rhythmic beat of the wipers arcing their way across the windscreen. Ten years ago he had left a steady job, started a small business of his own, following a trend; two years back it had gone bust, nothing spectacular about that. Now he was picking himself up, starting from scratch: working for a stationery suppliers, there in the East Midlands, East Anglia, glorified rep. He laughed. "If you're ever in the market for a gross of manila envelopes or a few hundred meters of bubble wrap, I'm your man."

As they reached the outskirts of the city, sliding between pools of orange light, the rain eased, the wind dropped. Life shone, dull, through the upstairs nets of suburban villas as they approached the Trent.

"Whereabouts?" Michael asked. They were slowing past the cricket ground, the last customers leaving the fast-food places opposite with kebabs or cod and chips.

"Anywhere in the center's fine."

"The square?"

"You could drop me off in Hockley. The bottom of Goose Gate, somewhere round there."

"Sure."

Shifting left through the lanes as they went down the dip past the bowling alley, he drew into the curb below Aloysius House. A small group of men stood close against the wall, a bottle of cider passing back and forth between them.

"Thanks," Lynn said, as Michael pulled on the hand brake. "You've been really great."

"It was nothing."

"If it weren't for you, I'd still be out there now, probably. Condemned to spend a night on the A52."

"Oh, well ..."

Lynn shifted across the seat to get out. "Goodnight."

"I don't suppose ..."

She looked at him.

"No, it's all right."

"What?"

"It's late, I know, but I don't suppose you'd have time for a cup of coffee or something? What d'you say?"

Lynn's hand was on the door and the door was opening and she knew the last thing she wanted to do, right then, was walk up that street and turn the four corners that would take her to her flat, walk inside, and see her reflection in the mirror staring back.

"Okay," she said. "But it'll have to be quick."

The all-night café was near the site of the old indoor market, opposite what had once been the bus station and was now a car park and The World of Leather. The only other customers were taxi drivers, a couple, who from the look of their clothes were on their way to Michael Isaac's night club up the street, and a woman in a plaid coat who sang softly to herself as she made patterns on the table with the sugar.

They ordered coffee and Michael a sausage cob, which, when it arrived, made Lynn look so envious, he broke off a healthy piece and insisted she eat it.

"I'm in the police," she said. The first cups of coffee had been finished for some time and they were starting on their second.

He showed little in the way of surprise. "What branch? I mean, what kind of thing?" His eyes were smiling; in truth, they had rarely stopped smiling the past half hour. "You have a uniform or what?"

"God!" she said and laughed.

"What?"

"Why is it that's always the first thing men ask?"

"Is it?"

"Usually, yes."

"Well, do you?"

Lynn shook her head. "I'm a detective. Plain clothes."

"Is that so?" He looked impressed. "And what do you detect?"

"Anything. Everything."

"Even murder?"

"Yes," she said. "Even murder."

The couple across from them were laughing, well-bred voices as out of place as good china; the girl was wearing a long button-through skirt in what might have been silk and it lay open along most of her thigh. From time to time, carelessly, the young man stroked her with his hand. They were probably nineteen.

"What's the matter?" Michael said.

Lynn realized she had started crying. "It's nothing," she said, unable to stop. A couple of the cabbies were looking round.

"It'll be the accident," Michael said. "Delayed reaction. You know, the shock."

Lynn sniffed and shook her head. "I was crying when it happened. That's what did it."

"But why," said Michael, leaning forward. "Why were you crying then? What was it all about?"

She told him: everything. Her father; fears: everything. In the middle of it he reached across and took her hand. "I'm sorry," he said, when she'd finished. "Really, truly sorry."

Lynn released her hand, ferreted in her bag for a half-dry tissue, and gave her nose a good blow.

"Shall I not walk you home?" he said, out there on the street.

"No, it's all right."

"I'd feel happier."

"Michael ..."

"Young woman such as yourself, doesn't do to be walking home alone at this hour ... Heavens, is that the time?"

"You see." Lynn laughing, despite herself. Tears gone.

"Come on," he said, taking her arm. "Show me the way."

She slipped free of his hand, but let him walk with her nonetheless, up past the Palais and into Broad Street and the new Broadway cinema, where she kept meaning to go without quite making it.

"*The Vanishing*," Michael said, looking at the posters. "Did you ever see that?"

Lynn shook her head. "No."

"It's a fine film," he said.

At the entrance to the courtyard, she turned and stopped. "This is it."

"You live here?"

"Courtesy of the Housing Association, yes."

Slowly, he reached for her hand. God, how I hate this part of it, Lynn thought. Deftly, she moved towards him, kissed him on the cheek. "Goodnight. And thanks."

"Will I see you again?" he called after her, voice echoing a little between the walls.

She turned her head for a moment towards him but didn't answer and Michael didn't mind: he knew he would.

Forty

The assistant chief constable's last words to Skelton: "However else this little lot turns out, Jack, keep track of the bloody money."

"Enough here," Graham Millington had said thoughtfully, weighing one of the duffel bags in his hand, "to keep the Drug Squad in crack till next year."

Skelton's instructions had been clear, hands strictly off, keep your distance, no diving in: watch and wait, the name of the game. As he came down the stairs after the briefing, the strain on his face clearly showed.

"If this bastard's tossing us around, Charlie," Reg Cossall said, "jolly Jack there's going to be scraping the shit off his boots for weeks."

Resnick and Millington had charge of the A17 team, Helen Siddons and Cossall were north on the A631. "Big chance, eh, Charlie," Cossall had laughed, "me and Siddons, parked off for a few hours, chance to find out what the old man's getting his Y-fronts in a state about. Taking precautions, mind." He winked, and pulled a leather glove from his side pocket. "Not be wanting to catch frostbite."

Two officers had been installed in each Little Chef since the previous night; cameras with infrared film and the kind of zoom lenses normally used for spying on Royals were trained on both parking lots and entrances. The pairs elected to make delivery sat with the ransom behind them on the rear seat, joking about how they were going to pull a switch themselves, take off for a month to the Caribbean, the Costa del Sol. Intercept vehicles, radio linked, were stationed at intervals along all major routes leading away from the restaurants. Once their quarry showed, he would be followed in an inter-changing pattern until finally he went to ground. All in all, resources from three forces were involved.

Watch and wait: the clock ticked down.

Divine sat on a packing case in the storage area, feet on a carton of oven-ready chips. Four in the afternoon, but he was eating his second Early Starter of the day. In between, he'd tried the gammon steak, the plaice, and a special helping of those hash browns that went with the American Style breakfast, just four with a couple of eggs. All in all, he thought the Early Starter was best.

"Ought to get something down you while you can," he called across to Naylor, who was over by the small rear window, peering out. "Not every day it comes free."

"Soon won't be able to see a thing out here," Naylor said. "Not a bloody thing."

"D'you hear what I said?" Divine asked, biting down into a sausage.

"Another half hour and he could come from those trees over there, right across this field, and none of us would see a thing."

"Jesus!" Divine exclaimed. "Might as well talk to your chuffing self."

Naylor came over and took a piece of bacon off the plate.

"Get your own!"

Naylor shook his head. "Like my bacon crispier than that."

"Yeh? I can see Debbie fancying everything well done, eh?"

Naylor gave him a warning look, shut it!

Divine wasn't so easily dissuaded. "Gloria, though, out there waiting tables, got her eye on you. Play your cards right, you could be away there. Quickie down behind the griddle."

The storeroom door swung open and Gloria came in, a big woman from King's Lynn whose white uniform needed extra safety pins to keep it in place. "Feet off there," she snapped, looking at the oven chips. "People got to eat those."

"Kevin here was just letting on," Divine said, "how he could really fancy you."

"That's nice," Gloria said, treating Naylor to a smile. "I always like the quiet type, they're the ones that take you by surprise. Not like some." Delicately, her chubby fingers lifted Divine's remaining sausage from his plate. "All that talk and then they're about as good for you as this poor thing. Look at it. First cousin to a chipolata."

Resnick checked his watch; less than five minutes since he'd looked last. All the while sitting there, hoping he wouldn't be proved right. Susan Rogel over again. Another wild-goose chase, another woman unaccounted for. Cold sleep in a shallow grave. Beside him, Millington unscrewed the top of his second thermos and held it towards him. Resnick nodded and waited while Millington half-filled the plastic cup.

Straitened circumstances, he thought it might taste better than the first time. "Wife not back into dandelion coffee, is she, Graham?"

"Gilding, sir."

"Come again."

"Gilding. You know, old furniture and the like. Restoration. Sent off for details of this course, Bury St. Edmunds way. Two hundred quid for the weekend. Eighty-five for the video. Daylight robbery, I told her, but, no, Graham, it's the cost of all that gold leaf, she says ..."

Controlling a grimace, Resnick sipped the coffee and continued to stare through the windscreen, letting his sergeant's chatter fade inconsequentially into the background. He couldn't quite rid his mind of the image of Dana, pale faced, listening to the replay of the tape. *Nothing ... nothing bad has happened to me, so I don't want you to worry ...* Dana, listening to her friend's voice, fears strung along the edges of her imagination. This woman, who to Resnick had been so lively, irrepressible, slumped in the chair with all the life drawn out of her. If he had no longer felt any connection between them, it was because Dana no longer had anything with which to connect. Well, partly that. Ever since that first astonishing, joyful evening, Resnick had been aware of the shutters coming down, drawn by his own hands.

"Look!" Millington said suddenly, interrupting his own conversation.

But Resnick was already looking. The green Orion had passed the Little Chef sign once, reappeared from the opposite direction less than two minutes later, and was now approaching it again.

"He's slowing right down," Millington said. "Go on, you bugger, turn in, turn in."

They watched as the vehicle followed the white arrow painted on the car-park surface, drove forward fifteen feet towards the entrance, stopped, took a left, and slowly reversed into the broad space between a green 2CV and a reconditioned Post Office van.

Through the binoculars, Resnick could see the driver's face behind the wheel, white, clean-shaven, middle-aged: alone.

"Time, Graham?"

"Four forty-two."

Having parked the car, the man was making no attempt to move.

"Want me to check out the license plate?" Millington asked.

"Not yet. For all we know he's got a short-wave radio scanning the police channels. Wait till he's out of the car. And then alert Divine and Naylor first."

Millington looked at his watch. "Four forty-four."

Resnick nodded. "Here comes the delivery car, right on time."

"This is it, then. What he's waiting for."

"Maybe. Maybe he's just tired, taking a nap."

"With both eyes open?"

The unmarked police car moved across the forecourt and drew to a halt as close to the main door as it could get. Resnick wiped away the first dampening of sweat. Headlights burned low against the field fence and the red tail lights blinked. The detective on the passenger side slid clear, leaned back across the seat, and lifted the black duffel bag clear.

"All right," Millington said, "pay some bloody attention."

Detective and duffel bag disappeared from sight.

"What's he doing?" Millington asked.

"Nothing."

"Come on, you bastard. Move."

Four forty-seven and the plain-clothes man reappeared, went briskly around the back of the car, and resumed his seat; without rushing, the car drew away.

"I don't believe it," Millington said. "He's not going to do a thing."

"Yes, he is."

Resnick held his breath as the door to the Orion opened and the driver set his feet on the tar-covered surface. "Radio, Graham."

But Millington was already giving the signal to Mark Divine.

"Right!" Divine said in the storeroom and was on his way. Out in the main body of the restaurant, he took his time, saw the man coming towards him through the double set of glass doors. At the cash desk, he hesitated, picked up a roll of extra strong mints, and placed the money in the cashier's hand. The man had to break step to get round him, Divine apologizing, stepping into his path by mistake, apologizing again, and heading for the door.

"Smoking or non-smoking, sir?" the cashier asked.

"I'm just off to the Gents' first," the man said. "But either's fine."

"Orion's licensed to a Patrick Reverdy," Millington said in the car, "address in Cheadle."

"Long way from home," Resnick said, glasses focused on the restaurant door.

When the man emerged from the toilet, he was still rubbing his hands together after using the dryer. Naylor was now sitting in the smoking section near the door, stirring sugar into his coffee. He watched as the man told the waitress he was expecting a friend and accepted a double seat towards the rear window. While he was waiting, he ordered a toasted tea cake and a cup of tea. Home-going traffic built up steadily on the road outside. Resnick talked briefly to Skelton, keeping him informed; at the other location, Siddons and Cossall were drawing a blank.

Another ten minutes, tea cake consumed, the man checked the time, picked up his bill, and walked between the tables towards the cashier; paying his bill, he left a fifty-pence tip on the counter, turned towards the exit, changed his mind, and turned back again towards the toilets. Naylor's stomach muscles knotted tight.

"He's staying too long," said Millington, staring at his watch.

"Maybe he's being careful," Resnick replied.

When the man stepped back into the restaurant with the duffel bag in his hand, Naylor's breath stopped. Nonchalant as you like with it, little swing with the right hand. "May be nothing," the man said to the cashier, "but someone seems to have left this in the Gents'. Thought you might want to keep it safe out here. All this talk of bombs, someone might panic, stuff it down the loo." He was holding the bag out towards the cashier, but so far she had made no move to take it. "Don't worry," he said, "I stuck it against my ear and had a good listen. Nothing ticks."

✦✦✦

Divine detained the man before he drove away and while Resnick checked back with Skelton, keeping him up to scratch, Millington came over and had a word. Nothing serious, no reason to get alarmed. The man's driving license showed his name to be Reverdy; he'd driven there to spend an hour with a woman he'd met at last year's Open University summer schooL "Lives in Spalding, but can't always get away. Married, you see."

"And you drove all the way from Cheadle?" Millington said.

"I know," Reverdy said. "The things you do for love."

In her car, parked at the far side of the garage on the A631, Helen Siddons set down the receiver and sighed, grim-faced. "Okay, that's it. Let's head back. It's over."

"Just so's the day's not a complete blow-out," Cossall mumbled, "I suppose a quick fuck's out of the question?"

If she heard him, Helen Siddons gave no sign.

Forty-one

Skelton was waiting for Resnick inside the double doors, falling into place alongside him on the stairs; no early run this morning, exhaustion in the superintendent's movements, the veins that showed red in his eyes. Twice he had tried contacting Helen Siddons but her phone had been disconnected; sleepless he had lain beside the cold rebuke of Alice's back.

"About the only thing that's bloody clear, Charlie, one way or another, the bill for this one's going to be firmly nailed to my door."

Resnick shook his head. "I don't see what else we could have done. As long as there's still a chance the girl's alive, we had to play along."

At the landing, Skelton turned aside, shoulders slumped. "Half an hour, we'll review where we are."

But within half an hour both local radio stations had played extracts from the second tape on the air. It had been delivered by hand, a messenger with a motorcycle helmet and scarf wound about the lower part of his face, no chance of recognizing who it was. Someone in the news room had given the tape a cursory listen, switching off after several minutes when it became apparent what they'd got. After phone calls to department heads, solicitors, copies were made and sent to the police; one question asked—the assertion that an earlier tape had been received, demanding a ransom, was that true? The police spokesperson would neither confirm nor deny. That was enough.

Radio Nottingham put the item at the top of its scheduled news; Trent interrupted its programing with a special bulletin. Each newscaster gave a brief introduction covering Nancy Phelan's disappearance and the lack of subsequent success in tracking her down before referring to an apparently unsuccessful attempt by the police, yesterday, to apprehend a man who claimed to have kidnapped Nancy and who had made a ransom demand. The extracts from the tape which followed were remarkably similar.

The instructions given to the police were clear and precise, as were the warnings. Unfortunately for everyone concerned, these were not heeded. It was simple, you see, all they had to do, these people, was follow what I told them and then my promise could have been kept and Nancy Phelan could have been reunited with her family and friends, safe and sound. But now ...

I hope you're listening to this, Jack, I hope you're listening carefully, you and those advising you. Remember what I told you, Jack, if anything bad happens it's going to be your fault, your fault, Jack, not mine. I hope you can cope with that, that responsibility.

Lynn had called Kevin Naylor early and arranged for him to give her a lift. Hedged in between the traffic on Upper Parliament Street, she recounted her mishap with the car.

"Sounds as if it could've been a sight worse."

"Say that again."

"Not dead yet, then?"

Lynn touched the side of her head. "Just a little sore."

Kevin grinned. "No, I mean chivalry."

"Oh. No, I suppose not."

"Seeing him again?"

She was looking through the window at the knot of people waiting to cross at the lights near the underpass, a man with a fluorescent orange coat sweeping up rubbish outside the Cafe Royal. "I shouldn't think so." She had no idea how strongly she believed that, nor whether she wanted it to be true.

They were drawing level with the Co-op when the news item came on the radio and Kevin reached for the switch, turning up the volume so they could hear the voice on the tape.

✦✦✦

Robin Hidden had hardly left his flat for days. Phone calls from his office, inquiring about his absence, had gone unanswered. Mail lay downstairs beside the Thomson's directories and the bundle of newspapers someone had once tied up with string and left, intending to take them to the recycling bin. Robin ate tinned tomatoes, cheese, muesli with powdered milk; he left the television picture on all the while, volume down, the radio just below the level of normal conversation. He did crosswords, ironed and re-ironed his shirts, scraped every vestige of mud from his boots, pored over maps. Offa's Dyke. The Lyke Wake Walk. Wainwright's guides to the Fells and Lakes. The Cleveland Way.

He was writing the same letter to Mark, again and again, so important to get it right. Explain. Mark was his best friend, his only friend, and he had to make him understand why Nancy had been so important to him, the ways in which she had changed his life.

That morning he had been up since shortly before six, cold out and dark. Frost on the blackened trees and thick on the roofs of cars. He drank tea absentmindedly, struggling with draft after draft, his thoughts like a tangle of wool which spooled along the page for sentence after sentence, seemingly clear, before becoming snagged impossibly down. Nancy, now and then, then and now, over and over, again and again. The only woman who, for however brief a time, had allowed him to be as he was, accepted him as a man. Who had loved him. She had loved him. Another sheet of paper was screwed up and thrown aside to join the others scattered round the floor.

Dear Mark,

I hope you don't mind …

At the first mention of Nancy's name, the pen rolled free from Robin's hand. The broadcaster's words, the voice on the tape, blurred in his mind even as he heard them, bits and pieces of a dream he had never dreamed. Almost before the item had finished, he was reaching for the phone.

Neither Harry nor Clarise Phelan had been listening to the radio at all; the first they heard of the existence of the tape was when a newspaper reporter arrived in the dining room of their hotel, where they were having breakfast, and asked for their reaction to what had happened.

"You give us a lift to the police station, pal," Harry said, already on his feet, putting on his coat, "and I'll tell you on the way."

"Charlie ..."

Skelton pushed his way into Resnick's office without knocking, no gesture of recognition towards Millington, who was sitting this side of the desk.

"Field the girl's parents for me, will you? They're downstairs kicking up a stink and I've got to finish this statement for the press and okay it at headquarters."

"I thought that was none of my concern any more. Inspector Siddons, isn't she liaising with the Phelans? Or did I get that wrong?" There was an edge to Resnick's voice that took the superintendent by surprise. Resnick, too.

"Christ, Charlie ..."

It was the first time in memory Resnick had seen Skelton with his shirt in less than good order, his tie at half-mast. He knew he should be feeling more sorry for him than he was, but he was in the middle of a bad day, too. Not so long before he'd had Robin Hidden on the phone in tears, sobbing out every word; best part of fifteen minutes it had taken him to calm the lad down, agree to talk to him if he came in. Resnick glanced at his watch: that'd be any time now.

"Charlie, if I had the slightest idea where she was, I'd get her on to it. Truth is, so far this morning she hasn't showed."

With a mumbled word and a nod, Graham Millington slipped away to his own desk; he could see all too well which way this particular conversation was going and the last thing he wanted to find himself doing was trying to appease a distraught father with a build like a good light-heavyweight.

"Graham," Resnick said.

Oh, shit! Millington thought, not quite through the door.

"Why not see if Lynn's still around? Have a word with the Phelans together. If Inspector Siddons arrives, she can take over."

"If I'm going to deal with it," Millington said, "I'd sooner it was from start to finish."

Resnick gave Skelton a quick glance and the superintendent nodded. "Fine."

"What if they want to listen to the tape? The one with their daughter's voice?"

"Yes," Skelton agreed, hanging his head. "Let them hear it all. They should have heard it in the first place. I was wrong." He looked at Resnick for several seconds, then left the room.

Helen Siddons had not been wasting her time. She had acquired the original tapes and their packaging from the radio stations and had them sent off for forensic analysis, though by then so many hands would have touched them as to render that next to useless. But it was a process that had to be gone through. In case. She had listened to the second recording and compared it to the first, taken both to two experts and sat with them, listening through headphones, each nuance, again and again.

These things they were agreed upon: the northern accent identified on the first tape, less obvious on the second, was almost certainly not a primary accent. Certain elements in the phrasing, the softness of some of the vowel sounds, suggested Southern Ireland. Not Dublin, perhaps. More rural. A childhood spent there and then a move to England, the northwest, not Liverpool, but harsher—Manchester, possibly, Bury, Leigh, one of those faded cotton towns.

And the note sent in the Susan Rogel case, Helen Siddons wanted to know, was there any way of telling whether it was written by the same person?

There could be, in certain instances it might be possible, but she had to understand, written and spoken registers were so different. The farthest either of them was prepared to go, it could not be discounted the source was the same man.

For Helen that was enough. All of the suspects in the Rogel case, everyone the police had interviewed, seventeen in all, transcripts of their interviews would have to be double-checked, some would have to be contacted again if necessary She was quite convinced now, the perpetrator in both instances was the same: and, more likely than not, he was already known.

Forty-two

All day, Lynn had been aware of this uneasy sense of expectation. Through the usual raft of paperwork, the follow-up interviews on the Park burglaries, a session with Maureen Madden about an alleged rape victim who had, twice now, recanted on her evidence and who they thought was being threatened, all through the haze of sexual badinage with which Divine and his cronies clouded every day, the constant ringing of telephones, the unthinking cups of tea, she could never shake off the feeling of waiting for something to happen.

Distracted, Resnick had paused at her desk in the late afternoon, asking for news of her father, automatically passing good wishes.

"Pint?" Kevin Naylor called, putting on his coat by the door.

Lynn looked at her watch. "I'll see."

When finally she went down the stairs, out past the custody sergeant's office, the entrance to the police cells, she knew it was Michael she was looking for—exchanging words with the constable at reception, kicking his heels on the street outside. He was nowhere.

Knowing that she'd regret it, promising herself she wouldn't stay too long, Lynn headed across the street to the pub.

"You ask me," Divine's voice rose above the noise, "she's been dead since a couple of hours after she was lifted."

Lynn wasn't about to waste her breath telling him that nobody had.

"What about this ransom business?" Kevin Naylor asked.

"Load of bollocks, isn't it? Some clever-clogs tossing us a-bloody-round. You know yourself, it's happened before."

"Come on, Mark," Lynn couldn't keep sitting there saying nothing, "her voice was on the tape."

"So? What's to stop him forcing that out of her first?"

"All in two hours?"

Divine raised his eyes towards the smoky ceiling. Why were some women always so literal, jumping on every word you said as if it were gospel? "Okay, maybe it was a bit longer. Two hours, four, six, what's it matter?"

"To Nancy Phelan or to us?"

Divine emptied his glass and pushed it along the table towards Kevin Naylor, his shout this time. "All that matters, what we should be looking for is a body. Never mind all this undercover crap out there in the sticks."

"Wasn't what you said at the time," Naylor reminded him. "Not with another Early Starter on your plate."

"You can talk! Here, you should've seen our Kev and this Gloria, tongue'd dropped any further from his mouth he'd been hoovering up the floor with it."

Oh, God, Lynn thought, here we go again. "I'm off," she said, getting to her feet.

"Not now, look, I'm just getting these in. Pint or a half?"

Lynn thought of what was waiting for her at home, half a frozen pizza, a bundle of ironing, her mother's call. "All right," sitting back down, "but make it a half."

A light rain had started to fall, not enough to persuade Lynn to use her umbrella as she took the cut-through beside Paul Smith's shop and came out by the Cross Keys, opposite the Fletcher Gate car park. Later the temperature was due to drop and most likely it would freeze. Last night, on the bypass out near Retford, a Fiesta had skidded on black ice and collided with a lorry loaded high with scrap; a family of five, mother, dad, two lads, a baby of sixteen months, all but wiped out. Only the baby had survived. She thought about her own good fortune, the car that had come so close to clipping her when she had swung, blinded, wide from her lane.

As she turned through the archway and began to cross the courtyard, the keys were in her hand.

Midway across, she hesitated, looked around. Muted by curtains or lace, lights showed from windows here and there about the square.

Soft, the sounds of television sets, radios overlapping. A cat, ginger and white, padding its way along the balcony to the right.

Michael was on the landing, halfway up the stairs, sitting with his back against the wall, legs outstretched, breath on the air, a newspaper folded open in his hands.

"You know," he said, drawing in his legs, "I can read this thing from cover to cover, front to back, every word, and if you asked me five minutes later a single thing about it, I wouldn't have a clue."

Lynn had still to move.

"Here," he offered the paper towards her, "test me. Name the prime minister of Bosnia-Herzegovina. The Father of the House of Lords. Define once and for all the obligations of the Treaty of Maastricht. I couldn't do any of it."

"How long have you been here?" Lynn asked.

"Oh, you know, I haven't exactly been counting, but possibly one or two hours."

She turned away, past the chalked graffiti, to look at the light falling in a spiral at the foot of the stairs. Rain drawn across it like a veil.

"You're not angry?"

"For what?"

"Me being here."

Angry? Was that what she should be? Looking at him sitting there, Lynn's shoulders rose and fell and she tried to avoid the smile sidling into his eyes: how long had it been since anyone had waited for her five or ten minutes? "No, I'm not angry."

He was on his feet in a trice. "Shall we go, then?"

"Where?"

Disappointment shadowed his face. Doubt. "You didn't get my message?"

"No. What message?"

"About dinner."

The iron of the railing was cold against her hand. "There wasn't any message."

"I left it where you work."

"You don't know where I'm stationed."

"I phoned personnel."

"And they told you?"

He had the grace to look a little sheepish. "I told them I was your cousin, from New Zealand."

"Somebody believed you?"

A laugh, self-deprecating. "I've always been quite good at accents, ever since I was a child."

Lynn nodded, moved one step higher, two. "Where was that? That you were a child?"

"What do you think?" he said. "Is it too late for dinner or what?"

He had booked a table at the San Pietro. Red tablecloths and candles and fishermen's nets draped from the walls. Crooners murmured through the loudspeakers in Italian, more often than not to the accompaniment of seagulls and a mandolin.

"I've no idea what this place is like," Michael said, pulling out her chair. "I thought we could give it a try."

The waiter appeared with the wine list and a couple of menus.

"Red or white?" Michael said.

"Nothing for me, I've had enough already."

"Are you sure? You …"

"Michael, I'm positive."

He ordered a small carafe of house red for himself, a large bottle of mineral water for them both. For a first course, he had prosciutto ham and melon, Lynn a mozzarella and tomato salad. They were well into their main dishes—fusilli with gorgonzola and cream sauce, escalope of veal with spinach and sauté potatoes—when Michael asked his first question about her day.

"I suppose I shouldn't have been surprised you were late, this terrible business, it must be driving you mad."

Lynn set down the fork she had half-raised to her mouth. "Which business is that?"

"That poor missing girl."

"What makes you think I'm working on that?"

"Are you not? I suppose I thought you all would be, trying to find her, you know, twenty-four hours a day."

"Well, I'm not, not directly."

"But you must know all about it. I mean, what's going on."

She lifted up her fork again; the veal was tender, sweet to the taste, the breadcrumbs surrounding it not too crisp.

"This latest business, this ransom that was never collected and everything, isn't that all very weird? Didn't I read that setting that trap for him cost so many thousand pounds?"

"You seem to know as much about it as I do."

"Ah, well, it's only what I read in the papers, you know."

"I thought," Lynn said, "you forgot all that the minute you'd taken it in."

Michael smiled back at her and summoned the waiter, ordered himself another carafe of wine.

"You're sure you won't?"

"Quite sure."

For the remainder of the meal, he asked her about the damage to her car, her father's health, talked about plans for setting up on his own again once the recession had really started to turn around. Distribution, that's the thing, wholesale; anything but stationery, deadly stuff, try as you might, never get it to really move. And he'd glanced up at her, grinning, to see if she'd got the joke.

They were back in the courtyard, the cold biting round them; Lynn with her scarf wound twice around the space between her upturned collar and her hair, Michael's hands deep in his pockets all the way back from the restaurant, but now …

"You know," Lynn said, "I don't think I'm ready for this."

"What would that be now?"

"Whatever it is you're wanting."

His hand was on her arm, inches above her wrist. "To be friends, is there anything wrong with that?"

"No. Except that's not all you want."

He was close enough to have kissed her with scarcely a dip of his head, not a tall man, not really, three or so inches more than she was herself. "Am I so transparent, then?" he smiled.

Something happened to his face, Lynn thought, when he smiled. He came to life from inside.

"And am I not going to get my kiss, then? My little peck on the cheek?"

"No," Lynn said. "Not this time."

When she glanced down from the balcony, he was still standing perfectly still, looking back up at her; before she could change her mind, she let herself quickly in, bolted and relocked the door.

Michael only then starting to walk away, whistling softly. Not this time, he was thinking. Well, doesn't that mean there'll be another?

The bath as hot as she could take it, Lynn lowered herself through the rising steam. How clearly had he known she had wanted him to kiss her, standing there with little more than their breath between them? His mouth pressed against her, no matter what. So long since a man had thought of her that way, made love with his eyes. Despite everything, she shivered, imagining his touch.

Forty-three

Alice Skelton was in her bathrobe, towel wrapped around her hair, cigarette between her lips. It was twenty past six in the morning. She had heard his daughter—that was the way she tried to think of Kate now, it made things easier—returning home closer to three than two. Not bothering to be quiet about it any more, no more guarded whispers as she gave some youth a last wet kiss and reached down to slip off her shoes. These days—these nights—it was a slamming of doors and a shout of thanks, and whoever had driven her home turning back up the volume of the car stereo before the end of the drive. Alice had lain awake, said nothing, waited for the raid on the fridge, the toilet flush, the bedroom door. Christ, girl, she thought, what would I have done with my young life if I'd enjoyed your freedom? Would I have screwed it up any less or more?

Beside her, rolled as far towards the edge of the mattress as was possible, Jack Skelton slept on, his body twitching every now and then as if cattle-prodded by his dreams.

At four, Alice had given up all pretense and gone downstairs. Sweet biscuits. Ice cream. Coffee with a little gin. Cigarettes. Finally, just gin. She ran an early bath and lay back in it, her head resting against a plastic cushion, listening to the World Service: *Londres Matin*, the early morning news in French.

Out and dried, she had been considering going back upstairs and getting dressed when the phone rang.

"Hello? Mrs. Skelton? This is Helen Siddons."

"It's also practically the middle of the night."

"I'm sorry, I wouldn't have called at this hour if …"

"If it wasn't important."

"That's right. Is your husband there?"

If he's not with you, Alice thought, I suppose he must be. "I expect he's still sleeping, don't you? He tires easily these days."

"Could you get him for me? It is …"

"Important, I know." She let the receiver fall from her hand and it banged against the wall, bouncing and bobbing at the end of its twisted flex. "Jack," Alice called up the stairs, "someone for you. I think it's the massage service."

Helen had been backtracking through the Rogel interviews, never quite certain what she was looking for but trusting it would leap out at her when she found it. Motive, opportunity, some connection that somehow they had missed. Something which they had failed to find important then, but now …

Those who had been brought in for questioning fell into three broad categories: anyone who might have had a grudge against the three principals involved, known villains with a penchant for extortion, and finally a more haphazard collection of people who had been in the area at the time, possibly acting in a manner that aroused suspicion. In the case of primary suspects, their backgrounds were well-documented, profiles fairly full; other individuals, notably those from the last group, had been lingered over less lovingly. At the time, that hadn't been seen to have mattered. But when those people were brought into the limelight, the gaps in knowledge were prodigious.

Helen wondered how assiduously some of these stories had been checked—the first alibi but not the second or third? And what was known about them once they had been eliminated from the inquiry? She guessed, very little. In some cases, nothing. How easy, then, for one of them to lie low a short spell, up tracks, and move away. Start over again somewhere else.

"Take someone with you," Skelton said. "Another detective, someone who can do some leg work if it's needed. Divine, for instance. He could drive you."

Mark Divine was less than happy, playing chauffeur to a sodding woman! Still, at least he was getting a decent motor; top a hundred in the fast lane with no trouble.

"Divine," Helen Siddons said. She was wearing a dark suit with a mid-length skirt, her hair pulled back and severe. Divine had in mind she'd not have been out of place in that video he'd rented last night: *Death Daughters From Hell.* He could just picture her wielding a whip.

"Yes, Ma'am." Divine coming to mock-attention, giving her as much of a come-on as he dared with his eyes. Never knew, if they got a result, might not be above letting her hair down on the way back.

"One word out of turn from you, Divine, and I'll have your balls cut off and dried and strung up for auction at the next divisional dinner-dance. Understood?"

Lynn had sifted through the mass of material on and around her desk, checked the CID room notice board, the message log; during the course of the morning, she contacted the officers who had rotated duty on the desk, got through to the switchboard, and asked them to go through all incoming calls. Finally, it seemed incontrovertible—no personal message had been left for her inside the past thirty-six hours. For whatever reason, Michael had lied.

"Problem?" Resnick stopped by her desk on his way back to his own office. A bulging brown bag from the deli was leaking gently into his hand.

Lynn shook her head. "Not really."

"Worrying about your dad?"

"Sort of, I suppose."

"Any news when he's going in for the operation?"

"Not yet."

Resnick nodded; what else was there he could say? He had promised to call the Phelans this afternoon with a progress report, not that any progress had been made. Whoever had sent the ransom tape, they were in his hands. Every other trail, such as it had been, had long gone cold. Behind his desk, he opened the bag and stemmed a rivulet of oil and mayonnaise with his finger, then brought it to his mouth. Only a few drops fell over the Home Office report on responses to private policing. How long was it since he had spoken to Dana? He should ring her, make sure she was all right. If she suggested meeting for a drink, well, what was wrong with that? But the number snagged in his brain like a wedge of ill-digested food stuck in his throat.

Lynn spent the afternoon with several copies of Yellow Pages and the other business directories. On her eleventh call, the receptionist said, "Mr. Best? He's often out on call, but if you'll hold on I'll see if he's available."

"Excuse me," Lynn said quickly. "But that is Mr. Michael Best?"

"That's right, yes. Can you tell me what it's pertaining to? If he's not here, perhaps someone else can help."

"Look, it's okay," Lynn said. "Don't bother now. I'll catch up with him some other time."

That evening she turned down all offers of a drink, left pretty much to time, skin beginning to tingle as she neared home. But there was nobody stretched out across the stairway reading the newspaper, no note slipped beneath her door. So many times she went to the window and looked down over the courtyard, always expecting him to be there. At about quarter past nine, she realized that she'd dozed off in the chair. By ten she was in bed and asleep again, surprisingly unconcerned.

Forty-four

As if it weren't enough of a liability being born black, her parents had to christen her Sharon. One of the few names in current English instantly recognized as a term of abuse. "Don't want to waste your time with her, right little Sharon!" In addition to all the innuendo and insinuation she'd grown up with from childhood, to say nothing of the outright bigotry, the head-on insults—"Black scrubber! Black cow! Black bastard!"—for the past five years she had been the butt of Essex girl jokes too numerous to mention. The fact that there was no resemblance whatsoever to this mythical blonde in a shell suit with breasts where her brains should be seemed to make little difference. It was all in the name. It could have been worse, she sometimes consoled herself, she could have been Tracey.

Sharon Garnett was thirty-six and had been a police officer for seven years. She had trained as an actress, two years at the Poor School, worked with theater companies, mostly black, doing community work on a succession of shoe-string grants; two small parts in TV soaps, the obligatory black face with a heart of gold. A friend had made a thirty-minute video for Channel 4 with Sharon in the lead and for five or ten minutes it had looked as if her career might be about to take off. Six months later she was back in a transit van, touring a piece about women's rights from an abandoned hospital in Holloway to a youth center in Cowdenbeath. And she was pregnant.

It was a long story: she lost that baby, sat at home in her parents' Hackney flat, day after day, not speaking to anyone, staring at the walls. One afternoon, between three and four, the sun shining and even Hackney looking like a place you might want to live—she remembered it well, right down to the smallest detail—Sharon went into her local nick and asked for an application form.

"Open arms where you're concerned," the sergeant had said, "racial minorities, you're actual flavor of the month."

Despite the occasional remark, the groups that grew silent and closed circle as she entered the room, the excrement-filled envelope with "Eat Me" stenciled on the front found one day in her locker, Sharon's training passed pretty much without incident.

Surprise, surprise, her first posting was Brixton, policing the front line. Out on the streets with her black woman's face and shiny uniform, she exemplified the ways in which the Met was changing; black men called her whore and her sisters spat at her feet as she passed.

Three applications for detective were turned down; finally, back to Hackney with the domestic violence unit, but that wasn't what she wanted. She had done her share of caring and consciousness raising already; if she'd wanted to be a social worker, Sharon told her inspector, she would never have applied to join the police.

Fine: back on the beat.

Eighteen months on, a relationship splintering around her, she left London, joined the Lincoln CID; nice, quiet cathedral city, Sharon as out of place as papaya in a Trust House Forté fruit salad. Oh, there was burglary and plenty of it—the recession bit deep here, too—drug-dealing in a minor kind of way, anything and everything you could imagine to do with cars as long as they were other people's. The most excitement Sharon had was when a small-scale row about shoplifting on a prewar council estate suddenly flared into a riot: youths throwing petrol bombs and insults, ten-year-olds hurling stones as the police retreated, outnumbered, behind their shields. It had taken reinforcements from outside the area and the arrival of a specialist support unit to regain control.

Since then she'd been seconded to King's Lynn. Even quieter.

It was quiet now, thirty minutes shy of sunrise, frost heavy across the hawthorn and the oak, the dark ridges of ploughed fields. Sharon was hunkered down behind an ancient Massey-Ferguson tractor, with two of the other officers, passing back and forth a thermos of coffee unofficially laced with Famous Grouse. The coffee was hot and their breath, dove-gray in the clearing air, testified to the cold. She drank sparingly and passed it on; last thing she wanted to do, crawl off somewhere and squat down for a pee, difficult enough without wearing tights over her tights the way she was that morning.

"They'll never bloody show," one of her colleagues said. "Not at this rate."

Sharon shook her head. "They'll show."

She had been working this investigation for five months now, ever since the first incident had been reported, seven pigs slaughtered on a farm this side of Louth, dragged off and butchered in the waiting van. Market stalls the length and breadth of Kesteven had flourished special offers of pork belly, legs, chump chops.

"Times like these," Sharon's governor said, "people do what they can."

She supposed it was true: reports of sheep rustling on Dartmoor and in the Lakes had tripled in the past two years.

"Look! There!"

Her heart began to pump. Headlights, dull in the slow-gathering light, steered between the intervening trees. Sharon spoke into the radio clipped to the shoulder of her padded jacket, instructions that were concise and clear.

"Good luck," somebody said as he moved swiftly past her.

The breath inside Sharon's body threatened to stop. The lights were clearer now, funneling closer, the van shifting out of silhouette against the slowly lightening sky. Resting on one knee, the other leg braced and ready, Sharon's mouth ran dry. Over by the sheds, a few of the animals moved around morosely, rooting at what remained of the straw that had been thrown on to the frozen ground.

The skin beneath her hair tingled as the van slowed and slowed again. Before it had come to a halt, three men jumped out, dark anoraks, black jeans, something bright in one of their hands catching what little light there was.

"Wait for it," Sharon breathed. "For fuck's sake, wait!"

Two of the men launched themselves at the nearest pig, one seeking to club it hard behind the head. The animal squealed, terrified, and slithered as the club came down again. Running to join them, the driver of the van lost his footing and went sprawling, longbladed knife jarred free from his hand.

"Go!" Sharon called, sprinting forward. "Go! Go! Go!"

"Police!" The shouts sang out around them. "Police! Police!"

Sharon jumped at the man who had already gone down, the heel of her trainer driving into his back and flattening him again into the ground. Satisfied, she carried on running, leaving whoever was in her wake to wield the handcuffs, drag the man away. The hardwood stave that had been used as a club lay in her path and, without stopping, she scooped it up.

Angry voices tore around her, curses and the sharpening clamor of the pigs. One of the thieves broke free and took off in a run towards the van. Sharon watched as two of her colleagues set off in pursuit, feet catching in the ruts that rose like frozen waves from the ground. Two of the others were involved in scuffles, while a third was already on his knees, head yanked backwards with a choke-hold tight about his neck.

The runner had managed to start the van and now it lurched towards them, one of the officers hanging from the side, an arm through the window, grabbing at the wheel. Sharon jumped back as the vehicle slewed round and stuck, the driver's foot on the accelerator serving only to dig deep into the ground, showering black earth high into the air. A fist landed on his temple and a cuff secured him to the wheel as the ignition cut off.

"Sharon!"

A warning turned her fast, pulling back her head to evade the butcher's cleaver swinging for her face.

"Nasty," Sharon said, and struck out with the club, catching her attacker's elbow as the arm came back, hard enough to break the bone.

Only when their prisoners had been properly cautioned, farmed out into different vehicles for the drive back to Lincoln, the sun showing at last, faint through the horizon of sparse trees, did Sharon wander back across the churned-up ground to where the pigs were rooting eagerly. It took no time at all for her to realize what was at the center of their attention was a human hand.

Forty-five

The pig farm had been made secure: diversion signs were in place on all approach roads; attached to four-foot metal stakes, yellow police tape, lifting intermittently in the northerly wind, marked off the area where the body had been found. Men and women in navy blue overalls were moving out in a widening circle from the spot, carefully raking over the ground. Others were examining the track, preparing to take casts of tire tracks, boot marks. Nancy Phelan's body, freed from its shallow grave, lay in the ambulance covered by a sheet. In a maroon BMW, smeared with mud, the Home Office pathologist was writing his preliminary report. Harry Phelan, driven through the morning traffic by a grim-faced Graham Millington, had walked off across the farm track and into the adjacent field as soon as he had identified the body. Now he stood, stock still, hands in pockets and head bowed, while, back inside the car, his wife, Clarise, wept and wanted to walk out and hug him but did not dare.

It was still well shy of noon.

Resnick stood in topcoat and scarf, talking to Sharon Garnett, his face pale in the winter sun. Close to five nine and bulked out by the duck-down jacket she was wearing, Sharon was in no way dwarfed beside him. She had known about the disappearance from the television and posters which had been circulated with Nancy Phelan's picture—not so many women missing, thankfully, that the connection didn't spark fast in her mind. Well before her pork butchers had been driven away, she had made her suspicions known, found herself talking to Resnick within minutes.

"How long," she asked, "do you think she's been in the ground?"

"Difficult to tell. But my guess, not too long. The pigs would have found her otherwise, even in temperatures like these."

"Does it help?" Sharon asked. "Finding her here?"

"To pinpoint the killer?"

She nodded.

"It might narrow down the field. It all depends."

"But there'd have to be a reason, wouldn't there?"

"Go on."

"I mean, why here? On the face of it, it doesn't make a lot of sense."

Resnick looked around at the flat landscape of broad fields. "It's out of the way, you'd have to say that for it."

Sharon smiled a little at the corners of her mouth. "Everywhere round here is."

"It takes time to bury a body," Resnick said. "Even if it's only a few feet deep. And if anyone threatened to disturb you, you'd see them from a long way off."

"He'd have to know it, though, wouldn't he?" Sharon said. "Know of its existence, that for long periods of the day there was nobody around. Stuff like that. I mean, you wouldn't just drive along with a body in the back, see somewhere, think, oh, that looks a likely place."

"You could."

"Yes, but is that what you think?"

Resnick shook his head. "No, I think whoever it was knows this area well, this farm, this track. My guess would be he already had the idea in his head, possibly even before he kidnapped the girl. Bury the body here."

Sharon thought about her first sight of the hand, the rooting pigs. "But then he must have known, sooner or later, the body would be found?"

"Yes," Resnick said, "I think that's part of the point."

"What point's that?"

"I'm not yet sure."

The pathologist was on his way towards them, trousers tucked down in green wellingtons. "I'll have to do the proper tests of course, but I'd say she's been dead, oh, possibly three days, four. My guess is she was killed first, the body kept somewhere, then brought here. Signs of deterioration are remarkably few."

"Cause of death?" Resnick said.

"Oh, you saw the bruising round the neck. Strangled, almost certainly."

"How?" Sharon asked.

The pathologist glanced at her over the rim of his spectacles, as if recognizing for the first time that she was there. He made no attempt to reply to her question.

"How was she strangled?" Resnick asked.

The response was immediate. "Not with the hands. A ligature of some kind. Possibly a piece of rope, though that might have torn more of the skin. A narrow belt?"

"How soon," Resnick asked, "before we can have a full report?"

"Twenty-four hours."

"And before that?"

"I'll get something to you as soon as I can. Early afternoon?"

Through this exchange, Sharon had been doing her best to rein in her anger. "You have any women in your team?" she asked Resnick, as the pathologist traipsed away from them, back towards his car.

"One, why?"

"You always back her up as well as you just did me?" Any thought that she might have been paying him a compliment was dashed by the look in her eyes.

Harry Phelan was standing in the same position, a scarecrow in the center of a ploughed field, nothing growing there to protect. Clarise had started towards him, ventured as far as the gate and no further. Resnick put an arm round her shoulders and at his touch she began to cry again, her head resting sideways against the broad front of his coat.

"It's Harry I'm fretful for," she said, sniffling into bits and pieces of damp tissue. "All of the energy he's got, he's put into willing Nancy still alive. Even on the way out here, he kept saying, she's all right, you see, whoever this is, it'll not be her. Not Nancy, it'll not be her."

Resnick left her to trudge into the field, Harry turning his head once to see who it was, but moving no farther. They said nothing for some little time, two men at either end of middle age. Not for the first time, Resnick felt useless, hopelessly inadequate to the task. How do you begin to comfort a man who has just identified the murdered body of what was once—in his heart still remained—his child? If he and Elaine had ever had children themselves, would he have known any better? Would circumstances, one day, ever have enabled him to understand?

"If the ranson had been paid this would never have happened." There was no anger in Harry Phelan's voice now, no passion. He was a man whose life had been sucked out.

"We don't know that," Resnick said.

"If it had gone all right, not got messed up, with the money ..."

"It's possible she may have been killed before."

Harry looked at him, too numb properly to comprehend. Lapwings rose up as one from the farther end of the field, flew a half circle, and landed back down between where they stood and the side hedge. Vehicles were starting up back at the farm, revving their engines purposefully; Resnick knew that he should go but he kept standing there.

"Shall you catch him, d'you think?"

Resnick took his time about answering. "Yes," he finally said, thinking on balance that he meant it.

"Nothing will happen to him, will it? Even if you do. Some crackpot with a bunch of letters after his name'll stand up in court and spout something and they'll shut him away in some hospital for ten years and then let him back out."

Resnick didn't reply.

"If you do set hands on him," Harry Phelan said, voice flat as before, "for pity's sake keep me clear of him. Because if you don't I'll not be responsible for what happens."

After a few more minutes, Resnick turned side on and looked at Harry waiting till the other man returned his gaze; then, together, the two of them set off back across the field.

Sharon Garnett was waiting for him back at the car, slightly tense, legs a little apart, her face set with determination. Resnick thought it likely he was about to get another lecture. "I was wondering," she said, "you ever have vacancies in your team?"

Resnick took a moment to collect his thoughts, not what he had been expecting. "From time to time," he said, "people get promoted, transferred." He didn't tell her that not so very long back one of his men had been stabbed to death when he sought to break up a scuffle between youths in the city center.

"What happened here," Sharon was saying, glancing back across her shoulder to where the body had been found, "I did all right, didn't I?"

Resnick nodded. "I should think so, yes."

"So if I were to apply," the slow smile starting up again near the edges of her mouth, "I could rely on you for a recommendation."

"After what you said before, I'm surprised you'd even think about working with me."

She stepped back and gave him a slow once-over, amused. "Basically, sir, I'd say you were okay. You just need somebody around to give you a bit of a nudge."

Resnick held out his hand. "Thanks for the help. Maybe I'll see you again."

"Right," said Sharon, "maybe you will." And she turned to get back to her own business, too much to do to stand there and watch him drive away.

Forty-six

They were heading east, back through Newark towards the city and not a decent passing space in sight. Frustrated behind the wheel, Millington chewed instead mint after extra-strong mint, never letting them remain in his mouth long before crunching them between his teeth.

"Drop a plumb-line down from the first ransom drop to the second," Resnick said, "what do you get?"

Millington flicked on the indicator, changed down ready to overtake. "Long as it had a kink in it, where we've just come from."

Resnick sighed and shook his head. Out through the nearside window, a farmer was forking feed from the back of a tractor, cattle making their way towards it, waveringly across cold land.

"I wonder what it's like," Resnick said. "To be in Harry Phelan's position. Something you must have half-known all along, there in the back of your mind, and then ... Jesus, Graham! Dug up in a ploughed field. How the hell d'you begin to live with that?"

Millington didn't know. Tight on the wheel, his hands were smeared with sweat. How could either of them really know? Two middle-aged men, neither of whom had ever fathered a child.

Resnick got through to the station on the car phone and asked for Lynn Kellogg. Briefly, he filled her in on what they'd found. "Get yourself over to Robin Hidden soon as you can," he said. "Take Kevin along if he's free. Best if Hidden hears it from you if you can get to him in time. He's going to have the media crawling all over him any time."

"Right," Lynn said. "I'll do what I can."

"And, Lynn. That friend of his, up in Lancaster or wherever, suggest he goes up there for a bit, keeps his head down."

"Right."

Millington cursed quietly, forced to pull in behind a high-sided lorry which the single carriageway left him no room to overtake. Fingering another mint from the packet, he offered one to Resnick, who shook his head.

The phone sounded and it was Lynn calling Resnick back. "Just to be clear, when I talk to Hidden. We're no longer looking at him as a suspect here?"

"No," Resnick said. "Just another victim."

When Millington dropped him off at the London Road roundabout it was so gloomy the floodlights at the County ground, some quarter of a mile up the road, could scarcely be seen.

"Tell Skelton I'll be there in half an hour."

"He's going to love that," Millington said. Resnick didn't care; this was something he had to do himself. Climbing the slight hill towards the Lace Market and turning left on to Hollowstone and up towards St. Mary's Church, he stepped into the full force of the wind. There was a hole in the stone wall a third of the way up the hill, giving way to a space large enough for a short man to stand up in. Two figures were huddled inside, newspaper and cardboard around their legs and feet; Resnick guessed another three or four had slept there that night.

When he turned right in front of the church, there was Andrew Clarke's red Toyota illegally parked outside the architects' office, Clarke's name, the senior partner, in tasteful lower case on the glass beside the door.

Yvonne Warden was chatting to the receptionist at the desk, fresh cup of coffee in her hand, green plants luxuriating quietly to either side. Framed photographs of office blocks and hotels the firm had designed hung from the wall, alongside copies of the original plans.

"If you want to see Andrew," she began, "I think he's still in a meeting ..."

"It's all right," Resnick said. "That's not why I'm here."

Dana was at her desk in the library, looking through a box viewer at a slide of one of Philip Johnson's Houston buildings, a high-rise version of one of those gabled houses she'd fallen in love with by the canals in Amsterdam. A shame, she was thinking, Johnson never got to follow through on his design for a Kuwaiti Investment Office opposite the Tower of London that was a replica of the Houses of Parliament, twice life-size. At least the man had a sense of fun.

She looked around at the soft click of the door and when she saw it was Resnick she said hi and smiled, but halfway out of her chair the smile died.

"It's Nancy, isn't it?"

He nodded and held out both hands, but she turned aside and walked towards the window; stood, resting her head against it, eyes closed, holding on. The glass was cold against her face.

Resnick didn't know any other way to do this. "Her body was found early this morning. She'd been buried in a field. She'd been strangled."

Dana jolted, as if a current had passed through her, and her forehead banged against the window hard. Carefully, Resnick eased her back against him, until she was leaning against his chest, her hair soft on his face. Her breathing was like rags.

"Do her parents know?"

"Yes."

"Oh, God!" Slowly this time, Resnick still holding her, the top of her body arched forward until the crown of her head was once again against the glass. Someone came into the room and, on a look from Resnick, went quickly away again. "She was so … beautiful," Dana said.

"Yes, she was."

Dana turned, shaking, into his arms and Resnick held her, trying not to think about the time. By now Skelton would be taking counsel, issuing orders, readying himself for a press conference. As the senior officer present when Nancy Phelan's body had been lifted from the ground, Resnick himself would have to go before the television cameras before the day was out. From the square, faint, came the sound of the bell on the Council House ringing the hour.

"You'd better be going," Dana said, releasing herself and moving past him to where she kept the tissues at her desk. "God, I must look a mess."

"You look fine."

Dana sniffed and summoned up something of a smile. "Only fine?"

"Terrific."

"Did you know I've got another job?"

He shook his head.

"Yes, in Exeter. Starting next month." She laughed. "Andrew gave me such a wonderful reference, they could hardly understand why he'd agree to let me go."

"Are you sure you'll be all right?" Resnick said.

"In Exeter?"

"Now."

Dana sighed. "Oh, yes. I'll be ... I'll be fine. Just like you said. Fine."

Resnick squeezed both of her hands, kissed her softly on the mouth. "Phone me, if things get bad."

Michelle had sat down early with the baby, thinking it had to be almost time for *Neighbours*; what she got was the last third of the news. Some black woman standing in front of some farm buildings, answering questions to the camera. Michelle thought it was something about—what was it?—Salmonella or mad cow disease until the photograph of Nancy Phelan appeared top left of the screen. Quickly, she shushed Natalie down and leaned forward to turn up the sound. Almost immediately, the picture switched and there was this man, round-faced, sad-looking, Michelle thought, speaking about the same thing. Detective Inspector Charles Resnick, read the caption bisecting his tie. "Deep regret," he said, and "renewed effort," and when the interviewer, out of sight, asked whether he thought Nancy Phelan's death had come about as a direct and unfortunate result of police incompetence the inspector's mouth tightened, his eyes narrowed, and he said: "There's no way of knowing if that's the case. Any attempt to suggest otherwise would be pure speculation."

Not that that was going to stop it happening.

Back across the Trent, Robin Hidden had disconnected his phone but could do nothing about the steady stream of local newsteams and reporters who beat a path to his door. Finally, he clambered over three sets of gardens, sneaking between rose bushes and around artificial ponds, until he found a path back on to the street.

He bought a paper at the newsagents to get change and rang Mark's number from memory. His friend had been replacing some tiles in his bathroom and had heard what had happened on *The World at One*. "Why don't you come up?" Mark said, without waiting to be asked. "I've still got some time off. We could have another go at Helvellyn. Three thousand feet up in the snow."

"Are you sure?"

"Course I'm sure."

"I'm not exactly going to be good company."

"Robin, for heaven's sake! What else are friends for?"

There were tears already in the corners of Robin's eyes. Across the paper, the headline read MISSING GIRL'S BODY FOUND and underneath, POLICE PLAN FAILS. *Just after dawn today*, the report began, *the body of Nancy Phelan, missing since Christmas Eve was discovered, naked and apparently strangled, buried in the mire of ...*

Numb, Robin walked on till he came to the footbridge over the river, turned down past the Memorial Gardens, and continued on until the roundabout by the old Wilford Bridge. Shoulders slumped, he leaned on the masonry to catch his breath. Through the sour gray of the day, all he could see was the image of Nancy, that last time together, getting out of the car and walking away. The air stuck in his lungs like a fist.

Going by on a bike, rod resting across the handlebars, a fisherman turned his head and stared at him curiously.

Robin pushed himself on, without any real aim, down through the close streets of the Meadows until he came out near to the railway station. Although he had only the clothes he stood up in, he knew he wasn't going back to the flat. Mark could lend him an anorak, his spare pair of boots, he'd done it before. The ticket and anything else he needed, he could pay for with the credit card in his wallet.

Forty-five minutes to wait for a train, Robin bought an orange juice from the buffet and carried it along to the end of the platform, collar buttoned up against the curl of the wind. The train that would carry him across country was one of those little Sprinters, two carriages at most, but if he stood where he was, before long one of those expresses would come hurtling in. He looked through blurred eyes at the dull shine of the rails, heard Nancy's name falling softly from his lips.

Forty-seven

The briefing room was cramped and airless, too small for the number of officers clustered inside. Pinned along one wall, stretching away from a color photograph of Nancy Phelan, smiling and alive, were grainy black and white 8×10s of her in death. Other photographs showed the location where her body had been buried, strips of colored tape pinned to them, marking spots where tire tracks had been found, so far unaccounted for, a boot mark, incomplete and etched into a hardened ridge of soil. A map of Lincolnshire and East Anglia showed the two roadside restaurants where the ransom money had been left, the locations north and south of a line that swung gently eastwards as it traced, inland, the curve of the coast around the Wash. Almost directly between, circled in red, was the spot where the pig farm was situated and where Nancy's body had been found.

"Stinks of stale farts in here," Cossall said, moving towards the rear of the room.

Divine looked offended. "Only just let that one go."

Along the corridor in the computer room, extra civilian staff were in place, entering and accessing the information obtained so far, including what Helen Siddons had retrieved from the investigation into Susan Rogel's earlier disappearance. All this would be checked against the national Holmes computer. Once connections were established, it was from here that fresh action would be generated.

"More sodding paper," as Cossall liked to put it, "than you'd need if you had four hands, two arses, and a bad case of diarrhea."

Jack Skelton had recently returned from a press conference where he'd come within an inch of losing his temper. To listen to the most prevalent line of questioning, you'd imagine that Nancy Phelan had been abducted and murdered by a combination of the city's police force and the Conservative government through the good offices of the Home Secretary.

Wearing a black suit, hair pinned back, shoes with a slight heel, Helen Siddons was leaning slightly towards him, talking earnestly.

Resnick sat with eyes closed, arms folded across his lap, trying to ignore the way his stomach was rumbling while he marshaled his thoughts.

Skelton nodded to Helen, who stepped smartly away, got to his feet and signaled for silence. "Charlie, what have we got so far?"

Notepad in hand, Resnick got to his feet, moving towards a more central position. "Right, preliminary pathologist's report states death by asphyxiation; bruising consistent with the use of a leather belt or similar, no more than a centimeter and a half across. Marks under the hair, towards the back of the skull, left side, consistent with a fierce blow to the head. Whichever weapon was used, it may have been padded or covered in some way, as, although the bruising's severe, there are only minimal cuts to the skin. Other bruising, particularly to the arms, legs, and back suggest Nancy struggled with her attacker, possibly in the immediate time before she was strangled."

"Good for her," said a voice from one side.

"Much sodding good it did her. Poor cow!" said another.

"Probable scenario, then," Resnick went on, "for whatever reason, either he's coming for her or she's trying to make her escape, the two of them struggle, he subdues her with a blow to the head, strangles her while she's unconscious." There were other permutations, worse still.

"As far as can be ascertained," he continued, "there was no sexual attack, no evidence of semen inside or outside the body. There's no recent evidence of sexual intercourse."

"Bloody waste," Divine said quietly.

"Thought you were one of those," Cossall said, overhearing him, "didn't give a toss if they were alive or dead."

"The fact that she was buried where she was," Resnick was saying, "makes examination of the body difficult. There were some samples of skin tissue found under her nails, however, and here and there particles of fertilizer-enriched soil which don't seem appropriate to the ground she was buried in. Tests are continuing on all of these."

"Time of death, Charlie," Skelton prompted.

"Again, not easy, due in the main to unusually low temperatures. But the best guess as of now is that she'd been dead for four or five days, with the body only being transferred to the point where it was found as little as six hours or less beforehand." Resnick looked around. "I don't need to spell out for you what this means: she was almost certainly already dead when the attempt to follow the ransom instructions were carried out."

Muted cheers and more than a few prayers answered. At least they didn't have to take the blame for that.

"Not a lot else from here," Resnick said, flipping over another page of his notebook. "As you know, there's a partial print of a boot, composite rubber, wellington or similar, size eight or nine. Tire marks are marginally more interesting, weight and spread suggests a medium to large saloon, but I think we're being a bit hopeful going that far."

"Hopeful isn't sodding in it," intoned an anonymous voice, miserably.

"What we still lack is anything positive to link whoever killed Nancy Phelan with the person who returned her clothes to the flat. Analysis of the skin tissue found under her nails might give us that, if we can find a match in our records."

"And pigs might do the proverbial," Cossall remarked sourly.

"Something to add, Reg?" asked Skelton.

Cossall smirked and shook his head. Resnick stood his ground. "What we might have, however, is a better suspect than any of us thought. Someone a few of us have actually seen."

In the hubbub that followed, Resnick moved back towards his seat and now it was Helen Siddons' turn. The level of conversation rose again as she stepped forward and she was careful to wait, eyes surveying the room, until it had died down and she was sure of everyone's attention.

"Most of you will know something about the Susan Rogel investigation and will be aware there are certain basic similarities with this one. Woman disappears without trace, after a brief period a ransom demand is made, and when an attempt is made to make payment, the money is ignored. So far, so good. Here, though we have a body, in Susan Rogel's case we've turned up nothing and it's not outside the realms of possibility that she engineered her own disappearance. Except … listen to this.

"Thirty minutes after the time appointed for the ransom to be collected, a car pulled in at the pub where the money had been left near the outside toilet; the driver went inside and ordered a half of bitter and a ham roll, left ten minutes later, still finishing off the roll and went to the Gents'."

"Must've pissed with his left hand," Divine said.

"When he drove off, he was followed and detained. At first, he got a big shirty, thinking it was a random breath test, but as soon as he realized it was something else, he was as co-operative as you like. Ended up asking almost as many questions as we did. Claimed he'd started studying once for a law degree, but for some reason had dropped out. Still thought about going to university, reading criminology.

"He said he was currently working as a sales rep for a firm called Oliver and Chard, based in Gloucester. Specialized in work clothes, farms and factories, you know the kind of thing, overalls, protective clothing, reinforced boots. He was on his way to a dairy farm in Cheddar and after that had a call to make in Shepton Mallet. Car he was driving had been hired from Hertz that morning; normally he used his own, but he'd been experiencing difficulties getting it to start."

Helen Siddons looked right to left around the room; not too many people were staring at their shoes.

"His name was Barrie McCain. Of course we checked him out with his employers, appointments log, car hire, everything. It all tallied. There was never any follow-up; there didn't seem to be any reason. Not until Patrick Reverdy turned up at the Little Chef and fished the duffel bag of money out from the toilet."

"This McCain," Reg Cossall said, "I presume we wouldn't be going through all this if he was still working for the same firm."

"Gave in his notice," Helen Siddons said, "the week after the noncollection of the ransom. Some story about his mother being ill Manchester way, Wilmslow, the personnel manager thinks she remembers. He'd been a good salesman, friendly, they'd been sad to let him go."

"Photograph," Cossall said, "too much to hope for."

"Company policy is to keep one on file. McCain kept forgetting to bring one in. After a while, they got fed up asking. Figures were so far up in his area, they didn't want to get the wrong side of him. However," continuing among the moans and groans, "D.C. Divine described the man he saw close to in the Little Chef, the one calling himself Reverdy. According to the personnel manager, in outline it fitted him to a T. Similar height, five eight or nine, medium to slight build, sometimes she said he used to let his moustache grow a little but before it became established normally he shaved it off. McCain was seen at close quarters by two other officers—getting a photo-fit together is a priority, I think, as soon as this is through."

"Thanks, Helen," Skelton said. "Charlie. All right, the rest of you. Without shutting off other avenues, there's a lot to work on here. I want every element of this Reverdy's story checked forwards, backwards, then checked again. McCain, too. If we can clear connections between them, anything that's more than circumstantial, for the first time we might be ahead of the game."

Forty-eight

Lynn was in the bath, lying back, listening to GEM-AM. She had been in there long enough for the condensation that had steamed over the glass front of the wall cabinet to begin clearing, the pine-scented bubbles to all but disappear; the water was starting to feel cold. She considered running some more hot, finally decided long as she'd been there, it wasn't time enough for the tank to have properly heated through. Another few minutes and she would have to get out. On the radio, a commercial for quick-fit exhausts came to an end and back came the music. They seemed to have been playing Everly Brothers' songs, off and on, all evening. Another one now: "Till I Kissed You." Her mum used to love their stuff, sing it around the kitchen when Lynn was young. Days when she still had something to sing about. She'd even been to see them once, the Everlys, her mum. Yarmouth, it would have been. Phil and Don. Hadn't there been something about one of them being ill? Not being able to appear. Drink or drugs. Don or Phil.

Lynn pushed herself up in the bath and the water splashed, chill, around her waist. Maybe it was some kind of Everlys anniversary. Perhaps one of them had died and what she was listening to was a tribute. She hoped not, one thing her mum didn't need, another reason to be sad. For long enough for the picture to form, Lynn closed her eyes and saw Robin Hidden's face.

That morning, when she'd told him about Nancy's body, he had turned gray listening to the words. Right there as Lynn stood watching, Robin, face crumpling in like a balloon losing air, the life being sucked out of him. "Why don't you sit down?" The words stale even as she said them, stale and inadequate. "Would you like me to make some tea?" But he had, and Lynn had negotiated her way between the unwashed pots and empty packets and found the PG Tips.

"You haven't got any milk."

"I know. I'm sorry, I ..." He had looked back at her, helplessly. He still hadn't found the way to cry.

"You stay there," Lynn had said. "I'll nip down to the corner shop and get some."

By the time she had come back, the tears had been there, clear in his eyes. They sat in the airless room, drinking tea, while he told her about the first time he had met Nancy, the time he got a cramp during his run; the first time and the last.

"I should have g-gone after her," he said. "Instead of letting her walk off the way she did." Panic and guilt jostled in his voice. "If I'd r-run after her it wouldn't have happened."

"You weren't to know that."

"But if I had."

"Look, it was her choice. She didn't want to be with you. Not any longer. If you'd gone haring after her, she wouldn't have thanked you."

Tears tumbled down Robin Hidden's face. "N-now she would."

When he sobbed, she'd gone and stood beside him, patting his shoulder, telling him it was okay to cry, feeling genuinely sorry for him at the same time as she sneaked glances at her watch.

"Don't you think," Lynn had said later, pieces of tissue wadded and damp on the floor, "it would be a good idea if you got out of here? Went away somewhere. You've got family."

He hung his head. "I don't want to go there."

"Friends, then. Isn't there this friend ...?"

"Mark."

"Yes, Mark. Couldn't you go and stay with him? Give him a ring."

"I suppose ... Yes, I suppose I sh-should."

"I would. If I were you. Climbing, isn't that what you do?"

"Yes."

Lynn had looked back once from behind the wheel of her borrowed car, half expecting to see him looking down, but between the half-drawn curtains the window had been bare. "How am I ever going to get used to it?" Robin Hidden had said. "The fact that I'll never s-see her again. Not ever."

Lynn realized, as she released the plug and climbed out of the bath, that she had been thinking of her father all that time; then and now.

When it came to it, how would she get used to never seeing him again? At least, not alive. "Dream, dream, dream," sang the Everly Brothers. Reaching out, Lynn switched off the radio. She was still drying herself, one foot on the side of the bath, when the doorbell rang.

Michael was standing outside, a bottle of wine wrapped in green tissue paper balancing in the palm of one hand. "I thought you'd have had a busy day. Time to relax, maybe, wind down."

Lynn had pulled on her terry-cloth dressing gown, belted tight. She could see his eyes, quick to where it hung open a little at her breasts. That look.

"If it's not convenient, I'll just leave this and go, why don't I? Early as it is, you could be ready for your bed."

She stepped back and let him inside. "Wait a sec while I get dressed."

Michael smiled.

"There's a corkscrew in the kitchen," she said over her shoulder, moving to the bedroom. "Drawer to the left of the sink."

She put on blue jeans, a cream sweater over a cotton roll-neck, sports shoes on her feet. Michael was sitting on the two-seater settee, leafing through that evening's *Post*, two glasses of red wine stood on the low table before him. "Amazes me," he said, "the way people open themselves up like this." The front page held a picture of a weeping Clarise Phelan being led towards a waiting car by her husband. *MY AGONY by murdered girl's mother.* "I mean, wouldn't you want to keep those feelings private?"

Lynn took her glass over to the easy chair angled towards the small, rented TV.

"I expect, though, you've seen some progress now, what with the poor girl's body and all."

"Oh, yes," Lynn said, "as a matter of fact, we have. Quite a few new leads just today."

"And you," Michael tasting his wine, "you're more at the center of things?"

"In a way, yes, I suppose I am."

He put down his glass and crossed the room, not hurrying, smiling all the time with his eyes. As he leaned down towards her, Lynn instinctively braced herself, a vestige of fear. His mouth was strangely soft and his lips as they slid over hers were pleasantly warm and curranty from the wine. His tongue pushed gently and she let it in.

"I've been thinking about that for the longest time," he said. He was sitting on the arm of the chair, leaning across her, face pressed close against her neck. "Really, the longest time."

"A few days, that's not so long."

"Oh, no. Longer than that."

She shifted her head away till she could see his face.

"You didn't recognize me, did you?" Michael said.

Not taking her eyes from him, Lynn shook her head.

"And you don't now?"

"No."

His hand was stroking her arm, fingers beneath the sleeve of her sweater. "It was the monkey suit …"

"The what?"

"Dinner jacket, evening dress, black tie. I've noticed it before, the way it changes a man." He smiled again and she noticed for the first time a chip of green in the gray-blue of one eye. "Moss Bros, cheaper than a trip to your local neighborhood plastic surgeon." The smile widened. " 'Let me get those.' Remember?" He took a twenty-pound note from his top pocket and passed it in front of her nose. "You were wearing a blue dress. Such beautiful shoulders. And your hair, your hair was pushed up at the back like this …"

She caught hold of his wrist and held it fast; his pulse she could feel beating against her ear.

"You do remember now, don't you? Or did I make that poor an impression?"

What she remembered was the black suit, smart, one face amongst others, ranged along an overcrowded bar. The voice, pursuing her away, offering to buy her a drink later, but surely the voice was not the same?

"That policeman you were with then, wasn't that him I saw being interviewed this evening on tele? The one talking about the body?"

Lynn nodded. "My inspector. Resnick."

"Good, is he? At his job. What would you say, a good copper?"

"Yes, that's what I'd say."

Michael made to move his hand from her hair and she let it go. He brought down his face to kiss her again and just before he did she said, "Meeting me on the road that evening, when I almost crashed the car—was that a coincidence or what?"

His mouth brushed against her lips. "Oh, I don't think there's any such thing as blind coincidence, do you? I prefer to think it's all pre-ordained, part of some wider plan. Whatever ..." Kissing her again, "... will be, will be." More strongly, she kissed him back. "No songs," Michael sighed, "like the old songs."

"I think I'd better go."

They had slid to the floor between the chair and the settee, Lynn's sweater was bunched up by her neck, the belt loosened at the top of her jeans. Michael lay with one leg between hers, not looking at her, tips of his fingers making small circles on her skin.

"You're sure?" Lynn said.

"I think so." Still not looking at her, strange for a man who usually did nothing but. "Early start tomorrow, busy day."

Lifting his leg, Lynn rolled away from him; sitting up, she smoothed her sweater into place. "Me, too," she said.

"Catching up with your man."

"Could be." On her feet, she tightened her belt. "We can always hope."

"Yes," Michael said. "Can't we?"

Lynn leaned forward to kiss him, but he slid his face away. She picked up the wine glasses, one from the table, one from the floor.

"Here," Michael said, "let me take those. I need a drink of water. Trouble with red wine, leaves you with such a thirst."

While he was in the kitchen, Lynn slipped into the bathroom and looked at herself in the mirror, ran a comb through her hair. She was more than ordinarily flushed.

"Till I see you again, then," said Michael, over by the door.

Lynn turned the handle to let him out. "Phone me, next time. I don't always want surprises. Phone me first."

He kissed her deftly on the cheek and stepped outside. "You best get back in quickly, you don't want to be letting in the cold."

She could hear his footsteps echoing down the stairs as she locked and bolted the front door. Resnick picked up his phone on the seventh ring; faintly, in the background, Lynn could hear music playing. "Hello," she said. "It's me, Lynn."

"It's not your dad," Resnick said. "Nothing's happened?"

"No. It's the investigation."

"Nancy Phelan?"

"Mmm."

"What about it?"

"I could explain easier if we met somewhere. It's not too late for a drink."

"The Partridge?"

Lynn glanced at her watch. "Twenty minutes."

"Done."

She set the phone back down and it was some sixth sense, a split second before she heard the sound, that swung her round.

When Michael had gone into the kitchen for a glass of water, he had slipped the catch on the window that led on to the walkway. "Now I wonder," he said, "exactly what you and your colleague were going to talk about. Over your friendly pint." He had an old-fashioned tire jack in his hand, wrapped around with rubber and cloth; if he could avoid it, he didn't want to damage her face. Not unless he had to: not yet.

"Michael ..." she began.

"No," he said, smiling even as he made that slow shake of the head. "Don't waste the words."

She made a lunge past him but his arm was fast and the jack struck her twice, the first time high on the shoulder, hard enough against the bone to make her scream; the second blow was to the back of her head as she fell, face first, unconscious, to the floor.

"Well, now, Mr. Resnick," Michael said towards the telephone, "let's see how good a good copper you really are."

Forty-nine

Resnick had not been in long when Lynn rang, back from a couple of hours at Marian Witczak's house in Mapperley, listening to her account of New Year's Eve at the Polish Club. She had dropped a note through his door earlier, inviting him, and Resnick, partly through guilt at having let her down, partly to avoid another evening frustratedly anticipating the glories of his Billie Holiday box set, had accepted. In Marian's drawing room, comfortable in armchairs guarded by ornate antimacassars, the ghost of Chopin hovering around the grand piano, Resnick had sipped plum brandy and listened to what he had missed—the politics, the polkas, the member who had drunk his way through fifteen flavors of vodka before clambering on to one of the tables and re-enacting the Polish cavalry's defense of Krakow down to the last despairing fall.

He had walked home with lengthening strides, head clearing rapidly in the cold air. Time enough to find a little supper for an insistent Dizzy, grind and brew coffee, before answering the telephone and hearing Lynn's voice. Going back out again, especially for another drink, was close to the last thing he wanted, but he knew she wouldn't be suggesting a meeting unless it were important. Resnick dialed the DG taxi number from memory and lifted his topcoat from where it hung in the hall.

Both bars of the Partridge were fairly full and Resnick checked them carefully, right and left, before settling for a half of Guinness and a seat between an elderly man whom Resnick knew by sight, nursing his last pint of mild for the night, and a group of four who were still arguing their way through last Saturday's match, ball by ball. When his own glass was more or less empty and there was still no sign of Lynn, Resnick went to the phone and dialed her number. No reply. He checked with the station to see if, for whatever reason, she had gone there. No one had seen her since early evening. Resnick finished his drink and picked up another cab, across the street by the clock from the old Victoria station.

No lights showed through the windows of Lynn's flat, no response to knock or bell. When he peered into the glass and saw his own face reflected there, he saw a fear that so far he could only feel, not understand. The door had not been double-locked and he considered gaining access with the credit card that otherwise he rarely used, but noticed, when he looked again, the catch on the kitchen window was unfastened. No difficulty hauling himself up and through the space, flicking on the light.

"Lynn?"

Two glasses stood on the metal drainer, freshly rinsed. A corkscrew, cork still attached, lay beside a sheet of crumpled tissue. Resnick found the bottle in the main room, unfinished, on its side; a little wine had spilled out on to the carpet and made a stain, still damp. The coffee table had been shunted aside, the chair pushed at an odd angle against the wall. There was a second cluster of stains, darker and less sweet; Resnick touched the tip of his finger against the carpet and lifted to his nostrils the unmistakable taint of blood.

Graham Millington was at the head of the stairs, talking with two of the uniformed men they'd pulled in from routine duties. One of those nights when club brawls would either peter out of their own account or end in more than tears. Millington had been asleep in front of the television when the call had woken him, his wife tucked up already with a cup of Horlicks and a biography of Henry Moore. "What d'you call that?" he'd asked, looking over her shoulder at a photograph of one of Moore's sculptures. "Hole in heart patient?" "Isn't there football on, Graham?" she'd asked, long-suffering. She had been right: Wolverhampton Wanderers and Southend United. Millington had felt his eyes going before the first yellow card.

"They don't appreciate being dragged away from their shut-eye," the first constable was saying.

"I don't give a bugger what they appreciate," said Millington, "not till we've something more than nothing."

It was Divine, not a happy man himself, called out just three short moves away from maneuvering last year's Miss Ilkeston past checkmate, who came up with the first witness. His knock brought Corin Thomas to the door of his flat, smelling more than slightly of beer, overcoat on, chip pan in his hand. "Soddin' central heating's packed up again," Thomas said. "Too much to hope you've come to fix it?"

Divine told him it was. "You're dripping oil," he pointed out, "all over the lino."

"Better come in, then." Once the chips were starting to sizzle, Thomas told him what he had seen, a man and a woman, pretty much clinging to one another, going down the stairs past him and staggering over towards a parked car.

"Didn't occur to you to report it?" Divine asked.

"Love it, wouldn't you, if, I jumped on the old phone every time someone round here got half-pissed."

"Is that what you thought they were?"

"She was, no mistake. Hardly keep her feet at all, if he hadn't been half-carrying her. All but went over, the pair of them, more than once."

"The woman," Divine asked, "you recognize her?"

"Oh, yes. That one from lower down. Kellogg. One of your lot, isn't she? What all the hoo-ha's about, I suppose."

"What about the man?" Divine asked. "Ever seen him before?"

Corin Thomas shook his head.

"Sure?"

"Yes. It was dark, but, yes, there's lights enough down there. Good enough to make out someone you know."

"You could describe him, though?"

Thomas shrugged. "I don't know. I mean, I didn't exactly stare. Minding me own business, like. But, yes, the bloke, he'd be closer my height than yours. Five seven, eight. Far as I remember, darkish hair. Forties, maybe. Didn't get that good a look at his face."

"Recognize it if you saw it again?"

Thomas thought about it as the chip fat bubbled. "I might. Couldn't say for sure."

"Shame," Divine said, "but you're going to have to have your chip butty another time." Reaching across, he turned off the gas. "I know you'll want to help; do whatever you can."

✦✦✦

Resnick and Skelton were leaning on the balcony outside Lynn's flat, while Scene of Crime operated the proverbial fine-tooth comb. Most of the windows were lit up around the courtyard. Men and women, uniformed and in plain clothes, moved with purpose from door to door, up and down stairs. Breaths of both men blurred white on the air.

"No good, Charlie," Skelton was saying. "No way we can be even close to sure. She rings you, wants to talk about Nancy Phelan. Sometime in the next—what?—forty-five minutes, she's disappeared."

"And you don't think there's a connection?" Resnick was experiencing difficulty keeping his voice under control.

"We don't *know* there was any connection. Whatever happened, could have been sheer coincidence ..."

"We don't have to know there's a connection, we can work it out for ourselves. Making those kind of connections, that's what we *do*. Or have you forgotten we're supposed to be bloody detectives?"

Skelton fidgeted his wedding ring round his finger. "Charlie, you're not in danger of letting your feelings get the better of you here?"

Resnick gazed, amazed, around the room. His breathing was ragged and loud. "We're not supposed to think, now we're not supposed to feel, what the hell are we supposed to do? Other than keep fit and wear a clean sodding tie!"

"Charlie." Skelton laid a hand on Resnick's arm, lowered his voice. "Charlie, I know what you're feeling. Think a lot of her, I understand that. All I'm saying, what we mustn't do, go off at half cock. Wasted time, wasted effort, she'd not thank us for that."

Resnick hung his head. "Yes, I know. I'm sorry. Forget what I said."

"Most likely has to be," Skelton said, "either she had someone round for the evening, few drinks, got nasty, out of hand. Either that, or someone broke in, there was a struggle ..."

"I can't buy that. Why wouldn't he just take off soon as he got the chance?" Resnick looked Skelton in the eye. "The first, maybe, yes, possible."

"But you still think it's more?"

"Yes."

"You think it was him. Whoever did for the Phelan girl."

"Yes."

"But, how, Charlie? How, for God's sake? Somehow, some fluke, she got to know him? Found out who he was? Goes some way to stretching the imagination."

"Suppose," Resnick said, "it worked the other way. Suppose he was the one who got to know her?"

Get Corin Thomas talking and it was difficult getting him to stop; all the way back to the Canning Circus station, he kept Divine and the driver less than enthralled with accounts of where he'd been earlier that evening (a desultory trip round the city center pubs, looking for women), where he'd been the previous year on holiday (a fortnight of days eyeing up the talent on the beaches, all the while becoming red as a Forest shirt, followed by a desultory trip round the night clubs, looking for women), and what it was like driving a single-decker for Barton Buses. Poor bastard, Divine thought, no wonder he hated being dragged away from his chip supper, highlight of his tossing week.

Inside the station, they shut Thomas up long enough to sit him down in a corner of the CID room, tell him what he had to do. Divine and Naylor had spent a good couple of hours with the appropriate officer, trying to get the photo-fit to do precisely that. Problem was, part of the problem, once you got past the color of the hair and the shape of the mouth—small, both of them were agreed, turning down a little at the edges—there wasn't a lot about the individual calling himself Reverdy that was remarkable. Except, that is, for the eyes. And the one thing Divine and Naylor could not agree on was the color of the eyes.

Not that eye color seemed to faze Corin Thomas over much. "You realize I never got much of a look? I mean, you do realize that?"

They understood.

"And the light out there ...?"

They understood about the light.

"Well, in that case—and I wouldn't want you to hold me to this, not in court, like, not something I'd want to swear about on a Bible—but, yes, I'd say, what I'd say, the bloke I saw going across the courtyard with that mate of yours, I'd say, yes, it could be him."

"Boss," Divine stood beaming at Resnick's door, "the bloke from the Little Chef, him and the one who's got Lynn—looks like they might be one and the same."

"Right." Resnick was on his feet, on the move. "Just got confirmation from Manchester CID. The car he was driving belonged to Reverdy right enough. Stolen some time in the last ten days. Owner was away. Holiday. Insurance documents in the glove compartment."

"Think he pulled the same stroke again?" Divine asked. "Lifted something to pull this?"

"Likely. Let's check the lists. See if you can tickle the witness's memory about the car. We might have one or two more by now, corroboration."

"Right, boss."

"Kevin," Resnick called.

"Sir?"

"Copies of that photo-fit, priority. Big a distribution as we can."

"Straight away."

As Naylor set off, Resnick pulled a copy of Reverdy's statement; the Cheadle address wasn't an invention, like a lot of practiced liars, this was a man who'd found it paid to stick close as possible to the truth. Resnick was reading through the pages as he walked back to his office, wondering which elements might lead them where they had to go before it was too late.

Fifty

Lynn had woken with a dull pain somewhere in her head and a taste like cleaning fluid in her mouth. At least, the way she imagined it tasted. Probably, it was the smell. As soon as she had had the thought, her neck and shoulders spasmed forward and she threw up. Christ! Wet, on the inside of her leg. Looking down, Lynn saw her leg was bare. The pain in her head was sharp now and more precise, high at the back of her skull. Her eyes watered and stung and a rope of spittle and saliva hung from her mouth. She began the move that would allow her to wipe it away, but of course her hands were tied. Clasped. When she shook her arms, which were stretched behind her back, she recognized the clink and touch of handcuffs.

Oh, Christ!

Lynn blinked her eyes into focus. She was inside a caravan, secured to one corner, something—a chain, she guessed, twist her head as she might, she couldn't see—attached to the handcuffs prevented her from moving more than inches either way. She had been stripped down to her cotton top and blue knickers and there were goose bumps all the way along her legs. That and the pale trail of her own vomit, as if snails had slithered their slow way across her thighs. At least, she thought, I followed my mother's advice about accidents and underwear. You never know ... She knew, this was no accident. *Oh, I don't think there's any such thing as blind coincidence do you?* Suddenly, she was shaking, startled by tears.

"You're awake, then?" Michael was standing in the doorway, a tray balanced on the fingers of one upturned hand. "Considering the time of year, it's a beautiful day."

Behind the sleeve of his brown sweater, Lynn glimpsed the pale blue of open sky, smudge of darker green. Reaching behind him, Michael swung the door to.

The interior of the caravan was unremarkable: a small formica table and skimpy chairs, a narrow bunk along one wall, a Calor gas cooker, some cupboards, a sink. Near the center a gas heater burned low. Opposite her, fly-specked, a calendar showing the month of January below a color photograph of tulip fields, two years out of date.

"Here, I thought you'd be ready for this." On the tray he set near her on the floor were a mug of what appeared to be tea, the steam still rising softly from it, a slice of bread dabbed here and there with butter, some kind of cereal mushed up with milk. "You must be hungry. You slept a long time."

His eyes were never still. Lynn listened for the sound of traffic, other people; only the slow thrum from some kind of motor could be heard—besides their breathing, his and hers.

"You will eat?"

She didn't answer, looked at him, wanting his attention. Needing it.

"Wouldn't it be awful, when they found you, if you had just faded away?" He scraped the underside of the spoon against the edge of the dish before bringing it towards her mouth. "One thing I wouldn't want them to say, you were neglected. Not looked after. I wouldn't want them to be thinking that."

The tip of the spoon passed between her lips and tapped against her teeth and Lynn was reminded of his kiss. She opened wide enough to let it in. The cereal was lukewarm and tasted both of sugar and of bran.

"Good?" Michael inquired pleasantly. "Is that good? Should you like some more or is it a drink of tea?"

The tea was more difficult, she had to tilt back her head and still some of it escaped and ran down on to her neck.

"Here," he said, opening a tissue from his trouser pocket, then folding it again into a pad, "let me do something about that."

Unwillingly, Lynn flinched from his hand.

Michael just smiled and tried a second time. He noticed then the damp residue drying on her thigh. "A little accident," he said. "Is that what this is?" Carefully, he refolded the tissue before gently releasing spittle on to it, a gesture Lynn had seen her mother make a hundred times. "There now," Michael said, dabbing at her leg, "that's better now."

Damn you, Lynn thought, I am not going to cry again.

Smiling, Michael lifted another spoonful of cereal to her mouth and gratefully she swallowed it down.

Robin and Mark had made an early start; there was still some mist hanging quite low and when that finally cleared they knew there would be snow on the tops. But the local forecast was good and besides they were well equipped, compasses and extra clothes and food, regulation survival kit in their rucksacks. Robin had scarcely spoken of Nancy since he had arrived and Mark had been content to leave it that way, thought it best. What Robin needed most of all, Mark reckoned, was something to take him out of it, not long, cloistered conversations centered on nostalgia and regret. Not that, if it came to it, he would be anything less than sympathetic.

They had been walking now, steadily gaining altitude, for a little over an hour. Mark had set off in the lead and after a while they had changed places, Robin pushing on ahead, lifting the pace. Even though they were still at the lower levels, the effort was enough to test their breath and, of necessity, conversation was kept to a minimum.

"Look. There."

Mark stopped and followed the direction of Robin's arm, eastwards to where the sun had finally broken clear above the peaks.

"Didn't I tell you?" Mark said. "Didn't I tell you this was going to be a great day?"

Robin smiled before turning back and continuing to climb.

Lynn had asked for the rest of her clothes back, complaining of the cold. For reply, he had turned the heater up a notch and laughed. An eerily musical sound. She thought now she had heard him earlier, moving around outside, singing. No way of knowing if that were true. Somebody else? A dream? "I thought you were meant to be looking after me," she'd said.

He had left the caravan instantly, returned with an old piece of sacking, and thrown it down across her legs. "There."

When the door had opened for him to leave, she had heard it more clearly, the same insistent sound. Possibly a generator, the report on the tape's background noise had said. If she twisted her head a little she could make out the lettering, faded into the weave of the material: *Bone Fertilizer—Saddleworth & Sons.*

Michael came back half an hour later, whistling quietly. Lynn watched as he drew round one of the folding chairs and sat there, one leg crossed over the other, relaxed. "I'm sorry," he said, "that I lost my temper." He smiled. "That's unusual for me. I don't like it, never have. The way it affects you when that happens. Out of control. That's not what I want for us. I'd rather we continued to be friends."

"We could have been, Michael. You know that. That's why this is such a shame."

"And we're not now? Is that what you're saying?"

"Not exactly, Michael. Not any more."

Disappointment passed across his eyes. "But why ever not?"

"After this? After what you've done?"

"To you? What have I ...?"

"Not only to me."

"I've been good to you. I like you."

"Really?"

He moved off the chair and sat close beside her on the floor.

"You've got a strange way of showing it, that's all I can say."

"But I do, you know I do." She could feel his breath against her thigh.

"How much, Michael?"

He looked at her, questioning.

"Enough to let me go?"

"Maybe." His hand was resting on her thigh, a little above the knee, the thumb tracing small circles on her skin. "I'll have to think about it. I don't know."

"What will it take, Michael? What will I have to do?"

"What?"

"For you to do that? Let me go?"

He looked at his hand as if it belonged to someone else, before pulling it away. "It isn't like that."

"It isn't?"

"Threats. Promises. We don't have to do that."

"We don't?"

"I could have you …"

"Could you?"

"I could have had you …"

"Michael, it's true."

"What …?"

"That night at my flat. You could have had me. Whatever you wanted."

He was looking away, shoulders hunched, head down. "You think I didn't know. The way you were lying there …"

"Then why didn't you? What stopped you?"

"Nothing stopped me. I stopped myself. I …"

"No good like that, is it? Straightforward. Normal, Normal sex. Two people. Me and you, Michael. Me and you."

"Stop it."

"Is that what it is, Michael? Is that the problem?"

"Stop."

"Part of the problem?"

"Stop it!" He kicked the chair away and it smashed against the wall. His hands were clamped over his ears. He was shaking.

"Michael," Lynn said, "I could help you. Really. But you have to trust me. You have to."

She had no idea if he had heard her or not. Without another glance, he walked from the caravan and locked the door behind him. Oh, Christ, Lynn thought, all of the energy suddenly sapped out of her, I hope to God I haven't just pushed him too far.

He didn't come back for well over an hour and when he did he came in humming softly to himself, a small tape recorder in his hand. "I thought you'd be wanting to send a message to your friends. That inspector now—Resnick, wasn't that his name?"

Robin and Mark had continued their climb, the conditions causing them to detour once or twice from the marked path, but now they were back on track and moving towards Striding Edge. Both left and right, whichever way they looked, lower peaks were topped with snow. Gray and white, the mountain rose up before them.

They had stopped once, drinking from their flasks, eating chocolate, Mark breaking off a piece of Kendal Mint Cake.

From nowhere, Robin said, "Perhaps she's better off in a way, Nancy, where she is."

Not knowing how to respond, Mark had said nothing, but nodded, waiting for Robin to go on. But there was nothing more. Ten minutes later, everything was stowed away again and they were on the move.

The Edge was a narrow traverse, broad enough only for climbers moving in single file, the drop close to sheer on either side and deep. Robin and Mark had been across it many times.

"Want me to go first?" Mark asked.

"N-no, it's okay. I'm fine." The sun caught his shadow as he went carefully forward, flattening it against the rock floor. Watchful of his footing on the icy surface, taking his time, Robin continued to the midpoint and his face, when he turned, was lost in a blaze of light. He stood there, stock still, for perhaps five seconds, looking back at Mark from the center of that golden haze and then, without a word, stepped sideways into space.

Fifty-one

Michelle woke to the sound of rain sweeping against the windows, the blip-blip-blip as it dripped through the gap in the roof into the plastic bucket below. Beside her, Gary's breathing was steady and when she turned towards him, twisting her leg beneath his, she could smell cigarette smoke in his hair. Out drinking again last night. Herself, too. She couldn't remember when they'd spent so much time at the pub. Not feeling so good about leaving the kids alone, not even for half an hour, but they'd been fast off by then and once they were sleeping they almost never woke. Besides, Gary, he'd only have got into a mood if she'd said no. Just one drink, she'd said when she'd arrived, but Brian, flash bugger, had been flush again, laughing and making a fuss of her, insisting she and Josie have Bacardi and Coke, rubbing his hand up her leg too, the moment she sat down. Gary, thank God, he'd been too far gone to notice.

Michelle was more certain than ever Brian was into something dicey. Brian and Gary both, the way they kept up the clever looks and nudges, going off into corners and getting their heads down, whispering. Not that Gary seemed to have got so much out of it, whatever it was. Some things, she thought sadly, never changed.

She looked down at Gary now, his features softened by the half-light; one of those blokes, no matter how old they got, who never really looked any different to when they were kids. The ones who were always looking the wrong way, stuck standing at the end of the wrong line. He stirred and, suddenly tender towards him, Michelle bent her head and kissed him and smiled as he flapped a hand towards his face as if at a fly. Downstairs, the baby was waking, the day's first cry.

Michelle rolled away from Gary towards the edge of the bed.

Resnick had been unable to sleep at all. Twice he had tried, forcing himself to lay down at one and half-past three, both times getting back up after thirty minutes of flailing around, unable to clear thoughts of Lynn from his mind. Awake, he had paced distractedly from room to room, phoned, periodically, the station to see if there had been any developments, any news; in the kitchen, he had toasted bread, eaten it with cheese, strong Gorgonzola that had tasted of nothing. He had been so certain the trawl through the Open University lists would yield something. McCain and Reverdy, neither of them usual names. But blind alleys were all it had brought them, blind alleys and false trails. Wasted time.

Resnick remembered Harry Phelan's face, distorted by anger: *Forty-eight hours, that's what they reckon, isn't it? Forty-eight hours. If you don't find them in that, likely they're sodding dead!* Harry Phelan, standing in an open field, while behind him, inside the waiting ambulance, his daughter's body lay covered by a plastic sheet. Resnick willed himself not to look at the clock.

Maureen Madden, Kevin Naylor, anyone and everyone Lynn might have talked to, Resnick had quizzed them, anything she had mentioned about seeing somebody, a new boyfriend, a man. She had said something to Naylor about her car breaking down on the way back from her parents', someone stopping to lend a hand, offering her a lift. Nothing more than that.

Resnick stood in the top room of the house, one of the cats in his arms, staring out into the rain.

Michelle had just got to the bucket in time, the water only an inch from the top. Emptying it quickly into the bath, she had replaced it before hurrying downstairs and mopping up at the back where the rain had driven in through the gaps at the edge of the door Gary had failed to fix. The cup of tea she had made herself was little better than lukewarm.

In her cot, Natalie lay on her back, gurgling away happily now she had been changed and fed.

"Oh, Karl, just look at you!"

Left in the kitchen to his own devices, he had managed to get more Rice Krispies on the floor than in his bowl. The last of the fresh milk was dribbling from its carton into the sink.

"Karl, for heaven's sake!" The boy backed away, blinking, wearing Gary's old County shirt, long past his knees. "Come on, mind out of the way. Let me get this cleared up before your dad comes down."

Karl trundled into the doorway and bumped into Gary, still prizing the sleep from his eyes.

"Bloody heck, Karl! Look where you're going, why don't you?"

"Hang on a minute," Michelle said. "You'll be treading all that into the floor."

"What the hell's it doing there in the first place?"

"Karl had an accident."

"Karl *was* a sodding accident."

"Gary, that's not fair!"

"Not fair, it's sodding true, though, i'n' it?"

"Gary, don't. Look, he can hear."

"So what's that matter? Doesn't know what we're on about, hasn't a clue, have you, pal?"

"Asthdent," Karl said just inside the door. "Asthdent."

Michelle shook her head, pushed Gary aside while she swept the remaining Rice Krispies into the dustpan.

"Make him come back here and eat it, that's what you should do. Teach him a bloody lesson fast enough."

Michelle shot him a look and tipped the cereal into the bin. "There's tea in the pot. Likely cold. If you want fresh, you can make it yourself." And she shooed Karl into the other room and closed the door behind them: let him take his rotten temper out on himself.

The cats had decided it was time Resnick saw to their welfare. Dizzy had attracted his attention, weaving in and out of his legs, nudging his head against Resnick's ankles.

Downstairs in the kitchen, radio tuned to the World Service, Resnick had forked Whiskas into their bowls, ground the first coffee beans of the day, and looked to see what else there was for breakfast other than toast.

Near the back of the fridge he found a section of smoked sausage, which, when he held it close to his nose, failed to give off any warning signs. Using a sharp knife he sliced the sausage into rings and pushed them to one side of the board, lifted a pan on to the stove and poured in some olive oil, set the gas to low. A few cloves of garlic he peeled with his hands, making much use of his nails. An onion, and then he'd be there.

Bud made his familiar pathetic wail and without looking Resnick used his foot to shift Dizzy from the smallest cat's bowl.

The onion he sliced into half and half again, knife cutting down, smaller and smaller each time. By the time he had finished, he could scarcely see what he was doing for the tears. Resnick sniffed and fumbled for a handkerchief; finding none, he reached for the tea towel instead. When his eyes were clear he saw at last something he should have recognized before.

Two of the cats' bowls were overturned as he ran to the door, Pepper leaping for safety to the refuge of the largest pan. Only with his coat on, car keys in his hand, did he remember the gas, and dash back to the kitchen to switch it off. Hearing him coming, Miles and Bud cowered in corners, Dizzy stood his ground and arched his back.

"Where's Karl gone now?"

"I thought he was with you."

Gary was up some steps he'd borrowed from the neighbors across the street, trying to do something about the hole in the roof. Already there'd been a stream of shouts and swearing and, from experience, Michelle knew he was about to explode. But when Michelle had come back in with the baby, Karl, who she'd thought was stretched out on his stomach watching cartoons, was nowhere to be seen.

"Gary, where …?"

"I told you, I haven't fucking seen him!"

From their bedroom, the answer came in a scream. Karl was alongside the wardrobe when Michelle got there, continuing to scream, staring at his hands. The knife lay on the floor before him, smeared with blood.

"Oh, Jesus!"

When she ran to him, Karl turned away and threw himself against the wall.

"Karl, Karl, it's all right. Let me see. Let me see, now, sweetheart, let me see."

Gary stood just inside the doorway, saw the knife. "What the fuck you been doing, you stupid little bastard? What the fuck you, doing, sticking your nose where it's got no business? Eh? Eh?"

"Gary. Shut up and leave him alone."

"I'll leave him alone."

"Gary!"

He grabbed Michelle by the arm and half-pulled, half-pushed her out of the way. Karl saw the blow coming and threw up his hands, but the force of the punch knocked them aside and the fist struck the boy smack on the side of the head.

Karl let out a cry and toppled into the corner, weeping.

"Gary, you bastard! You pathetic, cowardly bastard!" Michelle had snatched the knife from the floor and set herself between father and son, handle grasped in both hands, blade pointing towards Gary's chest. "You dare touch him again. You dare!"

Gary stared back at her, breath uneven, hands falling slowly back to his sides. What the hell did the stupid bitch reckon she was doing, turning the bloody knife on him? But when he tried moving half a pace forward, it was clear she was not about to budge. With a curl of his lip, Gary turned away. Until she had heard him lurch heavy-footed down the stairs, the slam of the front door, Michelle wouldn't move. Only then did she drop the knife on to the bed and pick the terrified child up into her arms.

Resnick hadn't been the only one for whom sleep had been more or less impossible. Kevin Naylor had finally given up at around three and taken the spare duvet into the front room so as not to disturb Debbie, settled down in the armchair, and watched a discussion between an American academic, who seemed to have written a book about bondage, and a fiercely unfunny female comedian, the pair of them arguing about the effects the increase in estrogen in the water was having on the male sperm count. Fifteen minutes of that and he quickly showered, changed, wrote a note for Debbie, and set off for the station.

There had to be something, something they'd overlooked. In the CID room, he began to go through Lynn's desk, drawer by drawer, file by file, paper by paper. Almost an hour later, increasingly agitated, frustrated, he came close to missing it. The Yellow Pages scarred with the rings of numerous coffee mugs, he had gone through pretty thoroughly, but all that was marked were pizza deliveries, Indian take-aways, taxi firms. Kevin picked up the Thomson Directory that had been underneath it and gave it a quick flick through. The first time he noticed nothing, only on the second, carrying the directory across the room to add it to the general pile, did he spot the biroed asterisk, name printed at an angle in the column beside it.

SCHOTNESS STATIONERY LTD. Wholesale Supplies.

The address was a factory estate near the Clifton flyover.

The name written beside it was *Michael Best.*

Naylor's fingers fumbled the numbers twice and when he did get through, the phone rang and rang.

"Shit!"

"Something a problem, Kevin?"

When he saw Resnick in the doorway, Naylor could have given him a hug. Almost. "Look," he said, grabbing the directory from Lynn's desk. "Look here."

Taking the book from him, Resnick set it back down again to read it. "Good lad," he said. "Well done."

Naylor was too excited to blush.

Resnick checked his watch. "Too early to expect anyone there to set us straight. Meantime, what you can do is this. Names we took of everyone who was at that Christmas Eve do at the hotel where Nancy Phelan disappeared, that's all on file?"

"On the computer, yes."

"Right. Get it up on screen. I wouldn't mind betting Michael Best was one of the guests."

Across the room, Resnick picked up one of the photo-fit posters awaiting distribution. Not a perfect likeness, which was maybe why he'd not seen it immediately, but now he didn't think there could be any mistake. "*Later, then. Let me buy you a drink later.*" A dark-haired man in a dress suit, his eyes pursuing Lynn down the bar.

"Sir. Take a look at this."

Schotness Stationery were one of two small firms who had shared their celebrations on the third floor of the hotel and M. Best was listed among their guests.

Resnick was reaching for the nearest phone when it rang. It was Sharon Garnett, calling from King's Lynn. "Just had something delivered for forwarding, addressed to you, personally. It's a tape."

Fifty-two

Lynn woke to the sound of Michael masturbating close by where she lay. Without moving her head, she could see the outline of his body, rocking forwards and back in the almost dark. Closing her eyes again, she could only listen as he gasped towards his climax, unable to block out the final shuddering sigh as he came.

Lynn waited, held her breath. She had talked him into letting her have back her jeans, complaining of the excessive cold. He had loosened the chain that held her cuffs a little at nightfall, sufficient for her to be able to draw her arms up against her back. Nevertheless, she was stiff, sore; the side on which she had mostly lain was numb.

She heard Michael moving and realized he was looking down at her to see if she were awake. Tense, when his finger touched her cheek she managed not to react. For several minutes he stood there, bending forward, stroking her face. When she thought she could endure it no longer, he went away.

The caravan door clicked shut and she heard the key turning in the lock. Nothing now that she could do but wait. Continue waiting. Any attempt she had made the previous evening to engage Michael in conversation had come to nothing. Just, now and then, that recognizable smile—you think I'm going to fall for that? Think I don't know what you're doing?

Somewhere, Lynn knew, they would be looking for her. Resnick and others—officers that she had never met and would never know—using everything at their disposal, searching, following every clue. But what were they? What were the clues? She had come so close that last evening to telling Resnick Michael's name. Instead, she had put down the phone. Put off the moment. Why? As long as she lived, she might never know. Not that that need be so very long a time.

✦✦✦

Resnick was in King's Lynn within the hour, motorcycle escort all the way, headlights and sirens. Sharon Garnett's sergeant greeted him with a strong handshake, a quiet, "Anything we can do to help you land the bastard," as Resnick walked past. They sat in a small low-ceilinged room with a view out over wet cobbled streets. Quite close, a church bell was insistently ringing. "I wish they'd give over with that bastard thing," the sergeant remarked. Sharon looked towards Resnick, waiting for a signal to play the tape.

Though he was expecting it, Lynn's voice made him start and he missed the first few words.

> *... I have to tell you that I'm all right. I mean, I've been given something to eat and drink and so far nothing bad has happened to me. I'm being well looked after, I suppose. I'm not in any pain. The reason ...* She hesitated. *... the reason I'm here is that ...* Another hesitation, longer. Some movement of the microphone. Crackling *... the reason ...* Without a break, the man's voice, close to anger, interrupting. *She's here because she thought she could outsmart me, that's the way of it. Outwit me. Use me, that too. Get inside my defenses. And she's got to learn, you've got to learn, like I told you, that's one thing you can't none of you do.* Another pause, short, and then, *And that includes you, Mr. Resnick, that includes you.*

"That's it?" Resnick said. "That's all?"

Sharon nodded. "We played it right through, both sides."

"Nothing about a ransom, then," the sergeant said. "Not like last time."

"That was a game," Resnick said.

"Nasty bloody sort of a game."

"His kind. But it's gone beyond that now. He knows that."

Sharon Garnett looked at him. "You know who he is, don't you?"

"We've got a good idea."

"How come?"

"Staring us in the face," Resnick said. "More or less."

A fresh-faced PC knocked on the door and waited for the word to come in. "Inspector Resnick? Call for you. Shall I put it through here?"

It was a short journey from the stationery warehouse to where Michael Best lived in a rented house on the outskirts of Ruddington, south of the city. A short street of anonymous, flat-fronted buildings that stopped abruptly at the entrance to a field. Curtains twitched as the two cars slowed to a halt outside number five; the front door opposite opened and a man and woman came out to stand on their path and gawp. A word or two from Kevin Naylor sent them, reluctantly, back inside.

Millington was in no mood for niceties. He gave the nod to Divine, who grinned and sent the sledgehammer crashing against the front door, through wood and glass, and with a second swing they were inside.

The upper part of the house seemed hardly to have been used, a few boxes, mainly empty, a broken stiff-backed chair which someone had made an unsuccessful attempt to mend. Balls of dust fluffed around their feet where they walked. The bathroom was downstairs at the back, a converted scullery with black spots of damp high on the walls; toothbrush, toothpaste, shaving things were missing. In the kitchen the cupboards contained mostly tinned food—Baxter's pea and ham soup, HP baked beans, seven tins of sardines. A nub end of bread at the back of a chipped enamel breadbin, going green.

In the small front room a framed photograph of Michael Best and an older woman, enough like him to be his mother, hung above the tiled mantelpiece. She with her head half-turned towards him, Michael looking slightly bashful, self-conscious, the woman's pride clear in her eyes.

Shelved in the alcove behind the one armchair, Michael Best's library of books on running a smallholding, horticulture, tips for the independent businessman, the commercial growing and marketing of flowers. There were a pocket guide to Byzantine Art, a selected poems of Andrew Marvel, two paperbacks by Thomas Clancy. Beside a handy guide to hyacinths and gladioli was a copy of *Killing for Company*, the story of Dennis Nilsen.

"So what?" Millington said when Divine flourished it with something close to triumph. "I've got a copy of that at home myself."

Divine redeemed himself by finding the letters, hand written, either copies or unsent.

Dear Patrick

It was good to hear from you and to know that you are well. Things have moved on a little here and it looks as though my plans for setting up on my own should see fruition by this summer, autumn at the latest. I have been looking in the area around King's Lynn, which as you know is where my mother originally comes from, and think I may have found something ...

Dear Mother,

I'm so glad the flowers arrived safely, and the card, and that you say they made a nice display. I only wish I could have been with you, but as you know, I'm virtually holding down two jobs what with all the traveling and trying to make sure I don't lose the chance to ...

Dear Mr. Charteris

I am writing to you with considerable regret concerning your decision not to grant in full the loan we recently discussed. I had hoped that during our meeting I had been able to convince you ...

Dear Lynn,

I hope this letter from someone who is as yet a complete stranger ...

At the bottom drawer, underneath the letters, there was an application form for the Open University Science Foundation course, filled in but never sent. There were OS maps of Norfolk and Lincoinshire, with locations marked in blue-black biro, some of them circled in red; creased and well-used, a Little Chef motorists' map for 1993. In an envelope there were color photographs of a woman taken indoors using flash, bright spots reflecting back from the center of bewildered eyes.

"Any ideas?" Divine said, holding them up.

"Susan Rogel, I wouldn't mind betting," Millington said. "Let's get

Siddons down here to be sure. Meantime, get through to the boss, arrange for copies of these maps to be faxed across. I hope to Christ we find the right place and in time."

Lynn could hear a dog barking, quite far off; the same note, almost, it seemed, without interruption. She had heard Michael singing earlier, close by, the sound of hammering, ten minutes at most and then it had stopped. Her bladder was starting to burn. What she prayed for was the sound of approaching cars. A key turned in the lock and Michael came in.

He was wearing a white shirt, old corduroy trousers, boots on his feet. "Let me just get these off now. No sense getting mud over everything." He set down the bucket he was carrying and pulled off first one boot and then the other, placing them outside the door.

"Rain's given over," Michael said. "Going to be a nice day." He approached her with the bucket, fished from his pocket a small key. "If I trust you to help yourself with this, you're not going to be doing anything stupid?"

Lynn looked back at him but didn't answer.

Michael moved round behind her and knelt down on one knee. "Don't want me to be doing everything for you, not like a baby." He unlocked one of the cuffs and it swung against the back of her leg. "Get those jeans off, why don't you, and I'll move this bucket underneath you."

"Do I have to do this while you watch?"

"Why not? It's only natural."

Lynn shook her secured hand in sudden anger, rattling the chain. "Natural? Like this? What the hell's natural about this?"

"Temper," Michael smiled, on his feet above her, "temper. You know what I think about temper."

"All right," Lynn said, head down. "All right." With her free hand she eased her pants down along towards her knees; the instant she sat down, as she'd known it would, the urine streamed from her, splashing back against the underside of her thighs.

"Now then," he said, moments later, lifting the bucket away, "what have we got here?" Folded in his pocket, several sheets of toilet paper. "Will you or shall I?"

Staring at him all the while, she dabbed herself dry and dropped the damp tissue in the bucket when he held it out.

"I suppose now," he said, locking the cuff back around her wrist, "you'll be expecting something to drink?"

With her free hand, she took hold of his hand but immediately he pulled away. She waited until he was almost at the door. "I was watching you," she said, "this morning. The way you were just watching me."

He stopped in his tracks and she thought he was going to turn around, angry, even strike her, but instead he carried on, out through the door, and soon she heard him again, moving around outside the caravan, alternately whistling and singing a snatch of a song she had only ever heard him sing.

Fifty-three

By the time Michelle came away from casualty, Natalie grizzling in her arms, it was mid-morning. Karl's hand had taken nine stitches and was securely bandaged. Lucky, the doctor had said, none of the tendons were touched. The staff nurse, checking Karl's name against the records, had noted this was his second visit within a short space of time. "I explained all of that when the social worker had me bring him in," Michelle told her. "He had an accident, ran into the door." And this time, the nurse thought, he just happened to pick up a knife someone had left lying around. Wrigglesworth, the social worker's name was on the card; the nurse made a note to call his office as soon as she got a spare moment. The local police would be informed as a matter of course.

LOCAL CLIMBER KILLED IN FALL read the placard outside the corner shop.

"Fish fingers, Karl? Is that what you'd like?"

"Ish fingus," Karl beamed, jumping up and down, hand forgotten. "Ish fingus."

When she unlocked the front door and called Gary's name, she was relieved there was no reply.

"What do you think?" Lynn said.

He had brought her tomato soup from a can, heated up for lunch; sliced bread, buttered, then folded in half. Freed one hand so she could eat. Michael sitting on one of those insubstantial chairs, chattering away quite happily, not eating himself save for what remained of a chocolate bar, all the while watching her. Concerned.

"Is that all right? The soup, I mean. Precious little choice in the village and, besides, I'm never sure which kind is best. Heinz, I think, that's what they say. I like to buy that Scottish one, but they never have that. The bread was all they had left. I shall have to go earlier tomorrow."

"Michael, why won't you answer me?"

"What?" he said. "Sorry, what did you say?"

"I asked, what do you imagine's going to happen?"

He seemed to give it some thought. "Oh, I suppose we'll stay here for a while. Quite cozy now since I got this thing, don't you think? Throws out quite a good heat."

"Michael ..."

"What I've got to do this afternoon, though—well, I suppose tomorrow would do—see about hiring some kind of rotavator. That soil out there, I'm not turning it enough by hand."

"Michael, you're not listening."

He blinked. "Aren't I? I thought ..."

"I mean me."

"What about you?"

"What d'you think's going to happen about me? About this ... situation?"

He looked at her for a long time before answering. "Oh, we're not getting on too badly now, are we?"

Five years ago, on an application to open an account at the Halifax Building Society, Michael Stuart Best had given his place of birth as Dublin; as a guarantor he had cited his father, Matthew John Best, an address in Germany, serving with the British army overseas. Applying for a small business loan two years later, he had stated that he was born in Greater Manchester and that his father was deceased.

"He talked about it just the once," the sales manager at Schotness Stationery had told Graham Millington that morning, "the accident which took his parents off, like. Both of 'em. Aye. Lucky to get out himself, strapped in the back, see. On their way to visit relatives, Norfolk way. Terrible. Something you never get over, a thing like that. Good salesman, though, say that for him. When he was in the mood, talk the birds down out of the trees."

A quiet chap, the general verdict had been, Divine and Naylor going round the neighbors in Ruddington, knocking on doors. Kept himself to himself; friendly enough, though, not standoffish. Nice, the way he used to buy flowers, drive out to take them to his mum in the nursing home every Sunday.

They had made a room available in the local station; Skelton was there now, something of a sparkle back in his eye. "She was right," just about the first thing he'd said to Resnick when he arrived. "About the Rogel case. Helen. The connection."

Resnick didn't give a shit about Helen. The person he cared for here was being held prisoner, her captor a man who had killed one woman already, probably two.

They were steadily narrowing the marked locations down and Resnick continued to pace from desk to wall and wall to desk again, willing the phone to ring.

"Tactical unit's ready to move, Charlie. Helicopter on stand by if we want it. Two ARVs on their way, one from the city, one from Leeds."

Resnick's thoughts had jumped back several years to the unexceptional living room of an unexceptional house save that, cold in the small garden, Lynn Kellogg had just come upon her first dead body, a woman with blood drawn like ribbons dark through her hair. "How are you feeling?" Resnick had asked, and Lynn had fallen, fingers of one hand hooked inside his mouth, face pressed against his chest.

"Charlie?"

Before he could answer, the phone startled to life and Resnick fumbled it into his hand. Listening, his forefinger traced lines along the surface of the map before them. "You're sure?" he asked. "No room for doubt?"

"No," Sharon Garnett said. "None at all."

Before turning to Skelton, Resnick withdrew two of the remaining pins from the map and set them aside, leaving just the one in place. "Got him," he said, his voice now strangely calm.

"On your way," Skelton said. "I'll call up the troops."

Michelle had been mixing Natalie's food when Josie came to the door, short of breath from running almost the length of the street on high-heeled shoes.

"The law, they've nicked Brian. Gary's done a runner."

Michelle stared back at her, open-mouthed. "What's Gary ... Brian ... I don't understand."

"Christ, girl, where the fuck've you been? Brian's been dealing since before Christmas, I thought you knew."

"But Gary, he'd never ..."

"Oh, Gary. You know what your Gary's like. Wanted to feel big, go along for the ride. Anyway, look, what it is, I've got to go see Brian's brief. Okay if I bring the kids down, dump 'em with you?"

Michelle nodded, arms tight across her chest. "Josie, what'm I going to do?"

"My advice. Pray they lift Gary before he gets back here. Once he's inside, change the locks, move. Anything. Gary's a loser, always will be. Whatever happens, you'll be better off on your own."

Michael was sitting at the far end of the caravan, thumbing through a catalog, making notes in the margins, occasionally copying prices down on to a sheet of paper. From time to time he would purse his lips and whistle. "These now," he remarked from time to time, "they'll look something special, you'll see." In some part of his mind, Lynn thought, the two of them, Michael and herself, were living together on this piece of land, working happily side by side. The perfect couple. "Your father," Michael said once, looking up suddenly. "Maybe there's a way you could phone him, find out how he is. Set your mind at rest." But that had been close to half an hour ago and he'd mentioned no more about it. Lynn wondered if Skelton had asked for a news blackout or whether her mother, pottering in the kitchen, had been startled by her name. Tears pricked her eyes at the thought and for the first time she was close to breaking down.

"Nancy," she said with a sniff, needing to say something, needing to talk. "Did you know her too? Beforehand?"

Michael seemed surprised, his mind full of calculations, seedlings, yields. "That was nothing," he said eventually. "Casual. Not like this."

The main buildings were several hundred yards from the caravan and the ramshackle shed nearby, with its buckling walls and rusting corrugated roof. "It's more than I can ever manage myself," the farmer said, "since I had this trouble with my leg. When he come along last year looking to rent that parcel out, seemed like a fair blessing."

Resnick nodded and passed through to the back of the house.

Sharon Garnett handed him the binoculars, pointed in the direction of the cream caravan standing on blocks in the corner of the far field.

There were marksmen in place on three sides, the nearest flat on his belly only ninety yards away, elbows braced in the ridged earth. Just moments before, he had had a partial sighting of the target through the caravan window, moving left to right across his vision. He swore softly when he failed to get the order to fire.

"I'm going to try," Resnick said, "to get to the shed."

"Michael," Lynn had said, "why don't you leave all that for now? Come and talk to me."

In response, he had laughed. "I'm not stupid, you know. You won't catch me falling for some old trick."

Lynn had rattled her handcuffs against the chain. "What can I do?"

So he came over and sat beside her, wary, as if maybe expecting for the first time that it would all come springing back at him. What had attracted her in his eyes had disappeared and been replaced by the uncertainties of a child.

"You were going to tell me about Nancy," Lynn said.

Michael moved closer, his leg almost touching hers. "She wasn't like you. Screaming and swearing and kicking out at me every chance she could get. The rest of the time pretending to be nice, nice as could be. Making all those promises, things she would do for me if only I'd let her go." He laughed.

"What happened to her, it was her own fault. There was nothing else I could do."

"You kidnapped her. You killed her. How can that be her fault?"

"Don't!" The chair spun back, knocked from beneath him. "Don't talk to me like that. As if you had any right. Who d'you think you are? I'm in control here, me. And you'll just do well to remember that. You hear?"

"I'm sorry."

"Oh, so you say. Got you frightened now, have I? Well, maybe that's not before time."

"I mean it, I'm sorry."

"Yes? You expect me to believe that? What you always say, all of you, when it's too late."

"All of who, Michael?" Lynn asked. "All of who?"

But by then it was too late; he had heard the sounds of the helicopter, distant, coming nearer.

Not quite in position at the shed, still some twenty yards away, Resnick heard it too and swore repeatedly as he began to run, heavy-footed, cursing whoever had given the order too soon.

The caravan door burst open and Lynn emerged first, pushed out, Michael close behind her, one arm tight about her neck, the knife held unsteadily in front of her chest.

"Police," Resnick called, stumbling, running, stumbling again as the helicopter circled above them. "Armed police," came the distorted warning. "Stand still. Stand still where you are."

They ran. Lynn's ankle twisted beneath her and she fell sharply sideways, Michael grabbing at her arm and dropping the knife as he did so, grasping for her hair and catching nothing, Lynn rolling fast as soon as she touched the ground.

For a moment, Michael gazed about him and saw Resnick running, arms flailing, towards him; he felt the currents of air from the helicopter tugging at his clothes and hair. He turned and began to run again, back towards the caravan; the marksman in the field was up on one knee now, the back of Michael's head smack in his sights.

"Michael!"

Lynn called his name, yelled with all her might, and he faltered in his step and turned towards the sound of her voice. Resnick's dive struck him halfway up the body, head into his midriff, elbow sharp against his chest. Winded, Michael toppled backwards, kicking wildly, as Resnick, breath rasping, clung on so hard it took three officers to prize him free. They cuffed Michael Best and read him his rights before dragging him away.

Only then did Resnick turn to where Lynn had sunk back to her knees and begin to walk towards her, walk, then run. No holding the tears now, no stopping till finally he lifted her into his arms and held her, sobbing, safe, the daughter he had never had, the lover she would never be.

John Harvey

John Harvey was born in London in 1938. After studying at Goldsmiths' College, University of London, and at Hatfield Polytechnic, he took his Masters Degree in American Studies at the University of Nottingham.

Initially a teacher of English and Drama, Harvey began writing in 1975 and now has over 90 published books to his credit. After what he calls his apprentice years, writing paperback fiction both for adults and teenagers, he is now principally known as a writer of crime fiction, with the first of the Charlie Resnick novels, *Lonely Hearts*, being named by *The Times* [London] as one of the 100 most notable crime novels of the last century.

Flesh and Blood, the first of three novels featuring Frank Elder, was awarded both the British Crime Writers' Association Silver Dagger and the U.S. Barry Award in 2004. His books have won two major prizes in France, the Grand Prix du Roman Noir Étranger for *Cold Light* in 2000 and, in 2007, the Prix du Polar Européen for *Ash & Bone*. Also in 2007, he was the recipient of the CWA Cartier Diamond Dagger for Sustained Excellence in Crime Writing.

After a gap of ten years, Harvey has returned to the character of Charlie Resnick in his most recent novel, *Cold in Hand*.

Having lived in Nottingham for a good number of years, Harvey has recently returned to London, where he lives with his partner and their young daughter.

www.mellotone.co.uk

Bloody Brits Press

LIVING PROOF
A Charlie Resnick Mystery

John Harvey

"*Harvey's seventh procedural is smartly paced, slyly humorous, unsentimental about police work, violence, and other alienations of affection—altogether one of his best. Just like his first six*" —Kirkus Reviews

When a man is found in the middle of Alfreton Road in the early hours of a Sunday morning, stark naked and bleeding heavily from a chest wound, he is the latest victim in a series of vicious attacks on men. But inquiries in the mean streets of Nottingham's red-light district have brought the investigations to a dead end.

Charlie Resnick is the man for this job. And as if he hasn't had enough to deal with, he now has to provide police protection for a celebrity at the annual crime convention—an author with some very unpleasant "fan" mail. Chronically short-staffed as he is, Resnick fears it's only a matter of time before his lack of manpower has fatal consequences ...

Living Proof is the seventh Charlie Resnick Mystery

ISBN 978-1-932859-58-4 $14.95

Available at your local bookstore
or call toll-free 866-390-7426
or order online at www.bloodybritspress.com

Bloody Brits Press

STILL WATER
A Charlie Resnick Mystery

John Harvey

"Still Water *goes beyond fiction to provide a deeper perspective on the complexities of lust and love*"
—San Francisco Chronicle

"*John Harvey is lights out one of the best*"
—Michael Connelly

The battered body of a young woman is found floating in the still water of a city canal. Police suspect a serial killer, which makes it a case for the newly formed Serious Crime Squad. Not Charlie's case, then; not his worry.

But soon another body is found, and this time Charlie has a personal interest. His lover, Hannah, knew the murdered woman, knew too her husband was fiercely jealous. And very free with his fists. Arguing that her friend was the victim of domestic abuse, not the target of some anonymous killer, Hannah persuades Charlie to take on the case.

Investigating the murder, Resnick runs head-on into deeply disturbing questions about the nature of love, about the relationship of abuser and abused, and about our complicity in our own destruction.

Still Water is the ninth Charlie Resnick Mystery

ISBN 978-1-932859-60-7 $14.95